1914

Audley End House
February 1914

Annie Gingell broke the thin layer of ice that had formed on her water jug overnight. She gasped as her fingers touched the freezing water, and again as she wiped the wet flannel over her face and under her arms. She dried herself with the rough huckaback towel hanging by the washstand and, using the light of her bedside candle, dressed quickly and made her bed, remembering to fold the sheet corners the way Mrs Gifford had taught her.

She hurried to the kitchen, which felt warm and welcoming. She stoked the range and shovelled two large scoops of coal on to the fire, opened both flues and stood back to watch the flames leap into life. Mrs Warwick had left the kettle on the hob overnight, so it would take little heating to come to the boil. As she was about to make her way upstairs, Annie heard footsteps approaching and the jangle of keys as Mrs Gifford appeared in the doorway.

'Good morning, Miss Gingell. I see you have stoked the range.'

'Yes, Mrs Gifford. I'm just on my way up to the coal gallery.'

Annie climbed the wide oak staircase, taking the stairs two at a time. His Lordship had guests staying, so there would be an extra fire and another bath to get ready this morning. She pushed open the heavy wooden door to the coal gallery. She loved the warmth of this room. She checked the fire under the copper, threw in three shovelfuls of coal and placed a large wooden bucket under the tap. She then took a hip bath from the top of the cupboard and put it ready to be carried to the guest bedroom. Finally, she collected a piece of best palm oil soap from the store and placed it in the bath. Next she filled a cast-iron scuttle with as much coal as she could carry and hauled it to the guest wing. She

The Costermonger's Daughter

Christa Skinner

ISBN: 13: 979-8-5872-2835-1

The characters and events portrayed in this book are fictitious. Any similarity to real persons, living or dead, is coincidental and not intended by the author.

Cover design by: Dave Seddon

DEDICATION

For my husband Paul and our children Amy and Jake

CONTENTS

ACKNOWLEDGEMENTS

I should like to thank the Coffee Shop Writers group for their valuable contributions and for listening, Cathie Holden for her wise words and developmental editing, Dave Seddon for his excellent book cover design, and my husband Paul for his patience and painstaking copy editing and proofreading.

tapped gently on the first door along the dark corridor, waited and then slipped quietly into the shuttered room.

'Good morning, madam. I've come to make up the fire.'

'Very well, but do it quietly!'

'Should I open the shutters, madam?'

'If you must.'

Annie flung open the wooden shutters and peered out into the early morning light. A thin layer of misty dew hovered over Place Pond, where the heads of a pair of swans appeared, gliding through the haze. The watery sun caught the bronze finials of the turret towers, which glistened through the murk, and below her a network of spiderwebs, silver with dew, wrapped themselves around the hedges. She stoked the fire and added more coal.

'Will you be wanting a bath bringing to your room, madam?'

'Of course!'

Annie slipped out and scuttled down the corridor to collect the hip bath. She was startled by someone at the top of the staircase. It was Arthur, the new footman.

'Oh, you gave me such a shock, Arthur! What are you doing here?'

'Thought you might need a bit of a hand carrying those heavy buckets, a little thing like you!'

'Don't worry about me, Arthur, I'm used to it.'

Arthur winked.

'Well, seeing as I've climbed all the way up here, let me help you with the bath, eh?'

Annie felt herself colour under his gaze. She followed him into the coal gallery and, grabbing the soap she'd placed on top of the bath, followed him back to the guest room door. He placed the bath quietly on the floor and, turning to her, smiled.

'There you are.'

'Thank you, Arthur. Now you best get going. You don't want to be caught up here.'

Arthur winked again, paused and opened the door for her. Annie placed the bath in front of the fire and went back to the coal gallery to get the first bucket of water. She would need to make four trips to fill the bath. Having tipped in the final bucket, she tested the water temperature, placed the soap and towel next to the bath and slipped quietly out of the room. On the way down she stopped to look at herself in the oval mirror outside the coal gallery. She teased a loose bit of hair back under her mobcap and smiled at her reflection. She didn't need to pinch her cheeks today as they already had plenty of colour. She heard the clock in the Long Gallery strike 6.30, so hurried downstairs to lay the table for servants' breakfast. She put a knife and fork on either side of each plate, making sure that the handles were exactly in line, particularly those next to Mrs Gifford's and Mr Lincoln's plates. She then collected the nursery tray from the kitchen and carried it up to the top floor. On her way down the hall clock struck seven, time for servants' breakfast. She was hungry this morning. She sat down in her usual place next to Ethel and Daisy and was surprised to see Arthur sitting opposite her. Mr Lincoln said grace and, as she looked up, her eyes briefly met Arthur's. For the second time this morning she felt her cheeks glowing. He smiled and turned away. On the way to prayers Ethel caught up with her and grabbed her hand.

'He likes you, you know.'

'Who does?'

'That new footman. Arthur, isn't it? He couldn't take his eyes off you.'

'Don't be silly, he's just being friendly, that's all.'

'Is that what you call it then? You mark my words Annie Gingell, he likes you!'

That evening at the guests' dinner Annie thought he looked very handsome in his yellow and black striped livery. More than once he caught her eye as he collected dishes to be taken up to the dining room. She pretended she hadn't noticed, but secretly her heart was singing.

April 15th

It was the second Sunday in the month and her day off. Annie got up early to make the most of the day. She put on her hat and coat, picked up her bag and set off past the Tea House Bridge and up over the hill. She climbed over the wooden railings that bordered the estate and cut through Audley End Park on to Abbey Lane. The early morning sun sliced through the elm trees lining the lane, blinding her. She walked up the High Street and turned into Castle Street, crossed the road and headed up to Middle Square. As she was about to turn into her yard, she heard her mother's voice.

'Gruff, get up! If I 'ave to tell you again, I'll murder you.'

Annie smiled and went back out to the street. She hurried down to Salmon's Grocers. Mr Salmon was only there for a short time on Sunday mornings and she wasn't sure if he'd have closed for the day. Finding the shop open, she slipped inside. The bell above the door jangled as she went in. The smell of freshly sliced bacon, carbolic soap and brown paper bags welcomed her as it had done since she was a child. Reggie Salmon was sitting behind the counter, reading the *Sunday Pictorial*. He smiled as she stepped inside.

'Well, look who it is. If it ain't young Annie. How are you, my lovely? You got the day off then? I bet your old mum will be pleased to see you. They treatin' you right up at the Big 'Ouse?'

'It's hard work, Mr Salmon, but I don't mind. Me mum says she knows lots of girls who'd give their right arm for a job up there. Can I 'ave a half ounce of Condor Sliced, please? It sounds like me dad won't get out of bed, so I'm hoping the baccy might sweeten 'im up a bit.'

'Course you can, my darlin.'

Reggie Salmon gauged half an ounce and cut into the sweet-smelling tobacco, then wrapped it in a thin strip of newspaper. He dusted his hands on his brown overalls and winked.

'Yes, your dad 'ad a drop of beer up at *The Castle* last night. On 'is way 'ome he was singin' like a nightingale he was. The whole street could hear 'im. He's probably got a bit of a head on 'im this mornin'.

'I expect he has, Mr Salmon. Can I have a ha'porth of mixed for me mum, and four ounces of aniseed balls for the kids?'

'Righto, luv.'

Mr Salmon put the handful of mixed toffee in the middle of a large square of newspaper and folded the corners to make a small packet, then shook the jar of aniseed balls on to the scales. They hit the scoop like bullets. Without checking the weight, he tipped them into a small brown bag and twisted the top tightly. Annie knew that he always added a few extra for his regulars.

'There you are, Annie. Put it on the slate, shall we? Now you say hello to yer old mum and dad for me.'

Annie smiled, picked up the small packet of tobacco and two bags of sweets, and set off back towards Middle Square. She was met by her brother Fred and little sister

Nora, who, seeing Annie, ran to meet her, shouting,

'It's our Annie, it's our Annie!'

Annie bent down, scooped her up and swung her round. She screeched with delight. Fred grinned but hung back, then glanced along the street, checked there were none of his chums about, and gave his sister a quick hug.

'You alright, our Annie?'

'I'm fine, and how are you two?'

'We're fine too. How long are you staying?'

'I've got to get back by six, but it's early now so we'll 'ave all day, won't we?'

Fred eyed the bag in Annie's hand.

'Are them sweets for us, Annie?'

'They might be. But just you remember, young man, them's what asks, don't get.'

Annie put the tobacco and two twists of sweets into her bag.

'I 'eard mum soon as I got in the street, Mr Salmon says dad 'ad a drop of beer last night.'

'He won't get out of bed this morning. Mum's in a right tizz.'

'Come on then, let's go and see her, shall we?'

They turned into the yard. In front of them two rats fought over a dried scrap of fat, and in the lean-to next to the water tap, slouched the grizzled shape of Snobby Williams, in his hands, a bottle of cheap gin.

'You been 'ere all night? Go home, Snobby.'

Annie helped him to his feet and watched as he staggered, gin-drunk, towards the road, before sprawling on all fours. He waited a moment for the sky to right itself, hauled himself back on to his feet and wandered off in the direction of his shop at the top end of the street. Mum was stirring the contents of a heavy black pan, which bubbled on the range. Boiled cabbage steam rose into the air of the tiny kitchen and settled on the walls, already sour with damp. Annie thought how handsome her mum still looked, her tail of greying hair hanging like a rope down her back. Pol hadn't heard them come in.

'Gruff, I've told you....'

Then, sensing someone behind her, she turned and saw Annie. Instantly a smile crept into her voice. Her bright bird eyes, moistened as she clutched her eldest daughter's shoulders and stood back to admire her.

'Well, Annie, don't you look a picture? Gruff, Stanley, come and see who's here!'

'Is that our Annie?'

Dad's beer-stained voice echoed down the stairs, followed by the scratching of claws as Scout the dog tried to gain a purchase on the bare wooden stair treads. He slid into the kitchen and covered Annie's face with slobber as she bent down to stroke him. The back door, swollen by the recent rain, shed a few more splinters as it was kicked open by Stanley, who appeared, grinning broadly. He stopped dead and stared at his sister.

'Well, look at you, you look beautiful! They give you them clothes up at the Big 'Ouse? Turn round then.'

Annie twirled.

'I had to buy 'em. Can't be seen in my old rags up there!'

As she twirled again Gruff Gingell appeared in the doorway.

'Ain't you gonna give yer old dad a hug then?'

The air in the kitchen seemed to disappear as he lurched towards Annie. He was still bragging drunk. His bone-white hair hung tousled and unkempt. His cheeks glowed, the colour of a rash. His breath reeked of cheap beer.

Pol sighed, put her hands on her hips and turned on her husband.

'Is this any way to welcome yer daughter home fer the day?'

'I'm sorry luv, I might 'av 'ad a drop too much last night. Now come 'ere, Annie, and give me that hug.'

Annie wrapped her arms round her dad's neck and gave him a squeeze. He tottered unsteadily, kept upright for a second and then fell against the doorframe.

'Whoa, steady on, Annie, 'ave a care fer yer old dad.'

'You should be ashamed of yourself, Gruff Gingell! That Snobby Williams has only just gone 'ome. 'He spent the night in the yard. It's a wonder 'e didn't freeze to death! Now you take Scout and get yerself up the road to the City. The rat-catcher will be up there by now. See if you can win a few bob. Scout's hungry. I haven't fed 'im this mornin' so he should be catchin' well. And make sure you've sobered up by the time you get home!'

'I've got some baccy fer yer, dad. You can have it when you get back.'

'Oh, my little darlin', you're such a thoughtful girl.'

'Now you get goin', Gruff! You ain't eatin' or smoking anything until you've done something useful.'

Gruff grabbed Scout's collar and carefully stepped out into the yard. Pol smiled and went back to stirring the large pan of stew.

'He'll be the death of me that one. And now with all this talk of war... I don't know. But sit down, Annie, and tell us all about what's happening up at the Big 'Ouse.'

****

It was early evening when Annie set off. The low sun poked through the trees, making thin shadows on the ground. Behind a crumbling red brick wall Audley End House reached up as if trying to grab the clouds. Stanley had walked Annie back to the edge of the estate. He'd grown tall in the past six months and looked much older than his seventeen years. He'd been working as a costermonger with Gruff for the past year and now took the horse and cart around the villages selling fish and vegetables. He'd become a good horseman and accompanied his father to the regular horse fairs held on the Common. He'd got a good eye for a horse and had a way with them.

'Dad's lucky to have you working with him, Stanley. Has he been drinkin' a bit lately?'

'It's not just the drinkin' Annie, it's the fightin'. Last week he got into a fair old brawl with Sixer outside the Castle. It was a good job old Clip Clop was there. He and Fred Driscoll broke it up. Dad and Sixer spent the night in the lock-up. Don't suppose mum mentioned that, did she? Some days he spends more on the beer than he earns. Mum's takin' in more washin', I'm doin' an early mornin' bread round before helpin' dad, and after school Fred does a bit of stoking up at Snowflake Laundry. It ain't easy to put enough food on the table to feed five.'

'I know, Stanley. At least with me out of the way it's one less mouth to feed.'

Stanley pushed his hands further into his pockets and smiled at Annie. He was about to say something but hesitated. The clock of St Mary's Church sounded the half hour.

'I've gotta go, Stanley, or I'll be locked out. You've gotta keep an eye on things. Go fetch 'im out of the Castle *before* he's spent his wages, or tell Mr Pledger not to serve 'im more than one drink.'

Annie lifted her skirts and climbed over the low wooden stile into the field, which led across the estate to the servants' entrance at the back of the house. She leaned over the fence, smiled and gave her brother a hug.

'I'll see you as soon as I can get away. Be strong.'

She ran across the damp grass. The dew was rising and her skirts clung to her thin ankles.

'I'm thinking of signing up, Annie', Stanley shouted.

A stiff breeze had blown up and swallowed his voice. She hurried to the servants' door and headed straight for the servants' hall to find supper over. The men were sitting in a circle listening intently to Arthur, who was perched on the edge of a stool. He glanced up at her, his eyes ablaze, then continued, talking in a lowered voice.

'What's going on?'

The men leapt to their feet, hastily pushing back chairs, which scraped the tiled floor as Mr Lincoln swept into the room.

'Mr Scoggings, you are new here and obviously have a good deal to learn about how we do things. Might I suggest that you refill the lamps in here and then go and check the fires? The rest of you are fully aware of your duties, which do *not* include idly sitting around talking!'

Arthur winked at Annie as he passed her on his way to the lamp room. He didn't seem the least bit put out by Mr Lincoln. Annie grinned. *He seemed to have a bit of spirit did Arthur Scoggings*! The servants' hall emptied. Annie sat listening to the ponderous tick of the clock. She wished she'd been able to hear what Arthur had been saying to the men.

The following day Arthur caught her as she was laying the

fire in the Library. He seemed a little nervous. His hair was smoothed glassily against his head and his eyes darted backwards and forwards. Checking they were alone, he cleared his throat.

'Annie it was my day off on Monday and I was walking past *Hart's Printing Works* when I saw a poster for the new Charlie Chaplin film showing at the cinema. I'd be honoured if you'd care to come with me when you're next free.'

Annie could feel her heart racing. Despite knowing that she ought to go home on her next day off, she found herself saying,

'Yes, Arthur. That would be lovely!'

'Well, that's done then, isn't it?'

'How will I let you know when?'

'Tell you what, why don't you leave a message in one of them books over there?'

Arthur picked one of the lower shelves and took out a small book. Its leather was rich, its spine stamped in gold and edged with a line of fleur-de-lys. It sat third along the shelf, and was one of a set of identical books that recorded the minutes of Parliament from the eighteenth century. He carefully opened it and pointed to the third page.

'There we are. The third page of the third book on the third shelf from the floor, section C. That's where you can leave the message. And I can leave you a message in the same place. How does that sound?'

'Suppose someone from the family opens it?'

'No, you can tell no one has opened most of these books for years. Don't you worry about that.'

He cocked his head to one side.

'It sounds like someone's coming. I'd best get downstairs. I'll look forward to hearing from you then.'

Annie's hand fluttered up to her burning face. She studied the shelves of books running from floor to ceiling, noting the exact position of the book he'd chosen. She stood in the dark room for a moment, trying to slow the loud thumping in her chest. The air was heavy with the must of old books and dry paper. She felt light-headed as she stooped to finish preparing the fire.

April 20th

Annie crept into the Library and slipped her note into the third page of the third book on the third shelf in section C. Her next day off was to be the 26th April. She hoped that six days would give Arthur enough time to arrange a day off too. She crossed her fingers hoping that the family weren't expecting guests on the 26th, which would mean he'd have no chance to get away.

Three days later Annie finished setting the fires in the Library and, once again, nervously ran her fingers over the leatherbound books on the third shelf in section C. Her heart leapt as she slid the book out and a note fell on to the floor. She hurriedly picked it up and thrust it into her pocket, before replacing the book and rushing down to servants' breakfast. Arthur beamed at her as she sat down at the far end of the table next to Ethel. Breakfast was agony. Finally, she had a chance to read the note as she made her way up to the Coal Gallery.

April 19th

Dear Annie,

I thank you for your note and am very pleased to say that I have managed to swap days with Alfred, which will allow me to have the 26th off.

There is a matinee performance of The Tramp starting at 3

o'clock, which would give us time to have a walk and picnic in the park beforehand if you agree. I would be very happy to arrange the picnic but please let me know if this idea meets with your approval.

I look forward to your reply and hope that I'll be able to spend an enjoyable day with you.

Yours sincerely,

Arthur

April 26th

Annie waited by the cloud hedge. She was early. Ethel's dress hugged her waist a little too well and showed a bit too much of the grey ankle boots she'd borrowed from Daisy. She tried to pull the dress down further over her hips but her fingers fluttered over the fabric creasing it in all the wrong places. As the estate clock chimed twelve, there was a rustling behind her and Arthur appeared, grinning, by her side.

'You look a picture, Annie Gingell!'

His hair was plastered down with oil. A tiny rivulet ran down over his left ear forming a shiny streak down the side of his neck. Annie wanted to laugh and itched to wipe it off. She'd never seen Arthur wear anything other than his footman's uniform or his smart livery before. His own clothes seemed to sit as uncomfortably on him as her borrowed outfit did on her.

'You don't look so bad yourself, Arthur Scoggings!'

'I managed to butter up cook and talked her into giving me a few leftovers from the pantry, so we won't go hungry. Shall we cut through the kitchen garden and out into the park? I know the perfect spot for a picnic, down by the river.'

Annie turned and beamed at him. A sudden movement over and above his shoulder made her look up to where Ethel and Daisy craned their necks to stare down at them from the high mullion window of the coal gallery. She smiled to herself, wondering how they'd managed to climb up high enough to see out, and, what they were saying to each other.

'What are you smiling at then?'

'Look up at the coal gallery window.'

Arthur turned, and grinned at the faces of Elsie and Daisy, peering down at them. Annie laughed.

'They are so nosey those two!'

'Well let's give them something to look at then!'

With that, he waved up at them, winked at her, and held out his arm. She smiled and slipped her arm through his. As they reached the gates to the kitchen garden Annie pulled away and ran giggling in front of him.

'Best not to walk through here like this, I don't know what Gabriel and Mr Coster would think.'

'Let them think what they like, Annie. I'm proud to be seen walking out with you '

As it happened there was no sign of either Mr Coster or Gabriel. They made their way to the stile at the edge of the garden and climbed over into the park, where Arthur quickly put Annie's arm back through his and led her towards a sheltered spot by the river. Annie knew this part of the river well and gasped in delight, seeing the rope swing that she and Stanley had played on as children still there, tied to the low branch of a huge horse chestnut tree that clung to the side of the riverbank.

'How did you know to bring me here, Arthur?'

'I didn't, I just thought it would be a good place for a picnic!'

'Well, it's perfect. I haven't been 'ere for years. We used to 'ave such fun here when we were little!'

Arthur laughed and placed the picnic basket on the ground, took out a small blanket, which he spread at the foot of the ancient tree, then sprung onto the rope swing, kicking the side of the bank to propel himself over to the opposite bank, where he turned, grinning at her.

'Throw the rope back, Arthur! I'm coming over too.'

'But your dress, Annie. It might get splashed.'

'Oh phooey! I need to see if I can still do it, Arthur, and no stupid dress is going to stop me. Look away for a minute!'

Catching the rope, she tugged Ethel's dress up over her knees, kicked off the pale grey boots and jumped on to the large rope knot before launching herself across the water. Arthur grabbed her round the waist as she landed next to him and helped her up the bank.

'Well, I can see you've done this before, Annie Gingell!'

'Not for a long time I 'aven't, but it's good to see I can still do it.'

'My turn again now.'

Arthur jumped on to the swing and hurled himself over to where the picnic basket sat waiting. Clambering up the bank, he threw the rope back to Annie, turning his back as she pulled her dress up again. She landed as he turned to steady her. Their eyes briefly met, hovered, then they quickly looked away from each other.

'Well, madam, if you'd like to be seated, luncheon will be served.'

Annie leaned up against the trunk of the tree and slipped her feet back into the boots, which she'd left laced as Daisy's feet were much bigger than hers. Arthur placed two plates on the blanket, then on a third plate arranged cold meat pie, two hard-boiled eggs and a bowl of cold potatoes. He sat back next to Annie to admire the spread.

'Not bad for leftovers, eh?'

'It looks lovely, Arthur.'

They ate in silence for a few moments. Annie hated silences and filled it as quickly as she could.

'Arthur, what made you come down here to work?'

'I didn't have a lot of choice, Annie. Being one of seven, my parents couldn't afford to keep us all at home, and there weren't many jobs to be had in Manchester. So when I saw the advertisement for a footman at Audley End House I applied. I'd no idea where Saffron Walden was. I'd never been down South before, and I hadn't got the faintest idea what a footman was even, but my dad said I ought to apply seeing as I'm quite tall.'

'And good-looking!'

Annie turned and grinned at him as his face flushed slightly. She paused before pulling a handkerchief from the pocket of her dress, and leaned over to wipe the oily trickle from his ear and neck.

'Arthur, you've got enough oil on your hair to fry onions. Can't you feel it running down your neck?'

'I'm not used to using this stuff, that's the problem. Some of the lads put it on for me. I thought it looked alright!'

'Well, let's just say, I think you look better without it.'

'That's telling me then, innit?'

'So, what do you think of us down South. Do you like being a footman?'

'It's alright, Annie, but as far as I'm concerned it's just temporary until I can find something better. I've got ambitions. I want to make something of myself.'

Annie was stung by the certainty of his words. He intended to move on as soon as he could. Arthur suddenly turned to her and grabbed her hands in his.

'But Annie, I wouldn't have met you if I hadn't got this job, would I?'

He gently tilted her chin towards him and kissed her softly on the lips.

No one had kissed her on the lips before. It was a kiss she would remember for the rest of her life.

'Well, Arthur, I hope you won't be leaving just yet.'

'What about you, Annie? Do you want to be a housemaid for the rest of your life?'

'Of course not, Arthur, but like you, my mum and dad were finding it hard to feed all of us kids and, seeing as I'm the eldest it made sense for me to find work in service, where I could get my board and lodgings for free. 'One less mouth to feed at home', my mum said. So I know I'm helping them too. I'm lucky as well, as I'm local and can get to see my family whenever I've got time off, except today of course!'

Arthur's arm encircled Annie's shoulders as they lay down looking up at the overhanging branches of the chestnut tree.

'What would you like to do then, to make something of yourself, Arthur?'

'Well, I'm not against work in service, but I'd want to be a head steward, or a butler. Someone senior.'

'Well, if you work your way up, you could be someone senior, but it won't happen just like that, you'd have to work at it.'

'I know, but there are other jobs in life which allow you to be your own boss, where you don't have to take orders from the likes of Mr Lincoln. That's what I'd like, to be someone who gives orders, not takes them.'

'There are some days when I feel like that too, Arthur. I think His Lordship treats us quite well, but when I see how they waste perfectly good food, which gets thrown to the pigs, and I think about how hard it is for ordinary people to find enough to eat, it makes me cross.'

'Well, you must have ambitions too, Annie. You don't need to accept that you will always be at the beck and call of Mrs Gifford.'

The estate clock struck two. Arthur rolled over on his side and locked Annie's eyes in his gaze.

'Don't worry, Annie. I won't be going anywhere yet, and don't you forget it.'

He winked and jumped to his feet, pulling her with him. They packed the empty plates into the basket, followed by the rolled blanket.

'We can leave the basket in the orchard at the back of the kitchen garden. We could hide it under one of the fruit trees.'

They walked hand in hand back to the estate, left the basket under an apple tree and headed into town. Annie had never been to a film before but had heard of Charlie Chaplin and that he was very funny. They joined a queue that had already formed outside the cinema. A billboard by the entrance advertised two films, '*The Tramp*' starring Charlie Chaplin, and a second called '*Pool Sharks*', starring WC Fields. Arthur explained that he was a famous music hall artist, and that it was his first film. As the queue grew longer, Annie's excitement grew. The doors finally opened, and Arthur showed their tickets to a young woman, who clipped them before they went to find their seats. Someone called an usherette checked the ticket numbers and showed them to their seats. On stage sat a pianist playing a tune

Annie didn't know. The auditorium gradually filled up until every seat was taken. They had to stand up several times to let people squeeze past to get to their seats. Finally, the lights dimmed, and the pianist changed to another tune as the curtains opened. From behind them a bright light cut through the darkness, projecting moving images onto a huge screen on the stage. Annie marvelled at the story being played out in front of her, laughed at the antics of Charlie Chaplin and enjoyed the accompanying piano music, which set just the right the mood for the action.

Arthur grabbed Annie's hand as soon as the lights went down and leaned over to plant a kiss on her cheek, before clapping wildly as the film began. Annie's face muscles ached as she laughed more than she'd ever done before. The film finished after what felt like fifteen minutes, but was in fact an hour. There was a wave of heads quickly moving apart as the lights went up, and the audience blinked into the sudden glare. The pianist then stood to announce an interval before the second film, and requested that they join in singing two well-known songs. Arthur's voice was rich and tuneful as he joined in. Annie wasn't sure of all the verses but joined in the chorus. She was relieved when the pianist introduced *'I'm Forever Blowing Bubbles'*, and joined in every verse.

The lights dimmed again, announcing the second, shorter film, which was another comedy, giving WC Fields an opportunity to show off his snooker skills. Arthur's arm was firmly around Annie's shoulders, as they sat side-by-side, guffawing with laughter. Annie laughed until tears rolled down her aching face muscles.

As they walked slowly back through the park, Annie's eyes danced with laughter as Arthur broke off a thin branch from a tree, using it as a stick as he imitated Chaplin's distinctive walk.

'You take him off really well. That's what you should be, Arthur – a comic actor!'

He turned to her and swung her round until they tumbled dizzily onto the grass. Laughing, their lips met and Annie was kissed for the second time in her life. It left her breathless.

'I think we should get back, Arthur, as I must go and see my mum and dad. It's been a lovely afternoon and I haven't laughed so much ever!'

June 28th
Middle Square, Saffron Walden

Gruff kicked open the kitchen door and threw the paper down on the table.

'Read that, Pol!'.

Pol flopped down in a chair and stared at the headline:

'ARCHDUKE FERDINAND AND WIFE ASSASSINATED'

She skimmed the article, keeping an eye on the pot of potatoes, which were almost cooked.

'It says they were killed by a Serbian-backed terrorist. Well, I think that's terrible, but what has that got to do with us? Why is it such a big headline?'

'It's all to do with countries protecting each other Pol, and mark my words this means trouble.'

'Well, I can't see it's got anything to do with us, we've got enough to worry about with all this talk of problems with Ireland, and now maybe a war. Stanley's got it into his head that he will be old enough to go and fight. Over my dead body! Now sit down and let's eat'.

August 3rd
Audley End House

Arthur cleared the family breakfast plates on to a silver tray and carried them down to the kitchen. Breakfast had been dominated by talk of the looming possibility of war. He'd slipped Lord Braybrooke's discarded newspaper under a large plate and then hidden it under his jacket. Lying on his bed later that evening, his eyes lingered over the headline, his pulse racing.

'GERMANY MARCHES ON BELGIUM
ASQUITH ISSUES ULTIMATUM

Belgium's neutral status was violated today as Germany marched into its heartland. Addressing a packed House of Commons, Prime Minister Herbert Asquith informed ministers of the following:

'We have made a request to the German Government that we shall have a satisfactory assurance as to Belgian neutrality, and that all German troops will leave the country before midnight tonight.'

Arthur slept fitfully, waking early, with a sense that the world was about to change.

August 4th

Glancing over Lord Braybrooke's shoulder, Arthur was able to scan the morning headline as he served the silent family their breakfast.

'BRITAIN DECLARES WAR ON GERMANY'

Lord Braybrooke's strident voice drowned the strangled gasps of his wife and daughter as he read out the statement made by the Foreign Office:

'Owing to the summary rejection by the German

Government of the request made by his Majesty's Government for assurances that the neutrality of Belgium would be respected, his Majesty's Ambassador in Berlin has received his passport, and his Majesty's Government has declared to the German Government that a state of war exists between Great Britain and Germany as from 11 p.m. (12 midnight German time) this evening, Tuesday August 4th.'

Lord Braybrooke folded the newspaper and placed it on the table. Looking over at his wife and daughter, whose breakfasts remained untouched, he boomed,

'Good for Asquith! Quite apart from respecting Belgium's neutrality, a country whose sovereignty we have agreed to protect, Britain needs to shield both its global empire and its sea trade.'

He paused, taking a bite of toast and sipping his tea.

'Germany's obvious attempt to dominate the continent threatens our industrial and imperial supremacy. We simply must not allow it to strip us of our trade and colonies, and trample over our rights and liberty!'

Arthur's body prickled as he lingered, clearing the table of its untouched breakfasts. Peering over his glasses at the pale faces of his wife and daughter, Lord Braybrooke continued:

'This is no great surprise of course. Asquith has been building up our troop numbers for months, so they'll be ready for immediate mobilisation. But England will expect that every man will do his duty, so there's bound to be further recruitment drives.'

Arthur felt a surge of excitement as he carried a tray of teacups down to the scullery for washing. As he turned to go back up to the dining room, Alf Lewis appeared from the boot room, carrying two pairs of freshly polished shoes.

'Here Alf, have you heard, war's been declared with Germany!'

Alf's face fell.

'What?'

'I'll try and pick up His Lordship's paper when he's finished breakfast. If I can, I'll let you have a look, and then we can pass it on to the other lads.'

With that, he rushed up the stairs and found the dining room empty. The newspaper sat where Lord Braybrooke had left it. Picking it up, he slipped it inside his jacket and quickly finished clearing away, before heading back to the kitchen and into the servants' room, where breakfast was about to begin. Mr Lincoln sat at the head of the table, looking grim. Clearing his throat, he swept his eyes around the staff and announced,

'I'm afraid that I have bad news. As from 11 o'clock last night we are at war with Germany.'

There was a collective gasp. Annie shot a glance at Arthur, who winked at her and then quickly adjusted his face as Mr Lincoln glared at him, before continuing.

'It seems that Germany has marched into Belgium and Mr Asquith is concerned that we might be next. There is no need for panic, but I must warn you all that there are very likely to be some changes on the estate. We must wait and see how the situation develops, but for now we will all carry on as normal, and I do not expect idle gossip to interfere with the smooth running of the house.'

Breakfast was eaten silently, as normal. Alf, sitting opposite Arthur, silently questioned him, raising his eyebrows. Arthur nodded in response, touching his jacket to indicate that he had the newspaper hidden inside it.

That afternoon Annie had an hour free. She slipped into the Library and pulled out the book she hoped would contain a message from Arthur. Her heart leapt as she found a note written on a small piece of cream paper. She quickly pushed it into her pocket and ran upstairs to her room to savour it.

August 4th

Dearest Annie,

If you can get away, meet me under the cloud hedge after servants' dinner tonight.

Your loving Arthur

Annie smiled and added it to a small pile of notes she kept in a box at the back of her bedside locker.

Servants' dinner dragged. Mr Lincoln said nothing more about the day's news but the atmosphere around the table was tight, like a fist. Annie managed to steal away briefly after helping Ethel and Daisy clear away. To avoid bumping into Mrs Warwick or Mrs Gifford, she took the passage furthest away from their sitting rooms, where they would be sipping an after-dinner sherry. She waited by the towering yew hedge, planted to hide the service wing from the scornful eyes of His Lordship's guests. At last, there was a movement from behind the hedge. Her heart pumped wildly as Arthur appeared, grinning. Throwing his arms around her, he pulled her close and smothered her face with kisses. He finally pulled away, holding her hands and gazing at her as if for the first time.

'Annie, I could hardly look at you at dinner for fear I'd reach out and touch your hair, your face, your hands. You're beautiful, and I can't believe you're mine!'

Annie entwined herself around him as his hands roamed over her body with a familiarity she loved. She looked up into his eyes. They were ablaze, but in a way she hadn't seen before. He grabbed her hand and led her to a partly obscured bench at the end of the hedge. Holding hands, they sat side-by-side looking across the front lawn to the black swan swimming alone along the river Cam, which flowed across the lawn.

'How little he knows of the looming crisis, Annie.'

She turned to him, fixing her gaze on his.

'Annie, they're going to need soldiers, lots of extra soldiers if we're to win this war. Every man will be expected to do his duty.'

He paused, before grabbing both her hands in his.

'I'm thinking of signing up, Annie.'

Rolls of thunder broke inside her as she pulled her hands from his and up to her face, as she allowed his words to settle inside her head.

'But Arthur, think of the danger! You have a good job here. Are you really prepared to give it up to fight in a war that might kill you?'

'Annie, it's something I have to do. It doesn't mean I'll be leaving here yet, probably not for months. That's if I'm even accepted. I won't be the only one from the estate to sign up either, you mark my words!'

'You're breaking my heart, Arthur.'

Standing up, she turned to leave.

'I don't want to talk about it now Arthur. What makes it worse is that you look excited about going to war. I can see it in your eyes!'

'Annie, please don't go. At least promise me that you'll let me know when your next afternoon off is.'

'I'll think about it, but I have to go now. Mrs Gifford will be wondering where I am.'

With that, she ran back to the kitchen, stopping the tracks of her tears with a swift swipe of her hand.

Castle Street

A large placard had been placed outside Salmon's shop. Stanley propped his delivery bike up against the shop wall and stopped to read it.

'WAR DECLARED ON GERMANY
CAN BRITONS STAND BY WHILE GERMANY CRUSHES AN INNOCENT PEOPLE?
ENLIST TODAY!'

Inside the shop, high-pitched voices filled the air. Stanley picked up a paper and signalled to Reggie Salmon to put it on the slate, before slipping out of the door, setting the bell ringing. Outside, he sat on the pavement and leaned up against the wall to read the news. Beneath a photograph of large crowds lined up along the Mall and gathering in front of Buckingham Palace, a reporter described the scene:

'All along the Mall people gathered singing 'God Save the King.' Outside Buckingham Palace crowds waved flags and sang "Rule Britannia". At the first stroke of Big Ben chiming eleven, huge cheers went up, as the war telegram giving instructions to "Commence hostilities against Germany" was flashed to ships and establishments under the white ensign all over the world'.

Stanley's face flushed, his eyes shone, his feet pedalled faster than ever as he rushed to finish his early morning bread round. Desperately hoping that seventeen was old enough to enlist, he kicked open the kitchen door. Pol thrust a copy of *The Daily Mail* in front of him, open at an advertisement for the New Army being recruited by Lord

Kitchener.

'Read this, Stanley. How old does it say you have to be?'

His heart sank as he read out the age requirement for new recruits.

'All applicants need to be at least eighteen years old, and nineteen to serve abroad.'

Triumphantly, Pol snatched back the paper and fixed her eldest son with eyes of steel.

'Now let that be the end of your ideas about signing up, my lad!'

'Well, I'll sign up next year then, when I *am* old enough!'

'Oh, will you? They're saying it'll all be over by Christmas, Stanley, so I think you'd better give up on that idea too.'

Stanley pushed past her and ran upstairs to his room, where he threw himself on to his bed.

1915

Kitchener's scepticism about a short war had proved correct and, as the war continued into 1915 with little sign of victory, the need for more men to fight had become obvious, and Annie's worst fears had become a reality.

February 21st, 1915
Recruiting Office
Saffron Walden

Smiling to himself, Arthur Scoggings pushed his hands further into his pockets, propped himself against a wall and watched his pals lie.

'Name?'

'Reginald. Reginald Pearson, sir.'

'Age?'

'Nineteen, sir.'

'Health problems?'

'No, sir.'

'Well, let's be 'avin a look at yer. Lift up yer shirt, open yer mouth!'

Reggie puffed up his chest and opened his mouth wide.

'Can you read these letters?'

'A, F, D, B.'

'Stop! Well lad, you're just what we're looking for. Sign 'ere. Next!'

Careful not to catch the recruiting sergeant's eye, Arthur winked at Reggie and stifled a chuckle as Tommy Jenkins stepped up, followed by Sid Lewis, Ernie Roberts and, finally, the Steven's brothers, Bert and Fred, who being on the short side (a little under five foot four), were told to go away and grow an inch.

They'd all lied. They were just eighteen, one year too young to fight abroad. It wasn't the first time they'd lied about their age. Several of the boys had grown up together, played cricket together and were now going to war together.

They were then put into groups, one Bible per group. Arthur held the Bible for his group.

'Right lads, we're now going to swear an oath of allegiance to the King. Repeat after me.'

'I swear to faithfully defend His Majesty, his heirs and successors against all enemies, and to obey the authority of all generals and officers set over me, for as long as this war may last.'

Arthur and his pals stared straight ahead, not daring to look at each other as they repeated the officer's words.

'Right. Well done, lads! Now off you go. You'll be hearing from us shortly.'

February 27th
Salford, Manchester

As he was the youngest of eight, Arthur's mum and dad were relieved when he'd got the job at the Big House, and for Arthur it had been a huge step up in his life. At home, being the youngest he'd always been the last in line. On bath days he'd had the last bath, usually in cold water, with a grey slick hovering on the surface. At meal times he was last to be served, which in his house meant the smallest portion. And for as long as he could remember he was the last to wear the family clothes. This didn't make sense as he was bigger than his older brothers, especially George, whose cast-offs he'd always been expected to wear. The trousers had always sat a couple of inches above his ankles and his jackets never quite buttoned up. His feet were badly calloused, having been squeezed into shoes a couple of sizes too small. But that's just the way it was. At the Big House he'd been given new shoes, a smart footman's livery and day uniform, his own bed and four good meals a day.

'One less mouth to feed', his mum had said.

And now, just over a year later, his parents beamed with pride when he appeared at their door to tell them he'd been accepted into the estate workers' 'Pals' battalion and was about to start his training.

His dad slapped him on the shoulder and turned to his wife:

'He's going to make something of himself, you mark my words'.

Arthur was a big, good-looking lad. His dad had shown him how to puff out his chest to make sure he met the qualifying standard. He easily passed for nineteen compared to some of the scrawny boys they'd enlisted.

A week and a half after they'd signed up, they received letters telling them to report to the local recruiting station to be measured for their uniforms. Mr Lincoln had given them three hours off. As soon as servants' breakfast was finished, they and sixteen others set off to walk into town. Fred and Bert Stevens hung around the door, enviously watching them go. Arthur felt sorry for them.

Ragged queues of young men waited outside the local recruiting office beneath posters of Lord Kitchener, who stared down at them, fixing them with steely eyes and pointing an imperious finger. *'Your Country Needs You!'* it read. It was an irresistible call to arms for young men still with everything to prove. They joined the queue to be measured and were finally issued with a stiff khaki jacket and trousers, a flat field cap, a shirt, two pairs of woolly socks, two pairs of long johns, two pairs of short johns, puttees, a trench coat and black boots. To carry their kit they were given a type of knapsack, which the recruiting sergeant called a webbing. They were then given a metal mug, water canteen, trench spade, some sort of cutters and a long knife, which they were told to hang from the various canvas loops attached to the webbing.

Arthur could barely stand up. The trench coat was heavy and the new wool trousers irritated his legs. He tried hard not to scratch them. Every time he bent over, the kit dangling from his webbing fell forward, almost toppling him over. His boots were already hurting his ankles.

Back at the Big House Fred Stevens leant on his spade as Arthur and his pals took the shortcut through the kitchen garden on their way back up to the main building.

'Let's try yer 'at on, Arthur.'

Fred pulled the peak of Arthur's cap down over his forehead, then gave it to his brother Bert, who appeared at the door of the bothy. He wiped his muddy hands on his jacket, then held the new hat for a few moments.

'Hard luck, fellas. You need to eat a bit more of Mrs Warwick's bread and dripping.'

'Maybe you're right, Arthur.'

'Don't give up lads. Try again in a couple of months!'

March 2nd
Audley End House

Tents had appeared on the front lawn of the estate. Large groups of new recruits from all over Essex were arriving in heavy army trucks. They stood around in groups of ten, waiting to be allocated tents.

A company of the 5th South Staffordshire Infantry, many of them in civvies and flat caps, others wearing temporary Kitchener blue uniforms and carrying wooden practice rifles, joined the growing number of men and were immediately directed to the final row of round white bell tents that had been erected on the cricket pitch, next to the river. A group of swans eyed them quizzically as they dumped their rucksacks and equipment at the mouth of their tents before installing themselves inside

Men from the Royal Essex Regiment were assigned the next line of tents, which were closer to the main house.

The estate workers 'Pals' company had been assigned to the 4th Essex Territorial Battalion, which would be trained alongside the full-time soldiers of the Royal Essex Regiment. They would retain their jobs on the estate until called up to fight. During training they had beds in the house, rather than having to sleep ten to a tent on the lawns.

The weather had turned exceptionally cold and icy. Many tents lost their footing, their pegs having lost their hold. Several tents collapsed, exposing blankets and clothes plastered in mud from the ice melt, which under foot had formed pools of murky brown water. Muddy boots were hung from roof poles in a futile attempt to stop them filling with the filthy water, but they never dried out. Wooden beds were arranged around a central pole, fanning out like spokes of a bicycle, always ten to a tent.

In the House life carried on as normally as possible. But with most of the men now spending up to ten hours a day training, the female staff found themselves stepping into many of the male servant roles. Ethel and Daisy had been moved to the kitchen gardens. Ada had volunteered to help with His Lordship's cows and Fanny was being trained to drive a tractor. Ellen, who'd worked for Mr Lincoln as a stillroom maid, now served at table and occasionally worked as under butler. Annie thought herself very lucky to be moved into the kitchens to help Mrs Warwick, who was now Head Cook, replacing Monsieur Lambert, who'd joined the 'Pals' regiment. However, she was still expected to carry out housemaid duties each morning. For her, like everyone, life had become harder.

As she laid the fire in the Library, Annie heard the bugle sounding the 5.30 reveille. She peered out at the bleary-eyed men as they slowly emerged from their tents, blinking into the grey dawn as they silently drank large steaming mugs of tea. Arthur would be down shortly on his way to the parade ground, a roughly cut square, hewn out of the former rose garden and filled with asphalt.

With Arthur training long hours every day, she'd hardly seen him recently. She hoped to catch him before she was needed in the kitchen. She continued to stare out of the window, scanning the faces of the trainee soldiers beneath the window. After ten minutes Arthur had still not appeared, so she checked to see she was alone before quickly pushing a note into the third book on row three in section C of the bookshelves. She then rushed down to the kitchen to help with servants' breakfast.

All talk was now about war. Mr Lincoln wouldn't allow such discussions in the servants' room, so conversations were held secretly, in snatches.

Ada was full of it.

'I 'eard the lads were in trouble yesterday. Marching through Widdington they were. They were singing: *'Do your balls swing low, do they jingle to and fro'* and the village priest heard them!'

Annie stifled a laugh as Mrs Warwick came into the kitchen.

'Miss Smith, that's quite enough. Now get back to work, all of you! Miss Gingell, I'm going to need some walnuts for tonight. That wretched new garden boy forgot to bring them up this morning. You'd better go down and get them now.'

'Yes, Mrs Warwick'.

Ada caught her as she was about to set off for the kitchen garden.

'Lucky you. I wish I could go. The new garden boy brought the vegetables up this morning. He's got such a lovely smile, smiled straight at me he did.'

Annie hadn't met him yet, but she was secretly hoping to catch a glimpse of Arthur, who'd be doing bayonet practice in the field next to the kitchen garden.

She stepped out into the morning with a strange fluttering in her stomach. She tilted her face to catch the warmth of the sun on her cheeks as she hurried along. The snowdrops were now competing for space with the first of the aconites, and on the lake a pair of moorhens sieved the water for insects.

As she approached the kitchen garden there was a thunderous roar as line after line of men charged at rows of straw-filled sacks, stabbing bayonets into the belly of their targets, which exploded into a cloud of dusty stalks. She slowed her pace, trying to pick out Arthur. She found him watching her. He winked, and then took his turn to charge. For a moment his face became ugly, brutal, his body ferocious. Was this the funny, gentle Arthur she thought she knew? She couldn't bear to watch him, and hurried past trying to shut out the hideous roar of the men's voices.

Reaching the kitchen garden, she pushed open the huge wooden gates and found to her relief that the high garden walls muffled their horrible cries. She spotted the new garden boy in the far corner, next to the beehives. He was draping each hive in black and appeared to be talking to himself. He didn't hear her approach and was unaware of her eyes studying him until, feeling her presence, he turned to face her. It was then that she realised he'd been talking to the bees. He smiled shyly at her.

'Hello.'

Annie understood what Ada meant about his smile.

'Hello. Mrs Warwick has sent me to collect some walnuts.'

She paused.

'You're new here, aren't you? My name's Annie.'

'And I'm Gabriel,' he beamed. 'I started last week. I'm sorry I forgot to bring the walnuts up to the House with the rest of the vegetables this morning. Is Mrs Warwick very cross?'

'No. Her bark is always worse than her bite. You'll soon get used to her. Gabriel, who were you talking to just now?'

'I was telling the bees about my granfer's passing. He died last night.'

'I'm sorry to hear that, Gabriel. But why were you telling the bees?'

'You must tell 'em when someone dies. If you don't, they'll be spiteful, for bees is understanding creatures an' knows what you say to 'em.'

'What exactly do you say to them? I don't think I'd know what to say.'

'I just told 'em that they should stay at 'ome. They shouldn't fly as granfer is dead and gone.'

'How do you know they understand?'

'Oh, they understand all right.'

Mr Coster appeared round the side of the potting shed, carrying a tray of seedlings.

'I was stung all over by bees when I was a lad. And no wonder, I never told 'em I was going to put them in a new 'ome. Everybody knows that before you goes to put bees in a new 'ome, you must knock three times on the top of the hive and tell 'em. Same as you must tell 'em when anyone dies in the House. Now what brings you 'ere, young Annie?'

'Mrs Warwick sent me for some walnuts for Her Ladyship.'

'There's plenty of them in the mushroom shed. Gabriel go and fetch a bucketful.'

Annie followed Gabriel into the musty gloom of the mushroom house. The damp stench of compost hung in the air. Deep wooden trays lined the walls, from which sprouted clusters of tiny cream mushrooms. In the corner, next to a window laced with cobwebs, was a stack of shallow wooden crates full of dimpled brown walnuts. Gabriel scooped the ripe nuts into an enamel bucket, which he carried out into the sunlight. Annie followed as he carried the bucket to the garden gate and set it down on the ground. He stared out at the young men in uniform, bayonets poised to attack.

'They said the war would be finished by last Christmas, but they was wrong. I 'ope that'll be me in one of them smart uniforms next year.'

'You enjoy your time here, Gabriel. Don't go talking like that. There's more to war than a smart uniform.'

Gabriel picked up the bucket of nuts and pushed the handle into Annie's hands. She grabbed it and turned to face him.

'You heard that last October twenty of our local boys were sent back. Me mum saw them at the station. She said they were in a terrible state!'

Gabriel winced.

'And just before Christmas, eight Saffron Walden lads were killed. You think about that before you go rushing to sign up. Now I'd better be getting back. Mrs Warwick will wonder where I've got to.'

Annie set off for the House. She decided to take the shortest route, to avoid the gaze of the soldiers, so skirted round the back of the kitchen garden by the side of the Tea House Bridge. As she passed the bridge a bee flew almost into her face. She gasped and went to brush it away but it started to circle around her head, and then very slowly over her head. She looked up at it as it flew to about a foot beyond her face and hovered again, before flying away. She stopped and listened to the silence. Bayonet practice had finished for the morning.

'Where on earth have you been, Annie? You'd better get on with shelling those nuts. I'll be needing them in the next hour.'

Annie went through to the scullery, drew up a stool next to the bucket of walnuts and began cracking the shells. As she worked, she pictured Arthur thrusting a bayonet into a bag of straw, which in her mind became an enemy soldier. *How would it feel to kill a man*?

That evening she stole into the Library and took out the third book on the third shelf in section C. Arthur had left her a note. She quickly replaced the book and slipped the piece of paper into her apron. She had half an hour before preparing baths for the guests as they returned from the day's hunt. She made her way up to her room in the attic and fell onto the bed before opening Arthur's note.

April 10th, 1915

Dearest Annie,

I was really sorry to have missed you this morning. I tried to come to the Library before bayonet training, but Mr Lincoln was about and I couldn't risk being seen.

Thank you for your note. I know you don't like what I'm doing, but I hope you've now begun to understand why I have to do my duty. We're all doing our best to help our country. I finished my bayonet and sniping course today and will be starting a month's bombing training, followed by machine gun handling, which I think will mean even longer days. It's hard for us all.

When I catch sight of you going about your work Annie, it lights up my day. Tonight I'll wait behind the yew hedge. If you can slip away, I'll be there at ten and will wait until half past.

Until later.

Your loving Arthur

Annie held the note up to the ceiling and reread Arthur's message. Rising excitement moved from the pit of her stomach up towards her mouth. He'd covered her with kisses last time they met behind the hedge. She turned over on the bed and wrapped her arms around herself, remembering the smell of him, the softness of his voice and the feel of his hands around her waist.

The clock in the corridor chimed the half hour, reminding her that she was needed in the coal gallery. The guests would have returned from the hunt muddy and tired, and would now be wanting baths. She carefully folded the piece of paper and from the back of her drawer removed a small cardboard box. Opening it, she took out a bundle of notes tied together with a piece of red ribbon she'd worn in her hair as a child. She gently undid the ribbon and added the note to the top of the pile, before carefully tying a small bow and returning them to the box, which she placed at the back of the drawer before sliding it closed.

Rushing down to the coal gallery, she stopped to look at herself in the large oval mirror hanging on the landing outside the gallery. She noticed the colour in her cheeks and smiled at her reflection. She pushed open the heavy oak door. As she did so she could hear light footsteps scurrying out of the door at the far end of the gallery and the sound of laughter. *What is that Ada up to?* she thought. *I hope she hasn't been dallying with young Thomas again.*

She stopped herself. *What was she thinking? Of course, it couldn't be Thomas. He was training with Arthur. So who could it be? All the young men were training.* She turned to the copper and shovelled two large scoops of coal into the fire before picking up a hipbath. As she did so, there it was again: the low buzzing of bees. Annie placed a large bar of best palm oil soap into the bath and carried it through to the guest corridor. She knocked on the end bedroom door before taking the bath into the empty room and placing it near the fire. She took baths and soap into each room lining the corridor, setting them down by the fire, before returning with freshly laundered towels. Each bath would have to be filled with hot water from the copper. Being of slight build, Annie struggled to lift the heavy wooden buckets, which doubled in weight when filled with water. The heavy oak door of the coal gallery juddered as she pushed it open. She was relieved to find that both Ada and Ethel were already filling buckets.

'Phew, am I glad to see you two!'

Ada turned off the tap and strained to lift the bucket without slopping hot water over the floor.

'I swear these buckets is gettin' heavier!'

Ethel placed her bucket under the tap and slowly straightened up. Placing both hands on her hips, she stretched and arched her back as she waited for the bucket to fill.

'My back's bad today.'

She bent to turn off the tap, before looking up at Annie.

'Mrs Warwick wants you in the kitchen, Annie. You'd better

get down there. 'Er nerves is playin' 'er up.'

As Annie hurried through the Long Gallery, she could hear the members of the hunting party on their way up to the guest rooms. Their voices echoed in the stairwell and the wooden stairs creaked as they climbed them. She stopped briefly under her favourite portrait. It was of a pale-faced young boy, wearing long silk skirts. He carried a nest of baby birds. She'd decided he was probably about three or four years old. His eyes always seemed to follow her as she passed, as if inviting her to speak to him. Unlike the other portraits in the house, he had no name. She'd liked to have known who he was.

'Who *are* you?' she asked.

'What are you doing talking to that picture, Annie?'

Fanny the scullery maid grinned.

'Mrs Warwick sent me to get you. She says she needs you down in the kitchen now, and that the meal won't cook itself.'

'I'm sorry, Fanny. I'm just on my way down there now.'

The dinner stretched on interminably. It was 9 o'clock and the desserts had still to be served. Annie helped Mrs Warwick put the finishing touches to a large blancmange and a platter of exotic fruits. She daintily arranged the fragile pieces around a large pineapple, which had been grown in the estate vinery. She then carefully moved the two finished platters to the footmen's table, ready to be carried up to the dining room. She glanced at the large pendulum clock above the sink. It was now 9.15 and there was still the cheese course, followed by coffee. *She might just be finished in time to meet Arthur*. It was quarter past ten by the time the last footman had cleared the dirty china from the table. The guests would now be having coffee. Standing on tiptoe, Annie could just see out of the bottom corner of the tall window behind the cold sink. She spotted a slight movement at the end of the yew hedge. Arthur was waiting for her. She moved away from the window as Mrs Warwick swept in from the scullery. Perspiration stained her blue blouse and ran down the furrows of her forehead onto her cheeks and nose. She took out a large handkerchief and mopped her face.

'Annie, will you come away from that window and go and help with the pots. A party this size means more china, cutlery and pots to wash, and if we want to get to bed tonight, we must all help each other!'

Annie felt her heart sink as all hopes of seeing Arthur died.

'Yes of course, Mrs Warwick.'

June 12th
Middle Square

Pol was hanging out the washing when a letter arrived for her neighbour Elsie Parker. She was smoothing out a dripping sheet when the scream came.

Pol had known Sidney Parker since he was a baby. She'd watched him grow into a fine young man, who'd signed up almost as soon as war was declared. Stanley had grown up with him and, because of him, had begged her to let him sign up. She was pleased that he was two years younger than Sidney, still too young to fight.

Sidney had trained to be a machine gunner. He'd been wounded by a bullet passing through his shoulder and lung, before burying itself in his right hand. After five months in hospital he'd volunteered to go back to the front, where he received a leg wound. He was considered to be an excellent gunner and had been selected as a regimental sniper. He'd been fearless, attacking from the support trenches, before moving through the communication trenches to the front line. Finding them blocked, he'd gone over the top from the second line.

Elsie Parker had held herself together through months of anxiety, but nothing had prepared her for the arrival of the War Office telegram, delivered by the post boy. He rode his bicycle into the Square and, without meeting her eye, pressed the notification into her hand and mumbled,

'I'm so sorry, Mrs Parker'.

Pol slipped into the house and found Elsie slumped in a chair, staring at the threadbare rug beneath her slippered feet. The telegram had fallen from her lap and lay face down on the floor. Pol touched her friend's arm, then went over to the sink. She filled a kettle and set two cups on the table

'He's gone, Pol. He's gone!'

Elsie's face collapsed as Pol rested her hand gently on her shoulder. Pol sat silently waiting for the sobs that racked Elsie's body to subside. She poured them both strong tea and waited until Elsie was able to speak.

News of Sidney's death spread like a rash. Pol waited until Gruff and Stanley appeared at the kitchen door that evening, before gathering the family together around the scrubbed-pine table, which had borne witness to the giving and receiving of news for as long as Pol could remember.

'Sit down all of you.'

Rubbing soapy hands on her apron, she swept the table with eyes on the verge of tears, allowing them to rest on Stanley, who had been Sidney's best friend since childhood.

'There's terrible news. Sidney has been killed.'

'He can't have been. He said he'd be home soon!'

Stanley pushed back his chair and ran from the kitchen. Above them they could hear the rusty springs of his bed groan as his body convulsed with grief. Pol went to follow him upstairs, but Gruff grabbed her arm.

'Leave him Pol, a boy of his age don't want his mum seein' him cry like a baby.'

Pol sagged into her chair.

'I suppose you're right Gruff, but Sidney was his best friend.'

'He was our friend too!'

Pol looked around the table at the anxious faces of her two younger children.

'What happened to him, mum?'

'I don't know. All his mum knows is that he was killed in action in Gallipoli.'

Gruff leaned over to Pol and covered her hand with his.

'He was a hero Pol, he died for his country.'

Pol shook her head with the futility of it all.

'Gruff, he was only nineteen, still a kid. He should have had his whole life ahead of him. And he was an only child, which makes it even worse. I only hope this will put a stop to Stanley nagging me to let him sign up.'

They sat in silence, a silence that slowly absorbed the painful truth into itself. In the room above them Stanley sobbed into his pillow.

Pol looked at Fred and Nora, both of whom were fighting back tears.

'Now you two, I hope this is a lesson to you. There's nothing glorious about war. People get killed. Sidney won't be the only one from this street, you mark my words.'

****

Almost a week later Pol met the post boy as he was about

to push his bicycle into the yard He had a letter for Elsie. Taking it from him, she scanned the envelope. It had come from Canada.

'I'll give it to Mrs Parker'.

She knocked gently on Elsie's door and found her upstairs sitting on Sidney's bed, staring though the open wardrobe door at Sidney's clothes. She sat quietly next to her for a few moments, before pressing the letter into her hands and going to the window, leaving Elsie to read its contents. The room held its breath until finally Elsie moaned and collapsed on the bed. She threw the letter at Pol.

'Read it Pol, read it!'

It had come from a Private J Thayner, a former comrade of Sidney's. It had been sent from a Canadian hospital to tell her how Sidney had died. Pol's eyes brimmed with tears as she read:

'On Saturday morning the First Essex Battalion were ordered to advance. Sid was one of the first over and was killed instantly by a bullet to the head. Thank God, he wouldn't have known much about it. He was a brave man, my only chum and my sniping mate. Sid was buried half a mile behind the front line. His is one of 584 graves ....'

Annie saw the headline in the paper as she tidied Lady Braybrooke's bedroom the following morning.

'LOCAL HERO DIES AT GALLIPOLI'

Beneath the headline was a photograph of Sidney Parker in full army uniform. His battalion proudly on parade in the Market Square, surrounded by flag-waving neighbours and locals, all gathered to see their men off to war. She felt her knees buckle and grabbed the edge of the bed. She knew she had to go. She needed to be with Stanley and her family. Mrs Warwick allowed her the afternoon off to return home, but insisted that it was to be an exception, compassionate leave normally only being granted for the death of a relative.

As she approached Middle Square, Annie took stock of the street she'd grown up in. The houses seemed to sag, leaning together for support. She remembered her childhood, running in and out of Sidney's house, playing war with her brothers in the fields at the end of the street. In their games the dead and wounded lived to play the next game. Not so now. This was real. She turned into Middle Square. A painful silence hung in the air. Pol was stirring a large pot of soup and dropped the spoon as Annie pushed open the kitchen door and threw herself, sobbing, into her arms.

'I knew you'd come home, Annie.'

They clung together. The warmth of her mother's body soothed her as it had when she was small.

'How's Stanley?'

'He's taking it badly, Annie. He didn't go with Gruff today. He's refusing to come out of his room. I was hoping you could talk to him.'

They sat opposite each other at the table. Annie ran her fingers up and down the deep ruts of its ancient scrubbed wood surface.

'No mother should have to grieve for her son. It's not the right order of things. Elsie's had so much worry with that boy, but he's always bounced back in the past. But not this time. I don't know what I can do to help her.'

Annie looked into her mother's eyes. They were mired in wrinkles.

'I'll go and see her, mum. Then I'll go and talk to Stanley.'

'You're such a good girl, Annie. Take a bowl of this soup with you. Try and make her eat.'

Training Camp
Audley End House
July 23rd

Arthur's back ached. He threw his trench spade down and lit a cigarette. Leaning against a wall of freshly dug earth, he turned his face to the sun and inhaled deeply.

'Scoggings! You won't have time for a smoke when you're ducking shells. Put your back into it man! These might be practice trenches but if this one's going to be seven-foot deep, you'd better get a move on, son! When you've finished 'ere I've got a nice little supply trench that needs digging – only five-foot deep, so might be a bit of a rest, eh?'

Sergeant Barker peered over the edge of the trench, and plunging a seven-foot measure into the mud, decided that Arthur needed to dig a further two feet to meet the required depth.

'It shouldn't take long, Scoggings, a strong lad like you!'

He moved further down the line of sweating recruits.

'Come on lads, time's getting on. You wouldn't want to miss marching practice, now would you?'

'Bloody hell, he doesn't give up, does he?'

Arthur stubbed out his cigarette and threw the butt into the oozing mud that caked his boots and swallowed the half-smoked stub. He'd left a note for Annie on his way to drill this morning. The prospect of seeing her, of maybe kissing her, made his heart swell as he dug. His training had almost finished, and as he glanced along the line of men bent double, trenching spades digging deep into the Essex soil, he felt proud to be among the ragbag of servants, grooms and gardeners who had now been transformed into a superb fighting force. Their company was ready to be mobilised.

They'd marched nine miles that afternoon, but instead of returning to quarters, they were ordered to gather on the parade ground. They waited in small groups anticipating an announcement. The sun slowly disappeared behind the mansion, throwing it into silhouette. Speculation was increasing and a nervous excitement spread from group to group until their mounting laughter stopped abruptly as Captain Cornell stepped into the fading light.

'Attention!' screamed the company sergeant.

As one, the company fell into line, each man's body taut and alert.

Captain Cornell cleared his throat.

'At ease men. Well, gentlemen, we are off at last!'

The men flinched, shocked by the immediacy of the announcement.

'Your training has been tough, but in just a few months you have been transformed into a fighting force fit to serve your country'.

Clasping his hands importantly behind his back, he nodded to Sergeant Barker, who stepped forward, holding a large brown box.

'You will remember that when you agreed to overseas service you signed the 'Imperial Service Obligation'.

Pausing, he indicated to Barker that he should begin handing out brooches.

'Each and every one of you should feel proud to wear this very special badge, the 'Imperial Service Brooch', to be worn on your right breast.'

One by one the men pinned the badge under their right breast pocket.

'No doubt, you all want to know *when* you will be deployed. We will move off at 0140 hours on July 30th'.

He paused.

'But not before a jolly good send-off! Write your postcards to loved ones today and prepare your kit for inspection in the Town square the afternoon of July 29th. We'll march through the town behind the band.'

That evening Arthur waited behind the cloud hedge. He felt excited at the prospect of finally putting into practice everything he'd been taught, but knew Annie would be upset to hear his news. He lit a cigarette and tried to decide how best to tell her. As he waited, he heard the estate clock strike nine. He began to feel uneasy. *What if she can't get away? What if she hears the news from someone else before I can tell her?* At that moment there was a movement behind him, followed by a pair of hands covering his eyes. He swung round and pulled Annie to him. She fell giggling into his arms. Sex was something he'd fought hard not to allow himself to think about, but with his hand resting just above her buttocks, he felt a burning desire.

Annie pulled away, a sharp sensation in her pelvis.

'No, Arthur. The way you make me feel frightens me.'

He folded her hands into his and kissed them.

'Annie, there's nothing to be afraid of, you know I'd never hurt you. But I think what I'm about to tell you will upset you'.

She grasped his hands tightly.

'Tell me!'

'The battalion are leaving at the end of the week.'

'Where are they sending you?'

'We don't know, Annie.'

'When will you be back?'

'When the job's done, I expect.'

'How can they send you away without even telling you where you're going or how long you're going to be away for?'

He pulled her to him.

'I'll be back as soon as I can, I promise, Annie.'

'And if you don't come back? It will be the end of everything that matters Arthur. You're all the world and life to me.'

'I know I'll be back, Annie, I know I'll survive.'

They clung together, hoping to dispel their shared fear.

July 29th
Town Square, Saffron Walden

Arthur hadn't managed to see Annie. Sergeant Barker had organised daily practice marches, with each march becoming progressively longer. There were endless kit inspections and sniper, bayonet and rifle practices. He managed to write a short note and slip it into the usual place in the Library, but hadn't received a reply by the time the company were ready to march into Saffron Walden.

Annie and the remaining servants at the house had been given the afternoon off to cheer on the estate boys as they prepared to leave for war. She put on her best frock and shoes, arranged her hair the way Arthur liked it and set off with Ethel and Daisy. They climbed over the stile on the edge of the estate and headed towards the Town Square. People stood seven or eight-deep, lining the route to the Square. Children sat on the kerbside, holding homemade flags. A group of young lads had climbed on to the drinking water fountain in the middle of the Square and clung precariously to its facade. She spotted Pol, Gruff and

Stanley, standing on the opposite side of the Square, and waved to them. A small platform had been erected in front of the Town Hall, and a group of local councillors in full ceremonial costume sat next to the Mayor, resplendent in his scarlet robes and gold chain of office. A light wind ruffled the feathers of his tricorn hat as he smiled and chatted to a group of local worthies sitting to his right. An air of expectation and excitement filled the Square as people craned their heads in the direction from which the battalion would arrive.

The sound of a drum announced the arrival of the men. The crowd fell silent. Annie pushed her way through the crowd and squeezed into a gap on the kerbside near the Mayor's podium. From there she had a clear view of the approaching troops, their bayonets and cap badges glinting in the watery afternoon sun. Marching behind their regimental band and banner, they entered the Town Square. She scanned their young faces as they passed, searching for Arthur. The band struck up 'It's a Long Way to Tipperary', the crowd cheered and waved flags wildly in time to the music. She still couldn't see Arthur. She stood on tiptoe, raking the lines of khaki uniforms. Suddenly there he was, marching so close to her she could touch him. *She had to let him know she was there*! She yelled his name at the top of her voice. Without moving his head, he winked, as the company wheeled off to the right to face the Mayor's podium. Her heart pounded and her body glowed with pride.

Sergeant Barker faced his men.

'Attention! Present arms!'

Captain Cornell turned to face the Mayor, who now stood by his side. Together they walked along each line, inspecting the men. Smiling broadly, the Mayor exchanged a few words with individual soldiers. He stopped next to Arthur.

Annie strained to hear what he said and was thrilled when Arthur's smile briefly touched her face.

The leader of the Town Council stepped forward, cleared his throat and gave a stirring 'Good luck, boys' speech. He was followed by the Mayor, who expressed the pride felt by the town, so many of whom had gathered together to wave their boys off to war.

The band struck up again and, as the men marched from the Square, Annie's pride turned once again to anxiety. Her gaze remained fixed on Arthur's back. She drank him in, remembering the feel of her arms around his neck and the strength of his arms around her. *When would she see him again*?

The crowd lingered for a while before slowly starting to wander back home to their bereft houses. Several mothers, having held themselves together, dissolved at the sight of their precious sons disappearing from view and safety, to face heaven knows what?

Stanley followed Pol and Gruff as they made their way over to Annie. Gruff beamed at her.

'You look a picture, Annie!'

Stanley hugged her.

'That will be me next year. Didn't they look grand in their uniforms?'

Pol glared at her eldest son.

'Have you forgotten about Sidney already?'

'It's because of him that I'm going, ma. I've got to finish the job 'e started.'

'Over my dead body, my lad. There's more to war than wearing a smart uniform.'

'Come on Pol, leave the boy be'.

Gruff turned to Annie and hugged her to him. The familiar smell of stale tobacco and alcohol lingered on his breath. She tried to smile at him, but instead buried herself in his arms and sobbed.

'There, there, don't you go upsetting yourself, Annie.'

'What if they don't come back? It wasn't so long ago that Sidney marched out of this Square. He didn't come back!'

Pol put her hand out and wiped the tears that streamed down Annie's cheeks.

'Did you just wave goodbye to someone you care for?'

'His name's Arthur, mum. He's a footman up at the Big 'Ouse.'

She broke into another chain of sobs.

'Now, Annie, he wouldn't want to think you're upsetting yourself, would he? He wants you to be proud of him, to be strong for him. Now, wipe those tears away, you can't go back to the Big 'Ouse with a face like that.'

Annie dried her eyes and forced a smile.

'You're right, mum. I'll try to be strong for him.'

'There's my girl.'

Annie wiped her eyes and smiled at Pol.

I'd better be off. Mrs Warwick'll be needin' me in the kitchen. There's a big party tonight and a picnic tomorrow to prepare for.'

'That's right, you keep busy. The time will soon go, you'll see.'

Stanley, Pol and Gruff gave her a final hug before heading off back to Castle Street.

Ethel and Daisy had hung back but now appeared by her side. Ethel grabbed Annie's hands.

'Well, I told you Arthur was sweet on you, but it looks like you're just as sweet on him. You're a dark horse, Annie Gingell! He'll be back, don't you worry about that.'

Several other servants from the estate had noticed Annie's distress. She felt exposed and wanted to hide from their enquiring eyes. She took a couple of deep breaths and turned to Daisy and Ethel.

'Come on, we'd better get going.'

With that, the three girls hurried back to the House. Having cut across the fields, they arrived back at the estate before the men. Annie knew there would be no time to speak to Arthur before the battalion finally left in the early hours of the morning, but she secretly hoped she might catch a glimpse of him from the window in the servants' corridor. She ran up the back staircase and peered out. She could hear the band approaching the Lion Gate, where crowds cheered and waved flags. She rushed to her room, threw her uniform on and stood by the window, doing up her buttons and tying on her apron. The regimental banner finally appeared under the vast arched gate, followed by the marching band and then the battalion. Heart racing, she scanned the rows of khaki-clad men until she spotted Arthur.

One last look, she thought.

She loved the shape of him, his proud upright bearing, she loved the way he walked, the strength of his arms carrying the rifle and bayonet she hoped would protect him. As they marched into the parade ground beneath her, she looked down at herself and realised she'd buttoned up her dress wrongly. With shaky fingers she started to rebutton her uniform, quietly whispering to herself:

Come home safely, please come home safely.

She hadn't heard Daisy, who now stood behind her at the window.

'He'll come back to you, Annie. He'd be mad not to. Now come on, we'd better get down there.'

Ethel squeezed Annie's hand as the three of them ran down to the kitchen. Mrs Warwick was standing over the range, enveloped in clouds of steam.

'Thank goodness you girls are back. Now, Annie, I want you to baste the meat and then help me with the pâté. You'll need to line five copper moulds with slices of ham and then add the pâté mix. Ethel, go to the pantry, get a large bunch of parsley, chop it finely and bring it in here, then start preparing the vegetables Gabriel brought up from the garden this morning. Daisy, I want you to move this turbot pan to the table and carefully strain off the liquor then arrange the fish on this platter. When you've done that, start making the crayfish sauce. The crayfish have been steamed, you need to peel and chop them. I'll do the rest. After that you can start preparing the fruit for the dessert and check we have a pineapple for a centrepiece.'

They worked silently until Mrs Warwick suddenly threw up her hands in the air.

'How on earth are we supposed to serve a five-course meal for twenty guests when we've no footmen to serve at table? Mr Lincoln has said that you girls will have to step up, which means I'm left without any help down here!'

At that moment Mr Lincoln appeared at the kitchen door.

'Ah, Mrs Warwick, I hear you're discussing the arrangements for this evening.'

He then turned to Annie, Ethel and Daisy.

'Now, when you've finished here, I'd like you to come to my office and we'll run through the procedures for serving at table.'

Mrs Warwick sighed and put a large pan of water on to boil.

The jangle of keys in the corridor announced the arrival of Mrs Gifford. She swept into the kitchen and addressed Mrs Warwick.

'I've just spoken to Mr Lincoln who wants Annie, Daisy and Ethel to wait at table this evening. Will you manage down here without them?'

'If we can have most things prepared before they sit down to eat, then I'll manage at a pinch, but it won't be easy.'

'I do understand, Mrs Warwick. Now, Annie Ethel and Daisy, you must work quickly. As soon as you've finished, you must change into your best black uniforms, put on fresh caps and clean, starched aprons. We can't let standards slip just because we're short-staffed. Then, take your instructions from Mr Lincoln.'

'Yes, Mrs Gifford.'

It was past midnight when the three girls had finished clearing the kitchen ready for the morning. It was the first time she and her friends had witnessed such vast consumption of good food. Arthur had told her about the rations given to the men fighting in the trenches, so it felt so wrong to be throwing away perfectly good food left by some of the guests. She felt angry that these privileged people continued to eat all this extravagant food whilst the rest of the country were taking such care not to waste anything.

August 1st
Liverpool Docks

Arthur had discovered that his unit, the 4th Essex, was to join the 5th Norfolk, another Pals territorial battalion, made up of staff from the Royal Sandringham Estate. Together, they were to become part of the 163rd Brigade and were bound for Gallipoli.

In the grey pre-dawn light they joined lines of soldiers queuing to board *'The Aquitania'*, a luxury liner commandeered for the war effort, due to her vast size, and capacity to carry large numbers of troops and equipment. Estate foremen, butlers, head gamekeepers and gardeners, now NCOs, their status dictated by class, queued next to farm labourers, grooms and household servants, who made up the rank-and-file privates.

'Bloody hell, never thought I'd set foot on anything as smart as this. They won't believe me when I tell 'em back 'ome.' Like bloody royalty us!'

Tommy Jenkins grabbed his kitbag and loped up the gangplank on to the ship. Arthur, Reggie and Sid followed. None of them had been on a boat before, so it took a while to become accustomed to the rolling motion, as more and more men spilled into the bowels of the vessel, where rows of bunks had been erected.

The officers made their way to the sumptuous cabins lining the upper decks whilst the men grabbed bunks next to each other and stored their kit under the lower beds, before reporting to the sick bay, which they discovered was situated next to the engine room at the far end of the ship.

'Bloody good place to have a sick bay if you ask me!'

Reggie let out a loud chain of coughs.

'These fumes are enough to bloody well kill you!'

They joined the queue of men lining the gloomy corridor and rolled up their left sleeves. An army doctor dispensed inoculations with practised efficiency, yelling,

'Next, next!' as each man proffered his arm.

There was a thunderous groan as the engines ground into life and the ship lurched violently to one side, throwing a number of soldiers into the waiting line of men.

'Whoa, careful there!'

'Can't 'elp it, mate, the bleeding floor's moving!'

'You're going to 'ave to get used to this, we 'aven't even got out of the 'arbour yet.'

The corridor erupted into guffaws of nervous laughter.

Five hours later Reggie was violently sick, narrowly missing Arthur's boots, which he'd left under his bunk. From the neighbouring beds men groaned and vomited, the rank smell sucking oxygen out of the air. They'd been rationed to two pints of water per man, meant to last three days, but Reggie had become dehydrated, so Arthur and Sid gave him some of their ration.

'Better get you some seasickness pills, mate.'

Sid lurched along the line of bunks in the direction of the sick bay, returning half an hour later with enough pills to enable Reggie to sleep. The waves continued to thunder against the outer walls of the hull, sending shoes, kitbags and equipment sliding across the fetid floor. That first night no one slept. The bunkroom was freezing at night and unbearably hot by day. On the fourth day the high winds and waves subsided, allowing them to rest and to go on deck to take the air, but with so many troops packed into a very small space with inadequate lavatory facilities, dysentery, together with the side effects of inoculations and seasickness tablets, began to take their toll.

After ten days at sea they were finally ordered up on deck. Some men were too weak to join the briefing and remained in their bunks. They were still some distance from land but the sound of gunfire filled the air. General Sir Ian Hamilton, the British Commander-in-Chief of the Dardanelles campaign, stood grim-faced on the starboard deck. He cleared his throat and began.

'Tomorrow, we will be landing at Suvla Bay. We have brought you here to secure the northern bank of the Straits of Dardanelles, which provide a sea route to the Russian Empire, which as you know is one of the Allied Powers. You are an exceptionally well-trained force, and now the time has come to put your training to the test using courage and fortitude, which I have no doubt you will all do'. He paused. 'And make Britain and the Empire proud. Make your families proud. Be proud of yourselves and make Britain a land fit for heroes to live in! Now rest and prepare yourselves for the days ahead.'

He then turned and climbed the stairs leading to the upper deck, leaving his officers to dismiss the men.

They tried hard to close their ears to the sound of gunfire, but most men were wakeful that night. Arthur heard a couple of men sobbing.

The following morning they landed near the beach. They had to wade to the shore and immediately move inland. Several officers and men were shot down before they reached the beach. Not just from enemy rifle fire and snipers, but a battery of gunfire, which relentlessly hit them as they crawled and ran inland. Arthur couldn't count the number who fell in that short time.

Two days after they'd arrived in this arid hostile land they were ordered to attack, that same afternoon. Having been in the sun all day, the inexperienced troops were thirsty and scared, and now they were to launch a major assault on the Turks holding Anafarta Plain. Their aim was to clear them out, ahead of the planned allied advance. What they hadn't been told was that the enemy were well-armed and that they would be attacking them from below in broad daylight, with little cover.

August 25th
Saffron Walden

'Missing' notices had begun to appear in the local newspaper, arranged on the page like advertisements for soap or some other household commodity. Annie anxiously scanned the well-thumbed page until her eyes rested on a notice in the bottom right-hand corner. A photograph of Jack Abbot, a childhood friend, and one of the estate gardeners, smiled up at her. Above the photograph were the words:

MISSING SOLDIER
Private Jack Abbot
No 4524, 4th Essex Battalion
Missing since August 12th, 1915
Any information respecting the above will be thankfully received by his mother, Mrs V. Abbot, 169 Castle Street, Saffron Walden, Essex.

Jack had marched out of the Market Square with Arthur's Pals regiment exactly four weeks ago to the day. She'd tried not to think about why she'd heard nothing from Arthur, telling herself that the men had probably had little time to write home. Arthur had warned her that it might be a few weeks, and heaven knows how long letters would take to arrive from Gallipoli. She tried to stifle a gasp as Daisy glanced at her from across the table, her teacup raised to her mouth.

'What's the matter, Annie? You look like you've seen a ghost.'

Annie pushed the paper over to Daisy.

'Look at this. Jack Abbot from the 4th Essex, reported missing.'

Daisy put down her cup and studied the notice.

'He's one of the gardeners, isn't he?'

'Yes, one of the estate boys. He left with Arthur!'

'It says he's missing, not dead, Annie.'

'But what if something has happened to Arthur? Perhaps his parents have received news that he's missing? If they have, do they even know I exist? I've no idea if Arthur has told them about me. Will I have to wait to read about the fate of the 4th Essex boys in the local newspaper? I don't even know where his family live, so how can I contact them?'

'You're letting your imagination run away with you, Annie. No news is good news in my book. Now come on, there's nothing to worry about, Arthur will be back, you wait and see.'

Annie grabbed the paper out of Daisy's hands. She scanned the page of desperate notices and realised that she'd crumpled the edges of the page, distorting Jack's features, which had become ugly. She flattened the paper out on the table and focused on a second notice, placed under the photograph of a young local man she didn't recognise.

MISSING SOLDIER
Lance Corporal Stanley Hawkins
No 22694, the 4th Essex Battalion,
was reported missing on August 14th, 1915. He was last seen, wounded in the arm, at Anafarta on his way to the dressing station. News concerning him would be welcomed by his family at 76 Audley Road, Saffron Walden, Essex.

With rising unease, she read a third:

MISSING
Corporal Anthony J. Bear
No 6960, the 4th Essex Battalion,
last seen at Anafarta. If you have information about him, please contact his parents Mr and Mrs M. Bear, 66 High

Street, Saffron Walden, Essex.

'They're all from Arthur's battalion, Daisy! All young men just reduced to a number! How can I live without knowing, Daisy?'

'Annie, there's nothing to say that Arthur is missing, and you've just got to get on with living. Lord Braybrooke will be kept informed about his staff, don't you worry. Now come on, put that paper down, we have to get back to preparing for His Lordship's picnic tomorrow.'

A marquee had been set up in the middle of a stubble field to the east of the estate. A long wooden picnic table had been carried out by the two remaining male footmen, and Daisy had taken baskets of silver plate, knives, forks and spoons, which she had set out for twelve. The footmen carried out the polished glasses and twelve chairs, which they set down at the table before returning to the kitchen to await the food hampers being prepared by Mrs Warwick. The Audley End clock, being an hour in advance of railway time to allow an extra hour of daylight and shooting, chimed twelve times. Mrs Warwick glanced up at the large pendulum clock above the sink and wiped her forehead.

'Annie, have you got all the picnic baskets ready for the footmen?'

'Yes, Mrs Warwick,'

'I now want you to read out the menu so I can check each basket individually.'

Annie cleared her throat and read out the varied list of delicacies they had prepared that morning:

'Mulligatawny soup, hot hashed venison, hot chicken casserole, cold tongue, hot boiled apple pudding, cheese, fruit, coffee.

Drinks: 10 bottles of claret, 3 bottles of whisky, 3 bottles of port, 3 bottles of brandy'

'Right, quickly now, close the hampers and the footmen can load them on to the carts.'

By the time His Lordship's shooting party had arrived outside the marquee, put down their guns and settled the dogs, the tables were laden with sumptuous food. They greedily loaded their plates whilst Annie refilled glasses of wine, which were downed like water. The gluttony of the party, who barely took breath between mouthfuls and drank more alcohol in one meal than she had in her entire life, appalled Annie. The picnic lasted well into the afternoon. It was 5 o'clock Audley End time when the guests finally walked slightly unsteadily back to the house for baths, before preparing themselves for the evening meal.

Having helped Lily the scullery maid with the washing-up and Mrs Warwick with the preparation of the evening meal, Annie and Daisy were given an hour's break and were told to eat up some of the left-overs. They sat in the servants' room with platefuls of cold meat. Annie could hardly bring herself to eat anything.

'It's not right! His Lordship and his guests feasting on all this food while our boys are dying, fighting for their country. Their rations will be less than we'll be serving up for the first course upstairs this evening. I don't want anything more to do with it!'

Annie ripped off her apron and strode out of the kitchen. She waited for a moment before banging on Mrs Warwick's door.

'Come in. Oh, it's you, Annie. What on earth is the matter? Where's your apron?'

'I've taken it off, and I've come to say that I'm leaving!'

'Whatever for?'

'I can't stand back and prepare all this food for His Lordship and his friends to eat – and to waste – whilst the estate boys are fighting for their country and their lives on rations that are less than the first course being served upstairs. It's just not right!'

'Oh, for goodness sake girl, what difference will it make to the boys at the front if you give up your job here?'

'It will make a difference to me, Mrs Warwick!'

'Where will you go? And how will you find another job?'

'I'm going to help with the war effort. I'll get a job in a factory. They're looking for women to pack bombs and ammunition.'

'Well, my girl, that's all very well and good but where will you live? I'm sure your mother's house is fit to burst.'

'We'll manage, Mrs Warwick.'

'Does your mother know you're planning to leave?'

'No, but she'll understand.'

'Well, you can't just walk out. You must speak to Mrs Gifford as she'll need to replace you, but before you do, I suggest you think very carefully about your position here. You'd do well to remember that most girls would give their right arm to work in this house.'

****

Pol did understand Annie's anger, but secretly hoped she'd stay at the Big House. She couldn't afford to put another portion of food on the table. Annie would simply have to find a factory job before leaving Audley End.

Annie scoured the local paper for job advertisements and finally applied for a packer's job in the munitions factory in Ashdon. Two weeks later she was delighted to be invited for an interview. On her afternoon off she borrowed a delivery bicycle from Sillet's bakery and cycled the four miles to the factory. She arrived with five minutes to spare, so took out a small handbag mirror from the shoulder bag she had slung over her neck. She quickly wiped the beads of sweat from her forehead and tidied her hair, which hung in unruly coils over her eyes. A vast iron gate, flanked on each side by barbed wire fencing and a sentry box, gaped open. She wheeled her bicycle through and was immediately accosted by a khaki-clad middle-aged man, wearing a war service badge clipped to his jacket pocket.

'Can I help you, miss?'

'Yes, please. I have an interview this afternoon with Mr Wilkinson.'

'Your name, miss?'

'Annie Gingell.'

The man went into the sentry box and came back with a clipboard. He ticked her name off and then disappeared into the box again. She could hear him talking to someone on the telephone.

'I've got a Miss Annie Gingell here, sir. She's got an interview at three o'clock. Right you are, sir. I'll tell her to wait until he gets here.

'Mr West, the chargehand, will be here shortly. He'll show you to Mr Wilkinson's office.'

Then, pointing to a row of bicycles standing in racks, he looked at Annie and smiled.

'Now if you'd like to leave your bicycle in the rack over there, miss.'

Annie propped Mr Sillet's bicycle up next to a large black bike with a huge wicker basket, which caught in her handlebars. She was attempting to free them when a voice from behind her made her turn.

'It looks like you're in a bit of a muddle, Miss Gingell. Let me help you.'

'Oh, thank you.'

Having separated the two bicycles, the man smiled brusquely and introduced himself.

'My name is Mr West and I'm the chargehand here. I'll take you through part of the factory on our way to Mr Wilkinson's office, so that you get an idea of the layout. If you'd like to follow me.'

Annie had no idea what a chargehand was.

'Excuse me, Mr West, can you tell me what a chargehand is?'

He laughed.

'First time in a factory, eh?'

'Yes.'

'Well, I keep an eye on things in the factory. I make sure everyone's getting on with their work. There's no slacking on my watch!'

He led her into an enormous building with a roof even higher than the Great Hall in the Big House. Lines of identical machines powered by canvass drivebelts, attached to a gantry of metal wheels that hung suspended from the ceiling, ground and spun huge cylinders, shooting particles of silver-grey metal up into the air. Heaps of shavings littered the floor. Rows of men and women clad in khaki overalls and caps, bent over the monstrous machines. Women pushing sack trucks collected the finished cylinders and wheeled them to the far end of the room, where they stacked them in pyramids next to a narrow metal rail track, which ran into a siding and loading bay. Women working in pairs, bent double over the heavy finished cylinders, rolled them onto waiting flatbed trucks, which were then pushed along the track and out of the building by a woman driving a heavy-duty shunting vehicle. The noise was deafening. Mr West turned and, seeing the look of unease on Annie's face, shouted:

'Don't worry love, you'll get used to the noise!'

Laughing, he led her out of a side door, across a yard and into another building. Male and female changing rooms, washrooms and toilets led off a windowless corridor. Further along there were two doors. A brass nameplate on the first read 'R. Wilkinson, Factory Foreman'. Mr West then pointed to the second.

'That's Mr Howell's office. He owns the factory.'

Knocking on Mr Wilkinson's door, Mr West turned to Annie.

'Remember, you only go into these offices when you're asked to. Work hard, and always do as you're told, and you'll be alright here.'

'Come in!'

'I've got Miss Gingell 'ere, sir.'

'Thank you, West.'

'Well, come in. Sit down.'

He adjusted his glasses and smiled at her as she sat stiffly on the edge of a chair and glanced around the dingy smoke-stained office.

'Well Miss Gingell, I see that you haven't had any experience of factory work. I think you realise that what we do here is of vital importance to the war effort, and we therefore expect the highest standard of work and behaviour from our staff at all times.'

'Yes, of course Mr Wilkinson.'

'I understand that Mr West has shown you the shell-manufacturing plant. Our shells are sent to France, where they're used in trench warfare. It is imperative that safety regulations are adhered to by all members of staff, particularly workers in the Danger Zones.'

'What are the Danger Zones, Mr Wilkinson?'

'We have a number of buildings in the Danger Zone. As the name implies, the work carried out in these zones is potentially hazardous. It involves packing empty shells with explosive and detonators, and then sealing them ready for transportation to France. Do you think you're suited to work of that nature, Miss Gingell?'

'Well, I've never done anything like that before, but I'm willing to learn.'

'Good, good. Now you'll need to have a medical as we only take healthy staff on here. Assuming the medical goes well, you can report for training tomorrow. You'll be paid thirty shillings per week, payable on a Friday, and will be expected to work an eight-hour shift. We run three eight-hour shifts, six days a week. I need extra staff on the early shift in one of the filling rooms, which means your hours will be 6 a.m. to 2 p.m., every day except Sunday.'

Annie nodded. Mr Wilkinson leaned forward, folding his arms in front of him.

'Now Miss Gingell, you'll be given khaki overalls and a cap. You'll notice that the buttons are covered in linen. When you come to work you must wear nothing metal. No hairgrips, no hooks and eyes – anything that might cause a spark. Working in the Danger Zone will also require you to wear soft shoes with no tread. You'll be given a pair of rubber pumps. Matches and cigarettes are completely banned for obvious reasons, and if we find anyone carrying them, or flouting the safety regulations, they will be dismissed immediately and possibly sent to prison. Have I made myself clear, Miss Gingell?'

'Yes, Mr Wilkinson.'

'Now I'll get the nurse to have a look at you and, all being well, Mr West will show you Blocks A and B, which is where the empty shells are filled, detonated and sealed. He'll explain the process to you.'

With that, he picked up the telephone and called Mrs Bryant, the nurse.

Mrs Bryant, a flustered plump woman, looked at Annie's eyes, asked her to open her mouth, took her temperature, examined her teeth and declared her fit.

'Right, Miss Gingell, there are a few things I need to tell you. You'll find that the chemicals you'll be working with will make you sneeze and splutter to start with. This is all perfectly normal. You'll also experience a bitter taste at the back of your throat, but this will soon disappear as your body gets used to it.'

Annie swallowed hard, imagining the bitter taste in her mouth.

'So you should gargle and wash your mouth out each day when you have your lunch break. There are sinks for this in the washroom. You'll also need to wash yourself thoroughly at the end of your shift.'

She paused and pointed to a large weighing machine.

'Now jump up on there. We'll see what you weigh and then how tall you are.'

She scribbled both readings on her clipboard, before rummaging through a pile of khaki dungarees and caps piled on a table next to the weighing machine.

'Take these and put them on in the women's changing room. Now let me look at your feet.'

She grabbed a pair of rubber pumps and pushed them into Annie's hands.

'These should fit you. Take them with you, but don't put them on until you're told. While you're doing that, I'll call Mr West and ask him to show you Blocks A and B. Remember now, no hairclips or hooks and eyes!'

Annie made her way to the changing room and climbed into the huge pair of overalls she'd been given. The legs were far too long, so she had to roll them up three times before she could see her feet. She hadn't worn trousers before and they felt heavy and scratched her skin. The cap was barely big enough. She had to force it down over her ears to stop it popping up and falling off. She hung her own clothes up on a spare peg and picked up the Danger Zone pumps.

Mr West was waiting for her as she opened the changing room door.

'Right, Miss Gingell, I'll show you Block A first, which is where I believe you will be working.'

Blocks A and B were set in a dip surrounded on all sides by an earth embankment. A large board with a red cross painted over black skull and crossbones hung on the guard fence, which separated the Danger Zone from the rest of the site. Other squat buildings lay within the area, each surrounded by an embankment.

Mr West cleared his throat and pointed to the narrow-gauge railway line Annie had seen in the main factory.

'Miss Gingell, you'll see that the line runs directly from the manufacturing plant in and out of Blocks A and B. It's carrying empty shell cases in and filled cases out, where they're loaded on to the waiting trucks, ready for dispatch. He pointed to a loading bay beyond the filling houses and then to two other windowless buildings.

'These are the gunpowder magazines. This is where the raw explosive is stored. You'll see that they're set quite apart from the filling rooms. That's for reasons of safety.'

'How does the explosive get to the filling shed, Mr West?'

'There are concrete underground tunnels connecting the magazines to the filling rooms. Flatbed trucks run along lines bringing the material in wooden boxes straight into the sheds. Now let's go in'.

He pushed open a large wooden door and pointed to another door marked 'Shift Room'.

'In there you'll find a rack for shoes. Before we enter the filling room you must take off your own shoes and leave them in the rack. Then, in your stockinged feet, jump over the barrier into what we call the 'clean side', where you need to put on the rubber pumps that Mrs Bryant gave you. One of the girls will help you, and I'll meet you in there.'

He disappeared through a neighbouring door.

Annie was bending over, taking off her shoes, when a woman spoke to her. Standing up, Annie looked into the yellow eyes of a woman whose face and arms were varying shades of mustard. Her mouth was outlined in orange and bright orange streaks circled her nostrils. The woman smiled from the other side of a low wooden barrier.

Annie gulped and jumped away from her.

'My face is a bit of a shock, eh? You'll get used to it. Now take your shoes off, then jump over 'ere to the clean side.'

Annie's heart hammered against her ribcage as she rammed her feet into the rubber shoes. The woman introduced herself as Elsie Manning. She pushed open the heavily reinforced door to the filling room. Rows of women lined a long bench, pouring powder through funnels into shell cases and then ramming it down with a long piece of wood and a wooden mallet. At the back of the room canary-yellow powder was being sifted, sending a choking dust into the air. Every woman's face, neck, hands and nails were varying shades of yellow. Mr West approached them.

'Thank you, Miss Manning, I'll look after Miss Gingell now'.

'The girls in here are filling nine-inch shells with gunpowder. It's vitally important that the powder in each shell is properly compressed, with no air pockets. What you can see the girls doing here is called stemming. They're making sure that each shell is packed to capacity.'

Annie sneezed and spluttered. The back of her throat felt raw. A couple of the women glanced up at her and smiled. Mr West paused and then turned to face her. He continued:

'Miss Gingell, if you look further along the line, you'll see the women are pushing candle-shaped exploders into the shells. Beyond them the final group are screwing caps into the filled shells and loading them on to the conveyor belt at the end of the room. This takes them out of this building and into the finishing room in Block B, where large machines turn the shells and screw the caps on, sealing them as tightly as is possible. They're then loaded ready for dispatch in the loading bay outside.'

He looked at his watch.

'I think we'll just have time to take a quick look into Block B before you leave.'

Annie followed him into the adjacent building, which throbbed with the sound of heavy machines turning and sealing the finished shells. Mr West had to shout to make himself heard above the din.

'Well, Miss Gingell, I've already explained what happens in this building. You'll probably be starting next door, but it's good for you to see the whole process. Now if you follow me, I'll show you the canteen and the administration office, where you'll go to collect your wages.'

Annie returned to Block A and changed back into her own

shoes before following Mr West into the canteen, which stood opposite the shell-manufacturing plant. Rows of long wooden tables and benches stretched across the room, which was empty save for a short busty woman, who was filling a large tea urn with water. She stopped and smiled at Annie as Mr West introduced her as Olive Castle, the factory cook.

'So, yer comin' to join us then are you, luv?'

'Miss Gingell will be having her training tomorrow, Mrs Castle.'

There was a sudden deafening noise and a number of cups leapt off the shelves behind Mrs Castle. Annie jumped in alarm.

'It's alright, luv, you'll get used to that. The canteen is very close to the firing pits. Every now and then the windows break!'

Annie nodded and smiled, then followed Mr West out into the corridor. He knocked loudly on the door marked 'Administration' and showed Annie into a gloomy, high-ceilinged room lined with filing cabinets. A bare light bulb hung above a large wooden desk, behind which sat a middle-aged woman at a typewriter. The office clock chimed five as the woman stopped typing and smiled at Mr West.

'Do we have a new recruit, Mr West?'

'Yes, Mrs Parsons. This is Annie Gingell, who'll be joining us for training tomorrow and, if all goes well, will start working in Block A next week. I'll leave her with you now as I must get on. I'll see you tomorrow morning at six o'clock, Miss Gingell.'

He disappeared out of the door.

Mrs Parsons took out a pad and gestured to Annie to sit

down. She swivelled round to face her.

'Now Miss Gingell, there are a few procedures that you'll need to be familiar with when you come to work here. I'm sure you're aware of the very sensitive nature of the work that you'll be doing, therefore we require you to sign this form, which is an agreement that you will respect the secrecy and security protocols of the factory.'

Annie wasn't sure that she understood what protocols were but signed the form anyway.

'Now I need to know your full name, date of birth and address for your disc, which will be ready in the morning.'

Annie had no idea what the disc was for, but nodded and smiled before giving Mrs Parsons her details.

'Good. Now in the morning change into your overalls, remove all hairpins and make sure you're not wearing anything with metal hooks and eyes. Then come to see me and I'll give you your 'War Service' badge and identity disc, which you must wear at all times. You'll need to bring sandwiches unless you decide to buy food in the canteen. All hot drinks are provided and if you're on the early shift you're entitled to breakfast, which is served at 7.30. You'll collect your pay each Friday from this office. Any questions?'

'Not for the moment, Mrs Parsons. Thank you.'

Turning back to her typewriter, Mrs Parsons left Annie to find her own way out. She quickly changed out of the prickly dungarees and hat and hung them on a free peg, then stuffed the rubber shoes into a large pocket on one of the legs. She put on her own shoes and headed out and into the yard with the bicycle racks. She tried to dig Mr Sillet's bicycle out from under the black bike with the large basket that had toppled over on to it. The man from the sentry box called to her.

I'll 'elp you with that, luv!'

He struggled to lift the heavy bike whilst Annie tugged Mr Sillet's from underneath it.

'Did you get on alright then, miss?'

'Yes, I think so. Thank you for your help. I'll see you in the morning.'

Annie pushed her bicycle out of the gate and set off for home. The sun was low in the sky by the time she reached Saffron Walden. She wished she'd asked why the girls had yellow skin, and if it washed off at the end of the day. She hadn't even asked how dangerous the filling job would be. However, the prospect of earning good money and to be helping with the war effort excited her. But as she cycled up Castle Street, she decided not to tell Pol exactly what she'd be doing at the factory.

She burst into the kitchen with her good news.

Pol was sitting at the table with a copy of the local paper spread out before her. Annie sensed her mood before reading the headline:

'LOCAL PALS BATTALION DISAPPEARS

After weeks of rumour and vague official telegrams sent to relatives of the local Pals regiment, we regret to inform readers that all members of the battalion have now been listed as missing in action. Extensive inquiries via the American Ambassador in Constantinople to discover whether any of the missing men were in Turkish prisoner of war camps have been to no avail, and the King has only been informed that the Pals had conducted themselves 'with ardour and dash'. Relatives have contacted the Red Cross and placed messages in newspapers, hoping for news of their sons or husbands from returning comrades, but we are sad to report that to date no news has been received.'

A list of the local men appeared at the bottom of the article:

Abbott S. 7330 *Lance Corporal*
Andrews W. 7746 *Corporal*
Bear A. 5030 *Acting Sergeant*

Annie's eyes scanned the list of names arranged in alphabetical order, hoping that Arthur's name wasn't listed, but under 'S' there it was:

Scoggings A. *Private*

Numb, she hardly absorbed the final paragraph.

Any family wishing to place missing notices in this newspaper is invited to do so at no charge. We live in hope that our boys will return home.

Pol hugged her daughter as she stared at the newspaper headline, her face savage with hope.

'They're missing, Annie, that doesn't mean they won't be found when this bloody war is over. You must never give up hope.'

But they both knew that the Street was dwindling, occupant by occupant.

****

September 9th, 1915,
British Military Hospital,
Alexandria

My dear Annie,

I only hope this letter reaches you before you learn the fate of my old chums from the Pals.

For some reason I've been spared, which makes me think that my job has to be to finish what we all came here to do. I thank God that soon I'll be fit enough to return to the front, and I will make sure my chums didn't die for nothing. Then, when this awful war is over, I'll return to you, my love.

My memory of what happened to me is blurred, but I'll never forget that as we waded ashore at Suvla Bay we were hit by a hail of sniper fire. The sea was red with blood and we had to push our way through dead bodies floating on the surface. Tommy Jenkins was hit before we even got off the landing craft.

Once ashore, we were ordered to charge at the Turkish enemy. The Pals had drawn ahead of the rest of the British line as the fighting grew hotter, and the ground became wooded and broken. Colonel Beauchhamp yelled orders to keep pushing on to drive the enemy in front of us. We charged into the forest, where we were met with fierce fighting from the Turks, who bayoneted and shot our officers and men. We pushed on without back-up but were picked off by snipers entrenched in the ridge and up in the trees.

The next thing I remember was waking up in a German military hospital. A doctor spoke to me in broken English, telling me that I'd been shot in the head. A large bloodstained bandage covered my right eye and I had a sharp pain down my right cheek and ear.

The doctor told me that I was very lucky, as I'd been found by a German soldier who was with the Turkish forces. He told me that the idea of taking prisoners was very strange to the Turks, who would rather exterminate the lot of us, and that it was only because the German soldier had a good heart that I was saved and taken to a German Military Hospital.

I was treated well there but found it difficult to remember much. I'd got no idea if there were any other survivors of the assault and, if so, what had happened to them. I didn't want to believe the German doctor's description of their likely fate, so told myself that we'd probably advanced too far, and that when we'd found ourselves under intense fire had retreated and returned to the trenches. I made myself believe it and it wasn't until I was finally declared fit enough to leave that I learned the truth.

I managed to escape from the convoy taking me to the prison camp and made my way under cover of night to the coast at Anzac beach, where I was ferried along with others to one of the ships taking the withdrawing allied invasion forces to Egypt. It was then that they told me about the failure of the assault and the disappearance of the entire Pals Battalion.

It seems that there were few Pals survivors, and those that did survive were probably massacred by Ottoman soldiers.

I am so sorry to be the bringer of such terrible news, Annie.

The thought of coming home to you bucks me up in the dark hours when I lie awake. I hope and pray that you are well and live in the hope that I will see you again soon.

Your loving Arthur

Arthur placed the letter in an envelope and gave it to the night nurse, before turning over and trying to sleep. He pressed his head further into his pillow, trying to shut out the cries of the man in the next bed, who was asleep but reliving some recent horror. He hadn't told Annie about the night terrors that had begun to haunt him. They'd told him it was common and that he'd get over it. He'd be back at the front next week and wouldn't have time to dwell on things.

****

Howell's Munitions Factory, Ashdon
September 30th, 6.00 a.m.

It was Annie's third week at the factory. She had begun to get used to the rough cloth of her overalls and cap and was now less bothered by the noise of the heavy factory machinery. She clocked in, made her way to the changing room and climbed into her working clothes. She bent down to pull on her trousers and scratched her legs, noticing the yellowish tint of her skin. The striking yellow faces and bodies of the other girls no longer appeared strange to her. In fact everything she and the other munitionettes touched turned yellow, even the canteen benches and tables.

Mable Billings came into the room and sat next to her. She took off her socks and exclaimed.

'Even my toenails are yellow!'

'Doesn't it bother you that we're all turning yellow?' Annie asked.

'No. I've got enough to worry about without caring about a bit of yellow skin. Besides, it'll wear off after a couple of weeks, you mark my words.'

'But it won't wash off, I've tried.'

'No, course it won't. Now you know why they call us 'canaries'.

Mable tucked a lock of curly brown hair into her cap and stood up.

'Come on, it's five past six, don't let old man Wilkinson catch us gossiping!'

Annie had been told that as a safety measure the girls shouldn't open their mouths in the factory. As far as she was concerned there wasn't much point in opening your mouth anyway, as it was impossible to hear yourself speak. She had been given the job of filling aerial torpedoes with powder. She put on a pair of gloves and quickly joined the group of women already lining up filled shells onto the conveyor belt to be taken into Block B for finishing and loading, ready to be transported to the front. Mr West had shown her how to gauge the depth of powder needed in each shell before putting in the detonator and how to finish the shell off by clearing the screw heads ready for the final machine sealing. She set to work and, having finished a batch of twenty, left the building and walked into the machine room to check the speed of the conveyor belt, which appeared to have slowed down. As she opened the door a horrifying scream rose above the sound of thundering machinery. Annie looked up trying to see where the scream had come from, but was roughly pushed from behind by Fred Smith, who, with a wave of the hand, indicated that she should get back to work. The other girls appeared not to have heard anything. The scream became a howl, as the row of machines at the far end of the room ground to a halt. There was a scuffle, silence, and then the relentless grinding of machines once again.

In the canteen at lunchtime Elsie Manning whispered that she had been working on one of the machines when the girl next to her caught her hair in the unguarded machine. It peeled her scalp off all the way round her head. The girls bent towards her to catch her words, but glanced nervously at the door, springing away from their huddle as Mr Wilkinson appeared in the doorway.

'No doubt many of you heard about the accident this morning. The girl in question has been taken to hospital and we expect her to make a full recovery. Remember that what happens within the factory remains in the factory. Miss Gingell, please follow me to my office.'

With that, he turned in the direction of his office. Annie jumped up from her seat and followed him out of the canteen.

'Come in and close the door, Miss Gingell.'

He gestured for her to sit down.

'You're new here, Miss Gingell. Mr West tells me that you're a good worker. I'm sure an intelligent girl like you is aware of the Defence of the Realm Act, which prevents the press printing information about accidents as it might affect public morale.'

'Yes, I understand that Mr Wilkinson, but surely the best way to protect public morale is to prevent accidents happening in the first place.'

Mr Wilkinson smiled and walked over to where Annie sat. He rested his hand on her shoulder.

'And how do you suggest we do that, Miss Gingell?'

'The machines should have safety guards fitted.'

Mr Wilkinson's hand began to move down towards Annie's breasts.

'I can see you're a feisty little thing, Miss Gingell.'

He moved over to the door and turned the key in the lock. Annie froze.

'I like a girl with spirit.'

He fiddled with the flies on his trousers and lunged towards her, grabbing her and forcing her up against the wall. Pulling her overalls down, he dragged her underwear to her ankles. She tried to bite his hands and kick him in the groin, but he was a large man and easily overpowered her. He silenced her shouts, covering her mouth with his stubby fingers as he forced himself into her, thrusting with increasing urgency until he let out an ugly moan and pulled himself away. She slid down the wall and hugged her knees into herself sharply, aware of a sticky liquid running down her legs. He turned away from her and adjusted himself, before wheeling round, glowering at her.

'Get up, you filthy little whore. Don't you dare tell me how to run my factory!'

Annie wiped a thin trickle of blood from the inside of her thighs and forced herself to stand. She pulled on her knickers and overalls, the rough material rubbing against the raw flesh between her legs. Mr Wilkinson turned the key in the lock and returned to his desk. Without looking at him, she opened the door and ran to the women's' toilets, where she locked herself into a cubicle. A chain of violent sobs racked her body as she perched on the edge of the toilet seat. She sat for a few minutes, then swiped the salty tears from her face, cleaned herself up, and returned to the line of young women in the filling room.

Elsie Manning glanced over at her and mouthed, 'What did he want?'

'Nothing', she mouthed, turning back to her half-filled shell before the chargehand noticed.

Just before clocking-off time Elsie joined Annie as they stripped off in the communal washroom. The two women shared one of the washbasins that hugged the walls of the cold room.

'Where did you get them bruises on your arms, Annie?'

Elsie grabbed Annie's hands and twisted her arms outwards, revealing five finger-sized bruises on each arm.

Annie pulled away and plunged her arms into the basin, rubbing soapy water over the bluish marks, which were now beginning to creep up under her armpits.

'Who did this to you Annie, was it 'im, Wilkinson?'

'Why are you asking, Elsie?'

'Because you ain't the first, Annie. He shouldn't be allowed to get away with it, that's why!'

Annie dried herself and, putting her work clothes back on her peg, got dressed.

'He won't get away with it, Elsie.'

She left the room, put her card in the machine, walked out of the building and over to the bicycle shed. A sharp cutting sensation spread downwards from her hips as she lifted her leg over the crossbar and sat on the wide canvass saddle of Mr Sillet's bicycle.

Pol was stirring a large pot of meat stew when Annie pushed open the kitchen door, bringing a gust of chilly autumnal air in with her. Her cheeks glowed, but Pol only had to look at her daughter to see that things weren't as they should be.

'Whatever is the matter?'

Annie had decided not to tell Pol and Gruff, knowing they would stop her working at the factory. She needed to contribute money to the family and to help with the war effort.

'Nothing mum, just a bit tired, that's all. I'll be alright when I've had a little sit down and some of that stew.'

The following day she arrived at the factory a few minutes early. As she put her bicycle in the shed a young man wearing thick pebble glasses stepped out from behind a neighbouring bicycle and grinned at her. He held out his hand.

'Ronald Smith. Most people call me Ronnie. Glad to make your acquaintance. You're new 'ere, aren't you?'

'I've been here a few weeks, but you wouldn't notice me. I've got the sort of face people don't notice.'

'I don't know about that. I must have been walking around with my eyes closed then. Where are you working?'

'I'm in the filling room.'

'You happy there? I've heard that Mr Wilkinson runs a pretty tight ship.'

'It's alright. The pay's a lot better than when I was in service.'

'But not as good as it should be. You girls deserve better. The dangerous work you do needs guts.'

'Oh, it's not that dangerous.'

'Don't you believe it. There have been a few accidents since I've been 'ere, and that's not counting the explosion. No, you girls should be on the same wage as us men.'

'Well, aren't we?'

'No, you get about half what I do, you mark my words. Trouble is most men don't want you women 'ere. If you're happy to work for half wages what's to stop them employing a woman instead of a man? No, they're worried about their jobs. You girls are a threat.'

He smiled and walked towards the factory door.

Annie propped her bicycle up and ran after him.

'Ronnie, wait!'

Turning, he stopped and watched as she ran towards him.

'Is that what the writing on the wall by the locker room means?'

She tried to remember the exact wording of the slogan written on the wall to the left of the locker room door:

'Givers of life should not be trained to take it.'

'It doesn't need me to explain that, does it. It's obvious isn't it?'

'Well it's wrong. Women have every bit as much right to help their country as men do. And they should be paid as equals if they're doing an equal job to men!'

Ronnie dug around in his rucksack and thrust a crumpled

piece of paper into her hands.

'Ave a look at this and see what you think. If you're interested, come along to the next meeting in Saffron Walden.'

Annie quickly ran her eyes over the sheet. It was advertising a meeting of the National Union of Women's Suffrage Societies the following week.

'I thought these societies were just for women!' she yelled after him.

He turned.

'Nah, it's not them trouble-making Suffragettes. The Union don't believe in violence, they're Suffragists. My sister's a member. Men can join too'.

Annie folded the piece of paper and stuffed it in her pocket before changing into her overalls.

October 7th
United Reformed Church

The following week Annie made her way to the United Reformed Church in Abbey Lane. She joined a slowly moving queue of women that had formed outside the building. She looked around hoping to see Ronnie but there was no sign of him or anyone else that she knew. By the time she reached the doors all the pews had been filled. She turned to go, just as a young woman wearing a violet, white and green rosette appeared from within the church and stood on a low chair and smiled at the ragged group of women left outside.

'Standing room only now, ladies!'

Annie managed to find a space at the back of the room, where she was able to lean against a wall. Her back ached from bending over empty shells all day, and she found the cold dampness of the stone wall soothed her aching muscles. She craned her head forward and stood on tiptoes. From this slightly elevated height she was able to scan the tops of the heads of those who had come early and grabbed a seat. To her surprise there were a small number of older men, as well as a couple she decided were about her age. She then spotted Ronnie in the second row from the front, talking to a young woman sitting next to him. She wondered if it was his sister. The room suddenly fell silent and heads turned to the rear door, from where a small plumpish lady with cottage loaf hair appeared.

'It's her, it's Millicent Fawcett!'

The woman next to her leaned forwards, nudging her in the ribs as Millicent Fawcett walked briskly to the podium, her long tweed skirt brushing against the pew ends as she passed. Annie had seen photographs of her in the newspaper, but she looked much younger than her 68 years, despite the grey of her tightly swept back hair. She adjusted the rosette on her lapel and stepped up on to the stage. As she turned to face the packed hall, there was a spontaneous burst of applause. She smiled broadly and, with an immaculately clipped voice, welcomed everyone.

'I cannot tell you how pleasing it is to see so many of you here this evening.'

Then, casting her eyes around the room, she spoke directly to the small group of men sitting in the pews nearest to her.

'I particularly welcome you gentlemen to our meeting. However, please forgive me for saying, that no matter how benevolent men may be in their intentions, they cannot know what women want and what suits the necessities of women's lives as well as women know these things themselves. So, I thank you for listening, and for joining us this evening in a spirit of solidarity.'

Then, turning to the audience, she continued:

'I can never feel that setting fire to houses and churches and letterboxes, and destroying valuable pictures, really helps to convince people that women ought to be enfranchised. We must have government. But we must watch them like a hawk. However, it is impossible to practise parliamentary politics without having patience, decency, politeness and courtesy.'

There was a general murmur of agreement as people turned to each other and nodded.

'It's not just politicians who should be decent and fair people!'

All eyes cut to the back of the hall as Annie realised she was shouting. The indignation she'd felt since hearing she was being paid half Ronnie's wage boiled over.

'If two people are doing the same job, they should get the same wage. It's not right that men get paid more just because they're men. The factory managers shouldn't be allowed to get away with it!'

'Hear! Hear!' shouted the woman standing next to Annie. 'She's right. It ain't fair!'

Millicent Fawcett smiled at Annie, then thanked her before continuing:

'Of course, what the young lady at the back has said is very true, but we must be patient, yet relentless in our fight for equality. Think of our movement as being like a glacier, slow-moving but unstoppable. Our struggle will continue throughout this war, but much of our energy will now be diverted into supporting the war effort.'

There were loud cheers and cries of 'Hear! Hear!' from the floor.

'But what's been done to right the wrongs that women *still* have to put up with? What have you done to improve women's wages and working conditions?'

Annie's words were lost in the general hubbub, but a woman standing in front of her turned and thrust a pamphlet into her hands. It had been published by the Actresses' Franchise League and was advertising a series of plays, followed by discussions promoting women's suffrage. She tapped the woman on the shoulder and smiled

'Thank you.'

'Read it, I think it'll answer some of your questions.'

'I will.'

She noticed there was to be a play in Saffron Walden the following Wednesday evening. There was then much discussion about the war effort, but Annie felt she was already doing as much as she could to help. She was too ashamed to tell anyone about how she had been assaulted by Mr Wilkinson but knew she had to find a way to stop him treating other women the same way. This was the wrong she needed to have put right.

October 14th

The following Wednesday evening Annie waited outside the Baptist Church hall. The sky was heavy with rain and she shivered as her wet skirt clung to her legs. She'd cycled straight from the factory, as Ronnie had said she'd have to arrive early if they wanted seats at the front. She propped her bicycle up behind a low wall at the back of the church and ate the damp cheese sandwich Pol had packed for her that morning. She kept an eye out for Ronnie and had just finished her sandwich when he arrived, hands in pockets and cap pulled down over his ears. The attractive woman who had been sitting next to him at last week's meeting had her arm slipped through his and smiled as Ronnie introduced her.

'Annie, this is my sister Gladys.'

Returning her smile, Annie shook Gladys's outstretched hand, warming to her immediately. The three of them then joined the short queue that had begun moving into the hall. Much to Annie's delight they were ushered into the front row of seats. She sat on Ronnie's right, and had to lean across him to speak to Gladys, who had sat down on his left.

'It's the first time I've been to a proper play', she whispered.

Gladys smiled and pulled out a crumpled programme from her pocket. She handed it to Annie.

'This tells you something about the play. It's called *'Diana of Dobson's'* and is by Cicely Hamilton, so should be good.'

Annie scanned the list of characters and then began to read something called a 'synopsis'.

'Few women forget the first time they have been assaulted....'

Hardly able to stifle the gasp that was trying to force its way up from the depths of her chest, she continued to read:

'Few women forget the first time they were assaulted, the first time that someone felt they had the right to touch, to kiss, to take without asking...'

Ronnie and Gladys pretended not to notice her shaking hands as she tried to digest what she had just read. She wanted to finish reading the synopsis, but was sure that her insides had touched the outside, that her secret was there for all to see. She glanced furtively around, expecting all eyes to be on her, but was surprised to find that Ronnie and Gladys were talking to a woman sitting behind them, and the young woman to her right was engaged in a lively discussion with her companion. She continued to read:

'Women deserve the right to be safe in their working

environments and to have their independence without having to sacrifice their bodies to get it...'

She hadn't finished reading the programme, but handed it back to Gladys as the lights dimmed and all half-finished conversations were abruptly cut short. Harsh white lights beamed down like searchlights on to the raised platform in front of her, creating illuminated circles on the stage floor. Into them stepped three women, their faces thick with make-up. She was close enough to see their spittle, as their voices cut through the now silent audience. She gazed up at the three women as they transformed themselves into three 'live-in' shop girls at Dobson's Drapery Emporium, where they were bedding down for the night in the company's gossipy dormitory. One of the three, Diana, spoke with the accent of an educated young woman, the other two with the coarse tones of the lower classes. They discussed the drudgery of their work, the poor wages and food, the nastiness of their supervisor, Miss Pringle, and the hopelessness of their living conditions.

The play *had* been billed as *'A Romantic Comedy'* in three acts. But so far, the evening hadn't been what Annie had expected at all. She'd always thought that live-in shop girls were well looked after and earned far more than she did at the munitions factory.

Towards the end of the first act a number of unguarded comments made by Diana suggested that she had been assaulted by the company director, a Mr Piggot. Annie suddenly found herself on the verge of tears and hurriedly wiped her eyes.

It appeared that Diana had been left penniless and had had to rough it with the other shop girls, until she unexpectedly learned that she had inherited £300. She decided to tell Mr Piggot and Miss Pringle what she thought of them and then packed her bags for the Swiss Alps, saying 'I'll have a month of everything money can buy me, *then* I'll go back to the treadmill grind – but, I'll have something to remember – I'll have had my freedom.'

As the curtain fell Annie shouted:

'Good for you, Diana!' Then, looking around, she realised that she'd spoken her thoughts aloud. As the lights went up Ronnie and Gladys smiled at her.

'So, you're enjoying it then?'

'I got a bit carried away just now, I was so angry, I'm sorry.'

'Well, don't be, it's good that you feel so much for the characters, Annie'.

The young woman sitting next to Gladys then leant over and, fixing Annie with a knowing look, said:

'Yes, I felt angry too. You're not alone here you know. We all have a story to tell.'

Gladys leaned over towards Annie and squeezed her hand.

'Let's hope that Diana enjoys her month living a life of luxury, eh?'

The lights dimmed again. There was a loud creaking as the curtain juddered its way up, revealing Diana, now dressed in the finery of the aristocratic set. She'd passed herself off as a member of the 'ornamental class', hobnobbing at the Swiss resort of Pontresina. Her fellow guests assumed she was a rich widow and suffered her outspoken asides in defence of the 'useful class'. She was an obvious 'catch' and was courted by two suitors, one a brash, self-made tycoon, who'd benefitted from the cheap labour of others, the other a lazy former guards officer with insufficient inherited wealth to see him out, who was looking for a wealthy wife rather than for work. Diana accepted the attention of the second man but tested his commitment by challenging him to slum it as she had done. A test he failed miserably.

The final curtain fell to loud applause. Annie joined the many men and women on their feet cheering as the curtain was raised again, revealing the cast, now sitting in a semi-circle, smiling out to the audience.

To Annie's surprise, Gladys stood up and made her way to the steps at the side of the stage. She climbed up carefully, holding her skirts, revealing a glimpse of her black leather boots. She walked to the front of the stage and then, turning to the actors, thanked them before addressing the audience.

'What a wonderful performance!'

The audience erupted once more, and Annie found herself shouting at the top of her voice 'hurrah! hurrah!'

Gladys motioned for everyone to be seated and then swept the room with her eyes.

'There is much to discuss in this play, but as we are limited to only fifteen minutes, I won't waste time. Suffice to say that we have witnessed the plight of the overworked, underpaid female assistants at an imaginary workplace. However, I fear it is one that is common in many establishments. We see that the only alternative to their dead-end jobs is the unlikely prospect of marriage...'

'And what's wrong with that?' a tall bearded man bellowed from the back of the room

'A woman's place is in the 'ome, looking after the children.'

He then stabbed an accusing finger at the actresses.

'People like you aren't real women. Get back into the home, where you belong!'

Gladys, speaking calmly, thanked the gentleman for his comments and then continued:

'In this play we see a self-made man benefitting from the

cheap labour of young girls, who are entirely beholden to their employer.'

She paused. 'In more ways than one.'

There was the sound of a chair being pushed over as another man from the back stood up.

'What does that mean then? What are you suggesting?'

Gladys fixed her eyes on the group of men and women at the back of the room before answering.

'I will leave that to you to decide.'

Smiling, she continued:

'This play criticises a social structure in which it is acceptable for women to be paid consistently less than men, often for doing the same job. It also shows the effect that money, or the perception of it, has on people's expectations and estimation of others. We are living in a period of not just wage inequality but inequality of opportunities between the sexes. Only the few can afford the sunlit idylls that Diana strives for, and it seems that the majority who can, are men. Women have far less chance of ever achieving greater respect and feelings of self-worth in a society that condones this behaviour.'

A woman from the back of the room stood and glared at the women on the stage.

'I'd like to ask the actresses why they want to change the role that we women have always had. Do they really think that women are capable of holding political office? Do they really believe women are able to influence society in the way that men can?'

Another woman stood.

'You've only got to look at some of the vile acts of arson and theft carried out by women in the name of suffrage, to show that women are mentally unable to handle political matters.'

A woman shouted:

'Both sexes have different strengths. Women's highest duty must be motherhood, with all the responsibility that it brings. The whole institution of the family will be threatened if we give women the vote!'

A bald-headed man wearing a cravat stood and said:

'I agree with the previous speaker. I believe what she's saying is associated with the 'Domestic Feminism' movement, which espouses the belief that women have the right to complete freedom – within the home! Quite right, I say.'

Ignoring this contributor's point completely, the bearded man at the back of the room yelled.

'So should women all start wearing men's clothes and smoke cigars?'

Laughing, he turned for support to a group of men in the back row, lolling back in their chairs, one of whom shouted:

'You people only campaign to cover your own undesirability!'

Annie was on her feet, turning to face the man full on, she spat:

'And you, sir, are a rude, ignorant and narrow-minded buffoon!'

There were shouts of 'Hear! Hear!', until the actress playing Diana stepped forward, cleared her throat and waited. When the room finally fell silent, she addressed the audience.

'This evening we've tried to show you the reality of many women's lives. We've tried to show you women talking openly to each other about suffrage and their desire for more equal roles between the sexes. We don't wish to imitate men, we don't wish to threaten men's' jobs in the workplace, and we certainly do not condone violence of any sort in our struggle for equality. Finally, we do not see ourselves as unwomanly grotesques. Thank you.'

There was a round of applause, mixed with guffaws from the back of the room.

Gladys then brought the evening to a close by thanking all those who had spoken and announcing that, owing to the war, many members would be temporarily cutting back on their activities in order to divert their energies into the war effort. She also announced that the Actresses' Franchise League hoped to take specially selected groups of women to hold concerts and plays, under the auspices of the YMCA, to entertain troops both at home and in France.

The room emptied in a surprisingly orderly fashion. Annie remained in her seat with Ronnie, while they waited for Gladys.

'Well, you weren't frightened to speak up, were you?'

Ronnie grinned at her.

'Some of those men at the back need a good talking to.'

'And you are the person to do it, Annie Gingell!'

Gladys put her arm round Annie and gave her a hug.

'I think we've found a spokeswoman for the workforce at the munitions factory!'

Ronnie laughed.

'Why do you think I asked her along?'

As they left the hall the three actresses were packing the few props they had into a bag. Gladys spoke to the woman who'd played Diana.

'Have you got any spare programmes in that bag of yours?'

'Yes, I'm sure there's some in here somewhere.'

She rummaged in the bag and pulled out a wad of unused programmes and flyers, which she pushed into Gladys's hand.

'Actually, they're not for me. I think my friend Annie might like them. She paused.

'Annie, this is Gertrude, Eva and Mable.'

Annie felt suddenly shy as she shook each of their hands in turn, muttering that she was pleased to meet them, and how much she'd enjoyed the performance.

'Well, you certainly seemed to be enjoying it! We could do with more people like you who are prepared to speak out. Why don't you come along to one of our meetings sometime? As Gladys said, we're cutting back on our activities for the time being, but we'll still be holding regular meetings.'

'I'd love to. Thanks for asking.'

Annie beamed at the three women and turned to leave. Gertrude muttered something quietly to Gladys as they left the room. Annie couldn't hear what had been said but felt sure it was about her.

October 15th

The following evening Annie sat watching Pol as she peeled carrots into an ancient colander. The warmth of the kitchen had begun to make her drowsy, but a blast of cold air roused her as Gruff kicked the bottom of the door and appeared carrying the local paper, which he hurled on to the kitchen table.

'Look at this!' he said, pointing to the headline.

'STALEMATE!
GAS BLOWN BY SHIFTING WINDS CAUSES 60,000 ALLIED TROOP CASUALTIES'

'As if things aren't bad enough, now we bloody well find out that we've gassed our own boys!'

Annie had seen the effect of gas. Truckloads of young soldiers, their eyes bandaged, walking in a crocodile. Each man's hands resting on the shoulders of the man in front for guidance. These were now a common sight, snaking into the Red Cross Hospital that had recently been set up at Walden Place.

Pol put down her knife and read the first paragraph. She slumped into a chair, wiping her hands on her apron.

'Mrs Farmer from number 98 heard this morning that her youngest boy Henry's on his way back 'ome. Blinded by the gas. Makes me wonder how she carries on, 'avin' lost two already, and the other one reported missing. Mrs Abbott from number 96 told me that the poor woman leaves her backdoor open night and day, hoping that one day Leonard will just walk back in.'

She paused.

'I hope this puts an end to our Stanley's ideas about signing up.'

Annie picked up the paper. She'd continued to scour it daily for news of Arthur's missing Pals regiment, which appeared to have vanished from the face of the earth. Pol watched her daughter as she ran her finger down the list of local men reported killed in action.

'No news is good news, Annie, just you remember that! Now be a love and go up to the Common and fetch the washing in, it should be dry by now.'

Annie grabbed the old wicker washing basket and made her

way up to the Common. Rows of washing billowed in the gathering wind. She made her way to the line at the far end, where Gruff's pale-blue work shirt flapped in the growing gusts. She had things to do at home, so hurried to unpeg the washing. As she bent down to pick up the basket, she saw Stanley loping towards her with a wide grin on his face.

'It looks like I might get to see some action, Annie! There's talk of conscription in the New Year if they can't get enough men to sign up by Christmas.'

'Where did you get that from, Stanley? Anyway, you're not old enough!'

'I will be next year. Everyone's talking about it. Haven't you heard anything?'

'No, I haven't. And you can forget all about it. It's probably just rumour anyway. Don't you dare say anything to mum – she's got enough to worry about without you adding to it. Promise me you won't say a word?'

Stanley shrugged his shoulders and kicked the side of the basket.

'Alright, but she's probably heard anyway. She's just not saying anything.'

'Right, you can stop kicking that basket. It's got clean clothes in it. You can carry it for me.'

They made their way back to the house in silence. Stanley walked sulkily behind her into the kitchen and dumped the washing on the table, before heading upstairs to his room.

Gruff looked up from his paper as Stanley disappeared out of the door.

'What's got into 'im then?'

October 16th

Annie had got up early as she wanted to arrive at the

factory in time to put up a few of the flyers the actresses had given her. The play was to be put on in Ashdon the following week. Annie felt sure that some of the women would want to go. She'd written a short summary of the plot, which she was about to attach to one of the flyers in the locker room, when Mr Wilkinson appeared.

He leered at her.

'What are you doing?'

'I'm putting an advertisement for a play on the noticeboard.'

He went to grab the piece of paper from her hands.

'Let me see that!'

Annie stuffed it into her pocket and rounded on him.

'This room is for the use of the women who work for you, Mr Wilkinson, so may I ask why you felt it necessary to come in here?'

Ignoring her, he lunged towards her and tried to pull the piece of paper from her pocket. Stepping back, she held it up and waved it before him.

'I'll read it to you, Mr Wilkinson.'

As she read, Mr Wilkinson's leer turned to an ugly glare as he swiped the piece of paper from her hands and ripped it up.'

'You'd be better off trying to *please* your employer rather than wasting your time on this rubbish!'

He moved towards her, but she ducked under his arm and turned towards the door.

He barred her way.

'Oh no, young lady, you've displeased me. I think you should show me how sorry you are.'

He began to fiddle with his trousers.

'No, Mr Wilkinson, you aren't going to do that to me *ever* again!'

'Don't you tell me what I will or won't do. Just remember I could have you removed from this factory right now, young lady!'

'But you won't Mr Wilkinson.'

He lurched towards her.

'Don't you dare touch me!'

Mr Wilkinson grabbed her and tried to force her up against the door. Rolls of thunder broke inside her.

'No, you don't do that again!'

With that, she forced her knee into his groin. With a howl, his body jackknifed. His hands flew downwards, cupping his crotch.

There was a loud hammering from the other side of the door.

'Is everything alright in there?'

Mr Wilkinson attempted to regain his composure, readjusted his trousers and smoothed his hair. Glowering at her, he spat:

'You'll pay for this!'

He pushed her to one side, opened the locker-room door and, looking straight through Elsie, who mumbled, 'Good morning, Mr Wilkinson, I thought the door was locked, I'm sorry if ...', he limped out of the building.

Elsie found Annie picking up the pieces of paper littering the floor.

'What was *he* doing in here?'

Annie assembled the torn pieces together.

'He didn't want me to put this up on the noticeboard.'

Elsie read Annie's summary of the play and then looked at the flyer, which remained on the wall.

'He shouldn't have been in here. He's no right to say what we can and can't put up on our noticeboard!'

'Well, if he thinks that's going to stop me, he has another think coming. I've got just enough time to rewrite this before we start work. Elsie, could you put up some of these flyers in the factory for me?'

'You try and stop me!'

They changed into their overalls. Elsie then disappeared into the factory whilst Annie quickly scribbled the play summary on the back of one of the unused flyers. By the time the other women clocked in, the flyers had been placed in strategic places around the factory and Annie's review had been attached to the flyer on the noticeboard.

Ashdon Village Hall
October 26th

Annie arranged to meet Elsie and several other girls from the factory outside the washrooms at the end of the day. She waited until a largish group had formed before setting off for the village hall. She walked her bicycle along the footpath next to Elsie. Behind them, the group from the munitions factory followed in an unruly crocodile. A few stragglers had run and caught them up and, by the time they reached the centre of the village, they numbered thirty women. Annie smiled as they joined the queue waiting for the doors to open. She hadn't expected quite such a turnout, as most of the girls hadn't been to see a play performed before.

The doors were finally flung open and the noisy queue slowly melted into the hall. Somehow, they all managed to fit into the second row. Nobody minded squashing up to make room for Vera Roberts, who arrived red-faced and perspiring heavily, having run all the way from the factory.

Annie leaned over and mouthed to her:

'What happened to you?'

Vera mouthed back:

'Mr Wilkinson wanted to have a word with me.'

Annie thought, *huh, that explains why she looks so flustered*. She knew just what Mr Wilkinson's 'having a word' meant but nodded and smiled at Vera as the curtain rose and the hall lights dimmed. Spotting Annie in the audience, one of the actresses she'd met the previous week winked at her from the stage. Elsie nudged her and grinned. A few of the other girls looked along the row at her, proud that their friend Annie should be known in such elevated circles.

By the end of the after-play discussion a number of the munitions girls were indignant, others very angry. Several cheered Annie as she stood up to face down a few male hecklers, who'd positioned themselves in the row behind them. The discussion was brought to an abrupt close when a short plumpish woman wearing a violet, white and green sash appeared from the back of the hall and made her way towards the stage. Annie recognised her immediately.

Millicent Fawcett climbed the three steps up to the raised platform, which served as a stage. She walked to the centre, smiled and, looking directly at the hecklers behind Annie, silenced them with a voice of cut glass.

'Let us show ourselves worthy of citizenship whether our claim to it be recognised or not. As part of our contribution to the war effort the National Union of Women's Suffrage Societies plans to include clubs for soldiers and their wives, to form maternity centres and organise the training of women for acetylene welding.'

A man with boot polish hair who'd been sitting behind Annie stood up. She could smell his smoky breath as he yelled,

'Taking our jobs, that's what you women are doing, it's not right!'

'No sir, we are simply freeing you up to fight. Please sit down, you will find that more comfortable.'

The man, momentarily lost for words, meekly flopped back into his seat.

Millicent Fawcett continued:

'Remember that though war will make women's services more conspicuous, and prove women to be worthy of citizenship, their work in peacetime has been just as valuable.'

Then, with bird-like eyes, she swept the hushed room.

'Ladies, as a sex we are too often largely ignored, but we are very good at just getting on with things, albeit mostly in support roles. If you are interested in becoming a member of the NUWSS, please pick up a leaflet as you leave. Thank you.'

As they filed out of the hall, a tall woman wearing a violet, white and green rosette approached Annie. Smiling, she held out her hand.

'Good evening. I am a friend of Millicent Fawcett'.

Annie shook the woman's outstretched hand.

'Good evening'.

'I do hope you don't mind me accosting you like this, but I couldn't help noticing you and your friends. If I might come straight to the point, may I ask if *you* might be interested in joining the National Union of Women's Suffrage Societies?'

'Why are you asking *me?*'

'I can see that you're a woman with a good fighting spirit. Are you and your friends all working near here?'

'Yes, we work in the munitions factory in Ashdon.'

'And from what you were saying during the discussion just now, it seems that you are very dissatisfied with the conditions at the factory.'

'You bet we are.'

Elsie had hung back with Annie, whilst the others, eager to get home, had waved goodbye and picked up a leaflet before leaving the hall. Elsie held out her hand and introduced herself to the tall woman, who smiled warmly at them both.

'In joining the Union, you will find yourselves amongst other women who share your views. You will be amongst other women who are fighting to have their voices heard. But unlike the Suffragettes, who believe that deeds, and often militant deeds, speak louder than words, we Suffragists believe that if we are to be taken seriously by parliamentarians and the like, we must argue our case in a rational and respectful way. But that doesn't mean we lack spirit.'

Annie and Elsie looked at each other.

'We've not heard of the Suffragists before.'

'That is probably because we don't draw attention to ourselves in the same way that some of our sister groups do. However, now that we have this awful war to deal with, our sister groups have suspended all militant suffrage activities so that they can focus on war work too.'

Annie thought for a moment.

'If you don't mind me saying so, we shouldn't let the war be used as an excuse for lower wages being paid to women for doing the same job as the men, like in our factory. We're all helping with the war effort and should be treated equally.'

Annie realised that she'd raised her voice. It echoed in the silent hall. Elsie touched her elbow and turned to leave, apologising to the tall woman for holding her up.

'Please don't apologise. It is indeed refreshing to meet women who are passionate about our cause.'

She turned to Annie.

'We need strong women like you to help us lobby the government. I would very much like you to consider working for us, which would of course mean giving up your work at the munitions factory.'

Annie couldn't quite believe what the woman had said.

'But I don't even know what lobbying is. I need my job at the factory, not just to help my mum put food on the table, but to help our boys who are out there fighting. Besides there are things I need to do at the factory. We've only just started.'

'You would of course be paid.'

The woman then checked her watch and picked up a large carpetbag from the floor.

'I must go now, but remember that the members of the NUWSS have thrown themselves into the war effort.'

She reached into her bag and took out a small buff-coloured card, which she thrust into Annie's hand.

'My colleagues in the Actresses' Franchise Movement were most impressed with the passionate way you argued your case at last week's performance. You are obviously an intelligent woman, and certainly based on how you handled those hecklers tonight, I'd say that, with the right encouragement, you could go far in our organisation. Go away and think about what I've just said and if you change your mind, please let me know.'

With that, she swept out of the hall.

Annie looked at the card.

'Vesta Tilley!'

Elsie gulped, 'Isn't she that music hall singer, the one who dresses up in a soldier's uniform?'

'Yes, that's her! She sings that song...'

'On Saturday I'm willing, if you'll only take the shilling, to make a man of any one of you.'

Giggling, they made their way back to the centre of the village, where Elsie left Annie to cycle back to Saffron Walden.

****

October 27th

The changing room was buzzing when Annie arrived the following morning. A round of applause went up as she pushed open the door.

'Well done, Annie. You put them boys in their place last night. It's time we all had our say.'

Annie stepped up on one of the benches lining the far end of the room. As one, all eyes cut to her.

'We had a good time last night girls, but I think it gave us something to think about too.'

'You bet! About the way this place is run for starters.'

'Hear! Hear!'

Annie cleared her throat.

'So, what do we need to change?'

Eva Jarvis pushed her way to the front and climbed up next to Annie.

'We need proper guards on the machines. We don't want

any more accidents.'

'That's right. Hear! Hear!'

Mary Ellis then climbed up.

'What about the fillers? They need proper facemasks.'

Enid Broughall stood on tiptoes and, from the back of the crowd, shouted,

'And why do we only get half what the men get for doing the same job? It's not right.'

'She's right, it's not fair!'

Annie smiled at her friends.

'I think it's time we had our say, and Elsie and I are happy to go to Mr Wilkinson with your complaints.'

A loud cheer went up but was almost immediately silenced when the changing room door flew open and Mr Wilkinson erupted into the room.

'What's going on? Get to work, all of you!'

Annie calmly turned to face him.

'We have a few questions we'd like you to answer before we begin work today Mr Wilkinson.'

He scowled at her, his face puce, his voice strangled.

'You! How dare *you* tell me when you will and will not begin work. Get down from there and into the factory immediately!'

'No, Mr Wilkinson. We'd like you to listen to what we have to say.'

'I will *never* be told what to do by the likes of you. If you do not get to work within the next five minutes, consider yourself dismissed!'

'That's all of us then!'

Elsie had climbed up next to Annie and stared defiantly at

him.

'You will listen to us Mr Wilkinson, otherwise no work will be done today.'

Annie smiled inwardly as he groped the wall for support and glared at them with bulging, ferret eyes. She held his glare, then remembering Millicent Fawcett's measured tones, she turned to face the factory girls.

'Why are we women paid less?

'Yes. Why are we paid less?'

A chant started.

'Equal pay for equal work! Equal pay for equal work!'

Annie held her hands up for silence, then turned to Mr Wilkinson, who was now sweating profusely. He took a handkerchief out of his trouser pocket and mopped his forehead. His mouth flopped open as if to say something, but Annie locked eyes with his and fired a torrent of questions at him.

'Why are we paid less than the men in this factory Mr Wilkinson? Do we eat less? Do we have fewer people who depend on us?'

'Why aren't the machines in this factory fitted with safety guards? How many more girls will lose their scalps like that poor young woman a few weeks ago?'

'Why are we called 'canaries', Mr Wilkinson?'

'Why does our skin turn yellow? I'll tell you why – it's because we're all being poisoned.'

'It's the same in all the munitions factories!', Mr Wilkinson spluttered.

'So that makes it alright then, does it?'

Elsie stood, hands on hips, refusing to back down.

'So why do so many girls faint in the TNT room,

Mr Wilkinson?'

'Why do some girls have fits when they work in the cordite room, Mr Wilkinson?'

Without giving him time to spit out a reply, Annie rounded on him.

'Why are there piles of powder left by each shell in the filling room?'

'Why is the floor covered with heaps of metal shavings? And why are there ammunition boxes all over the floor when there are lathes whizzing and sparking right next to them? This is a very dangerous place to work, don't you think, Mr Wilkinson? There have been lots of explosions in munitions factories, but if people like you can sweep them under the carpet, it will happen again and again. How long will it be before we have an explosion here like they had in Silvertown or Woolwich, where the flames reached over the river and sent up a gasometer on the other side? Like a fireball, that was!'

Mr Wilkinson was speechless. He leaned his heavy bulk against the wall and gulped for breath, his air of superiority now wafer-thin.

'Well, what, what do you expect me to do about it?', he spluttered.

'Firstly, we expect you to show us some respect by listening to our concerns, Mr Wilkinson. Elsie and I will ask the girls to return to work, only on the understanding that you will meet with us to discuss our concerns today.'

'Don't be ridiculous! I don't have the time to spend listening to a couple of flibbertigibbets like you. I have a factory to run!'

As his voice increased in volume his dentures came gnashing down. He hurriedly lowered his head and gobbled them up again.

'Right girls, there will be no work for you today, or until Mr Wilkinson agrees to meet with us.'

Then, turning to him:

'If you wouldn't mind leaving, the girls will need to change out of their overalls.'

With that, she and Elsie stepped off the bench and headed to their pegs. The other girls followed suit. Mr Wilkinson's face had drained of colour.

'Wait! Wait!' he hissed. 'I'll see what I can do.'

'That isn't good enough, Mr Wilkinson. We need to know that you'll meet with Elsie and me today!'

'I ... I'll need to speak to Mr Howell first', he stammered. 'It's his factory. I'm just his foreman.'

'Well, you tell Mr Howell that Elsie and I would like to speak to him today, Mr Wilkinson.'

Then, turning to the girls, she insisted:

'We'll only start work when you've arranged a meeting.'

'Hear! Hear!'

'Whilst you are arranging that Mr Wilkinson, we'll have a tea break.'

Fuming, Mr Wilkinson sloped off to his office.

'Well, you showed him,' crowed Elsie, who had jumped back on to the bench.

'Let's hope Olive's got the kettle on. It's time for a cuppa, girls!'

The girls followed Annie and Elsie to the canteen but were stopped by Ronnie Smith, who was waiting outside the locker-room. He grabbed Annie and swung her round.

'I knew you could do it!'

'Whoa! I haven't done anything yet, Ronnie, just made a lot of noise.'

'I heard you. No one's spoken to old man Wilkinson like that before. Bloody marvellous you were.'

'Well let's see, Ronnie. We're taking a break now, but if the girls get to work today, you'll know we got our meeting.'

'Bloody marvellous! You're bloody marvellous!'

On that note Annie, followed by most of the female workforce, walked through the factory to a rousing cheer and applause from some of the men and loud taunts from a number of others, and the few women who'd chosen to return to work. They didn't have long to wait. As they sat drinking a second cup of tea the door to the canteen opened. A tall slim man with balding head and military moustache stepped into the room. Many of the girls, including Annie, had never seen him before but assumed he was the factory owner, Mr Howell. He stepped into the canteen, which had fallen silent.

'Would Annie Gingell and Elsie Manning please come with me?'

Annie and Elsie put down their cups, swung their legs over the bench and turned to face him.

'Are you Mr Howell?', Annie asked.

'Yes, and I own this factory. Now I'd like you both to step outside.'

'Before we do that, Mr Howell, I'd like you to promise the girls that you'll meet with us now, and that you'll listen to our concerns.'

He cleared his throat and addressed the silent room.

'I am prepared to meet with these two ladies now. I will listen very carefully to their concerns on your behalf, and see if we can work together to sort this out. In return I would like you all to get to work immediately.'

Annie smiled at her friends.

'Right girls, you heard it from him. Now finish your tea and return to work. Elsie and I will report back later.' With that, she and Elsie followed Mr Howell to his office.

****

The sky was battleship-grey as Annie got on her bicycle and pedalled home. It was late when she kicked open the kitchen door and sank into Gruff's chair next to the range. Pol beamed and nudged the kettle on to the hot plate.

'You look as though you could do with a cuppa. They kept you late at the factory, did they?'

Annie had said nothing to Pol about the problems at work, knowing that she would worry, but tonight she needed to talk.

'I've stirred things up a bit at the factory, mum.'

Pol poured two cups of tea and sat down opposite her daughter. Peering at her over the rim of her cup, she sipped her tea and waited.

'Mum, the conditions in the factory are bad. A couple of weeks ago a girl was scalped when her hair got caught in one of the machines.'

Pol gasped and shook her head.

'The machines are dangerous, mum. The women have also found out that the men are getting more money for doing the same work as them.'

'So how did they find that out?'

'I told a lot of them to go to that play last week in Ashdon. It was all about the way women are taken advantage of at work. A lot of them are now very angry, so I held a meeting and promised them I'd try to get a few things changed at the factory.'

Pol sighed and put down her cup.

'What are you getting into, Annie? We can't afford for you to lose your job – not now.'

'I won't, mum. Me and Elsie met the factory owner today and he's promised to make things safer at the factory, but says they can't afford to give us equal pay right now as any spare money needs to go into the war effort.'

'He's right, Annie. Everyone needs to pull together to improve things for our boys. You shouldn't be wasting your time stirring things up amongst the women. You've got to think of what's right for the country, not squabble about the way women are treated. Remember women are only in the factories because of the war. When it's over you and your women friends will be back in the home, where women belong. Leave the big decisions to the men, Annie.'

'I don't believe that, mum. I'm just as capable of making big decisions, and I don't intend to live my life just having babies and cooking.'

Pol winced. She studied Annie's determined face and knew there was little she could say or do to reel her wayward daughter in.

'It's your life, Annie. But whilst you're living under my roof you have to hold down a job to help this family survive.'

Annie knew there was no point continuing. 'Don't you worry, mum. You can count on my money just as long as you need it.'

Pol nodded and sighed as she pushed the local paper into Annie's hands. On the front page was a photograph showing Audley End House in the background and in the foreground a large stone cross, bearing the inscription:

'THIS CROSS WAS ERECTED BY KING GEORGE V AND QUEEN MARY TO HONOUR THE MEMORY OF THOSE OFFICERS AND MEN OF THE ESTATE WHO FORMED THE 4TH ESSEX PALS BATTALION OF THE 163RD BRIGADE AND FELL AT GALLIPOLI.

THEIR NAMES LIVETH EVERMORE'

Annie moved her chair over to the table.

A list of the men's names appeared below the large inscription. Hardly daring to breathe, Annie ran her eyes down the list of familiar names, her fingers crossed under the table. Arthur's name wasn't there! For a moment her heart leapt, then beneath the list of the dead, under the heading '*Lost in Action*' was inscribed a single name: 'Arthur Scoggings.'

Pol leaned over and squeezed her hand.

'He's missing Annie – that doesn't mean he's dead.'

'I know, mum. But if only I knew!'

'Of course you want to know. But you have hope, Annie. Think of the families of those young boys from the estate who won't be coming home.'

'I know, mum. I knew most of them. They were friends of Arthur's. I watched them training with him.'

A sudden urgent knocking on the door made them jump. Pol glanced at Annie and went to open it. A cold gust of air swept into the warm kitchen and settled around Annie's ankles.

'Where is she? Where is she?'

Mrs Turner, the red-faced landlady from the *Five Bells,* marched in and glared at Annie.

'What's this I 'ear – you stirring up trouble at the munitions factory? You should be ashamed of yourself, Annie Gingell! My Mary's now talking about leavin' unless she gets the same money as them men. Youngsters like you are getting above yourselves. Be grateful you've got a job, that's what I say. Today of all days, when young Frank Marking's family had the telegram boy knocking too!'

She glanced down at the newspaper.

'And all them lovely young lads from the Big 'Ouse killed. You should be 'elping the war effort, young Annie, not wasting time worrying about how much you get paid and what the conditions are like up at the factory. What do you think the conditions are like for our boys? Just remember, when this war is over, it's back to being a real woman for you, doing women's work!'

Pol guided her to a chair.

'I'm sure your Mary will change her mind when she hears that the owner of the munitions factory has promised to improve conditions for the workers.'

Annie clenched her fists under the table and looked up at the angry woman.

'Mrs Turner, we are glad to have a job, and no one has asked anyone to leave the factory. We all want to help the war effort, but we work at the same job as the men, in a very dangerous place. So why shouldn't we be treated the same as them? The war shouldn't be used as an excuse to pay us less, or treat us any differently to the men.'

Mrs Turner threw her head back and laughed.

'So, you think you're worth the same as any man?'

'Yes, Mrs Turner, I do. I also think my life is as valuable as any man's. It's not all about money, Mrs Turner. The munitions factory doesn't have to be as dangerous as it is. It wouldn't cost too much to put right some of the dangerous things that we see all around us up there, like unguarded machines and boxes of ammunition next to sparking lathes. It just takes someone to stand up and say so.'

Mrs Turner shifted uncomfortably in her chair.

'The factory owner has agreed to improve conditions for everyone, not just the women, and we have agreed to wait until after the war to sort out our right to equal pay. But believe me Mrs Turner, most of the women who've been doing war work won't happily go back to being tied to the kitchen stove.'

Pol stared at her daughter. She hadn't heard her speak like this before.

Mrs Turner stood up and, without a sideways glance at Annie, walked towards the door.

'Good evening, Mrs Gingell.'

Pol closed the door behind her and hugged her daughter, laughing loudly.

'Whatever did we do to deserve a girl like you!'

That evening Annie made her way to the Audley End kitchen garden. She climbed over the low gate near the beehives and watched the worker bees flying back and forth, carrying pollen in the tiny sacs on the back of their legs. She moved closer and, in a hushed voice, told the bees about the death of the Pals battalion. As she talked, a lone bee hovered over her head.

****

October 28th

There were a number of women already in their overalls when Annie walked into the changing room the following morning.

Elsie rushed up to her, eyes blazing.

'Wilkinson and Mr Howell are in there. They've got some men moving the boxes of ammunition, and there's a man putting guards around the machines!'

'What, *already*?'

Annie pulled her overalls from the peg. She struggled to pull the coarse canvas trousers up over her hips. Her heart thumped as she pushed her card into the clocking-in machine, before rushing over to the door leading to the factory floor. Elsie and a few of the other girls followed and watched silently as Annie flung it open. Seeing her, Mr Wilkinson scowled and yelled at one of the men to finish loading his box of ammunition on to a flat-bottomed truck that was already piled high with boxes. Mr Howell unfolded his arms and walked over to where Annie and the other girls were standing.

'Good morning, Miss Gingell. As you can see, Mr Wilkinson and I have almost finished relocating the ammunition boxes. The machines should all be fitted with guards by the end of the day and Mr Wilkinson will be distributing face masks to the fillers later on this morning.'

'Well, we didn't expect that to be done so soon, Mr Howell!'

'No time like the present is my motto, Miss Gingell. Now I trust there will be no more bother and you and your ladies will get back to work without any further fuss.'

'Well, we're very pleased that you've kept to your side of the bargain, Mr Howell. Thank you.'

'Right girls, you heard what Mr Howell said, so let's get to work.

****

When the siren sounded for tea break, Annie and Elsie made their way to the canteen.

'What I don't understand is how Mr Wilson managed to get them guards for the machines so quick. He must have had them already. It wouldn't surprise me if old man Wilkinson was supposed to have had 'em fitted before, but he never bothered.'

Elsie dunked a digestive biscuit in her tea and quickly stuffed it into her mouth before the bottom half broke off and sank to the bottom of her cup. Annie leaned back on her bench and stretched her arms above her head.

'I think you're right, Elsie, and, come to think of it, how does Mr Howell think he's going to put his hands on enough masks if he hasn't got them stashed away already?'

She paused as Enid Broughall and Mary Ellis joined them.

'We 'eard what you just said Annie. We was thinking the same thing. They 'aven't been treatin' us like they should for a long time now.'

Alfred Higgins, who'd worked in the factory before it had been adapted for munitions work the previous year, swivelled round on his bench and approached Annie's table.

'Just who the hell do you think you are, Annie Gingell? You've been 'ere five minutes and you're acting like one of them union leaders. Is it the men's jobs you and your like are after then?'

Annie put down her cup.

'No, I can assure you we're not after your jobs. Things in this factory aren't right and we just want them put right that's all. Are you unhappy then, that guards are being fitted to your machines, and the fillers have now got masks to protect them from the chemicals they stuff into them shells?'

Alfred Higgins didn't reply, but a number of the machine operators nodded at Annie, who turned to face Mary.

'I think Mary's right when she says you haven't been treated properly for a long time. But they have made a start and we need to bide our time before we upset them again. But we haven't forgotten about the girls in the TNT rooms, or the girls in the cordite rooms either!'

The siren sounded and as the workers stood ready to return to work, Mr Wilkinson appeared in the doorway holding a large cardboard box, which he opened, sending clouds of dust into the air. A chain of coughs shook his body, before he was finally able to clear his throat and announce:

'As Mr Howell told you this morning, there is a mask for everyone in the filling rooms. You can take one each and then return to your work.'

'Ow long 'ave you 'ad them, Mr Wilkinson?'

'Looks like they've been standin' on a shelf for a long time, Mr Wilkinson!'

Eva Jarvis was the first to take her mask from the box. She held it up in front of Mr Wilkinson, who was now blowing his nose vigorously into a large white handkerchief. Several of the other girls joined Eva.

'Why weren't we given these before, Mr Wilkinson?'

'Shame on you, Mr Wilkinson!'

'Think yourselves bloody lucky you've got them at all. Now get back to work!'

Annie stepped forward and taking her mask from the box, placed it over her mouth and nose, then, before fixing it behind her ears, she turned and glared into Mr Wilkinson's arctic eyes.

'Get your masks, girls! Better late than never, that's what I say! Now let's get back to work, eh?'

Annie tied the mask firmly behind her ears and left the factory for the filling room and the shell she'd been packing.

The other girls followed suit, leaving Mr Wilkinson to report back to Mr Howell.

Later that afternoon Mr Howell appeared in the filling room.

'Miss Gingell, would you please come to my office?'

Annie removed her mask and glanced over her shoulder to meet Elsie's gaze. She shrugged her shoulders and raised her eyebrows as she rushed to keep up with Mr Howell, who was striding across the yard to his office. He ushered her into a dark room with shelves from floor to ceiling, full to bursting with untidy files. Old bills and letters spilled out from their worn corners. The air was heavy with the must of old books and dry paper. Annie waited for him to speak.

'Sit down, Miss Gingell.'

Mr Howell sank into an oak swivel chair and peered at her over his vast leather-topped partners' desk. He picked up a lead pencil and sat with it poised over a sheet of headed notepaper.

'Miss Gingell, I understand that you are fairly new here, but you certainly seem to have made your presence felt, not least with Mr Wilkinson, whom I believe you have shown little respect for, despite his position here as foreman.'

'If Mr Wilkinson wants me to respect him then he must make himself respectable Mr Howell, if you know what I mean?'

Mr Howell raised an eyebrow and scribbled something on his pad.

There was a knock on the door.

'Come in!'

The door opened. Mr Wilkinson stood, holding the half-empty box of masks. Seeing Annie, he froze.

'Yes, Wilkinson, what did you want?'

'I just wanted to let you know that the fillers all have masks now, Mr Howell.'

'Not before time, Wilkinson. And the machines? Have they finally had the guards I ordered last year fitted?'

'Yes, Mr Howell. The men only have four left, to fit in Block B.'

'Leave that box with me, Wilkinson, and shut the door behind you.'

'Now where were we, Miss Gingell?'

'You said I had to show Mr Wilkinson more respect, Mr Howell, but I don't think he respects his workers. If you don't mind me saying, I think the factory would run much better if he showed a bit of concern for our safety at work.'

'Well, I think he has made a start, don't you Miss Gingell?'

'Yes, he has, but I think you and Mr Wilkinson will have to agree that there are still a number of other problems to be sorted out.'

'And what precisely are these *other* problems, Miss Gingell?'

Annie closed her fingers and drew them back, holding them in a tight bud.

'The problem of the girls fainting in the TNT room, and the girls who have fits when they're working in the cordite room. It's the ether in the cordite that does it. That munitions policewoman, Gertrude West, said so.'

'And how do you know that, Miss Gingell?'

'She was at one of Millicent Fawcett's meetings. She got up and spoke to us all.'

Mr Howell winced.

'Thank you for bringing the matter to my attention, Miss Gingell. I think that's quite enough to be getting on with for the time being.'

He scribbled something else down on his pad.

'I just don't want you to forget what you promised, Mr Howell, that's all.'

'Yes, yes, I'm quite aware of that, Miss Gingell. Now perhaps you'd like to return to work.'

As she stood to leave an almighty explosion shook the room, sending files cascading from shelves and shards of glass flying through the air. Metal girders and chunks of concrete crashed down on Mr Howell's desk. A cloying grey dust swirled around her head, filling her lungs with smut. She retched, fighting for breath. A wailing siren drowned the screams of Annie's friends in what was left of the filling room across the yard. To Annie, trapped beneath piles of debris, it seemed that the whole world shook.

'Give me your hand, Miss Gingell!'

Mr Howell was clawing at a chunk of concrete, which pinned her right leg to the floor. A splintered wooden beam lay across her chest.

'I can't move my hand.'

'I'll try to move the beam, then you'll be able to lift up your arm, Miss Gingell.'

Grabbing a broken length of metal, he began to lever the beam off her chest. Rivulets of blood and sweat trickled down the pleats of his face, whilst a spate of ragged coughs shook his body. The heavy beam had slowly begun to move when a second explosion threw him back against a sheet of twisted corrugated metal, as a thick blanket of black smoke enveloped the room.

'Are you alright, Mr Howell?'

The force of the second blast had lifted the concrete from her leg enough to enable her to pull it free. A sharp pain shot from her ankle up to her knee as she attempted to straighten it. She could hear Mr Howell's laboured breathing but the smoke made it impossible to see where he had landed. By twisting her body backwards and forwards, she managed to loosen the beam laying over her chest enough to pull herself from under it. She stumbled towards where she thought Mr Howell was.

'Mr Howell, I can't see you, let me know where you are.'

A thin rasping voice appeared to come from beneath what she thought was a piece of corrugated roofing.

'Over here, Miss Gingell.'

Picking her way towards the voice, she could just make out the shape of Mr Howell's shoe sticking out from beneath the piece of corrugated metal. Grabbing the ragged edge of the roofing, she dragged it off and threw it to one side. Mr Howell lay motionless, his face blackened and mouth wide open, gasping for air. She bent over him.

'Keep breathing, Mr Howell. Give me your hands.'

Mr Howell managed to lift his hands and place them in hers.

'I'm going to have to pull you up, Mr Howell.'

He choked, nodded and tried to sit up.

'It's alright, Mr Howell. Let me pull you.'

She pulled him into a sitting position.

'Now I want you to put your hands round my neck, Mr Howell, and we'll get you on your feet.'

Annie managed to pull him onto his knees before finally dragging him to standing.

'Lean on me, Mr Howell.'

She moved him towards the shattered windows and, stumbling over piles of rubble, managed to reach the door that had been blown off and now lay somewhere under their feet. She dragged him away from the remains of the building and propped him up against an iron girder that had survived the blast.

'Stay there, Mr Howell. I've got to find the girls!'

'But Miss Gingell, there might be other explosions!'

Annie ran into the crumbling ruins of the filling room. Another series of sharp pains shot through her leg as she tripped over piles of shoes strewn over the floor. The door had been blown off its hinges and thick smoke billowed out and up into the open sky. It hung there where the roof had once been. The moans and screams of buried workers filled the air. She tripped over the blackened body of one of the filling girls, her new mask melted into the grisly charred skin that had covered her face. Annie retched and crawled over piles of twisted debris that lay beneath the suffocating blanket of smoke that swirled over her head. A number of burned, dazed workers stumbled towards a gaping hole in what had been an external wall. Out of the corner of her eye Annie spotted a movement and crawled towards what was an outstretched hand. She grabbed it and yelled.

'Hold on to my hand. I'll get you out.'

The hand closed like a vice on hers. She kicked aside the remains of a door and pulled as hard as she could. The woman screamed as Annie wrenched her wrist out from beneath the shattered lump of wood that pinioned it to the floor. With another violent tug she was able to pull her free.

'Lean on me and head for that hole', she choked.

Together, they stumbled towards a pile of dust-covered shells that lay across their path. The force of the blast had thrown other shells into a corner, where they balanced haphazardly, disgorging their deadly contents. Annie dragged the woman towards a gap in the crumbling exterior wall and laid her down by an earth embankment. She then turned back into the filling room, just as another explosion sent rubble and unexploded shells up into the sky. She was thrown out of the building and landed face down in one of the ditches bordering the Danger Zone. Her nostrils filled with mud and she struggled to breathe. Next to her she heard someone calling for her mother. Clawing the mud from her nasal passages, she filled her lungs with fetid air and choked violently.

'It's alright, Annie. I've got you.'

A hand searched hers and circled her wrist. There was a violent pull and she was dragged up and over the top of the filthy ditch. Mud caked her trousers, dragging them down from her crutch. The metallic taste of blood mixed with concrete dust filled her mouth. She retched again and spewed the contents of her mouth over Ronnie Smith's trousers. He laid her on the ground and ran back into the blaze, to return a few seconds later carrying Elsie, whose overalls hung in shreds. He laid her on the ground next to Annie.

'Are you alright, Annie?'

'I've been better. And you?'

'The same.'

Annie watched as workers from the factory dragged more survivors from the wreckage. The moans and screams of the injured filled the air as other workers struggled to help their colleagues. Annie dragged herself into a jackknife position and tried to stand. The ground spun, her head felt heavy, a trickle of blood ran down into her ears and on to her neck. She turned to Elsie, who was slipping in and out of consciousness, a large pool of dark blood seeping from her trouser leg. The sound of an ambulance cut through the screams.

'Elsie, I'm going to get you into an ambulance.'

The world spun as Annie forced herself to stand. She grabbed Elsie's arms and yanked them over her neck then dragged her senseless body over to the nearest ambulance.

'You've got to take her. She's bleeding. Quick!'

A woman wearing a Red Cross armband helped Annie roll Elsie on to a stretcher before ripping the remains of her trousers off, revealing a large shard of bone protruding from her shattered leg.

'Can you fix her up?'

'We'll do what we can.'

Annie left the nurse and made to go back into the building. Firemen had arrived and barred her way as Mr Howell appeared by her side, barely recognisable beneath the thick layer of grime that coated his face like a mask.

'You mustn't go back in there, Miss Gingell!'

'But we've got to try, Mr Howell. There are still people trapped in there. We have to try!'

There was the sudden cry from what had been Mr Wilkinson's office.

'Help us, for God's sake help us!'

Annie ducked under the fireman's arm and, pushing aside broken window frames and chunks of roof, made a path wide enough to crawl through. Ignoring the fireman, she dragged herself in the direction of the voice. The wall of the office door had collapsed, miraculously leaving the doorframe standing. She pushed her way into the room and froze. Mr Wilkinson lay trapped beneath two wooden beams, his penis protruding from his unbuttoned fly, and next to him one of the young girls from the filling room with her overalls and underwear down at her ankles. The fireman tried to usher Annie away, his face barely able to conceal his distaste. Annie bent down to try to pull one of the beams from Mr Wilkinson, his eyes followed her, his humiliation complete. The girl's eyes remained closed. Annie wasn't sure if she was conscious or simply trying to avoid looking into the eyes of her rescuers. Mr Howell staggered through the debris and stopped dead, scarcely able to comprehend the scene in front of him.

'Please leave, Miss Gingell. See if you can help somewhere else.'

****

A thunderous boom, threatening to topple the ancient houses on Castle Street, stopped Pol in her tracks. She threw down her broom and, with the force of the boom reverberating through her body, rushed out into the yard. In the distance, in the sky over Ashdon, thick plumes of smoke spread like a billowing black blanket thrown over the sky. An unnatural silence hung in the air.

'It's the munitions factory. Annie's in there!' she howled.

Outside the *Five Bells* Mrs Turner screamed,

'Mary, my Mary's in there!'

Outside number five, Mrs Marking wailed for her daughter.

'Grace is in there, God save 'er. Please God, save 'er!'

The residents of Castle Street and the many squares leading off it poured out of their houses and huddled together in the road, staring in horror at the sky over Ashdon. A second blast lit up the distant skyline sending a mushroom of acrid smoke into the air. Pol fell apart. She collapsed against Stanley, who, hearing the explosion had run home.

'It's alright, mum, our Annie will be alright. You know what she's like, she'll be alright.'

'I 'ope so, Stanley, I 'ope so. I've been dreadin this I 'ave. I've such an awful clutching fear in my heart, Stanley. I have to know what's 'appened to 'er.

'I know, mum, I know. Now you wait 'ere. I'll go and harness one of Sillet's horses and we'll take the delivery cart over there and see for ourselves'.

As he turned to go, Pol grabbed his arm.

'We must take Mrs Turner and Mrs Marking too, Stanley.'

****

A fire engine, followed by an ambulance, shot past them on the road, their bells clanging urgently. The sky over Ashdon convulsed. Huge flames sliced into the choking black smoke that swirled like a dark whisper over the main factory building. Stanley urged the horse on.

'Come on girl, faster, you can go faster!' The horse quickened its pace, then, as if sensing what was about to happen, reared up as the ground shuddered like an earthquake, as a third blast almost overturned the flimsy wooden cart.

'Whoa. Whoa. It's alright girl, it's alright!'

Stanley's grip on the reins tightened as the terrified horse bolted.

'Whoa. Whoa. It's alright girl, it's alright.'

The three women fell silent and gripped the sides of the wooden cart as it hurtled towards the mountainous wave of dust, which surged towards them like boiling surf. Stanley continued to calmly coax the animal. Then, with a final jerk of the reins the horse came to a stop, nostrils flaring, eyes wild. Her huge flanks rising and falling with her terrified breathing.

'Come on now, girl, take it slowly now.'

The animal hesitated, then nervously moved on into the cloud of smoke that wrapped itself around them, plastering their stinging cheeks with thick black smuts. A gust of wind briefly lifted the fog, allowing them to see the main factory building looming up in front of them. It appeared to be largely intact, but the smaller buildings within the separate Danger Zone had almost been razed to the ground. Stanley knew that Annie hadn't told Pol she was working in that Danger Zone. As they approached the gates to the factory Stanley grew less sure of himself, and wanted his mother to say something reassuring as she'd always done in the past. He looked at her sitting next to him, her face creased with anxiety. He watched as she cut short the tracks of her tears, with her hand wiped across her wet cheeks. This was the moment that he'd think back on, as the moment he'd become a man. He leaned over and caught her fingers briefly in his.

'Look mum, the fire engines are there and they're putting out the flames, and there are three ambulances with trained Red Cross nurses looking after the injured.'

Pol couldn't bear to look at the devastating scene playing out in front of them. Mrs Turner and Mrs Marking sat behind them, mute, their faces contorted with fear. The sky was now funereal. Cries of anguish and pain filled the air.

'Now you three stay 'ere. I'm going in.'

'Stanley, be careful son!'

He tied a handkerchief over his mouth and nose and ran into the blistering heat of the smoke-filled yard. A woman with her hair in flames staggered towards him her eyes hollow, staring into some unknown distance. Taking off his jacket he threw it over the woman's hair and smothered the flames. The stench of burning hair made him gag as he gently guided the dazed woman towards an ambulance. His eyes watered, blurring his vision, as he made for the Danger Zone, where the wounded lay on the earth embankment like tattered rag dolls. A woman with a red cross on her armband bandaged a badly burned woman, who begged for something to stop the pain. Others lay dazed and bleeding. He scanned their faces looking for Annie. There was no sign of her. He stumbled over bodies, some with legs and arms at grotesque angles, only identifiable by the discs they wore around their necks. He helped a crawling woman out on to the embankment and laid her next to another young woman who was trying to stand.

'Don't try to get up, 'elp is here'.

He looked at her again and realised that he was staring into the blackened face of Mary Turner.

'Are you alright?'

She stared vacantly at him and nodded.

'I've got your mum 'ere. She's on Sillet's cart at the entrance. We'll soon get you out of 'ere, Mary.'

He paused.

'Ave you seen our Annie?'

'Mary pushed herself up on to her bloodied elbow.'

'She's alright Stanley, but you must stop 'er. She keeps going back in!'

She grabbed his arm as he made to go.

'You've got to stop 'er, Stanley!'

Jets of water made a rainbow-like arc in the sky above them, as firemen doused the flames that were rapidly advancing towards the gunpowder magazines at the outer edge of the Danger Zone. Choking back tears of relief that threatened to blind him, he heaved aside pieces of jagged roofing and forced his way through mounds of scattered debris and charred bodies, calling to his sister.

'Annie, Annie, where are you?'

'I'm over 'ere Stanley.'

He followed her voice and, stepping over a lifeless form at his feet, found her dragging a young woman out from under a sheet of corrugated asbestos.

'Thank God you're alright, Annie. Mum's outside. She's worried sick. You gotta go and tell her you're alright.'

'Help me get *her* out first. It's Grace, Grace Marking. She's in a bad way but she's still breathing. Be careful with her Stanley, I think she's badly 'urt'.

Together they managed to pull her limp body out from under the debris. Stanley stumbled with her in his arms to an ambulance that was about to leave for the hospital. Annie hammered on the ambulance door and pointed to where Stanley leaned against the side of the vehicle, carrying Grace's limp body.

'You gotta take 'er, she needs 'elp now. She's hardly breathin'!'

'There's no more room luv, we're full to bursting as it is.'

Annie grabbed the closed door and forced it open.

'You've got to take her –she's going to die!'

The driver sighed and jumped down from the cab.

'Grab that stretcher then! Come on, lift her on to it! Quickly! Now, that's the last one for this trip. There's no more room!'

They rolled an unconscious woman on to her side to make space on the floor for Grace. The ambulance doors slammed shut and the vehicle sped off past Sillet's horse and cart, its alarm bell cutting through the smoke.

****

October 30th

Two days later *The Weekly News* simply published thirty-five death notices, reporting that each of the thirty-five had *'died by accident.'*

'Just look at that! Is that all they can say about those poor devils who lost their lives bravely doing their bit for the country. It ain't right'

Gruff threw the paper down on to the kitchen table.

'You know why they can't write about what really happened. It's that *Defence of the Realm Act*. They don't want to cause alarm.'

Pol pushed a bowl of soup in front of Annie, who sat at the table, her bandaged hands and arms resting on its worn surface. Staring out of the window into the empty yard, she picked up her spoon and grimaced.

Pol watched her with anxious eyes.

'Now you must eat, Annie, to build up your strength.'

'I know mum, I will. Has Stanley eaten anything yet?'

'He will luv, just as soon as he wakes up. He was calling out in his sleep again last night. It's affected him badly. Mrs Turner says Mary can't sleep, says she keeps seeing the faces of those girls. Nobody should have to see that.'

There was a loud knock on the kitchen window. Gruff pushed back his chair and dragged open the swollen back door, revealing Mrs Marking, her hair unkempt, her rheumy eyes red and swollen. She stepped into the warm kitchen, slumped into Gruff's chair and burst into a torrent of tears that slid down the folds of fat in her face.

'I've just got back from the 'ospital. They've put both 'er legs in splints and they've stitched up 'er 'ands. She looks terrible just lying there, and she's still unconscious. They don't know if she'll come round even. I don't know what to do with meself.'

'It's probably best that she's unconscious, it's givin 'er body a chance to heal.'

Pol filled the kettle and sat down next to her. Gruff patted the distraught woman on the shoulder and sloped off out of the kitchen. Annie swallowed another spoonful of soup and then dragged her chair over to Mrs Marking, whose doleful eyes rested on hers.

'I've got you and Stanley to thank for saving Grace. I don't want to think what would 'ave 'appened if you 'adn't pulled 'er out.'

Her face buckled again and fresh tears cascaded down her cheeks. Pol placed a cup of tea in front of her and then rummaged through a drawer. Finding a clean handkerchief, she pushed it into Mrs Marking's hand. The woman wiped her eyes and took a sip of the hot tea.

'It feels like there's a curse on my family. First Frank, and now this.'

Pol reached over and cupped Mrs Marking's hands in hers.

'There's every reason to hope that Grace will come round, maybe even tomorrow. You said the doctors are fixing up her broken legs, and they've stitched up her hands. Now they wouldn't 'ave bothered doin' that if they didn't think she was goin' to recover, would they?'

'Well, maybe you're right.'

Annie placed her bandaged hand on Mrs Marking's arm.

'Now I've grown up with your Grace, and I know what grit she's made of. It's goin' to take a lot more than some stupid explosion to crush her, you mark my words!'

'You are a good girl, Annie Gingell'.

Mrs Marking took a last sip of tea and stood to leave.

'I 'aven't even asked about you and Stanley.'

'We're all right Mrs Marking, don't you worry about us.'

Stanley was standing in the doorway, dark brown crescents had formed under his eyes, and his unruly hair lay flattened against his cheek. Mrs Marking walked over and grabbed his arm.

'Thank you, Stanley, for 'elping to get 'er out'.

****

November 12th

A memorial service had been organised at Ashdon Church for the thirty-five munitions workers who'd perished in the explosion. The candle-lit church was almost full when Mary and Annie helped Grace up the steps into the vestibule and then into a seat in the back row. She bent over and placed her crutches on the floor under her pew and motioned for them to sit next to her. Annie's arms had almost healed but her hands were still in bandages. Mary still suffered nightmares, which had left dark pools under her eyes, but the three of them felt lucky to be alive. Stanley had driven them in the delivery cart and, having tied up the horse, slipped in and sat at the end of the pew, next to Annie. The organist waited for the heavy oak doors to close, before placing his hands in his lap and swivelling round to face the congregation.

A painful silence enveloped the church as the Reverend Herbert Warner, vicar of Ashdon, slowly climbed the steps up to the altar. He turned to face the assembled mourners, his crisp white robes falling around him like a shroud. He welcomed everyone and then picked up a small ledger and began reading one by one, the names of the thirty-five victims. The sound of hushed sobbing rose from different parts of the church as each name was read out. Annie scanned the congregation and recognised many of the mourners, albeit from the backs of their heads. Mr Howell now stepped up in front of the altar.

'I am here to thank each and every one of these brave colleagues, who worked tirelessly in the service of our country. The danger they subjected themselves to daily, with courage and fortitude, will live with me forever. I'd like to offer my heartfelt condolences to their families and, as a token of my gratitude, I'd like you all to accompany me at the end of the service to the factory gates, where a large memorial to them has been erected.'

He paused and then, sweeping the church with his eyes, cleared his throat.

'And to those individuals who were injured, some very badly, I'd like to thank them for their loyalty, bravery and contribution to the valuable work carried out at the factory. And to those, who in the face of extreme danger, helped to rescue their colleagues I offer my heartfelt thanks. But there is one person to whom I owe a personal debt of gratitude for saving my life, and that is Miss Annie Gingell, who not only dragged *me* to safety, but repeatedly risked her own life to rescue many others.'

He then looked directly at Annie.

'Thank you, Miss Gingell.'

Annie's face coloured. She nodded and looked down at her lap, unable to meet his eyes. Stanley leant over and squeezed her bandaged hand. She winced and smiled shyly at him, as a lone bee hovered over her head.

Stanley looked up at it and mumbled to himself,

'I thought bees were supposed to hibernate. What's 'e doin' in 'ere?'

Outside people climbed on to the factory trucks lined up

beyond the graveyard. Leaving the church, Annie stopped to look at the rows of ancient tombstones, standing in haphazard lines like rows of crooked teeth. A number of people smiled or pointed to her as they passed. She and Mary then helped Grace towards Stanley's cart. He jumped down and, taking her crutches, helped her into the seat next to him. A large triangular piece of polished marble, engraved with the names of the thirty-five munitionettes, had been erected to the side of the newly repaired gates. People gathered silently around it and looked for the names of their dead. Inscribed at the top of the memorial were the words:

TO THE HOWELLS MUNITIONETTES WHO DIED SERVING THEIR COUNTRY
WE SHALL NEVER FORGET.
OCTOBER 28th, 1915

The silence was only broken by the sound of muffled sobs. Annie looked down the list of names, picturing each person in her mind's eye, whilst whispering a quiet 'goodbye'. Looking up and over to where the filling rooms had stood, she was shocked to see that the site had been cleared and two new buildings had been erected. It felt like the old filling rooms and all the people who'd worked in them had never existed. Mr Howell was suddenly standing next to her. He smiled down at her.

'The sooner we get back into production the better, don't you think, Miss Gingell?'

'It just seems too soon, Mr Howell. We should be honouring the dead, not just carrying on as if they've been forgotten.'

'Look what it says on the memorial, Miss Gingell. 'We shall *never* forget.' I'm afraid the war won't come to an end because we've suffered such grave losses. Our boys still need all the ammunition we can produce to help them win this war once and for all. Think of it this way, we're honouring the work of our colleagues by continuing with it.'

Annie hadn't thought of it like that.

Mr Howell then moved to the side of the memorial and, pointing to the new buildings, he addressed the bereaved families and friends.

'As you can see, we have wasted no time in rebuilding the old filling rooms. I'm sure you will all agree that the best way to honour our dead colleagues is to continue their valiant work. Our job is to help our men win this ghastly war, by providing them with the ammunition they so desperately need.'

His words hung in the air for a few moments, before a hesitant handclap broke the silence. It was followed by another and then another until, out of the collective grieving, came a sense of patriotic pride. The clapping grew louder. Mothers, fathers, brothers, sisters and friends, some with tears streaming down their swollen faces, joined together to proudly remember their dead. Mr Howell spoke to several of the families before joining Annie. He smiled warmly at her.

'Would you step aside for a moment, Miss Gingell? As you know, Mrs Wright, our overseer in the filling rooms was sadly one of the victims. I wondered if you might be interested in that position?'

'Well, thank you for asking me Mr Howell, but I won't be coming back to the factory as I've been offered employment elsewhere. However, I know who would be interested, and that's Elsie Manning, when she's properly better. She's 'ad a lot more experience than me.'

'Well, I'm very sorry to hear that you're leaving us, Miss Gingell. May I ask where you'll be working in future?'

'I'd rather not say at the moment if you don't mind.'

'No, no, quite. I'll speak to Miss Manning when she returns to work.'

He pushed his glasses back to the bridge of his nose and held out his hand. Annie shook it and was surprised when he enclosed her hand in both of his.

'Miss Gingell, I'd like to wish you all the very best of luck in the future, and if ever you find yourself in need of employment, please remember that there will always be a job for you here. Goodbye, Miss Gingell.'

He turned on his heels and walked towards the factory gates.

'What was that all about then?'

Stanley was standing, grinning, by her side.

'Whatever it was you said to him, upset him badly. I could see that from over 'ere.'

'I just told him I was leavin', that's all.'

'What do you mean, you're leavin'?'

'I'm going to work for the National Union of Women's Suffrage Societies.'

'The what? What in 'eaven's name is a suffrage society?'

'It's a society that's fighting for votes for women, Stanley.'

'Oh. So, what will you be doin' then? Will you get paid – mum won't be 'appy if you can't give 'er anything.'

'Yes, I'll get paid, Stanley, for talking to people in high places and persuading them that women's voices need to be 'eard. But don't worry, I won't forget about 'elping with the war effort as well. *All* members of the suffrage society have thrown themselves into war work, as well as doing their union work. I'm going to do both!

'I don't know what mum's going to say.'

'She'll be glad that I'm not in that factory any more, that's for sure! I 'aven't said anythin' to 'er yet, so don't you. Leave it to me, Stanley.'

****

December 23rd

Arthur Scoggings stepped off the train at Saffron Walden. It was a raw morning and an icy wind cut through his khaki trousers, making his left leg throb and his limp more pronounced. An elderly man approached him.

'You alright, son? You look as if you could do with a sit down.'

'Thank you, I'm fine, but I'm looking for lodgings for a few days.'

'I might know just the person, son. Now, do you know Saffron Walden?'

'Yes, I know it quite well.'

'You'll know Church Street then. Try Mrs Luckings at number 36. She and her husband Charlie take in lodgers. You on leave, son?'

'Yes, just for a few days.'

He slung his kitbag over his shoulder, turned up his collar and buttoned his greatcoat. Pulling his hat down over the livid scar on his right cheek, he thanked the man again and made his way slowly in the direction of the High Street. Passing the Regal cinema, he thought about the first time he and Annie had held hands. He held up his hands, the same hands that had killed many men, the hands that had driven bayonets into young German flesh. *How could he have even thought that Annie would want to touch those hands again? How could he step back into the old world?* In the hospital he'd felt the slow draining away of his old self.

Something had been lost that would never be regained. But during his darkest days there was always the hope that Annie would be waiting. *But she hadn't replied to his letter. If she was waiting, would she be waiting for the old version of him? Would she turn away, repelled by his appearance? Repelled by the man he had become?*

He carried on down the hill towards Church Street, remembering the day the Pals had marched out of the town to the cheers of the local people. It felt like a different life. Yet Saffron Walden was unchanged, still the same shops, still the same houses. He turned into Church Street and stopped outside number 36. He raised his hand to grab the brass knocker, and was horrified to see how violently it shook. His impulse was to turn and go but, in his mind's eye, he'd pictured this day for so long, it would be foolish to run away now.

The door was opened by a short round woman with salt and pepper hair tied in a bun, her face rosy with blooms of burst capillaries. Looking at his uniform, she smiled with kind eyes.

'What can I do for you, luv?'

'I'm looking for somewhere to stay for a few days.'

'Well, you've come to the right place then. Come on in luv, you look like you could do with a cuppa.'

Arthur stepped inside a long dark hallway, just as a thin man, whose clothes hung on him like laundry drying on a tree, appeared from a room off to the right. Seeing his uniform, he smiled and offered his hand. Arthur was surprised at the strength of his handshake, which belied his physical appearance.

'Come in lad, we've always got room for a soldier!'

****

The cold evening air made Annie's cheeks glow as she made her way from the United Reformed Church towards Castle Street. Millicent Fawcett's words still echoed in her ears. She'd never heard of Edith Cavell until this evening, but the story of her betrayal by a Belgian collaborator and subsequent execution had both angered and upset her. She turned into the High Street, in her mind replaying Miss Fawcett's speech about Mr Asquith, who they all knew was no supporter of the suffrage movement. By quoting a speech he'd made to the country, Miss Fawcett had demonstrated that Edith Cavell had made a positive contribution to the Government's thoughts on women's rights. Annie could remember it almost word for word:

'Miss Cavell has taught the bravest men among us a supreme lesson of courage. And in this United Kingdom and throughout the Dominions there are thousands of such women, but a year ago we did not know it.'

With these words still ringing in her ears, she crossed the High Street, more than ever sure that, despite Pol and Gruff's objections, she'd made the right decision to join the Suffrage Society and to direct her energies into war work.

As she turned into Castle Street, she noticed a poster on Salmon's shop window supporting the National League for Opposing Women's Suffrage. It was entitled 'A Suffragette's Home' and showed a grim-looking man arriving home from work to a scene of domestic chaos, with weeping children, a dangerously smoking lamp and a note attached to a suffrage poster, 'Back in an hour or so.' She ripped it off the window, screwed it up and rammed it into her bag.

In the two months since the explosion she'd finished her training with the Saffron Walden branch of the Voluntary Aid Detachment, which she'd come to refer to as the VAD, and was now to be sent to Wrest Park Military Hospital the day after Boxing Day. She'd learned how to drive an ambulance and how to dress and bandage wounds. It had been a hard eight weeks, working for the NUWSS in the evenings, rehearsing a play with the Actresses' Franchise League to entertain the soldiers, directed by Vesta Tilley, and helping with the publication of a pamphlet promoting women's suffrage. Her head was full of new ideas and for the first time in weeks she felt excited. However, she now had to push her new ideas to the back of her mind and concentrate on her war work. As she reached her yard the sweet smell of toffee wafted into the air. Kicking open the swollen back door, she smiled at Pol, who stood over a cast-iron saucepan stirring a dark brown velvety mixture, which rolled and bubbled deliciously. Wisps of grey hair curled at her temples and streaks of caramel sweat lined her right cheek. Annie's mouth watered.

'Mum, whatever do you look like?'

'Don't say anything, luv, it's just about the right temperature.'

She spooned a tiny bit of the mixture from the pan and dropped it into a saucer of water she'd placed on the table. It hardened into tiny balls as it hit the cold water.

'Perfect!'

Pol poured the steaming mixture over a tray of pale-yellow dough.

'Mum, should you be making sweets? Haven't you read the posters the Food Production Department have been putting up, telling us not to waste food? There's one in Salmon's window, you must have seen that.'

'Yes, I 'ave, but it's Christmas and I think we deserve some little treat. Don't worry, Annie, this is an exception. You know how 'ard I try not to be wasteful, but with you going away ....'

Her voice trailed off as she turned away, sweeping her hand across her eyes.

'I know, mum. They look lovely.'

'Gruff managed to get a Christmas tree from one of his customers, and Stanley got a goose from Home Farm when he was over there, so we should have a fine spread.'

Annie squeezed her mum's shoulders and filled the kettle.

'It sounds lovely, mum.'

'Sillet's have said we can cook the goose in their oven when they've finished baking the bread on Christmas Eve, but Mrs Marking and Mrs Turner have asked him too, so we'll have to wait our turn, I just 'ope it's cooked in time for Christmas dinner.'

'I'm sure it will be, mum, but don't forget I'm going to be up the 'ospital doing our show tomorrow night so I won't be able to 'elp much this year.

'I know, luv, don't you worry about it, those poor devils up there deserve to 'ave a bit of fun. I've managed to get some crepe paper to wrap the sweets and I thought I'd hang them on the tree to decorate it. If I've got any left, I'll use it to wrap up some of them socks I've knitted and you can take 'em over with you. Give 'em something to open.'

'That's lovely, mum!'

December 24th

The following morning Annie found Pol sobbing by the Christmas tree. At her feet a soggy pile of sweets had leaked the colour of their crepe paper wrappings on to the floor.

'The damp has melted the sweets!' she wailed.

****

Arthur had a fitful night at the Luckings's house. He woke

screaming in the middle of a familiar dream. He was clambering over dead bodies, trying to get out of the line of fire. Rats scavenged at his feet, running in and out of dead soldiers' chest cavities, eating the flesh of his fallen friends. Retching, he pulled himself up into a sitting position and swiped away the salty rivulets of sweat that stung his eyes and blurred his vision. Three gentle knocks sent his pulse racing and made his heart pump wildly. There was a pause and Mrs Luckings knocked again.

'You alright, luv. Do you want a cup of tea?'

'Yes, yes please', he gasped.

He sat in their kitchen, clasping the steaming brew to his chest.

'It's alright, son, you ain't the first to have bad dreams. We 'ad a lad a couple of weeks ago – same thing – kept 'avin these dreams where he was back on the front line. '

Without warning Arthur found himself shaking, unable to steady his cup, which spilled hot tea over his pyjamas. Mrs Luckings took it from him and placed it on the table.

'Do you want to talk about it, lad? Sometimes it's easier to talk to strangers.'

'No, no, I'm alright.'

Arthur sipped the tea slowly whilst Mrs Luckings topped up the teapot and threw a rasher of bacon into a frying pan.

'You'll feel better when you get some breakfast down you, son.'

She cracked an egg into the pan and paused for a moment before cutting a thin slice of bread and spreading it with a thick layer of margarine.'

'Now you eat this up and you'll feel a whole lot better! 'Ere 'ave some more tea.'

Arthur forced himself to eat, but a series of spasms brought chunks of half-chewed bacon back into his mouth. He choked violently and pushed the plate away.'

'It's alright, lad. You'll eat when you're ready.'

'It just don't feel right, me being 'ere when all my pals died.'

Mr Luckings came into the kitchen and sat down opposite Arthur. He placed his hands palm down on the table and leant over, smiling kindly at Arthur, who stared down into his teacup.

'Take your time, lad.'

'I'll be alright, Mr Luckings, just need to get back and finish off the job. But I need to see someone first. Mr and Mrs Luckings exchanged glances.'

'You got a sweetheart, lad?'

'I did 'ave, but I don't know if she still is. I 'aven't 'eard from her since I marched out of 'ere last August.'

'Well, I expect there's a good reason for that. Now you go and find her, lad.'

Arthur washed and changed back into his uniform and greatcoat, then left, taking a key from Mrs Luckings, who waited for him in the hall.

'Good luck, lad! I hope you find her. We'll see you later then.'

Shutting the heavy front door behind him, he turned down Church Street and into the High Street. He walked as quickly as his limp allowed and, reaching the top of the hill, was surprised to find himself out of breath. He paused for a moment before heading in the direction of Audley End House. Reaching the Lion Gate, he looked up into the eyes of the old beast, which stood above the gate guarding the entrance. In the changed world around him the lion suddenly felt very familiar. He smiled up at him.

'Hello, old boy.'

He felt the eyes of the animal follow him as, deciding to avoid the main entrance, he took the path round to the kitchen garden. Climbing over the garden gate, he lowered himself down to where the beehives sat clustered together against a high flint wall. Gabriel, the garden boy, was sweeping the narrow brick path running between the greenhouses. He stopped as Arthur approached.

'Hello, Gabriel.'

'Hello? I'm not sure I know you.'

'Arthur, Arthur Scoggings. I was a footman 'ere before the war.'

'Of course, 'ow are ya?'

'Not the man I was, but a lot better than some. So, you haven't joined up then?'

'Nah, I waited for me birthday, but when I went to sign up, they told me that I was more useful growin' things 'ere than fightin. Pity really.'

'Gabriel, what you're doing 'ere is better than bein' sent to fight, believe me. Don't you forget that!'

Looking down at his muddy boots, Gabriel shook his head.

'You was with the Pals, wasn't you? We thought you were all dead!'

'All except for me.'

'We've gotta tell His Lordship. There's a Christmas party for us workers tonight. You gotta come – as my guest.'

'No, no, I can't, Gabriel. I've got to get back to my regiment the day after Boxing Day and I don't want anyone to know I've been 'ere, so please keep our meeting to yourself.'

'So why are you 'ere then?'

'I'm looking for Annie Gingell.'

'She don't work 'ere no more. She went to work at Howell's

Munitions Factory. There was a big explosion there a couple of months back. A lot of the girls were killed.'

'Arthur steadied himself against the side of the greenhouse.

'Well, what about her, was she killed?'

'I, I don't know... I'm sorry, it's just that so many people have died since you left.'

'Where is this factory?'

'It's in Ashdon. I read in the newspaper that Mr 'Owell, the factory owner, put up a memorial for the girls who died. By the factory gates, I think.'

'Gabriel, 'ave you got a bike I can borrow?'

'Yeh, but you need to bring it back. I use it to visit me family.'

'Of course, I'll bring it back later today,'

Gabriel led Arthur round the back of the bothie. He disappeared into the potting shed and dragged out an old black lady's bicycle from behind the door.

'I hope you find what you want when you get there.'

'Thank you, Gabriel. I'll bring it back later.'

Arthur pedalled out of the estate towards Saffron Walden. He skirted round the top of the Common and on to the Ashdon Road, gathering speed as he reached the open countryside. The low winter sun poked through the trees, making shadows across his path. The crisp cold air made his eyes water and stung his scarred cheek, and for the first time in his life he prayed – out loud. As he approached the munitions factory a glimmer of winter sun forced its way through the cloud, turning the stone memorial silver. Arthur's body began to shake as he propped the bicycle up against the gates of the factory and slowly walked towards the polished marble edifice. A list of names had been carved alphabetically into the stone, but Arthur started reading from the top, his heart pounding. He read each name out loud but paused, crossed his fingers and whispered *'please, not her'*, before stealing himself to read the names listed under G. Her name wasn't there! He grabbed the gatepost and steadied himself. As he waited for the world to right itself a tall man with a military moustache approached him.

'Can I help you?'

'I was looking for a name', he gasped.

'And who might that be?'

'Annie Gingell, sir. She's a friend of mine.'

'Well, I'm very pleased to say that Miss Gingell not only survived the explosion, but helped many of her colleagues, including myself. Without her acts of bravery there would have been many more names on this memorial.'

Arthur's heart felt as if it would burst.

'Do you know where I can find her, sir?'

'I very much regret to say that she is no longer employed here. I believe she now works for the National Union of Women's Suffrage Societies, but has recently completed her training with the Saffron Walden Voluntary Aid Detachment. An ex-colleague tells me she is shortly to be deployed.'

Arthur felt as if he'd been thumped in the stomach. *Was this the woman he'd* left *behind just a few months ago*? The tall man peered at him through pebble glasses.

'Would you like to sit down? You look rather unwell.'

'No, no thanks. I've got to find her. I've got to get back to my regiment in a few days.'

'Well, I think I might be able to help you there. I believe Miss Gingell is appearing in an entertainment for the injured troops at Saffron Walden military hospital this evening. Several of my staff will be going.'

'I didn't know there was a military hospital in Saffron Walden.'

'There wasn't until a few months ago, but Walden Place has been requisitioned by the government and is now a Red Cross auxiliary hospital, caring for the wounded sent home from the front.'

'Thanks, thanks a lot Mr?'

'Howell, Mr Howell. Please give Miss Gingell my regards when you see her.'

Arthur's heart sang as he began to pedal back. He thought of all the things he'd say to her, things he should have said before. Then his heart raced as he imagined all the things she'd say to him. But as he caught sight of the spire of St Mary's reaching up into the sky, he braked and leant heavily on the handlebars, steadying the bike between his legs. *Had she waited for him? Would she marry him? Had she found someone else?* He returned Gabriel's bike to the potting shed and walked to the edge of the estate, taking care to remain out of sight. When he reached a large five-bar gate leading into Audley End Park, he climbed over and cut through to Abbey Lane. From there he walked into the grounds of Walden Place. A number of military ambulances were parked in the sweeping driveway. The four o'clock winter light was fading fast as he crept up to the tall ground floor windows and pressed his nose against the icy glass. Inside, a number of soldiers in bath chairs, one with an arm in a sling, another with an arm amputated from the elbow, another missing both legs, played cards on one of the iron beds which lined both sides of the room. A couple of men with large bandages over both eyes sat passively listening. Nurses with red crosses on their armbands smiled and tended to their charges, whilst at the far end of the room a small stage was being erected by a group of relatively able-bodied soldiers. He moved back from the window and slowly made his way back to Church Street.

How would she look at him now? Would she see him in the same way she used to, or would she look at him with sympathy in her eyes, like these nurses mothering their patients? He couldn't bear her to look at him that way.

Christmas Eve evening

Annie had learned the words of her songs by practising in front of the chipped mirror in her bedroom. She knew she was word-perfect, but still felt flustered and nauseous – she'd never done anything like this before. As she waited in the wings, she took a quick peep at the rows of men in bath chairs, others sitting five to a bed and others lying propped up in beds that had been moved near to the stage. She spotted several girls from Howell's, including Elsie, who was flirting unashamedly with the soldier sitting next to her. A chant of 'why are we waiting' grew louder, and the air tingled with the promise of laughter and goodwill. The curtain was finally tugged back by a couple of nurses who'd volunteered to be stagehands. A chorus of cheers and whistles went up as Annie stepped out on to the makeshift stage. At the back of the room Arthur had found a chair and sat transfixed. He could scarcely believe that this woman, the focus of the soldiers' wolf whistles and lusty cheers was the same woman he'd held in his arms just a few months before. He peered through a gap between the bandaged heads of two soldiers sitting in front of him and watched the suggestive swing of her hips as she shimmied across the stage, singing like a nightingale. The crowd erupted as she winked, left the stage and reappeared, walking amongst them, ruffling their hair and smiling mischievously. He ducked down behind the men in front, who were now whistling and singing along at the tops of their voices to *'It's a Long Way to Tipperary'*. Every man in the room had fallen in love with Annie.

What an idiot he'd been. This woman could have any man in the audience, why would she want him? Arthur waited until she'd turned and was singing her way back to the stage, before quietly pushing back his chair and making for the door. A nurse approached him.

'Are you alright? You look a bit shaky.'

'I, I ... just need some fresh air, that's all.'

'Do you want me to come with you?'

'No, no, I'll be alright thanks.'

He turned for a final look at the stage. Annie was smiling triumphantly at the wolf-whistling men, who clapped wildly, but the sudden movement at the back of the room drew Annie's gaze towards him, and for a moment their eyes locked. He held her gaze momentarily, then pushed open the door, willing the darkness to swallow him up. Annie struggled to remember her lines, her heart pounded as she strained to hear the prompt – for the third time. She somehow managed to keep herself together until the interval, when she rushed to put her face to a small hole in the curtain. She scanned the room looking for Arthur. Had it really been him? There was no sign of him now. She grabbed one of the stagehands.

'Could you please ask the nurse at the back of the room if she could come backstage for a moment? I really need to speak to her.'

'Oh, you mean Hilda, do you?'

'I don't know her name, but she was talking to a soldier who'd been sitting at the back. He got up to leave....'

'Righto, I'll go and speak to her straight away.'

Annie watched as the woman made her way through the

audience and spoke to Hilda, who followed her behind the stage.

'The soldier you were talking to at the back, the one who left, what did you say to him?'

'He said he needed some fresh air, and I asked if he wanted me to go with him, but he said no, he was alright. He did look a bit peaky.'

'Where did he go?'

'I really don't know, he just left. I thought he'd be coming back in after he'd had some air, but there's no sign of him now.'

Annie took another look through the hole in the curtain. He'd gone, and she had no idea how she was going to find him, or how she was going to get through the second half of the show.

'Two minutes everyone!'

Annie waited for the curtain to be hauled back, then, trying to banish all thoughts of Arthur, she stepped out on to the stage. The audience erupted as she and Vesta Tilley burst into a rousing chorus of *'Pack up your Troubles.'* Despite the audience's enthusiasm, the rest of the show went by in a blur. No matter how hard she tried, Annie kept replaying that moment when they'd locked eyes. *What was he thinking? Why did he go? How was she going to find him before she was due to leave?*

There were two encores before the final bow was taken. Vesta Tilley hugged Annie.

'You were simply splendid! It's been a great tonic for the men.'

'I hope so, and thank you, Vesta'. Annie paused. 'I'm very sorry but I have to leave. There's someone I really need to see.'

'But, but of course...' Vesta could only stand by and watch as Annie quickly changed out of her costume and slipped unnoticed out of the rear door of the hospital. Frost sparkled on the step and the raw evening air stung her face, which she realised was still thick with stage make-up. Her instinct was to go to Audley End. A full moon helped light her way through the park and down to the mansion house, where it seemed that lights blazed from every room. As she got closer, she could see into the Great Hall. A huge log fire burned in the hearth and the flames cast a warm sheen on the faces of the estate workers gathered around the ceiling-high Christmas tree, singing carols. She crossed her fingers as she scanned the upturned faces of the carollers. Arthur wasn't amongst them. Stepping back from the window, she waited for them to move into the servants' hall, where she knew the party would be held.

Why did she think Arthur might be there? She didn't know where else to start looking. Her eyes ringed with tears that spilled down her cheeks, she wiped her hand across her face, smudging the thick black liner that ringed her eyes, creating jagged pools of purple, which bled into the rouge that had highlighted her cheeks. She wiped her hands on her dress and, looking up, spotted Gabriel making his way to the kitchen garden. Stemming the flow of tears with the heels of her palms, she ran towards him.

'Gabriel, Gabriel, please stop!'

He turned and squinted at her through the half-light. 'Who are you? 'Ow do you know my name?'

'Don't you recognise me, Gabriel?'

'Nah, can't say that I do.'

'It's me, Annie, Annie Gingell!'

Gabriel stopped and examined her smudged face.

'You don't look like the Annie Gingell who used to work 'ere. 'As someone 'it you? Are you in some sort of trouble?'

Annie suddenly realised that her face was a purple smudge and, despite herself, laughed at what she imagined she must look like.

'It's stage make-up Gabriel, that's all!'

'Oh, well I 'ope you don't mind me sayin like, but you look much better without it.'

He paused and then scrutinised her more closely. 'Well it's a funny thing seein' you again, we didn't know if you was still alive – what with the fire and that, up at 'Owell's.' He paused again, and then added,

'Did he find you then?'

Annie's heart missed a beat. 'Who?'

'That footman, Arthur Scoggings. He went off with the Pals. He was 'ere this mornin', askin after you 'e was.'

'What did you tell him, Gabriel?'

'That you didn't work 'ere no more, and that you'd gone up to 'Owell's. I told 'im about the explosion. He borrowed me bike to go up there to see if your name was on the list of dead.'

'Did he say where he was living?'

'Nah, didn't say much at all, just borrowed me bike and left. 'E brought it back like 'e said 'e would. I told 'im we thought 'e was dead. 'E didn't want to see anyone, maybe because of the scar across 'is face. Said 'e 'ad to get back to 'is regiment, in the next couple of days I think.'

Great waves of despair threatened to topple her.

'If he comes back, tell him he can find me at 6 Middle Square, Castle Street, but only until 2nd January, mind. Then I'm off to train as a nurse. It was good to see you,

Gabriel. 'Ave a nice Christmas!'

Annie slowly made her way back over the fields towards Castle Street. *Why did he leave the hospital? Perhaps he doesn't love me anymore, but why did he come looking for me then? Perhaps he was disappointed when he saw me again. Maybe I'm not the girl he remembered?* She turned into Middle Square and carefully pushed open the kitchen door, taking care not to knock the red berries that Pol had entwined in the holly and ivy wreath she'd hung on it. The kitchen smelled of Christmas and carbolic soap. Pol had just finished stuffing the goose and was scrubbing her hands with a coarse nailbrush.

'I can't get this blessed stuffin' out of me nails. 'Ow did it go then, did them lads enjoy the show? Put the kettle on, luv, I'll just take this over to Sillet's. They've finished baking for the day, so I'm puttin' our goose in the oven with Mrs Turner's and Mrs Marking's. It should be done lovely by morning. I won't be a mo, then you can tell me all about it.'

She carefully lifted the large roasting tin off the table and headed for the door, just as it was pushed open by Gruff, who staggered into the kitchen with a piece of mistletoe wedged between his lips.

'Give your old man a kiss under the mistletoe, Pol!'

'Not when you're in that state I won't. And I 'ope you 'aven't spoiled my wreath!'

She disappeared over to Sillet's bakery.

Gruff propped himself up against the dresser. He'd drunk himself into a stupor and grinned stupidly at Annie.

'Now look at you', he slurred. 'Anyone'd think you was goin' to a funeral. It's Christmas! Let's 'ave a smile, Annie.'

'It feels like I *am* going to a funeral', she whispered under her breath as she filled the kettle and put it on the hob.

Pol appeared, ruddy-faced, at the door and glared at Gruff.

'Ow much 'ave you 'ad to drink?'

She was holding a bunch of squashed red berries in her hand. 'Look what you've done to my wreath, you clumsy oaf!'

'It's only a few berries, Pol. It still looks good, luv.'

'What would you know about what looks good and what doesn't? As long as you've got a drink and a nice Christmas dinner in your belly, nothing else matters, does it Gruff Gingell? I spent all mornin' makin' that wreath.'

'And a bootiful wreath it is. Come on Pol, give us a kiss under the mistletoe. It's Christmas.'

Annie pushed past her parents, almost knocking Gruff over. She rushed upstairs and threw herself down on her bed, sobbing. Gruff sagged into his chair by the range and pulled off his beer-soaked boots.

'Look at the state of you, Gruff. No wonder our Annie's upset. Did you even ask her about her show?'

Gruff's large head hung forward, almost reaching his chest as he slipped into an alcohol-fuelled sleep, his snores and splutters drowning out his daughter's sobs upstairs. Pol sighed and took the boiling kettle off the hob. She carried two mugs of steaming tea upstairs and stood for a moment outside Annie's door before quietly letting herself in and sitting silently on the edge of the bed. She placed both mugs of tea on the small bedside table and waited until Annie's sobs subsided, then grabbed her daughter's hand.

'Now what's all this about?'

Annie turned to face Pol, propping herself up with her head against the wall.

'I saw 'im, I saw 'im, mum.'

'Who did you see?'

'Arthur! He was at the back of the hall during the show, but he left, and I don't know how to find 'im'. Fresh tears began to roll down her wet cheeks.

'Now, now, luv, at least you know he's alive, that's good news, ain't it?'

'Yes, but why did he go before I could speak to 'im? I looked for 'im up at the Big 'Ouse. Gabriel, the gardener's boy, said he'd come looking for me. So why didn't he want to talk to me when he found me?'

'I'm sure 'e 'as his reasons, Annie.'

'I might never see 'im again. Gabriel said he's going back to join his regiment soon, so I won't have another chance to speak to 'im before I go'. A fresh wave of sobs washed over her body.

'Well, it's better to know he's still alive than thinking 'e might be dead, luv.'

'But I thought he loved me, and now I don't know if he's stopped loving me. That's almost worse.'

Christmas Eve evening
Arthur

Arthur walked slowly back to the High Street, trying to ignore the pain in his left leg. He walked up and down, not wanting to go back to the tiny room at Church Street. He gazed through the quaint windows of the Cross Keys, where a fire burned brightly in the hearth and people sat at tables, laughing and drinking. Moving back from the window, he stared at his reflection. A face he hardly recognised stared back. The livid raised scar over his cheek itched in the cold air. He ran his fingers along its rough edges and wondered when the deep frown lines of a man twice his age had become etched across his forehead. He looked away and turned into Castle Street. His dashed hopes, and the prospect of briefly returning to his family for the remainder of his Christmas leave, deepened the despair that had begun to overwhelm him. How could he pretend to be the same son who had marched off to war just a few months ago? He turned the key in the lock and crept upstairs before Mrs Luckings was able to ambush him.

Christmas Day

Annie sat down to Christmas dinner. Never had she felt less like eating. Thoughts of Arthur had kept her awake well into the night and now, in the cold light of day, she forced the dream-filled hope that he might appear at their backdoor out of her mind. She watched as her family tucked into Pol's roast goose, unable to lift her knife and fork.

'Come on luv, eat up, the goose is perfect!'

Gruff stuffed another loaded forkful into his mouth and chomped loudly. His cheeks ballooned and gravy leaked on to his chin as he smiled at his eldest daughter.

'Come on, Annie, you don't know when you'll next have a good meal like this.'

Pol looked up. There were tears in her eyes.

'Let's not think about our Annie going away, let's just enjoy being together today. Now eat some of your dinner, Annie, it'll make you feel better.'

****

In Manchester Arthur sat with his family, allowing his parents to believe his dejected mood was due to his imminent return to army life. His mother dared not ask the questions she wanted answered. Instead she fussed over him, applying poultices to his scarred face and insisting he rest his leg.

On Boxing Day he and his father walked alone to the local

pub and sat in a quiet corner away from the merry crowds near the bar. Setting two pints of beer in front of them, Arthur's father, a veteran of the Boer War, slapped Arthur on the shoulders and then sipped his beer.

'No one can prepare you for the horror of it all, son.'

'Best not to talk about it, eh?'

'That's right, son. You've just got to get on with it.'

'But why wasn't I killed? I was the only one who wasn't killed, dad, and it doesn't feel right, it doesn't feel right.'

'You were saved for a purpose – don't forget that.'

'It doesn't feel like that to me.'

'Now you just go back tomorrow and finish off the job you were trained for, lad, and then come back and get on with your life. That's what you were saved for. Me and your mum are proud of you, and you should feel proud to be wearing that uniform. Especially now, with your Corporal's stripes. Now drink up, best be getting back to yer mum.'

December 27th

Arthur joined a group of young soldiers waiting to board the troop train taking them to the docks at Newhaven. He recognised several lads from school standing together in a huddle at the far end of the platform. Pulling his cap down over his face, he craned his neck forwards, watching the engine as it approached the platform. There was a flurry of activity as the wheels of the great lumbering locomotive ground to a halt as it belched plumes of acrid soot and steam into the air. Some hugged tearful girlfriends or parents, before throwing kitbags over their shoulders and surging forwards on to the train, fighting for a space at the open windows to wave goodbye. Others found places to throw their bags down and settle themselves on the floor for the journey. Arthur leant back against his bag, pulled his cap down over his face and shut his eyes. A shrill whistle sounded as the guard slammed the last doors shut and the train began to pull out of the station and gather speed.

'Shut the windows, man, the smuts are filling the bloody carriage!'

'There'll be plenty more of them where we're going. You'd better get used to it, chum!'

Arthur folded his arms over his chest and waited for sleep to come, but images of Annie winking and smiling at those wolf-whistling soldiers in the hospital plagued him. *She was enjoying her war! She hadn't waited. She hadn't even replied to his letters, and now she'd seen him, seen how he'd changed – why would she want him back? People change, but sometimes too much. How could he have thought that life would be the same as he'd left it? The whole world was changing...*

The screeching of brakes woke him. The train shuddered to a halt, sending a kitbag tumbling from an overhead luggage net on to his wounded leg.

'Sorry, sorry mate, are you OK?'

A pale thin man whose uniform hung loosely on him bent down and lifted the kitbag off Arthur's leg, which was throbbing and rubbing against the rough wool of his trousers. Arthur noticed the two stripes on each arm of his jacket.

'I'll survive'. He half-smiled, gathered up his bag and dragged himself to standing.

'Looks like this is Newhaven then.' The thin corporal held out his hand. 'Vic, Vic Clarke'.

Arthur shook Vic's thin hand. It felt cold and clammy, like the skin of a frog.

'Arthur Scoggings', he replied.

Their carriage rapidly emptied as men poured out onto the wooden jetty. They joined the mass of khaki-clad troops that spilled out on to the pier from numerous carriages running the length of the train. The salt-encrusted boards beneath their feet groaned as the throng of uniformed men slowly made their way to the gangplank of a large 'dazzle'-camouflaged paddle steamer. Arthur and Vic were propelled forwards by the bulging kitbags of the men behind them as they climbed up to the narrow entrance door leading into the bowels of the ship. Once aboard, the two of them made their way back to the upper deck and found a space where they were able to lean against the ship's polished wooden rails. They watched as a never-ending line of soldiers pushed their way up the sagging gangplank. Arthur's eyes turned to the quay below them, which was lined with Red Cross ambulances waiting to transport injured men to one of the auxiliary hospitals nearby.

'Best not to spend too much time looking at them ambulances.' Vic watched Arthur's hand involuntarily touch the partially hidden scar on his cheek. 'Where did you get that then?'

'Gallipoli'.

'Huh, you was one of them unlucky bastards that got sent there then?'

'I don't suppose it was any worse than any other god-forsaken place. And you? This isn't your first posting.'

'Nah. I was in Wipers before. Got shrapnel in me arms and a dose of trench foot. They patched me up and 'ere I am back again. At least now we should 'ave one of those steel helmets '

The gangplank was finally hauled up and the huge paddles sprung into life, churning up water in their vast wheels and spitting out seaweed into the foam beneath them. A deep throaty blast from the funnels signalled their departure and, to Arthur's amazement, some of the men were cheering.

'Poor blighters – they don't know what's in store for 'em', he muttered.

The sun had disappeared, and with it, the comforting glow of its last rays on the geometric designs that covered the ship. In the half-light the black, white and blue camouflage took on a more sinister appearance. The men sat in groups smoking and hugging their greatcoats to them as the night air temperature dropped to freezing. Arthur shivered.

'You'd better get used to this, Arthur. There ain't no warm fires in them trenches, mate.'

Picardy, Northern France

The first faint glimmer of light was just creeping into the sky when Arthur's battalion reached a hill that led down to Piquing, a small town in Picardy. Seeing the town below them, the men, footsore and exhausted, forgot their blistered feet and aching backs and, throwing their heavy rifles over their shoulders, broke into song as they marched cheerfully to their billets. Most had never left home before and had no idea where Picardy was. As they approached the village Vic explained to Arthur that they were near the river Somme in Northern France. As they drew near, Company Sergeant Major Jenkins turned to the men and, indicating a large barn complex set around a farmyard, pointed to a flint and stone barn. He bellowed:

'Here's your billet, lads. When you get down there grab a bed and get a few hours' shut-eye!'

Vic turned and grinned at Arthur.

'Looks like they ain't ready for us at the front just yet.'

It took a few minutes for the men's eyes to adjust to the

gloomy interior of the barn, but then began a scramble to grab a free bed. Vic threw his webbing down on the floor, sending up a cloud of straw dust. He rotated his aching shoulders and propped his Lee Enfield against the wall next to Arthur's. Both men peered through the gloom at the rows of identical bunks, each with a horsehair pillow and rough brown blanket, which were gradually being occupied by the weary men.

'It don't look particularly luxurious, Arthur, but make the most of a dry bed while you can, mate.'

Arthur rolled on to a bottom bunk, allowing Vic to take the top. Closing his eyes, he heard nothing until the shrill sound of a whistle woke him.

'Right lads. Kit inspection in half an hour, and I want those rifles spotless!'

There were groans from various bunks around the room.

Sergeant Major Jenkins, a short plump man, reached for the nearest bunk and ripped the blanket back.

'I might remind you that this ain't a bleedin' hotel!'

The men dragged themselves out of their bunks and into their boots. Arthur picked up his rifle and began polishing the barrel. Vic joined him, giving his just a quick wipe before chipping the dried mud from his boots. Taking a small tin of dubbin from a pocket in his webbing he massaged it into the worn leather before rubbing the excess off and buffing it up to a deep shine. Neither spoke. There was nothing to say.

Assembled in the farmyard outside the barn, with hens clucking at their feet, the men had their first proper look at their surroundings. One of them exclaimed.

'So, what the hell 'ave we been sent 'ere for?'

Vic lit a cigarette and leant back against the flint wall of the barn. His eyes squinted into the sun as he took a long drag on his cigarette before blowing the smoke into a perfect ring. He turned his eyes towards the young man.

'Make the most of this chum, this is the calm before the storm, believe me!'

'I thought we was goin' to be fightin', not feedin' the bleedin' chickens!'

Arthur turned away from the young soldier who he guessed had lied about his age too. Sergeant Jenkins appeared from a smaller barn a few feet from where they stood. He glanced round at the groups standing casually chatting and barked,

'In line you scruffy lot!'

The men stubbed out cigarettes, picked up their kit and shuffled into something resembling a regiment, placing webbings at their feet and raising rifles ready for inspection. Having performed a cursory inspection of the rifles, most of which had yet to see action and therefore only needed a quick dust and polish, Sergeant Jenkins focused on boots, buttons and uniforms, which had become muddied and dusty during the recent march. Finally, satisfied with the men's efforts, Sergeant Jenkins clambered on to a bale of straw, which added a few inches to his short stature, and addressed the group, surveying the novice soldiers, who looked away or down at their feet, unwilling to meet his eye.

'Right men, you might be wondering what you're doing here in the middle of rural France. Some of you may even have thought you'd be going straight to the front line. Don't worry lads, there will be plenty of time for that in due course, but for now you'll be carrying out other duties. We'll be remaining here until January 2nd, when we march to Abbeville, which lies on the banks of the river Somme and is the Headquarters of Communication. It is also home to three army hospitals. We'll be stationed there for approximately five months and your duties will be to guard the roads, railways – which are used to transport the wounded to hospital – stores and prisoners.'

He paused and scanned the disappointed faces of the new recruits.

'Remember, there are many active roles to be carried out in wars, not least that of sentry duty, which will require you to patrol key sites. Needless to say, we expect you to fulfil this role to the best of your ability. Now stand at ease!'

With that, he swivelled on one foot, climbed off the straw bale and marched stiffly back into his office, leaving the men to mutter in small groups.

December 31st

The men assembled in the Grand Place. Having spent much of the day cleaning uniforms and polishing boots and buttons, they marched into the square behind the battalion band. A number of local people cheered and waved French flags, others had made Union Jacks, which they held up to the men as they passed by. The local Mayor greeted them warmly, offering slugs of calvados to toast in the New Year. As the band struck up again the men sang gustily at the tops of their voices, finishing with a chorus of '*Land of Hope and Glory*'. Arthur looked around him, his gaze resting on the naive young faces of those who had no idea of what they were to face in 1916. Quite suddenly his eyes rimmed with tears as he pushed thoughts of Annie to the back of his mind and raised a glass with the rest of them, welcoming in 1916. For some this was their first New Year away from home, and for many it would be their last.

Saffron Walden
31st December

Every year for as long as she could remember, Annie and her family had joined their neighbours to welcome in the New Year. As the church clock struck nine, the residents of Castle Street joined hands, forming a circle around St Mary's Church. Annie stood hand in hand with Pol and Gruff. Next to them Stanley and the other Gingell children waited with their hands entwined with those of their friends and neighbours. Under a full moon a fiddle player struck up a tune and the circle slowly began to move in a clockwise direction, gathering momentum as the tune gained pace. Neighbours laughed, their breath swirling into misty funnels in the cold night air as they fought to keep in time with the increasingly rhythmic step. But beneath their laughter was an unspoken sadness. This year a number of young faces were missing. Annie brought to mind each one of them, as the fiddle player slowed the pace and the dancers gradually fell into a calmer rhythm, until Gruff dropped her hand, spun on his heels and peeled away from the circle, leading the line of frozen dancers out of the churchyard. Without unleashing their hands, they slowly snaked their way towards the *Castle Inn*, where they danced through the front and out of the back door. Some broke away to order jugs of beer at the bar, whilst others followed Gruff into the *Greyhound*, where Ted Haines had lined up beers at the bar for his regulars. The remaining dancers moved on to the *Five Bells*, from where the sound of the piano and loud singing filled the air. By this time Pol and many of the women with young children had slipped away unnoticed.

Gruff pushed his way to the bar and, having put a number of beers on the slate, handed one each to Annie and Stanley. Then, ushering them away from the singers surrounding the piano, he held up his glass and looked into the eyes of his two eldest children.

'Ere's to you our Annie, and to you our Stanley, may God bring you both safely 'ome to us'.

They clinked glasses. Gruff turned to Stanley.

'You know you'd be goin' to war over your mother's dead body, don't you son? If it weren't for this conscription they're bringin' in, you'd still be 'ere 'elping me. But I reckon if you're old enough to 'ave a pint with yer old dad, you're old enough to fight for your country.'

'Thanks dad, it's good to 'ave your blessing.'

Stanley smiled and gave Gruff a wink.

'I'm glad I'm old enough to be conscripted, and you don't need to worry about me, I can look after myself.'

Gruff then gave Annie a hug.

'You know yer mum's frettin' about the two of you. Now Annie, we don't want no more heroics from you, we've 'ad enough of them recently. Just go and do yer job and keep yer 'ead down.'

'I will dad, I promise.'

She paused and took a long swig.

'I promised mum I'd bring her a jug of beer, but before I go, let's drink a toast.'

Annie held up her glass.

'To 1916, and to you Arthur, wherever you are! Please live!'

1916

Wrest Park Army Auxiliary Hospital
January 3rd, 1916

Annie was thankful that the Suffrage Societies had thrown themselves into the war effort, urging paid members to reduce their activities temporarily to enable them to offer their services. The recent publication promoting women's suffrage had been well received, and Annie had been singled out for her contribution. Having determined to put the heartache and upheaval of the previous few months behind her, she'd decided to throw herself into hospital work.

On a raw January morning Annie stepped off the train at Ampthill Station with a group of twenty-three nervous young women, who, having completed their basic training, were about to embark on an experience that would change them, and their lives, forever. For some it was the first time away from home and the first taste of independence; for others like Annie, seeing Wrest Park House took them back to their days in service. Without warning, images of Arthur flooded into Annie's mind. Images of him in a vivid footman's livery, then stripped to the waist thrusting a bayonet, and finally his face so close to hers she could almost feel his presence. She forced the memory to the back of her mind as a tall fierce-looking woman in a matron's uniform appeared from the house and waited to greet them. She introduced herself as Miss Herbert. The girl standing next to Annie nudged her and whispered:

'She's the daughter of Lord Lucas Herbert, who owns Wrest Park.'

Miss Herbert cleared her throat and introduced two nurses in crisp blue dresses, starched white caps and aprons.

'Firstly, I'd like to introduce you all to Nurse Butler.'

The older of the two women stepped forward and smiled

broadly at the new recruits. Speaking with a cut-glass accent, her wild blue eyes danced, giving her an air of mischief and fun. Annie warmed to her immediately.

'Well, girls, welcome to Wrest Park. Shortly you will be taken up to your dormitories, then given your uniforms, after which you will be taken round the wards.'

The younger nurse, a celery stick of a woman, then stepped forward and swept unsmiling eyes over the girls, as Miss Herbert introduced her as Nurse Peterson.

'You will do well here, girls, as long as you remember that Nurse Butler and I are both trained nurses with many years of experience. You will be working under us, will take orders from us and will learn from us. Matron is of course a very busy lady, so don't bother her with unnecessary questions. Direct any queries you may have to one of us, and remember, don't act without seeking guidance first.'

Having been fitted out with fresh ankle-length blue dresses, long white aprons and starched plain white caps and collars, which chafed the girls' necks, leaving deep red furrows under their chins, the new volunteers followed Matron into the first of three wards. It was known simply as A Ward, which they soon discovered was for the most serious cases, and for this reason had been situated on the ground floor for ease of access. Before the war the room had been a grand reception room with a vast arched ceiling, marble pillars and fireplaces at each end. Nurse Butler was changing the dressings of a man who had lost both eyes and part of his nose and mouth. He flinched as she gently bathed his ghastly wounds with salt water. The man suddenly put up his hand, waving it in the air, searching for Nurse Butler's hand, which he gripped with nicotine-stained fingers.

'Is it a fine day, and are the birds singing?' he asked.

'Yes, the sun is shining and the birds are singing', she replied.

'Well, I have much to live for still.'

Matron moved on to the next bed, where a man lay asleep with his legs uncovered. He struggled to breathe and a horrible rattling sound escaped from his chest as he fought to speak.

'There are a lot of chlorine gas cases in this ward. This poor man was also badly burned when a shell exploded next to him. We can't cover the wounds on his legs until new skin has grown.'

A man who'd lost both arms called for Nurse Butler to help him drink from a glass of water by his bedside. Matron picked it up, firmly telling him not to gulp but to take small sips, as his lungs and throat had been very badly burned by the chlorine and needed to heal before he'd be able to drink normally again. In the bed next to him lay a man with both buttocks blown off.

'Nurse Butler has a way with these men. They love her,' explained Matron. 'In fact, A Ward is known for its jokes!'

The new recruits had fallen silent. Nothing in their training had prepared them for this level of suffering, or bravery. In the dormitory that evening the girls gathered around Annie's bed as she read from the small Voluntary Aid Detachment pocketbook they'd all been given. On the first page was a letter written by Kathryn Furse, the Commandant-in-Chief, to serving VAD nurses. Clearing her throat, Annie began to read,

'This paper is to be considered by each VAD member as confidential and to be kept in her pocketbook. You are being sent to work for the Red Cross. You have to perform a task that will need your courage, your energy, your patience, your humility, your determination to overcome all difficulties. Let our motto be '*Willing to do anything*' and '*The people give gladly*.' If we live up to these, the Voluntary Aid Detachment members will come out of this world war triumphant.'

Quite suddenly, the girl in the bed next to Annie's, who'd introduced herself as Nan, gasped and let out a chain of sobs. Her face crumpled. She mumbled into her hands as they flew up to her eyes in an effort to wipe away the tears that rolled down her cheeks.

'I don't think I can do this. I don't think I'm brave enough...'

Nan blew her nose and gazed at Annie.

'I've never done real manual housework. I've never used mops and polishes and disinfectants. I didn't even know how to make tea until our training. I didn't know the water had to be boiled. All that we left to the servants.'

Annie closed the book and smiled at her.

'Well, it doesn't mean you can't learn. This is new for all of us and we're going to just have to knuckle down and do whatever's necessary.'

February 15th

A letter had arrived for Annie. She took it out of her pocket and sat on the side of her bed to read it. She recognised Pol's writing and quickly ripped it open.

Middle Square,
February 11th, 1916

Dear Annie,

I hope you are keeping well and looking after yourself, and that they are treating you well at the hospital.

As you know, they have now brought in conscription for all men between eighteen and forty-one. I had hoped that our Stanley's 18th birthday being on the 3rd February would mean that he'd miss the first call-up, but we got the letter on the 5th saying he had to report to the conscripting office in Saffron Walden on the 9th (the first day of conscription!).

Well, it all happened so quick we hardly had time to take it all in. He went to the office at nine o'clock in the morning, they gave him his medical and uniform and he was sent off to the Big House for training that afternoon. He's going to be there for three months before they send him off somewhere to do what they call home service in this country. After that, he will be sent off to fight. God knows where!

The house seems so quiet what with you both gone. Your dad's moping around and having to do Stanley's work as well as his own now, and I try not to worry about you both but I have to be honest and admit that I do.

There's not any news. All everyone talks about is the war. I only hope it ends soon.

Come home safe as soon as you can.

From your loving mum xx

Annie folded the letter and placed it in a small cardboard box at the back of her locker and headed down to the wards. She was thankful that Pol would never see the hideous injuries inflicted upon so many of the young lads at the hospital. They'd been trained, yet were totally unprepared for the horrors of war.

By the end of the first month at Wrest Park the new recruits had felt the shuddering misery of getting up early in the icy darkness to go on duty, in a ward with windows covered in ice. They learned that fires in the wards needed to be stoked all night, and that emptying the contents of two or three rounds of bedpans per shift was part of their job. They learned to keep kettles going, and how to prepare food on a number of old oil stoves. They learned how to scrub wards with carbolic soap, to make beds, to wash and feed the patients and to dress wounds. They learned how to listen to harrowing stories many of the patients needed to tell, how to write letters for men too ill or too illiterate to write themselves, and how to hold the hands of soldiers during long nights of pain.

At the beginning of their second month Annie and Nan were assigned to one of a fleet of ambulances meeting troop trains at Ampthill station. Their wait in the pre-dawn dampness of the ambulance finally ended when a long low whistle announced the arrival of what looked to them like an ordinary passenger train, until they peered inside. Rows of stretchers lined the sides of the carriage laid out on shelves, one above another like bunk beds. Every passenger seat had been stripped out to make space for further stretchers, which littered the carriage floor. They stepped up into the train and, breathing through their mouths, grabbed the ends of the nearest stretcher. The stench of festering wounds was overwhelming. As they carried the first casualty to the waiting ambulance, the wounded soldier's crusted eyes briefly flickered open. He stared up at Annie in hope and, grabbing her hand, he whispered, 'Am I going to die?'

To Annie he looked younger than her brother Stanley.

'Of course you aren't. We're going to fix you up, you'll see.'

She smiled and tucked his outstretched hand under the bloodstained blanket that clung to his small frame, and then returned to pick up the next stretcher. As they set it down in the ambulance, Annie glanced across at the young lad, whose dull eyes now stared blankly out from his partially closed lids. She checked for a pulse, then gently shut his eyes and pulled the fetid blanket over his face, before returning to pick up the next stretcher. Nan wiped her face, blew her nose, and followed Annie. On the next litter lay an officer. Having laid him on the floor next to the young dead soldier, Annie looked at them lying side by side. War had become a great leveller. They transferred a further ten men from the train to the ambulance, which then had barely enough space for Nan and Annie to move between stretchers. Except for the occasional moan the ambulance remained silent as they sped back to the hospital. Nurse Butler and several of the VAD nurses were waiting to receive the new patients. Nurse Butler peered into the gloom of the packed ambulance and then turned to Annie.

'Well, how many have you got for us?'

'There were twelve, but unfortunately one young lad died shortly after we put him in the ambulance.'

Pulling back the blanket and glancing at the soldier, whose yellowish skin fell away from the bones of his young face, Nurse Butler turned to one of the nurses.

'Poor chap, leave him here. Nurse Smith, will you deal with the necessaries? Now what else do we have?'

Annie passed the clipboard detailing the name, rank and injuries of the wounded to Nurse Butler. She quickly scanned it and passed it back to Annie before going from stretcher to stretcher, checking names or looking at name tags before reassessing the nature and severity of each man's injuries. Working quickly and efficiently, she relayed her observations to Annie, who checked them against the list.

'William Broughall – Gunshot wound (GSW)
Eric Smith – Shell wound (SW)
Reginald Batson – Fractured tibia
Henry Jarvis – Amputated foot, suspected gangrene
Harold Sampson – Trauma to leg, head, scalp, abdomen and

knee
Albert Fox – Trench foot (TF)'

Having checked each man, Nurse Butler turned to Annie and Nan.

'Nurse Gingell, I want you to move these men into the 'louse house', strip and help bathe those who need help, and leave those who are able to bathe themselves. Some will need blanket baths. Give them clean pyjamas and then I will decide which wards to put them on. Nurse Matthews I'd like you to assist Nurse Gingell.'

Neither Annie nor Nan had seen naked men before. Nor were they prepared for the lice, which crawled over the men as they peeled the filthy, blood-soaked uniforms and underwear from their broken bodies. They had been trained not to show horror or fear, but not how to hide their embarrassment. The soldier with the fractured tibia flinched as Annie cut the tattered remains of his khaki trousers from around the bone that protruded from his leg. She cut the blood-soaked bandages binding his leg to a rough wooden splint and bathed the area around the wound, before carefully removing his boots. As she pulled off his socks, layers of putrefied skin clinging to the festering wool peeled off as she cut his foot free. She then gently pulled his trousers and underwear off. The man glanced down at his leg and through clenched teeth whispered:

'Don't worry, love, I've had a dose of the old trench foot before. Never 'ad a leg like this though, that's a new one for me...'

Annie smiled as she helped him into a warm tub.

'Don't worry, we'll soon sort you out.'

She left him to soak and turned to the next stretcher, which had been laid on the floor next to a growing heap of scattered muddy boots and piles of soiled clothing. The man's arm had been amputated at the elbow, and as she turned back the stinking brown blanket that covered him, she saw he had a host of smaller wounds from flying metal. The man gave a low moan as she gently picked the squirming lice from the surface of each wound before cleaning the infected areas with warm water. Next to her, Nan helped a soldier into a bath, his skin covered in blisters. The final stretcher held the officer, who babbled incoherently. She and Nan managed to wash and disinfect a large gaping wound in his chest before calming him down and helping him into a bath. She and Nan had just finished delousing and cleaning the injured when Nurse Butler appeared. Smiling at the now clean patients, she quickly dispatched each man to an appropriate ward according to their condition. She then turned to them both and winked.

'Well done girls! Now, I'd like you Nurse Matthews to clean up in here. All tubs will need scrubbing and muddy clothes sorting into two piles, one for burning and the other for washing. All boots need to be sprayed and put to dry.'

Then, turning to Annie:

'Nurse Gingell, once you've helped Captain Smythe into a bath chair and taken him along to A Ward, you need to go and clean yourself up, put on a fresh uniform and shoes then go straight up to the operating theatre.'

Tying the strings of a fresh apron and clipping a clean cap onto her head, Annie rushed up the stairs, two at a time, to the operating theatre. She had never set foot inside this room before, let alone been asked to assist. Nervously she waited for a moment to get her breath back, and then gently knocked on the theatre door.

'Enter!'

A doctor wearing a white surgical gown and mask was leaning over a man on the operating table with a large open wound in his left thigh. He looked up and peered at Annie over the top of his mask.

'Come in, Nurse...?'

'Gingell, Nurse Gingell, sir.'

'I'm about to pack this man's wound with salt bags, which will help purify the surrounding flesh. You'll need to hold him down.'

Annie positioned herself next to the soldier, who told her his name was Reggie Marshall. He grabbed her hand as the doctor pushed a number of small bags of salt into the gaping wound and then bound it tight. The pain must have been excruciating as the salt burned into his flesh. His fingers locked around her hand as he let out a cry, which Annie felt would lift the roof off.

Later that evening Annie and Nan assisted Nurse Peterson as she changed dressings and dispensed medication. As they went downstairs to A Ward, peals of raucous laughter filled the building. Looking into the ward, they discovered a soldier whose legs had been removed from the knees, propelling his wheelchair down the length of the ward whilst his fellow patients opened fire on him with slippers, pillows or anything else available. At the far end of the ward Nurse Butler, doubled over with laughter, clutched her knees to stop herself toppling over. Nurse Peterson turned to them, giggling like a naughty schoolgirl.'

'They're playing their favourite game, *'Shooting the Dardanelles'*. Nurse Butler invented it. It's so good to see that they can still laugh.'

Annie was stunned to see Reggie Marshall, despite his dreadful pain, joining in with the best of them. She and Nan caught each other's eye and laughed until welcome tears rolled down their faces.

March 31st

Annie and her cohort were to begin the final two weeks of their three-month period of Territorial Home Service at Wrest Park. She had mixed emotions. On the one hand, she felt satisfied that she'd consolidated her basic first aid training and had grown in confidence but, on the other hand, was disappointed that she hadn't been able to use her ambulance driver training. So, having just finished a night shift, she ventured into an area of the grand house that she hadn't been in before. She'd only spoken to the owner's daughter twice since she'd been at the hospital, but had decided to approach her directly. As she walked down a brightly lit corridor lined with family portraits, a door opened and Miss Herbert appeared, dressed to go riding.

'Can I help you?' she asked.

'I hope so, Miss Herbert.'

'Well, you had better come into my office, Nurse ...?'

'Gingell.'

'Oh yes, do come in, Miss Gingell.'

Annie followed her into a lofty wood-panelled room. A dark-oak partners' desk, covered with piles of papers and files, filled the large leaded bay window. She threw her riding hat on top of an open folder and propped her crop up against the wall, before flopping down into a leather revolving chair. She pointed to a smaller chair and asked Annie to sit down.

'So, what can I do for you, Nurse Gingell?'

'I've been here for two and a half months now and have learned a lot about nursing, which I've enjoyed, but I am a bit disappointed that I haven't had a chance to drive an ambulance. I'm worried that I will forget everything I learned about driving when I was training to be a VAD.'

'Quite right, my dear. You have every reason to be concerned. Leave it with me, I'll see what I can do. I have received splendid reports about your work here and have no doubt that you would make an excellent driver.'

Miss Herbert stood, picked up her riding hat and crop, and smiled at Annie, who thanked her and made to leave.

'You know Nurse Gingell, Matron describes you as a lively, cheerful little article.'

She rammed her riding hat down over her ears, paused and opened the door for Annie.

'There are four types of VADs, Miss Gingell: stalkers, who walk around looking alarmed; crawlers, who are little people who expect to be stood on; irresponsible butterflies, who flit from one thing to the next; and the sturdy pushers, who will do anything. I think you fit into the "sturdy pushers" category, Miss Gingell. Good morning!'

The following day Annie was given a khaki jacket, skirt and hat, shirt and tie, stockings and black shoes, and told to report to the ambulance depot in the old stable yard. As she arrived, a man in a VAD uniform was bent over the engine of one of the ambulances. He put down the oil gun in his hand and introduced himself as Reginald Dark.

'Right, Miss Gingell, this is your vehicle for the next two weeks. You will be expected not only to drive it but to maintain it. If anything goes wrong, you will have to fix it.'

Annie had no idea about the mechanics of an ambulance or what to do if it broke down.

'I didn't learn anything about how to repair it if it breaks down!'

'Well, now's your chance to learn.'

With that, he beckoned her over and had just finished

explaining the basic design of the engine, how to deal with freezing radiators and how to manage a temperamental vehicle, when an alert went out announcing the imminent arrival of an ambulance train at Ampthill station. Seconds later engines were cranked into life as ambulance crews ran to their vehicles. Annie grabbed the starting handle from under the driver's seat and was joined by two VAD nurses as she gave her ambulance a few hefty turns before the engine sparked into life. She jumped into the driving seat and, having only a few minutes to familiarise herself with the controls, put the ambulance into gear, put her foot hard down on the accelerator and joined the small fleet of vehicles heading for the station.

As she sped back to Wrest Park, aware that these men had already endured the long and painful journey by train and boat from France, followed by a further ambulance train from Southampton, Annie tried to avoid any unnecessary bumps in the road for fear of causing her charges any further pain. Half an hour later, having helped her crew unload ten men at the hospital, she turned round and drove back to the station to pick up a further ten. She wondered how the makeshift hospital would find enough beds for them all.

Arriving back at Wrest Park, she passed a number of ambulances taking groups of patients to convalesce at a local country house requisitioned by the War Office. The following day, as Annie made her way to the ambulance bay another group of walking wounded were being helped into waiting vehicles, to be taken to convalesce before being returned to the front. Despite beds being made available by the early discharge of these men, she was sure that the hospital had once again exceeded its official capacity of 156 patients.

Castle Street
Saffron Walden
April 16th

Annie turned into Castle Street and popped into Salmon's to buy tobacco for Gruff, and three scoops of aniseed balls for Pol and her young brother and sister. Mr Salmon was serving Mrs Turner and they both turned as the bell above the door announced a new customer. Mrs Turner's face dissolved, she grabbed Annie, enclosing her within her skinny frame, and squeezed her tightly, planting a damp kiss on her forehead before standing back and scanning her face, as if for the first time.

'Well, it's good to see you 'ome at last, Annie! Yer mum and dad 'ave missed you, what with Stanley doin' his trainin' and that. Yer mum says the house hasn't been the same since the two of you left, and I know how that feels, you mark my words.'

Annie disentangled herself from Mrs Turner's embrace.

'How's your Mary doing, Mrs Turner?'

'Well, she didn't go back to Howell's after the explosion. But like you, she's doing 'er bit. She's joined the VADs and has nearly finished 'er three months of nursing training with the St John's Ambulance. They need more nurses overseas....'

With that, she collapsed into the old kitchen chair next to the counter and pulled a creased handkerchief from her pocket. Wiping her eyes, she peered up into Annie's face.

'Ave a word with 'er Annie, she'll listen to you. God 'elp us, I can't bear the thought of 'er goin' away. She's 'opin to be sent to France!'

Annie's pulse raced as she tried to calm the older woman.

'I don't think she'll have a chance to say where she wants to go, Mrs Turner, but she's a strong girl, she'll be alright.'

Mr Salmon finished slicing a large joint of cooked ham and wrapped three slices in brown paper, which he handed to Mrs Turner, who had grabbed the edge of the counter and pulled herself to standing. Putting it in her basket, she turned unsteadily to leave.

'You're a brave girl, Annie Gingell, but 'ave a thought for us left at 'ome when you go off lookin' after our boys out there fightin'. We ain't getting any younger and this war is slowly killin' us all.'

She shuffled to the door and heaved it open, setting the bell clanging.

'Don't you mind her, Annie, she's just worried for you youngsters that's all. Now what can I get you?'

Gripping the tobacco and aniseed balls tightly in her free hand, Annie walked quickly up to Middle Square and kicked the splintered back door, which juddered open revealing Pol and Gruff sitting at the old pine kitchen table. Pol leapt to her feet and gathered her daughter up into her fleshy arms. Gruff hauled himself up out of his chair and waited impatiently to give Annie a hug.

'Well, look who's 'ere, what a lovely surprise!'

It had only been just over three months, but Annie noticed the change in her parents. They seemed to have aged. The house felt empty without Stanley. Gruff settled himself back into his chair and Pol ladled a large serving of soup into a bowl, placing it before Annie.

'Now eat up and tell us all about what you've been up to.'

That evening Annie couldn't sleep. She'd read the poster on Salmon's window advertising for more trained nurses to serve overseas. The idea of adventure, the chance to travel, of freedom was irresistible. Pol and Gruff had tried their best to persuade her to work in one of the military hospitals springing up all over England but, knowing their daughter, realised it was futile to try and hold her back. She'd decided to get the train to St John's Gate in London the following week to sign up with St John Ambulance Brigade as an ambulance driver. She had two letters of recommendation, one from Wrest Park and the other from the head of the VAD movement, certifying that she had completed her training and initial Home Service. From her knapsack she took out the letter with the Wrest Park Military Hospital heading and reread the final lines.

'Miss Gingell has proved herself to be a hard-working individual, capable of showing great courage and kindness. We cannot recommend her highly enough...'

Convinced that what she was about to do was the right thing, she folded the letter away and turned off the light, finally falling into a fitful sleep.

****

The journey up to London took longer than Annie expected, as many passenger trains had been requisitioned for use by the military. At Saffron Walden station she waited for over an hour before the long low whistle and plume of black smoke finally announced the arrival of the Liverpool Street train. An hour and ten minutes later Annie walked the mile and a half to the recruiting office at St John's Gate, pushing her way through the thronging rush hour crowds and stopping to gaze up at St Paul's Cathedral. A large banner bearing the badge of St John Ambulance hung above the entrance to a dingy office block, which had been set up as a temporary recruiting office. To the right of the door hung a large poster depicting a smiling woman about to climb into an ambulance, turning and appealing to fellow women to offer their service as ambulance drivers and nurses. A queue of women snaked its way around the street corner. Annie joined the queue and tapped the shoulder of the young woman standing in front of her.

'How long have you been waiting?'

The woman turned and smiled.

'I've only just arrived, but I heard someone say that she'd been here for an hour.'

Annie folded her arms and watched a group of six women join the queue behind her. Turning back to the woman in front, she sighed.

'Looks like we'll be in for a bit of a wait then. You done any driving before?'

'No, I've never driven anything in my life. I've only just finished my nursing training and three months hospital work with St John Ambulance. When I saw they were looking for nurses overseas I jumped at the chance to see a bit of the world. You?'

'I'm hoping to sign up as an ambulance driver. I haven't done much driving, apart from picking the wounded boys up from the ambulance trains and taking them to hospital. It's hard work, but I preferred it to working on the wards. I'm not saying I wouldn't do it again mind, but given the choice I'd rather be a driver.'

The queue suddenly moved around the corner, affording the two women a view of the gradually diminishing line in front of them. An hour later Annie and the young woman (whose name was Vera) stepped into the gloom of the recruiting office. Four women wearing uniforms of the St. John Ambulance Brigade sat behind two trestle tables. The two older women appeared to be carrying out the interviews whilst the younger two noted down the name, age, and rudimentary health details of each volunteer.

'Next!'

Vera smiled nervously at Annie and stepped forward. The woman checked her watch and beckoned to her to sit down. She began by asking her name and age. Annie leaned forward trying hard to catch Vera's full name. She suddenly felt a tap on her shoulder from the woman standing behind her in the queue.

'I think you're next', she whispered.

The woman behind the trestle table was tapping her pencil on the table and glaring at her.

'Next!'

Annie's stomach lurched as she stepped forward, spluttering an apology. She smiled at the recruiting officer, who sighed and signalled for her to sit down. Having taken details of her age, experience and health, the woman nodded and peered over her horn-rimmed glasses.

'So, what prompted you to come along today, Miss Gingell?'

'I've always wanted to travel and to see something of the world. This seemed to be the perfect opportunity.'

'Well Miss Gingell, I'm afraid you might be rather disappointed if that is your prime reason for signing up. The work involved is arduous and the hours long. There won't be much time for sightseeing.'

'Oh no, I didn't mean to sound as if I was expecting a holiday. It's just that I've never been abroad before and I thought it would be interesting to try something a bit different. I'm a hard worker and I've had experience as a nurse as well as an ambulance driver, as you'll see from my references.'

Annie handed the recruiting officer her two letters of recommendation. The woman pushed her glasses further up the bridge of her nose and read the first one from Wrest

Park, followed by the letter from the head of the VAD movement. She nodded to herself as she perused them both and then, swiping her glasses from her face, she beamed at Annie.

'Well, you do come very well recommended, Miss Gingell. We'd be foolish not to accept you. Are you offering your services as a nurse or an ambulance driver?'

Annie returned the woman's smile.

'I'd like to drive ambulances, please.'

'Well, I'm afraid we currently need more nurses, but that doesn't mean to say that if we require more drivers in the near future you won't be able to transfer to the ambulance service.'

Annie tried to hide her disappointment by readily agreeing to join the next contingent of St John Ambulance nurses due to leave for France the following week.

****

A week later, having promised Pol and Gruff that she would look after herself and come back home safely, Annie caught the train to Victoria, where she joined a large queue of nurses and VADs waiting to report to the Embarkation Officer, before catching the boat train to Folkestone. A few hours later Annie found herself leaning over the railings of a large steamer, waving goodbye to the white cliffs of Dover. The rolling motion of the boat only served to increase the excitement of the young women on board. For most of them this was their first taste of adventure and, despite feeling queasy, they nearly all chose to remain on deck throughout the crossing. Covered in smoke smuts and salty sea spray, Annie joined in the hearty cheers as the boat finally docked at Boulogne. A crush of women surged towards the exit, where a wooden gangplank was being lowered. Waiting for them on the dockside, an Embarkation Sister smiled and greeted the new arrivals, explaining that they would be taken either directly to their hospital or to a nearby hotel for the night if they'd been placed further afield.

Annie discovered that she had been assigned to a hospital in Etaples, some fifteen miles south of Boulogne. She and her group were to stay overnight at the Hotel de Louvre before travelling on the following morning. They were instructed to take only a suitcase and hand luggage to the hotel, whilst the large trunks containing their camp and active service kits, together with several uniforms, were to be stored on the quay and then sent on to Etaples.

Annie slept badly and awoke with minutes to spare before breakfast was due to finish. She leapt out of bed, cursing the other girls who shared her room for not waking her. Running down the stairs, she almost tripped and only managed to stop herself falling by grabbing the wooden banister, which creaked loudly as she pulled herself up. Breakfast consisted of crusty bread and jam and coffee. She wasn't entirely sure she liked the strong and slightly bitter flavour of the coffee, which was served in a bowl, but guessed she'd get used to it.

They were taken by motor ambulance to what the driver called 'The Land of Hospitals.' He turned to them and smiled.

'Welcome to the 'Land of Hospitals', ladies. We've just passed through the ambulance depot, which we call 'thumbs-up corner'. We have hospitals stretching for about four miles, and the entire district of Camiers and Etaples takes 6,500 patients. The St John Ambulance hospital you lot are going to takes 2,600 and has 85 nursing staff, including you VADs.'

Annie couldn't imagine a hospital of that size after Wrest Park, which took 150 patients. She lifted the canvas flap covering the window as they entered what looked like a city of huts and tents. Hospitals lined one side of the road, and officers' and nursing staff quarters the other. The urgent tramp, tramp of boots suddenly caught up with them, prompting the driver to slow down and allow a battalion of khaki-clad soldiers to pass. Leaning out of the window, he yelled:

'Goodbye and good luck!' before turning to us. 'Those poor lads are on their way up the line.'

'What does that mean?' Annie asked.

'They're on their way to the front line, poor devils.'

The sound of artillery fire could be heard quite plainly as the new recruits stepped out at the St John Ambulance hospital, which was to be their place of work for the foreseeable future. The hospital sat next to a railway siding, beyond which were sand dunes and, if Annie stood on tiptoe, she could just glimpse the sea. She was assigned a tent with three other VADs – Elsie Tranter, Nora Smith and Gladys Brooker – who, like her, had never travelled out of England before but, unlike Annie, were ill-prepared for the long hours and shocking injuries they had to dress. The smell of gas gangrene and death pervaded their days and haunted their nights. Gladys regularly woke screaming. A shift system with dayshifts starting at 7.50 a.m. and finishing at 8.00 p.m., and nightshifts beginning at 7.50 p.m. and ending at 8.00 a.m., started and ended with prayers. Annie, having had experience of theatre work at Wrest Park, was attached to a team of military surgeons and was on duty most days from early morning till very late at night, often not getting to bed until well into the following morning, often only to have to rush from the tent back to theatre for an emergency call.

One morning as she stumbled out of her tent, having had two hours' sleep, a large group of soldiers passed by on their way to the 'Bull Ring' for drill. As she waited to cross the road to the hospital one soldier caught her eye. He marched with a slight limp, but it was a gait she recognised immediately. She stopped dead, unable to move as Arthur, seeing her, flinched but turned his gaze away and marched ahead expressionless. Her heart exploded as she waited for the battalion to pass. Running up the stairs to theatre, she felt light-headed and had to stop for fear of fainting. Her body trembled as she pushed open the theatre door and rushed to help the surgeon stem the bleed from a soldier whose lower leg he had just amputated. Most emergencies were due to a patient haemorrhaging after amputation, and usually she was able to help control the blood flow by pressing down on the open wound. This morning she struggled to apply enough pressure and could feel the soldier slipping away. The surgeon, using his forearm to wipe a trickle of sweat from his chin, applied more pressure to the gaping wound, fixing Annie with grim grey eyes.

'Press harder, Nurse Gingell, press harder woman!'

Annie pushed down with all her strength, until together they managed to slow the blood flow sufficiently to allow her to tightly bandage the man's quivering stump.

'Well done, Nurse Gingell. I thought we might lose him for a moment. Would you wheel him into the recovery room and then, I think by the look of you, you need some sleep. How long have you been on duty?'

'Eighteen hours or so, but I did manage to get a couple of hours before the emergency alarm went off.'

'Well, it seems fairly quiet now, so go and grab some sleep while you can'.

****

Annie was thankful to find her tent empty, as Elsie, Nora and Gladys were all on dayshifts. She fell onto her tiny camp bed but, try as she might, she couldn't sleep. She knew she wouldn't be able to rest until she'd found Arthur. She needed to know if he still thought about her, if he still loved her, or if the war had killed his love and any dreams for a future that they might have had together.

The following morning, after she'd finished her final nightshift of the week, instead of going back to her tent she stole away to the 'Bear Pit', hoping to see Arthur's regiment. Lines of men were thrusting bayonets into straw sacks, reminding her of the time she'd watched Arthur training at Audley End. Another group were practising formation drills. She cast her eye from young face to young face, hoping to catch a glimpse of Arthur, but there was no sign of him. She was just about to leave when a group staggered out from what looked like a tunnel with a large door at the end, which had been forced open and from which the soldiers now poured out. They formed a ragged line, coughing and choking, some almost unable to stand. Arthur stood in the centre of them, staring ahead of him, his eyes fixed on some distant horizon, until the instructing officer bellowed:

'The gas released in that chamber, lads, was just to get you used to the real thing when you get there!'

Annie felt sick. She'd seen the effects of gas poisoning. She waited until the regiment returned to marching formation and realised that Arthur was on the end of his line. As they turned to leave the training ground, Annie positioned herself on the edge of the road next to where the regiment would be passing. She took out the piece of paper that she'd hidden in her pocket, checked that her tent number was clear enough to read, and as Arthur passed, thrust it into the top pocket of his khaki jacket. She then stood eyeing the men as they passed, making out that she was looking for one particular soldier. Spotting her, the commanding officer approached.

'May I ask if I might be of assistance?'

'Yes, I do hope so. I am looking for a Private Collins. He discharged himself from the hospital this morning and is in no fit state to return to his regiment.'

'No, I don't think you'll find him here, Nurse....?'

'Gingell, Nurse Gingell.'

'I'm afraid I don't know this man. You'd be advised to check with the General Staff at headquarters. Good day, Miss Gingell.'

With that, he turned and rejoined his men. Annie's heart pounded against her ribs as she headed back to her tent. *Had he seen her slip the note into Arthur's pocket? Had he guessed that she'd invented the story about Private Collins? What would Arthur think of her? Would he try to see her*? These thoughts plagued her as sleep once again evaded her. She was halfway between sleep and wakefulness when there was a rustling sound and the tarpaulin flap at the entrance to the tent lifted slightly. Startled, she sat up as Arthur quietly slipped in and knelt down next to her bed. She threw her arms round him and pulled him to her. They clung to each other, unable to speak, until finally he drew back and, cupping her chin, whispered:

'Annie.'

He'd said her name with more tenderness than he'd ever done before. It moved her deeply, nudging to the surface feelings that she hardly dared to acknowledge. Breathing raggedly, they melted into each other again until Arthur pulled away and took her face into his hands, his eyes hungry.

'I've missed you, Annie. There are so many things we never said. I love you, Annie, with all my heart.'

She took his hands in hers and caught her fingers in his. Tears ran down her cheeks as she fought to find words to convey how much this moment meant to her. She swung her legs over the side of the bed and knelt down facing him.

'Arthur, I love you so much it hurts.'

He grabbed her and, pulling her to him, encircled her in his arms.

'I thought you'd outgrown me, Annie. You looked so beautiful up on that stage at Christmas, singing like a nightingale, and all those soldiers falling in love with you.... I thought you wouldn't want anything to do with the likes of me anymore.'

'Is that why you walked away, Arthur? I looked for you after the show had finished. I didn't know where you'd gone, so I went back to Audley End. Gabriel, the garden boy, said he'd seen you... You were so wrong, Arthur, I've never stopped loving you.'

Arthur reached out and gently tucked back a stray strand of hair behind her ear.

'You broke my heart that day. But you know what they say, Annie, once your heart has been broken it grows back stronger and I think that's probably just about right.'

He paused, before pulling her to her feet.

'Marry me, Annie, when this bloody awful war is over, marry me.'

She reached up and gently ran her fingers over the scar running down the side of his face and left eye.

'Of course, I'll marry you, Arthur Scoggings!'

He reached into his pocket and brought out a small circular piece of plaited string, which he clumsily pushed on to the ring finger of her left hand.

'Our engagement ring, Annie!'

Laughing, he picked her up and swung her round, her feet brushing against the sides of the tent as they tried to stifle their laughter.

'Put me down, Arthur! Put me down! Someone might come in.'

She swivelled the string engagement ring around her finger. It felt rough against her skin.

'It's beautiful and I'll never take it off, Arthur.'

He wrapped his arms around her and then, pausing, whispered into her ear.

'I'm leaving tomorrow, Annie. We're going up the line first thing in the morning.'

The air vibrated around them. Annie felt as if she'd been struck. She pulled away from his arms, her eyes exploring his. She sat down heavily on the bed, taking a few seconds to absorb the immediacy of his leaving. He sat beside her and enclosed her hands in his.

'Don't worry, Annie, I'll be back before you know it.'

'I know, Arthur, I know you will.'

The sound of the hospital siren announcing another emergency brought Annie to standing.

'I have to go, Arthur.'

They stood for a few seconds more, clinging together, listening to their hearts, their breathing, taking in the smell of each other. She wanted to keep him close, safe.

'I must go, Arthur, they need me in theatre. Look after yourself, and come back to me.'

He turned to go, but swivelled round and held her for another few seconds before opening the tent flap and quietly melting into the midday bustle of the camp. A few seconds later she followed and ran across the road to the hospital.

****

Arthur
June 12th

Arthur glowed as he made his way back to the British Expeditionary Force's camp. He slipped into his tent, to find it empty. With just ten minutes to check his webbing and kit, he quickly gathered everything together. After the relatively slow pace of life during their five months of guard duties at Abbeville, the training camp in Etaples was harsh and the discipline tough for many of the soldiers who were new to army life. Despite being promoted to corporal, Arthur had begun to question it all, but seeing Annie again had renewed his sense of purpose. At the end of this awful war he would come back to her and they would be married. He could still feel her presence, smell her hair and hear her laughter as he gathered his equipment together and ran out to the parade ground. Sergeant Jenkins stood, hands tucked neatly behind his back facing his men, who'd laid out their webbings on the ground in front of them and were holding pristine Lee Enfield rifles ready for inspection. Seeing Arthur slip into the back row, he yelled:

'Where the hell have you been, Corporal Scoggings?'

'Call of nature, sir!'

'Get into line, man!'

Having checked that each soldier had sharpened and fixed a wire cutter correctly to the end of his rifle, Sergeant Jenkins handed over to Lieutenant Turnbull, who strutted along the lines, his eagle eyes checking each man's puttees, boots and uniform. Finally satisfied that his soldiers would march out of camp the following morning with their heads held high and looking like a credible fighting force, he puffed out his chest and outlined the schedule for the coming day.

'Right men, for those of you who have been keen to see action, you will be pleased to hear that the time has now arrived. Everything comes to those who wait! Tomorrow morning we march out of here at 0600 hours. We will march north to training trenches, where you will get your first taste of trench life. After that we will move south to the Somme battlefield front, to relieve the 13th Battalion of the Essex Regiment.'

A ripple of excitement, mixed with fear, passed from man to man as they realised that they were about to put into practice everything they'd learnt during their training. Lieutenant Turnbull cleared his throat.

'I suggest you spend this evening writing to your families and loved ones.'

With that, he dismissed the men and spun sharply on his heels before returning to the officers' mess.

Nothing could dampen Arthur's spirits as he sat on the edge of his bed writing to his parents. He knew they'd be worrying, so tried to allay their fears by making his letter light and cheery. To Annie, he wrote a more honest, heartfelt letter, knowing that she understood what he was about to face. His feelings for her spilled out over the page and made him all the more determined to return safely to her.

Neuville St Vaast
June 16th

Heavy rainfall, combined with the pounding of the solid

rubber tyres of lorries on the poorly built roads, had caused the vehicles to get bogged down in the mud, making it difficult to distribute the tonnes of supplies needed for the men at the front. The training trenches were set several lines back from the front line in a relatively quiet part of the trench network, but nothing protected the men's ears from the sound of artillery fire or their feet from the incessant rain, which churned the floor of the trench into a thick stinking mud bath. One of the first tasks given to the new soldiers was to carry supplies from the vehicles that had become half-buried in mud to the supply dugouts, ready to be distributed to the front, support and reserve trenches. The men toiled, sometimes ankle-deep in mud, carrying heavy crates of tinned bully beef, sacks of rock-hard biscuits and bags of porridge oats to the supply trenches, where they were stacked on raised steps to keep them out of the quagmire beneath. By the third day the new recruits had spent hours carrying out the thankless task of baling out water in a vain effort to help the mud harden and spearing huge rats, which threatened to outnumber troops, on the end of their bayonets.

'This ain't what I signed up for, Corp', a young private complained to Arthur.

'Be careful what you wish for, chum.'

Arthur pulled the dead rats from his bayonet and threw them over the edge of the trench into a large crater. They had now been holed up in the training trench for a week, but precious little training had taken place.

Beaumont Hamel
The Somme
June 23rd

The seven-hour march from Neuville St. Vaast sapped the

good humour from even the most stoic of the men. They'd marched through a lengthy thunderstorm and now low sagging cloud threatened further heavy rain, as they arrived damp and dispirited at the Beaumont Hamel trench, which was to be their home for the next eighteen days. The sound of heavy artillery fire made any attempt at conversation futile, so the men sat silently on the muddy fire steps that lined the sides of the dugout, waiting for Lieutenant Turnbull to issue orders. Finally, he appeared from the officers' quarters further up the line.

'Right men, you'll have time today to settle in. I hope you'll find your accommodation to your liking!'

A weak ripple of laughter passed down the row of muddy faces. Lieutenant Turnbull raised the volume of his voice as another shell exploded a short distance from where they sat.

'Tomorrow evening, which we will call Day 1, under cover of darkness we will commence cutting the enemy's barbed wire defences. At daylight on Day 2 we will release gas for one hour only, which will confuse the enemy as to our intentions and will serve to provide cover for you as you retreat.'

He paused as another shell burst somewhere in the narrow strip of land separating them from the German front line.

'The wire cutting is a vital first step in our advance and will continue for three days. On Day 3 there will be an early destructive shoot to help cut the wire, followed at 0900 hours by an 80-minute intensive bombardment of shellfire to remove the last remaining barbed wire. This will open up the field for a final infantry attack by Day 4. Some of you will be assigned to nightly raiding parties to judge the situation. Your job will be to report back on the effects of our efforts and to assess the strength of the opposition.'

Kicking a dead rat from under his foot, he bent down and picked up the lifeless rodent and hurled it over the ridge of the trench. Adjusting his field hat, he cleared his throat and continued.

'The field kitchen is at the end of this trench. I suggest you get some food and then bed down.'

The horsemeat stew had a few peas floating on its fatty surface and was accompanied by a hard, grey biscuit. Both were barely edible, but to the weary, hungry men they tasted better than their mothers' home cooking. Arthur and Vic found an indentation in the trench wall just big enough to allow them to lie with legs outstretched. They pulled their wet great coats up over their ears and settled down for the night. They were woken an hour or so later by thunderous rain and ominous flashes of lightning. Somewhere further up the trench someone screamed and called out for his mother.

'He's gonna have to get used to this,' muttered Vic, lighting up a cigarette.

Arthur pulled his coat further over his face and ears and lay for a few moments picturing Annie, wondering if she was thinking of him, before drifting back to sleep. By morning the saturated sandbags tucked into the trench walls had dripped water over his boots and trousers. Arthur sat up and shivered. Vic was having his first cigarette of the day and coughed violently. Up and down the trench men were waking and staring in disbelief at their surroundings.

'Good morning, lads. Rise and shine!'

A sergeant carrying a large demijohn of navy rum appeared and pushed a shell cap protector the size of an eggcup into Arthur's hand, into which he poured a measure of the strong black liquid. Arthur downed it in one and choked violently as the rum scorched his dry throat. He returned the shell cap protector and sat back to enjoy the warm sensation in his chest as the liquid found its way down to his stomach. Vic drank his ration and passed the vessel to the young private next to him. He held it out to be refilled and then attempted to swallow the stuff but vomited it up over the front of his coat.

'This is your morning ration, lads. Porridge is on its way. After that, get your wash rolls out and clean yourselves up. Have a shave.'

He stopped by the young private, who was wiping the vomit from his great coat.

'Get that cleaned up properly, lad.'

Then, staring at the new recruit's upper lip, he yelled:

'Where's your moustache, boy?'

'I, I haven't been able to grow one, sir.'

'Mark my words lad, you'll have grown one by the time we've finished with you. Now get yourself tidied up and shave that miserable bumfluff you *have* got!'

Vic leaned back against a wet sandbag and lit a second cigarette, inhaled deeply, then blew a perfect grey smoke ring, indistinguishable from the slate grey morning sky, as it drifted along the edge of the trench. A young private approached, close on the heels of the sergeant. Vic took another deep puff and smiled.

'Not a bad hotel this.'

'Glad you like it, Clark. Right lads, mess tins out!'

The private carried a large pot of tepid grey porridge, which he ladled sparingly into each mess tin. Despite its unappealing look the men devoured it. Having finished his porridge, Arthur took his dirty mess tin and washed it in a shell hole behind the rear wall of the trench. Having swilled the dregs of porridge away with last night's rainwater, he filled the tin and brought it back to where Vic and a number of other soldiers were still eating. He quickly threw enough water over his face to dissolve the caked mud that clung to his cheeks. The coldness of it made his skin tingle. He took out his razor, lifted his chin and was about to shave his neck when there was a high-pitched whizzing sound and the young clean-faced private next to Vic slumped forward, blood pumping from a large hole in his head. Dropping his razor, Arthur threw himself down into the filthy trench bottom on top of Vic and the other soldiers, whose mess tins now lay in the mud. Someone further up the line returned the sniper's fire, and then – silence.

'Bloody snipers', Arthur whispered. 'He wasn't wearing his helmet, the stupid kid.'

Keeping their heads low, Vic and Arthur cradled the dead young soldier before lifting the collar of his greatcoat to remove the mud-splattered identity disc that lay hidden under the folds of his shirt. They then gently covered him with his greatcoat and laid him on the fire step. Scraping off a layer of caked mud, Arthur managed to read the boy's name, 'Herbert Warner'.

He turned to Vic. 'We didn't even know his name. He only looks about eighteen.'

Sergeant Jenkins, bent double, pushed his way through to where the young lad lay and lifted the greatcoat, sighed and took the name disc from Arthur.

'Why the hell wasn't he wearing his helmet?'

'He'd taken it off to wash and shave, sir.'

'Bloody bad luck then!'

He peered over the top of his small metal glasses at Arthur and Vic.

'See to it that he's given a coffin. I'll arrange for the parents to be notified.'

He then turned to the cowering men still lying in the trench bottom.

'The rest of you, keep your heads down and prepare for duty in twenty minutes!'

Arthur and Vic made their way to the casualty station and returned with a simple coffin and, after saying a few words, lifted the young lad into it before replacing the lid and raising it on to the fire shelf for collection.

'The poor lad hadn't even grown his first moustache.'

Sergeant Jenkins reappeared and nodded briefly at the coffin, before ordering the men to pick up their kit and follow him. He led them to an area behind the reserve trenches that had been partly cleared of trees to form a makeshift parade ground. He climbed up onto a fallen tree and addressed the men.

'We have, very unfortunately, lost a young man this morning to sniper fire. He wasn't wearing his helmet. Let this be a lesson to you all. You must never drop your guard. Wear your helmet at all times, even when washing or shaving. Snipers are everywhere here, so get used to it!'

He glanced at a sheet of paper in his hand before resuming:

'We have a group of sappers who for months have been tunnelling under no man's land and are now almost directly under Jerry's trenches. They will pack Amenol explosive into chambers seventy-foot underground. They have been working discreetly, and a considerable amount of spoil from their digging has already been removed. Your task will be to remove the remainder from those chambers. I will shortly assign each one of you to a squad, and then, employing your trench spades you will work as discreetly and quietly as is possible to clear the tunnel of debris. It will then be wheeled to a hidden location, which will be revealed to some of you later.'

He paused and glanced round at the assembled soldiers before continuing. Referring to his list, he divided the men into squads of ten privates to one corporal. As corporals, Arthur and Vic had both been assigned new recruits.

****

The tunnel was approximately a hundred yards long and three feet wide, although in places it narrowed, forcing the men to walk sideways, crab-like. Even the shortest were unable to stand. They part-crawled, part-walked, doubled over, through the dank candle-lit tunnel. As they passed, eerie shadows were thrown up along its pitted chalk walls, as candles flickered in the fetid subterranean air. In places they were plunged into darkness, having to feel their way with hands outstretched sidewards, fingertips snagging against the rough tunnel sides that guided them. As they descended deeper underground the air became thinner. Several of the men complained of light-headedness. Finally, they reached a gallery high enough to allow them to stand. They stretched bone-weary limbs and gazed at the mountains of spoil lining two sides of the chamber. A high stack of sandbags formed the end wall, beyond which the miners had dug smaller chambers big enough to embed enough explosive to rip the trenches above apart. A collection of wooden wheeled carts sat idle in front of them. Beyond them, a group of sappers squatted, straining to listen to the faint thumps in the wet earth around them. One of them signalled to Arthur and his men to remain silent. Each man prayed that it was the sound of his own heartbeat, knowing it could be German tunnellers, priming explosives to kill them all. The thumping became fainter and finally ceased. The sapper signalled to Arthur that work could continue. The men toiled hour after long hour, loading spoil into wooden trucks, which were then manhandled to an area to one side of the tunnel opening, where men from Vic's squad bagged it up ready for disposal. No one asked where the spoil was to be dumped. No one spoke at all. They worked side-by-side, backs bent double, beavering feverishly, until Arthur gave the signal to down tools. Arthur's damaged leg ached almost unbearably as he led the men towards the tunnel opening, where shafts of light filtered into the murky gloom of the narrow passage. They spilled out into the glaring light of day and lay exhausted, waiting for the remaining men to emerge from the tunnel. Arthur counted his squad and realised there was still one man who had yet to appear.

'Who's missing?'

'Jones, Corp, he was a few feet behind me....'

Without warning, an almighty explosion shook the ground. Arthur was thrown on to an embankment as the earth in front of them rose up, like an enormous pie crust, slowly at first, then the bulging mass of earth cracked into thousands of fissures as it erupted, hurling hundreds of tons of earth skywards and tossing the men into the air like rag dolls. An eerie silence followed, broken finally by the coughing and choking of men clearing their mouths and throats of mud and dust, as they dug themselves out of the earth that threatened to entomb them. The tunnel entrance had been reduced to rubble, trapping Private Jones, Vic and his squad, and the sappers at the tunnel end. A trench spade lay half-buried behind Arthur, where he stood gasping for air. He grabbed it and started digging where the entrance had been. The chalk crumbled as he dug, dislodging large heavy boulders, which toppled towards him.

'It's no good Corp, we won't be able to get through that.'

'For Christ's sake man, there are men trapped in there, we have to try!'

One by one the men shook themselves free and started to dig, some with only their hands. A large boulder blocked what had been the entrance. Pulling together they finally managed to move it just enough for a man to get through. Arthur squeezed himself into the narrow gap and yelled:

'Is anyone there?' Silence. 'Is anyone there? Can you hear me?' Still no response. 'Shout if you can hear me!'

'It's no good Corp, there's no one alive in there, how can there be?'

'For God's sake man... '

Suddenly there was a quiet tapping coming from behind the rubble. Arthur pushed his way further into the tunnel, causing another fall of rock.

'Are you alright, Corp?'

The young private had pushed his way in behind Arthur, followed by three others carrying trenching spades. The tapping started again. It appeared to come from their left.

'Grab this and start digging!'

Arthur shoved his trenching spade into the young man's hand and began clawing at the rubble from where the tapping came. The other men began digging. Gradually the tapping became louder, clearer. Arthur pressed his ear to the rock and shouted:

'If you can, knock three times!' There was no response. 'For God's sake, knock, we need to know where to dig.' Nothing. Then a faint knocking. Three times, quite clearly. Another two men had now managed to squeeze through the opening, leaving little room to dig. Arthur grabbed one of the men's' spades.

'Use the spades to lever this rock rather than digging.

Spread out around it and force your spades into the crack at its base.'

'Right Corp!'

The seven men scrambled over piles of chalk and rubble and managed to fan out around the boulder.

'We need to dislodge it to the right. You five position yourselves as close together as possible to the left, balance your spade on your helmet and use it as a lever, and you two, help me push it over to the right'.

The men removed their steel helmets and wedged the rim under the base of the boulder, before laying their spades across the helmet's dome.

'Dig your spades as deeply as you can into the crack – now!' Arthur yelled.

The men strained and pushed but the boulder refused to move.

'Dig deeper for God's sake!'

The men gave everything, but still the boulder remained stubbornly buried in the chalk and earth surrounding it.

'It's no good, men. We'll have to dig at the rubble around it and hope we can get through that way.'

Arthur started to dig and chip at the mound of displaced chalk that lay impacted next to the huge boulder. A vein at his temple and the livid scar on his cheek throbbed. The younger men followed his lead and began hammering at the rock, which reluctantly submitted to their efforts and began to crumble. The tapping grew closer as the men sweated and dug. A huge crust of earth and stone suddenly gave way, covering the men in dust and rubble. A voice from the other side of the landslide was now clear enough to hear.

'Over 'ere, we're over 'ere!'

It was Vic. The digging party, spurred on by the sound of his voice, dug furiously, and with a final push the pile of rock tumbled, once again covering them with dust, rock and earth. A hole big enough for a man to crawl through opened up, revealing the trapped men huddled together at the entrance to a smaller disposal tunnel. Arthur thrust his arm into the hole.

'Grab my hand!'

Then, turning to his men, he yelled:

'Form a chain behind me. I'll pass them on to you.'

Arthur dragged the first man's limp body through the gap. The young face, contorted and covered with mud and sweat, was unrecognisable. He passed the man to the first soldier in the chain and then turned back to grab the next. The man screamed as Arthur grabbed his broken arm.

'Push him from behind!' Arthur shouted.

The man was propelled slowly through the gap.

'I can't breathe! I can't breathe!'

Arthur cupped his hands over the young man's mouth.

'Now breathe slowly, slowly does it, we're nearly there. Look towards the light.'

He turned and passed the soldier to the first man in the chain. Then, one by one, Vic's squad crawled through into the narrow chamber, followed finally by Vic and Jones. Mole-like, they grappled their way to the narrow gap at the original tunnel entrance where, having squeezed through, they collapsed blinking into the daylight.

****

That afternoon Arthur wrote to Annie at the Base hospital.

Beaumont Hamel
June 24th, 1916

My darling Annie,

We're finally dug in at a place called Beaumont Hamel, on the Somme. The weather has been pretty awful, rain and more rain. So much rain that the trench has filled with water and is now a mud bath. Despite this the men are, for the most part, in good spirits, and it was a nice surprise to be served a tot of rum this morning! The food isn't too bad. Last night we had stew and biscuit.

So far Jerry has been fairly quiet. Tomorrow we begin preparations for an all-out assault on him, so wish us luck.

I think of you all the time and fall asleep at night thinking of your lovely face, and you're the first thing I think of when I wake up. I feel strong because I know you're waiting for me. Please don't worry about me. Once we've got the job done here, I'll be back in your arms.

Take care my love. I will write again soon.

Your loving

Arthur

****

June 26th

The day dawned dull with low cloud and heavy rain, following an overnight thunderstorm. To fool the enemy about their intentions, the 4th Division released chlorine gas into no man's land for an hour. Arthur's unit, wearing newly issued box respirators, prepared to advance towards the German trench defences. Their mission: to cut through thick coils of barbed wire which formed the first line of the enemy defence, in preparation for an infantry assault scheduled for June 29th.

The men waited in nervous clusters, removing their masks to allow them to smoke. The signal was finally given. Having smoked the last Woodbine in his pack, Arthur threw the cigarette butt into the festering mud beneath his feet, where it landed next to the corpse of a decaying rat. The men pulled their masks over their noses and mouths, then, following Arthur, poured like ants over the top, into the narrow strip of land separating them from the enemy. They part-ran, part-crawled, keeping low to the ground, holding wire cutters attached to their short-magazine rifles. Arthur's arm ached with the weight of his Lee Enfield, his damaged knee throbbed. Signalling to the men to spread out, he crouched lower to the ground as an almighty blast hurled the man next to him into the air. He landed ensnared on barbed wire, where his body hung lifelessly, his torn trousers flapping in the morning wind. The howls of the injured were drowned out by another shell exploding to his right, sending vast clods of mud into the air. As it cleared, Arthur counted four more men lying face down at the bottom of a cavernous hole. A young lad lay moaning, his leg mangled and bloody; another yelped and writhed in the mud, crying for help. Trying to close his ears to their cries, Arthur urged the forward party onwards towards the enemy dugout. They began hacking at the barbed wire, which unlike the round wire used by the allies, was square in cross-section and made of hardened metal. Arthur lunged at the wire and lifted his rifle upwards. The jaws of the cutter closed, but slipped off the wire, making little impression on the hardened metal. He lunged again, the jaws slipped again and still made little impression. Standing next to him, Private Jones ripped off his mask.

'It's no use, Corp, these wire cutters are worse than useless against this stuff!'

'Rubbish man, you just have to try another way.'

Arthur wiped the sweat from his forehead and positioned the wire cutter over a smaller section of wire. Pressing hard down on the operating lever, the jaws clamped shut, cutting through the tough metal

'That's going to take all day, Corp.'

'Well, if that's how long it takes, that's how long it takes. Get on with it! And put your mask back on!'

Arthur signalled to the men to cut only small sections at a time. His blistered hands stung, sweat mixed with crusted mud streamed down his face and dripped off the end of his nose. He swiped it away with the filthy sleeve of his jacket. They cursed and cut for a further two hours before Arthur finally gave the order to retreat. Picking their way over the dead and dying, Arthur urged the men to get back to the dugout. Overhead, allied shells sliced through the fetid air before erupting, engulfing the enemy in a growing mushroom of mud and concrete debris. The men slowly clawed their way back, finally dragging themselves over the ridge into the tenuous safety of the dugout. Arthur then crawled back to where the young soldier with the contorted leg lay quietly whimpering. As he got closer, Arthur could see that the soldier's left leg was mangled by metal fragments, some of which had driven patches of his uniform deep into his thigh.

'It's alright lad, it's going to be alright, just hang on.'

Grabbing him by the arms, he dragged the injured man slowly towards the dugout. The young soldier who'd cried out for help now lay a few feet to his right with vacant, dead eyes staring up at the smoke-filled sky.

'I'll get 'im Corp'.

Private Jones had followed Arthur and now crawled towards

the dead soldier. He'd started to haul him out of the mud when the ground erupted again, throwing him and the dead man into the air. A few feet away Arthur, bent double and covered in clods of mud, had managed to drag the young soldier to the dugout wall, where two privates hauled him over on to the fire step.

'Over 'ere Corp!'

Private Jones lay sprawled over the corpse of his dead friend, a jagged bone protruding from the mud-encrusted sleeve of his jacket.

'I'm alright Corp, it's just a scratch!'

'Get back and get that seen too.'

The young man hesitated.

'Now!'

'I've still got one good arm, Corp.'

Between them they dragged the dead man to the edge of the dugout, where two young soldiers hauled his limp body on to the fire step. Another young recruit lay nearby, gripping his stomach, mouth wide open in a circle of agony. Blood pumped from the gaping wound in his torso. Reaching him, Arthur took off his jacket and held it over the throbbing wound, pressing hard down to stem the bleeding. A second young soldier had clawed his way through the mud and threw himself on top of his comrade, using his body weight to press down on the wound.

'Stay on top of 'im!'

Arthur dragged them both, inch-by-inch, over to the trench wall. The soldier's blood-drenched body was hauled over on to the fire step, where a medic waited. Finally, Arthur dragged the lifeless body of the young recruit into the trench.

June 27th

A much brighter, warmer day. Sergeant Jenkins had doubled the size of Arthur's unit in an effort to speed up the rate of wire cutting. Not only was progress slower than anticipated, but thirty per cent of the allied shells had failed to explode. Those that had, proved ineffective against Jerry's concrete dugouts, and low cloud allowed only poor aerial observation. Under cover of a further gas release by the 4th Division, Arthur's unit dragged themselves up to the wire for a final time, where they cut and hacked for a further hour. Arthur then signalled for the men to crawl back to the trench, whilst the sky exploded with an allied destructive shoot, followed by 80 minutes of intensive gunfire and shellfire, aimed at cutting the remaining barbed wire.

June 28th

The men awoke cold and wet. Thick mist and heavy rain made visibility poor. The trench had become a quagmire. Rats the size of small badgers scurried through the men's legs as they prepared to make a final sortie to report back on the effects of the initial bombardment. As the last of the gas supplies were released Arthur's unit struggled over the top, their boots sinking into the stinking mud. Relentless rainfall made it almost impossible to gauge the damage to the wire or the condition and manning of the enemy trenches.

June 29th/30th

The planned infantry attack had been postponed for forty-eight hours due to bad weather. The men sat around in dejected groups using stubs of candles to burn lice from the seams of their filthy jackets. Others spiked rats on their bayonets, smoked, or sat silently, waiting. Everyone was waiting.

'Get your letters written lads, then get some shuteye. Make the most of your holiday.'

Sergeant Jenkins clapped Vic and Arthur on the shoulder. 'That means you two as well!'

Arthur nodded, but made his way to the Casualty Clearing Station. Private Jones sat waiting to be transported to the military hospital in Etaples. A wooden splint held the broken bone in his forearm in place. He grinned at Arthur.

'Looks like that's the end of my war for a bit, Corp.'

'I wanted to thank you Private Jones, for your bravery. Without your help I couldn't have got those men back into the dugout.'

'My pleasure, Corp'.

He paused and then, pointing to two stretchers lying nearby in the mud, frowned.

'I didn't come out of it so bad, not like those poor sods.'

Arthur recognised one of the men as the young private with the badly mangled leg. He lay sleeping, waiting for the next field ambulance. A single scant sheet moulded itself around his body. Arthur could see that his right leg had been amputated. The second man groaned as he held a mud-caked hand over a large dressing covering his stomach. Arthur shook Jones's hand.

'Good luck, Jones, you'll make a fine NCO one day.'

He then pushed back the makeshift tarpaulin door and found a wet sandbag propped up next to an empty coffin. Sitting on the sandbag, he wiped a layer of mud off the coffin's surface with his sleeve before reaching into his breast pocket and taking out a sheet of damp writing paper. He smoothed the crumpled paper as best he could and began to write.

Beaumont Hamel
The Somme
30th June 1916

My dearest Annie,

Our major advance planned for 29th June has been postponed for forty-eight hours due to poor weather, which gives us all a welcome break. Today we're resting. We had an extra slug of rum again this morning, which was most welcome. We remain in reasonable spirits. I have some plucky young men in my unit who are giving their all. Their mothers would be proud of them. However, there is nothing glorious about this war and we all look forward to seeing our loved ones again.

I pray that you are safe, my love, and think of me from time to time during your long working days. I feel your presence around me, Annie, and without you in my thoughts I would be a much lesser man.

Please write, it will cheer me so.

Until we meet again.

Your ever-loving

Arthur

July 1st

Before dawn, the allied infantry moved into position along an eleven-and-a-half mile stretch of trench. Each man had been given a packet of Woodbines and now sucked on them like babies at their mother's breast. As the sun slowly came up, they wondered if they would see it go down that evening. Carrying essential rations, grenades, bayoneted rifles and digging tools, they stood shoulder to shoulder in silent rows running the length of the trench. They were to go over in waves. Vic's team were part of the first wave and stood two rows in front of Arthur's men, who were in the third wave. Behind Arthur, three more lines stood ready.

07.25 hours. Five minutes before zero hour. An enormous explosion made the earth quake beneath their feet, and black billowing smoke spread across the sky. Vic and Arthur ground their cigarette stubs into the mud as the sound of a whistle pierced the air.

Zero hour. The first wave of men spilled over the top, forming themselves into long close-formation lines, walking steadily forwards with bayonets thrust into the air.

07.32 hours. The second wave followed in close line-formation. Two minutes later Arthur's third wave moved in behind them, then the fourth, fifth and sixth waves of men until they'd all been herded over the top like lemmings throwing themselves off the edge of a cliff.

'Keep close, men! If the man in front goes down, step forward into his place!'

No sooner had Arthur spoken than a battery of machine-gunners emerged from the still intact enemy shelters and mowed the two lines in front of them down, ending the war for Vic Clarke and his unit. Arthur's men moved forward, stepping over the dead, the unforgiving mud swallowing their bodies up whole.

'Keep walking, men!'

A hail of bullets pinged off their steel helmets. More men dropped to both right and left. The air filled with the screams of men calling for their mothers, their wives, their girlfriends.

'Keep walking!'

Arthur's hand closed around the pin of his grenade. He and several of his men were now within throwing distance of the enemy trench.

'Hold back! Get to the base of the dugout before you throw. Then get the hell out of the way!'

Arthur pulled out the pin of his grenade and hurled it into the German trench. His men followed suit, before retreating and throwing themselves into a crater as the shells exploded around them, scattering body parts, chalk and concrete into no man's land. A number of men in the fourth and fifth wave had almost reached the enemy trench and were engaged in close-range fighting. They were thrown back by the force of the blast, their clothes ripped off them. One man screamed as the heel of his foot flew into the air. A young German soldier staggered towards him, his bayonet ready to stab the man as he lay half-submerged in the oozing mud. A cascade of bullets sliced through the air, grazing Arthur's ear as the German soldier slumped to his knees, shot by a young private who yelled 'If I don't get him, he'll get me!'

That evening Arthur wrote a letter to Vic's parents:

Beaumont Hamel
The Somme
July 1st, 1916

Dear Mr and Mrs Clarke,

It is with deep regret I write these few lines informing you of the death of your son Victor, which occurred today, July 1st 1916.

He was in the same platoon as myself and we were very great chums, which is why I think it my duty to write to you. He was well liked by all in the company and, with his death, we have lost a good comrade. He died doing his duty – leading his section in action. I can assure you of his good name, and that he will receive a proper burial. The platoon and myself share our sympathy with you in your sad bereavement.

Yours sincerely,

Arthur Scoggings

Etaples Base Hospital
July 10th

Annie's hands trembled as she tore open Arthur's letter. It had been a long day. There had been a convoy of four hundred men on stretchers, covered from head to foot in caked mud, some crawling with maggots, some stinking and tense with gangrene. All had been wounded at the Somme. One lad had both eyes shot through. They were smashed and mixed up with his eyelashes. He was quite calm and had asked her:

'Will I need an operation? I can't see anything.'

Annie had told him that he would never see again.

Tears cascaded down her face as she read. It had been a few weeks since his first letter and she'd thought he might be dead. She fiddled with the string ring that she carefully removed and kept in her apron pocket each day, only wearing it when her hands were clean and dry. She slipped the letter under her pillow, then lay down to rest, knowing that when she tried to sleep her ears would ring with the sound of the surgical saw at work, and that her mouth and nose would fill with the stench of gangrene. That day she'd assisted at ten amputations, one after the other. She reached under her pillow and reread Arthur's letter, and prayed.

The sound of a whistle announced the arrival of another ambulance train. Annie checked her watch – 2 a.m. Thrusting the letter back under her pillow, she left the tent and joined a number of other nurses making their way through the dark to the railway siding next to the hospital. Fifty-seven stretchers had been dropped in the oozing mud.

These men were the less severely wounded but, like all the others, theirs were the faces of war, staring up at the nurses with desolate soulless eyes in the hope that they'd be sent home. Knowing that all they could do was patch these men up and send them back to the front, Annie and her colleagues smiled and listened while cleaning and dressing their wounds, before leaving them on the side of the railway line for a train to pick them up and take them back to fight.

As they turned to leave one soldier screamed:

'You're the biggest criminals. You only heal us so there's someone left to kill! You bring soldiers worn to death back to life so they can be killed again, torn to pieces again!'

Returning to her tent, Annie checked the time – 4.30 a.m. She lay down and finally fell into a shallow sleep, with Arthur's letter tucked under her pillow. She was wakened three hours later by Gladys shaking her.

'Annie wake up, wake up!'

Annie groaned and turned over blinking up at Gladys.

'Get up Annie, you're wanted at General Staff Headquarters.'

'Why?'

'I don't know. Sister just told me to come and wake you. You'd better get over there.'

Annie threw on her uniform and, having splashed some water over her face, made her way to the squat concrete building that housed the General Staff Headquarters. She knocked on the main office door.

'Come in.'

Annie pushed open the door. The St John Ambulance Recruiting Officer smiled at her from behind a large oak desk.

'Do sit down, Miss Gingell.'

Pausing, she glanced at a page of notes in her hand. Annie could read her name on the top of the sheet of paper.

'I seem to remember you expressing a preference for ambulance work when we last met?'

'Yes, I'd like to drive ambulances if there's a vacancy.'

'Well, you'll be glad to hear that with the increasing volume of injured soldiers requiring transport to hospital from the Somme, we're in need of extra drivers.'

Annie's heart raced.

'You do realise of course that the work is dangerous, as you will be required to pick the wounded up from casualty clearing stations near the front. You will then transport them to the stationary Base Hospital here at Etaples. Casualty clearing stations are often under fire from the enemy, so you need to be aware of the risks involved, Miss Gingell.'

'I'm prepared to take that risk.'

'Well, that's decided then. You will be given driving goggles and gloves, a hat bearing the St John Ambulance badge, two white shirts, a tie, fitted jacket and wide skirt, sturdy shoes and gabardine raincoat when you report to 'thumbs-up corner', which is of course what we call the ambulance depot. I suggest you go there directly. I'll telephone them and tell them to expect you. Good luck, and good morning, Miss Gingell.'

She stood up and gave Annie's hand a hearty shake.

July 11th

The prospect of driving an ambulance again excited Annie. To be working near the front line would make her contribution more meaningful. It would also bring her closer to Arthur. Annie felt almost light-hearted as she made her way to 'thumbs-up corner.' As she approached, an older man, possibly in his early fifties, greeted her with a friendly handshake.

'Good morning, Miss Gingell. Welcome to the crew. My name is Peter Morris, senior ambulance driver. I hope you'll enjoy working with us.'

'I'm sure I will.'

'If you'd like to follow me, I'll show you to the uniform store and, once you've been kitted out, I'll take you to your ambulance.'

Annie followed Mr Morris into a flat-roofed building, which housed the ambulance service administration offices. Having been given her uniform, she walked to a large courtyard where several converted lorries and a few motor ambulances were parked. Mr Morris pointed to a small siren mounted on the roof of the administration block.

'This will be your alert, Miss Gingell. It might look small but it makes a lot of noise! Now, this will be your vehicle for the foreseeable future. I understand you've driven ambulances before, so I'll leave you for a few minutes to look over it.'

Hers was one of the mud-spattered motor ambulances parked at the end of the line. Annie rubbed the caked mud off a plaque on its side, which showed that it had been donated by the Midlands Automobile Club.

'Thank you, Midlands Automobile Club,' she muttered.

Storm curtains were clipped to the open front. Annie pushed them aside and noted that the top speed was

45 miles per hour and that the cranking handle had been stowed under her seat. Peering into the rear, Annie calculated there would be room for about nine or ten stretchers laid side by side. Mr Morris appeared and smiled at her. She liked his smile and grinned back at him.

‘All is in order I hope, Miss Gingell?’

‘It looks to be, Mr Morris. When do I start?’

‘Just as soon as you’ve put that uniform on, Miss Gingell. Is that soon enough?’

Annie rushed back to her tent, changed out of her nurse’s uniform and made her way back to the ambulance compound, just as the siren sounded and a handful of drivers appeared, running towards their vehicles. Grabbing the cranking iron from beneath her seat, she engaged it and gave it three sharp turns. The engine spluttered into life. She glanced over at the woman next to her and, jumping into the driving seat, shouted:

‘Where to?’

The woman smiled.

‘Follow me!’

Despite having treated so many mud-encrusted men, Annie wasn’t prepared for the narrow, slippery track that finally led to the Western Front. Several times the vehicle’s wheels skidded, almost throwing the ambulance over into the slimy mud. As they got closer, a great plume of thick choking smoke engulfed them. The sound of artillery fire, men’s screams and moans filled the air. Annie’s ambulance bounced and rattled along as she tried to keep up with the woman in front, who eventually slid to a standstill in an area set back from the rows of frontline trenches. Lines of wounded men on stretchers, waiting to be taken to base hospitals, littered the ground. Beyond them was an area of tents, some round, others larger and rectangular in shape, which Annie guessed housed the operating tables. Annie took her foot off the accelerator and let the vehicle slither to a halt. The woman in front jumped down from the cab of her ambulance and approached Annie, who climbed down to meet her.

'Well done you! That drive isn't the easiest. In normal conditions it's a fifteen-minute journey, but in this damn mud it takes at least forty-five minutes.'

She held out her hand.

'Phoebe, Phoebe Devonshire. Welcome to the team!'

Annie smiled at the woman as she returned her firm handshake.

'Annie, Annie Gingell.'

'Right, Annie, let's get some of these poor devils loaded up.'

Annie was forced to drive slowly, despite knowing that several patients needed to be seen rapidly. At times she had to rely solely on her reflexes and instincts to avoid slipping into enormous craters big enough to hold an entire ambulance, so she wasn't too surprised to discover that one man had died before she reached the hospital at Etaples. Nothing had prepared her for the constant enemy shellfire or witnessing four soldiers blown to pieces in front of her. Several trips later, and with the light fading fast and mud flying on to the windscreen, her vision became less and less reliable, until she was forced to drive at a snail's pace, whilst rain blowing under the flimsy storm curtains soaked both her and the cab. Arriving at the base hospital in the half-light it was now difficult to know where to unload the wounded. Exhausted men on stretchers covered every inch of available hospital space. The severely injured, hovering between life and death, their bodies viciously mutilated, lay on a carpet of blood and khaki, their uniforms in shreds.

Annie drove until dawn until, numb and exhausted, she drove back into the depot and collapsed with her head on the steering wheel, unable to face another stretcher or the sight of another man torn, bleeding and raving. She was woken by someone gently shaking her. It was Mr Morris, who helped her down from the sodden seat of her ambulance.

'Now Miss Gingell, I think it's time you got some sleep.'

Annie slept fitfully despite her exhaustion. She woke several times with visions of Arthur dying on a stretcher. She woke with her heart pounding, Arthur's voice ringing in her ears.

'How cheap life has become! It doesn't matter how many are killed. All that matters is that a man reaches a German trench before being hit. That's the average soldier's ambition in this bloody war!'

It felt so real, he felt so real. She sat up, looking round the tent at Gladys and Ivy sleeping soundly, then, having driven for forty-eight hours with just two hours' sleep, she made her way back to the ambulance depot, aware that her excitement for adventure had now become mixed with fear and trepidation.

August 31st

Wearing metal helmets, and with enemy shells falling all around, Annie, Phoebe and five other ambulance drivers drove in convoy, picking up wounded men from the front line. For long hours they fought to save the lives of men buried in dugouts and a recently shelled field hospital. Having worked as VAD nurses in England, both Annie and Phoebe also volunteered to man a new first aid station, little realising that it was within shouting distance of the German trenches. A few days later the German officers had started to recognise the two of them. One evening, when they were about to bandage and splint the leg of a young wounded soldier, Annie heard a low voice.

'Hallo...hallo!'

She lifted the tarpaulin entrance door and realised that the sound was coming from just beyond the trench, on the enemy side.

'Hallo...hallo!'

Checking the chinstrap of her helmet, Annie raised her head slightly above the parapet in the direction of the voice and, between the coils of barbed wire, found herself looking into the face of a young German officer who had stepped into no man's land, carrying a white handkerchief. Her instinct was to drop down beneath the trench ridge.

'Frauline, zere is no need to be afraid!'

With her heart thumping against her ribcage, Annie slowly raised her head and once again stared into the pale-blue eye of the young German.

He cleared his throat and stammered:

'Frauline, if you vear hat of nurse, not helmet, you can go in no man's land and ve von't shoot you.'

He turned and squelched back to the enemy dugout.

Annie gulped and watched as his slight frame disappeared over the top. Phoebe raised both eyebrows as she slipped back under the tarpaulin.

'Did he say what I thought he said?' she asked.

'I think he did!' Annie replied.

'But can you trust him, can you ever trust Jerry?'

'There was something about him, Phoebe, I think we could trust him.'

A short distance away the muffled sound of laughter drifted into the night. The following day an allied reconnaissance plane was shot down. It lay nose down in the mud about twenty feet away from their dugout. The pilot had bailed out and lay perilously close to the burning cockpit, from which ragged flames fanned out, threatening to engulf him. Wearing caps, Annie and Phoebe slowly edged their way into no man's land and over to the pilot. He appeared to be still alive. His legs were badly burned and probably fractured, but he was breathing. With their boots sinking into the stinking mud, together they managed to grab him under the arms and drag him over to the edge of the dugout, where a stretcher-bearer helped to pull the unconscious pilot to safety.

At the end of their shift Annie and Phoebe returned to base, carrying the pilot and several other badly injured men in their ambulances. Having delivered them to the hospital, they made their way back to the ambulance station.

'You see, being a woman sometimes helps!' Annie grinned at Phoebe. 'It means we can get to parts of the battlefield that the men can't, and we can save lives!'

Phoebe returned Annie's smile.

'Jerry probably thinks we can't hurt them as we're just "dainty, fragile" women. Huh, they've got a lot to learn!'

Annie patted her mud-splattered ambulance and joined Phoebe as they made their way into the admin block. She put her hand on Phoebe's shoulder and scoffed:

'They really have no idea how to treat women in a war zone. Let's hope that if nothing else, this war will prove that women are just as capable as men!'

As they pushed open the door into the office a grim-faced Mr Morris looked up from his desk and pushed a telegram into Annie's hand.

Saffron Walden
September 7th

On the corner of Castle Street a wooden board had been nailed to the window frame of Salmon's grocers. Five familiar names had been written on the board. Five young lives lost in Castle Street since Annie and Stanley had left Saffron Walden just over eight months ago. Stanley's name had been newly added. Annie ran her fingers over his name, trying to picture her brother in the *Five Bells*, drinking beer with her and Gruff last New Year's Eve, the night before they'd both left. Her eyes rimmed with tears as she slowly made her way up to Middle Square.

A desiccated Christmas wreath still hung on the outside of the kitchen door. Pol had vowed to leave it there until her two eldest children returned home. Annie pictured her mum opening the door to the telegram boy, holding out a quivering hand, taking the telegram from the young lad, whose words, quietly spoken, had destroyed her. She pictured Pol's face, savage with the hope that there'd been a mistake, and Gruff, falling apart. She pushed open the splintered door. Pol dragged herself up from her chair and clung to Annie, her body heaving as each wave of sobs engulfed her. Gruff sagged in his chair and mumbled into his beer. A framed photograph of a smiling, gentle-faced boy in an obscenely over-large cap had been placed in the centre of the table. It had been taken the day Stanley had marched out of the Square to war. Hearing their sister arrive, Annie's two younger siblings appeared in the doorway. Fred had turned fifteen since Annie had been away and now stood head and shoulders above her. He and fourteen-year-old Nora silently hugged their sister, nodded and sat at the table, trying not to look at the photograph that dominated the room and their thoughts. Fred wiped his eyes and stared at the floor, his puffy-eyed sister stared up at Annie, her face red and swollen.

'Why him, Annie? Why him?' she wailed.

She grabbed Annie's hand as her lips wobbled and her face crumpled.

'It's not fair! It's not fair!'

'We can't even bury him.'

Pol turned to Annie. 'We can't even bury him!'

'I know, mum. But he'll be given a proper burial. There are just too many dead to bring back home. When this is all over, they'll bury all the men who lost their lives, in proper graves over there in France.'

'I want 'im buried here. I want 'im buried near his family. It's not right that he should be left out there all on his own.' Pol collapsed into a chair.

Later that evening Pol and Annie sat together at the kitchen table. Gruff, crushed into a shadow, lay sprawled on the bed upstairs, whimpering as he slipped into oblivion. Annie looked at her mother, trying but failing to be strong for her daughter. Dark brown crescents had formed under her eyes, which were rimmed with tears. A painful silence had wrapped itself around the two women, who sat opposite each other, hands entwined. Pol shifted her gaze to focus on the photograph of her dead son, lines of grief etched into her weary face. Pointing to the room above, she sighed:

'I 'aven't got the energy to worry about 'im upstairs. He's weak. He's suffering like the rest of us, but 'is way of dealing with it is to lose himself in the drink. I found 'im lying in the gutter like a big grey slug this mornin'. As if I 'aven't got enough to deal with!'

Her voice trailed off as a chain of sobs racked her body. Annie's grip on her mother's hands tightened.

'Don't worry, mum, we'll sort something out.'

'How am I going to cope, Annie? This 'ouse is like a skeleton of an 'ouse now, what with you gone, our Stanley dead and Gruff drinking himself into the grave.'

She stared at Annie with glassy-eyed intensity.

'I've lost everything, Annie!'

'No, you 'aven't mum, you've got the rest of us kids. Fred and Nora need you, now more than ever.'

'But *you'll* be going back!' A fresh wave of sobs engulfed her. 'I can't bear to lose another child, Annie!'

'No mum, I'm not going back, I'm staying here.'

Pol's eyes momentarily lit up.

'I've got compassionate leave for now, mum, but I've written to the War Office and given them my resignation. I can get war work here eventually and help with the family at the same time.'

Pol smiled through her tears and hugged her daughter to her. Blowing her nose, she turned to gaze at Stanley's photograph.

'I mustn't become bitter and hard, others have suffered worse. '

She paused.

'It's just, I don't know 'ow we'll manage with Gruff not working and Stanley gone. I'm already putting in as many hours as I can up at the Laundry, as well as takin' in washin' and, without Stanley ....' Her voice trailed off again.

'Don't worry, mum, Fred's old enough now to start doing the round without dad. He's been helping him since he left school, so he knows how the business works.'

'It's a job for two people, Annie, you know that. Stanley looked after the 'orses he was the 'orseman. It's Gruff who does most of the sellin' and knows where to get 'is fruit and veg.'

'Well for the time being I'll be helping Fred. The two of us can manage until dad gets himself back together.'

Pol shook her head.

'Huh, there's not much 'ope of that.'

'We'll be alright, mum. You wait and see. Now try and get some sleep, you look all in.'

'I can't sleep, Annie! Every time I shut my eyes, I see our Stanley lying dead on some field somewhere.... all on 'is own!'

'Try, mum. Stanley wouldn't want to see you like this, would he? Try for him.'

'I can't lie down next to your dad, Annie, I just can't.'

'Well, I'll get you a cover and you can sit in the comfy chair in the front room.'

With the sound of Gruff's snores filling the stairwell, Annie grabbed a cover from her bed and brought it down to the tiny room at the front of the house, where Pol sat slumped and diminished, in a threadbare armchair, next to an empty fire grate. In her hand she cradled Stanley's photograph. She held it for a few moments, before quietly kissing his face and handing it to Annie.

'Put it back on the table, will you?'

Annie hugged Pol and was again shocked by the frailty of her mother's frame. She draped the cover over her shoulders and kissed her forehead.

'Now *try* and get some sleep, mum, I'm just next door in the kitchen.'

Annie listened to the gentle whistling of her mother's breathing, glad that she'd finally succumbed to sleep. She quietly pulled the door shut and sat at the table, forcing herself to meet the gaze of her dead brother. What had he been feeling when the photograph was taken? Was it fear or pride she could see in his eyes? Had he suffered like so many of the men she'd nursed? She turned the photograph away, unable to hold his gaze any longer.

She hadn't heard from Arthur for nearly a month and didn't know what to think. She fiddled with the circle of string on her ring finger, quietly muttering *'please be alive, please be alive,'* then, taking a sheet of paper from a drawer in the dresser and crossing the fingers of her left hand, she began to write.

Annie Gingell
6 Middle Square
Castle Street
Saffron Walden

September 19th, 1916

My darling Arthur,

I pray that you're still alive and that you get this letter.

My brother Stanley was killed at the Somme on 4th September and the family are taking it badly. My dad can't cope and has turned to the drink, so I've come back home for the time being, to do what I can to help my mum and my younger brother and sister.

I'm still wearing the ring you gave me. I'd die if I lost it. I think about you all the time and hope that you're safe so we can be together sometime when this terrible war is over. If you can write, please send your letter to the address above.

Look after yourself.

Your loving

Annie

It was when she went back to the drawer to look for an envelope that she discovered, pushed to the back, next to some unused stamps, several field postcards from Stanley. She reached in and picked up the small bundle that had been tied up with string. The most recent was uppermost. On this he'd ticked three boxes. The first, stating that he was quite well, the second, saying that he'd received Pol's letter, and finally the box indicating that a letter would follow at the first opportunity. He'd signed and dated it 3rd September 1916. Annie went to put the cards back and it was then that she spotted a letter in with the cards. She untied the string and, taking out the slightly battered envelope, recognised her mother's writing. The letter, addressed to Stanley, was unopened and had been returned. On the front was written *'Killed in action 4th September 1916'*, the day after Stanley had sent the service postcard. Annie shuddered and replaced the unopened letter back with the cards, retied the string and put them back in the drawer, before taking a fresh envelope and stamp from a small supply Pol had set aside to be used for letters to her daughter and now-dead son. Having addressed her letter, she put two penny stamps on the envelope, hoping that it would be enough postage for France. She'd never written a letter to anyone abroad before. She decided to walk down to the postbox at the bottom of Castle Street, to be sure that it would catch the first post in the morning. As she tugged open the splintered kitchen door, she almost stepped on a small basket holding a few vegetables and a bottle of milk. She picked the basket up and left it on the kitchen table, before quietly slipping out to the postbox. When she got back, she found Pol sitting at the table, the vegetables and milk untouched.

'It makes me ashamed to think of 'im laying up there! Most of the families on the street have lost someone or 'ave someone badly injured.'

She looked at the basket on the table.

'They're sufferin' just like us, but they still do kind things like this.'

Her eyes filled with tears again.

'Well, mum, you might not have the energy to sort dad out, but I 'ave!'

****

Early the following morning Annie and Fred hitched Kitty up to the cart. Annie climbed up next to her brother, who grabbed the worn leather reins and coaxed Kitty into a slow plod out of Sillet's yard and into Castle Street. Stealing a glance at her brother's hands, Annie realised that they were no longer the hands of a boy, but those of a capable young man.

'So, Fred, where are we off to then?'

'Well, we'll 'ave to go out to Wiseman's Farm first. Pick up some fruit and veg. Then I'll take you round to meet the regulars. It'll give you a feel for things.'

'Right you are Fred, you're the boss!'

They made their way out onto the Thaxted Road. The early morning sun sliced through the treetops and cast a warm flush over their faces. It had been an unusually warm September and the day promised to be another hot one. The gentle clip clop of Kitty's hooves soothed Annie, who sat quietly absorbing the stillness of the hedges and fields beyond. Her thoughts returned to Arthur and the hellish fields of stinking mud they called The Somme.

'Penny for 'em, Annie.'

Fred turned to her with a wistful smile.

'Oh, nothing Fred. Just thinking how nice it is here.'

They drew up to Wiseman's Farm and Fred jumped down

and went to help her down.

'Don't worry, Fred, I'm more than used to jumping down from high seats.'

They picked up several sacks of potatoes and turnips and loaded them onto the back of the cart before hauling up a large sack of apples and setting off. Kitty headed straight towards Wimbish, then on to Debden, Widdington and Littlebury, knowing which houses to stop at and which wayside troughs were full of cool drinking water.

'Well, I reckon she could do this round on her own,' Annie laughed.

'She could do it blindfolded. She even knows when we've sold everything. See how she's speeded up.'

Fred leaned forward and patted Kittie's steaming flank. It had been a very hot day and they both wiped streams of sweat from their faces as they made their way back to Saffron Walden. As they approached the crest of Windmill Hill, Annie noticed a number of small neatly dug plots at the bottom of the hill, each with what looked like rows of vegetables planted in tidy lines. The plots fanned out from the roadside and stretched back towards Bridge End Gardens. Suddenly Fred pulled sharply on the reins, coaxing Kitty over to the roadside.

'Whoa, old girl! Whoa!'

Jumping down, he examined the cart's wheels.

'Aah, I thought as much.'

'What's up, Fred?'

'It's the heat. It makes the wheels shrink and the tyres slip off if you're not careful. See?'

Annie climbed down and examined the wooden wheels at the back of the cart. The tyres had become slack and looked as if they were about to fall off.

'What can you do about that, Fred?'

'We'll 'ave to go down to Swan Meadow pool and get Kitty and the cart in the water for a bit. That'll make the wheels swell up again, then the tyres'll fit nice and snug.'

They made their way slowly down the hill and turned right into Freshwell Street. Kitty broke into a slow trot, anxious to cool down in the pond. As they stood side by side at the edge of the water, Annie found herself looking up at her brother, as she turned towards him and smiled.

'When did you do all this growin', Fred, you're bigger than me now!'

Fred smiled shyly before answering, 'I've got to be bigger now, 'aven't I?'

'I suppose you 'ave.'

Annie watched Kitty, who was craning her neck down to the cool water and drinking in loud gulps.

'Fred, what are those plots of land at the bottom of Windmill Hill? They're all planted up with vegetables.'

'They're called allotments Annie. The council has started renting bits of land so people can grow their own veg. Dad tried to get one but there's a waitin' list as long as my arm.'

'Well, did he put us on it?'

'No, dad said he'd be in 'is grave before his name'll likely come up.'

'Well it's worth *tryin'*, Fred. If we could get one, we could sell some of our own veg. It would save us some money.'

****

The following morning Annie made her way to the council offices. The door was open so she let herself into the small, gloomy reception room and stood in front of a large oak counter, behind which two women were busy filing a large stack of documents. Hearing the door open, one of them stopped and looked up.

'Be with you in a minute, love!'

A few minutes later she slammed the filing drawer shut and turned to Annie.

'What can I do for you, miss?'

'I'd like to have an allotment for my family please.'

'You do know there's a waiting list?'

'Yes, but I'd still like you to put us on it please'.

Having filled in the form that had been thrust across the counter to her, Annie smiled and returned it to the woman, who quickly scanned it and looked up when she discovered that the family's main breadwinner was 'incapacitated'.

'May I ask why your father is unable to work?'

'My brother, who helped our dad with his business, has just been killed at the Somme, and my dad is taking it badly and can't work.'

'Yes, grief is very incapacitating. But so many local families are suffering losses Had your father been killed, then we could possibly have pushed you up the waiting list as you would be classed as a needy family, but I see you have a brother of fifteen. Is he working?'

'Yes, that's just it. My brother and me are takin' over my dad's work while he's ill.'

'What work might that be?'

'He's a costermonger on the market Tuesdays and Saturdays, and sells fruit and veg to the villages the other days. If we only had an allotment, we could grow some of our own veg for the business.'

'I really don't think a single allotment would be productive enough to supply both your family and your business with vegetables, Miss Gingell. I'm sorry about your brother, and will add your family to the waiting list, but I'm afraid the likelihood of getting an allotment at the moment is quite remote. I hope your father feels able to support your family again soon and, in the meantime, I wish you and your brother the best of luck with running your father's business.'

****

Annie slowly made her way back home. As she passed Salmon's she paused to check the board. Another name had been added: Private Walter Hill from number 26. He'd been a trainee butler at the Big House and had been one of Arthur's friends. She stood for a moment, worn down by the weight of it all. Why hadn't she heard from Arthur? Tears streamed down her face as she fought to keep herself together. The bell over Salmon's door jangled and an arm gently cupped her shoulder. Reggie Salmon guided her into the shop and helped her sit down on the chair in front of the counter. He tore a ragged piece of wrapping paper from a pile on the counter and offered it to her.

'Here, wipe your eyes with this, Annie. I can see you've been checking the board. He was a lovely lad, just like your Stanley.'

Annie wiped her eyes with a small piece of the rough paper, then used the rest to blow her nose.

'How many more young lives are we going to lose before this horrible war is over, Mr Salmon? My generation are being swallowed up by it!'

Mr Salmon leaned back against the counter and folded his arms.

'I don't know how else to help me mum and dad. Me dad's

gone to pieces and is drinking himself to death. Me and Fred are doing his rounds. If we could only grow at least some of the veg we sell, we wouldn't have to buy so much from Wiseman's.'

'What about getting one of those new allotments up on Windmill Hill?'

'I've just been up the council office. They said we probably won't get an allotment. There's a long waiting list.

Her voice trailed off.

'Well, how about you have mine?'

Annie stared up at Mr Salmon's ruddy face.

'What? What did you say, Mr Salmon?'

'I said, why not use mine? I applied for one as soon as they were offered, but I've been so busy with the shop I haven't got round to digging it over yet. If you'd like it, you could give me some of your veg and you can have the rest. You'd be doing me a favour.'

Annie jumped up and flung her arms round his neck.

'If you're sure, Mr Salmon! It might be a way to get dad back on his feet again if I can get him out there diggin'.

Mr Salmon smiled. Turning to the row of sweet jars lining the counter, he put his hand into one and brought out two striped tuffins.

'And these are for the young'uns.'

'I don't know how to thank you, Mr Salmon!'

'You're a good girl, Annie, and what are neighbours for if we can't help each other out a bit. Now you get on home and tomorrow after I've shut up shop, I'll walk you over to the allotments and show you which one is mine. It's a corner plot so is quite a bit bigger than the rest.'

Annie hugged him again, picked up the tuffins and, setting

the doorbell jangling, stepped out into the midday sunshine.

The Somme
October 1st

Arthur picked his way through the jumble of barbed wire that ran the length of the British trench. Seven of his men spread out behind him and were forging their own way through into no man's land. Arthur peered through the fading light at the tangled wreckage of trees and the bloated bodies of two dead German soldiers, lying swollen and blistered a few feet in front of him. He turned back to the wire and began closing a number of gaping holes, twisting the rusty barbs back together. Further up the line he could see the arched backs of his men, bent double as they repaired the damage of the morning's bombardment. As he knelt to pull a length of wire out of the mud, a thundering blast shook the ground, hurling him into a filthy spume of mud, which engulfed him. A searing pain in his right arm forced him to look down. A splintered bone in his forearm had pierced the skin and was protruding at a strange angle out of his jacket and a damp patch on his mud-caked trousers was spreading like an amoeba up his thigh.

'It looks like you need a stretcher, Corporal Scoggings!'

The voice was that of Private Jones and was the last thing Arthur remembered, before waking up in a cold field ambulance taking him to a casualty clearing station, twelve potholed miles back from the front. He winced as the vehicle bounced over what felt like a fallen tree. He slowly lifted his head and, squinting through the gloom, realised that a splint had been bound tightly to his lower arm, forcing the bone roughly back into place. The throbbing of his arm, however, felt trivial compared to the racking pain in his leg, which had been bound so tightly he was unable to feel his foot. He lay back, casting his eyes around to view his fellow casualties. The man next to him moaned quietly before turning to face him.

'What 'appened, Corp?'

He moaned again. Arthur was about to speak when the raspy voice of another man lying behind them hissed:

'It was a bleedin' grenade! Right behind us when we was fixing the bleedin' barbed wire, that's what it was!'

Arthur tried to pull himself up and turn towards his men, but collapsed back onto his stretcher.

'Now Corporal Scoggings, you must lie down. You have a number of metal splinters embedded in your leg and you've got a compound fracture of your right forearm, so do try to keep still. It looks like the end of your war for the time being.'

The nurse steadied herself against the ambulance side as the vehicle suddenly lurched to one side. Arthur could hear the front wheels spinning in the mud as the driver tried to find a firmer grip on the muddy slope. Every jolt shot through his body like a knife blade slicing into him.

'It won't be long now boys, we're nearly there.'

'Where are we heading, nurse?'

'The field hospital. They will decide where best to treat you. Then some of you will be taken on to the base hospital at Etaples'.

Arthur's heart sang. The prospect of possibly seeing Annie again thrilled him.

It was several days later that Annie's redirected letter was delivered to his bedside in Etaples. Using his good arm, he tore open the letter but disappointment threatened to overwhelm him as he read its contents.

Saffron Walden
October 30th, 1916

Gruff leaned on his spade and wiped a trickle of sweat from the deep creases in his ruddy face. Sighing, he cast rheumy eyes over the heavy clods of earth that would need breaking up and raking before he could plant the autumn vegetables. He sighed again and stretched his aching back before taking up his spade and slicing into the biggest clods on the patch that he'd roughly dug over. Pol had given him an ultimatum: either he did his share of work or he found somewhere else to live. He knew that she meant it. It had been enough to jolt him out of his self-pitying misery. He even had to admit to himself that being out in the fresh air felt good. So, to spur himself on, he imagined the neat rows of fresh, overwintered vegetables, which would give him an early crop to sell in the spring.

'It's good to see you out and about again, Gruff!'

Reggie Salmon closed the small wicket gate that marked the boundary of the Gingell's allotment. Smiling broadly, he thrust a packet of a quick-growing variety of turnip seeds into Gruff's calloused hands.

'Thought you might like these to get you started. Put them in now and they should be ready by Christmas and they'll get your soil ready for your next planting.'

Gruff felt his eyes moisten as he took the seeds and returned Reggie's smile.

'I … I don't know what to say, Reggie.'

'Well, don't say anything. Now you'd better get back to it if you want to get them in the ground before it gets dark.'

With that he strode back to the shop, leaving Gruff to start raking the soil into a fine tilth, good enough to support the young plants.

October 31st

Annie left Fred to feed Kitty and put her back in her stable and crossed over the road to Middle Square. She carried a few unsold turnips and potatoes, which would help bulk out the meat stew Pol had cooking on the range. She kicked open the kitchen door and put the vegetables on the table. Pol sighed and thrust the *'Evening News'* over to Annie, pointing at the headline.

'Just look at this, Annie!'

'ONLY ELEVEN DAYS' SUPPLY OF WHEAT LEFT'

'It says we're 'aving to rely on cheap imports of wheat, and we 'aven't got enough, so we've got to grow more 'ere. It says we're only growin' enough for 125 days out of 365 days in a year!'

She slammed the paper down on the table and stared up at Annie, her eyes ablaze. For the first time in weeks she looked like her old self.

'It's bloody Jerry attacking our supply ships – that's what's doin' it! It says 'ere we need to start ploughing up fields and planting more wheat and potatoes. Says we need to release some of our home defence men to work on the land as we haven't got enough ploughmen and horsemen. But there's a shortage of horses for ploughing, we 'aven't got enough. Now they're bringing back some of the war horses. It says they're looking for women to retrain them.'

Annie snatched the paper from her and quickly scanned the article with a growing fluttering of excitement in the pit of her stomach. Later that evening, after the family had gone to bed, she spread the paper out on the kitchen table and noted down the address of the National Food Production Department and then sat down to write a letter of application. She'd worked alongside a lot of troubled and terrified horses. She'd seen how trauma had turned these docile animals into frightened, vicious creatures. *This could be a way for her to help some of those poor animals, as well as supporting the war effort*. She slipped out and posted her application before making her way home. She quietly let herself in and crept upstairs to Fred's room and knocked gently on his door.

'Fred, are you awake?'

Fred's bare feet padded across the creaking floorboards to open the door. His hair a messy haystack and his eyes heavy-lidded. He yawned.

'What's up, Annie?'

Annie pushed past him and flopped down on the edge of his bed.

'Can you and dad manage the round between you now that he's back on his feet and the allotment is all planted up?'

'Why are you asking, Annie?'

'They're looking for women to retrain war horses to work on farms. There's a shortage of horses for ploughing you see, and I've seen what war does to them, poor beasts, so I've applied. Hope that's alright with you?'

'But Annie, do you know how to handle them, especially the frisky ones?'

'I can learn, Fred. It would only be for a short while, and I'd be paid for it after a bit of training.'

'How much?'

'It says a pound a week'.

Fred yawned again and scratched his head.

'Well, we could manage without you now so why not, if that's what you want to do.'

'I 'aven't said anything to mum and dad yet, so keep it quiet will you for the time being? They mightn't want me, so there's no need to say anything until I know.'

'Mum's the word!'

'Thanks, Fred'.

She ruffled her brother's hair and winked at him before tiptoeing to the door and letting herself out.

November 15th

'Woah there, gently does it!'

Annie removed the blinkers from the terrified horse's head. She lowered her voice, gently coaxing him out of the lorry and into a large paddock, where she released him, and then stood back to watch. The stallion froze, his flanks heaving and eyes rolling. Then like a shot, he reared up, boxed the air with his muddy hooves and bolted to the far side of the enclosure. She turned to collect a second horse and led him slowly in to join the first. Finding himself free, he kicked his back legs into the air and, with nostrils flaring and mud-caked mane lifting heavily in the wind, he darted over to join the first horse. The two animals raised their heads, nuzzled each other, neighing softly, then sniffed the clean air and cantered around the perimeter of the paddock, before greedily grazing on the few tufts of grass growing in clumps between a couple of fence posts.

'Well, they look happy!' Mr Wiseman leaned on the fence next to Annie. 'We'll let them settle for a bit before getting them on halter reins, then we can start working on them. They'll be quite skittish for a while and won't take kindly to being reined in again after having tasted a bit of freedom, that's for sure. They won't trust you for a while, but we have to be patient, Annie.'

He smiled, left Annie and strode back across the yard and into the farm office. Annie leaned on the paddock's five-bar gate and watched the two war-weary horses explore their new surroundings. She breathed in, savouring the fresh air and pungent farmyard smells, which rekindled her senses. She listened to the silence, broken only by the swish of the horses' tails. They flicked hordes of flies, attracted by the distinctive smell of decay, from their muddy flanks and muzzles. She wondered if Arthur was still alive and how damaged he might be by the horrors he'd shared with these horses.

December 20th

Posters had been put up at various points around the town. A new one had appeared in Mr Salmon's window. Annie stopped on her way home to read it.

DON'T WASTE BREAD!
SAVE TWO THICK SLICES EVERY DAY
AND DEFEAT THE U-BOATS

Pushing open the kitchen door, she found Gruff sitting by the range reading the local paper, following the lines with his grubby fingers. He let the paper drop onto his lap and beamed at Annie. His skin glowed and, instead of a bottle of beer, he clutched a mug of tea in his muddy hands.

'Have you just got back from the allotment, dad?'

'Yes, love. Those quick-growing turnips are almost ready for picking. We'll have plenty to go with our Christmas dinner and have some left to sell.'

'That's good then, isn't it? Mr Wiseman's having to feed the livestock on turnips over the winter, so they'll be in short supply for eating come the New Year. It's not just him, it's all livestock farmers. They've been told not to feed wheat or barley to the animals. You need to get some more of them plants and get them in quick, dad.'

'Maybe you're right, girl.'

He picked up the paper again.

'Jerry's using subs now to sink supply ships headed for Britain. They're trying to starve us into submission, that's what they're doing!'

Smacking the paper with his fist, he passed it to Annie.

'Read it Annie.'

Annie cleared her throat and read:

'*The Director of Food Economy has suggested that everyone should cut their bread consumption by a quarter. Residents who do this will be given a certificate and a badge displaying the slogan "I eat less bread".*'

The kitchen door suddenly juddered open and Pol swept into the warm room, ushering in a rush of cold air.

'Shut the door Pol, I've only just started to warm up. That air's bloody freezing!'

Annie smiled as Pol plonked two dark loaves of bread on the table. They landed with a thump.

'This is all you can get in Sillet's now. They're 'aving to make it mixing barley, oats or rye flour together. There's no wheat for love nor money. Mrs Sillet was even trying to make it out of soya and potato flour. She says there's talk of voluntary rationing in the New Year.'

She flopped down in a chair.

'Make me a cuppa, Annie love. I was talkin' to Reggie Salmon just now and he says they're sayin' there's no more wheat or barley for farm animals over the winter. The Department for Food's advice is we should all eat more slowly, and only when we're hungry. He said they're tellin' people to buy bread by weight now.'

1917

January 2nd, 1917

Annie quickly led the horses back to their stables and was rushing out of the yard to go home when Mr Wiseman called her.

'Annie, have you got a moment?'

Annie was in a hurry to get to a meeting of the Women's Union of Suffrage Societies at the Reformed Church, where Millicent Fawcett was going to speak. She needed to get there early to get a seat but she followed Mr Wiseman into the office, curious to know what he wanted. He signalled for her to sit down and smiled at her.

'Annie you seem to have a natural way with horses and they respond to you in a way that they don't with anyone else. You've managed to gain their trust, and we now have two more useful horses. There are a number of fields at the edge of the farm that will need turning over ready for planting and I'd like you to start working with the rescue horses, getting them used to the plough. We can start tomorrow.'

'Right you are, Mr Wiseman. I've never done farm work before but I can learn.'

'Good, we'll start tomorrow then.'

Annie smiled to herself as she pedalled back home. She propped the rusty old bike that Mr Wiseman had dug out from the back of his barn up against the side of the house and dashed in and upstairs to change out of her overalls. Pol stopped stirring a large pan of stew and called up the stairs.

'There's a letter 'ere for you, from France!'

Annie almost fell down the stairs. She sank on to the bottom step and ripped open the envelope.

Etaples Base Hospital
Etaples
France

December 18th, 1916

My darling Annie,

As you can see, I'm writing to you from hospital in Etaples. It's taken me so long to reply to your letter as my right arm has been in a sling. The nurse did offer to write for me, but I wanted to wait and write it myself. I'm out of bed now, but still have my leg bandaged where they dug out a lump of Jerry's hand grenade. They're patching me up and I should be ready to go back to the front next week.

I can't tell you how disappointed I was when I arrived here and found you'd gone back to England. I had hoped we could spend a bit of time together, but it wasn't to be.

I was very sorry to hear about your brother Stanley. I know that you'll be helping your mum and dad to get over it, and that their need is greater than mine, so I mustn't be selfish and wish you were here.

I love you, Annie, and God willing, look forward to a time when we will be reunited forever.

Look after yourself,

Your loving Arthur

Pol watched Annie's face crumple as she reread the letter. She put her arm around her daughter's shoulders and hugged her tightly.

'Well, you know he's alive, love.'

'But he's been in hospital all this time with his arm broken and shrapnel in his leg, and that's only what he's *telling* me. They're patching him up and sending him back to the front to be shot at again. It's not right, mum. One soldier said to me that us nurses were criminals, putting men together again, just to be sent back and killed. He was right, mum!'

Another wave of sobs shook her body.

'He'll be back, love. He will, I can feel it in my bones. Now wipe your eyes and go get yourself ready for your meeting. Arthur wouldn't want you being so upset, would he?'

Annie folded the letter and carefully put it back in the envelope before going upstairs to change. She threw her overalls on the floor and put on a dress, then pulled her hair back into a chignon, tucking the stray hairs in with pins.

Arriving at the United Reformed Church, she joined the queue as it melted into the crowded room. She spotted a number of women from the munitions factory sitting near the front. Elsie Manning turned and, seeing Annie, beckoned her over to join them. As she sat talking to Elsie, Vesta Tilley, who was sitting in the front row, stood and made her way to the stage. Looking out over the audience, she caught Annie's eye and, smiling broadly, mouthed:

'See me in the interval.'

Annie returned her smile and nodded. Vesta then cleared her throat and, looking to the back of the church, welcomed everyone.

'I am sure I have no need to introduce our speaker this evening. Please welcome Millicent Fawcett!'

There was hearty applause as the diminutive figure of Mrs Fawcett swept into the room and on to the stage. She raised her hand in acknowledgement and signalled for silence. Annie thought she looked drawn and tired.

'As you know there has been some disagreement within the movement, which has led to a division between members. Some feel direct, and sometimes aggressive, action is the only means to draw attention to our cause. Others believe that we should give parliamentarians no excuse to argue that we are reckless and unfit to participate in politics. We have lost a number of members to the Women's Social and Political Union, who, despite their sometimes aggressive acts to bring attention to women's suffrage, are pacifists and do not support the war. I believe most of us here this evening are fully behind the war effort and, with the suspension of marches and reduction in our campaigning, find ourselves unable to stand by and do nothing.'

Elsie got to her feet, followed by Annie.

'Hear! Hear!'

One by one the women in front and behind them stood, clapping loudly. Mrs Fawcett held up her hands for silence before continuing:

'The National Union of Women's Suffrage Societies does not support the Women's Peace Congress.'

She paused and then, sweeping the hall with steely eyes, declared:

'I believe it is akin to treason to talk of peace!'

A hushed silence blanketed the room.

'Tonight I'd like to remind you all about why I'm a liberal, and what women's suffrage means to me.'

She paused and, in a clear silvery voice, began her address.

'I cannot say I became a Suffragist. I always was one, from the time I was old enough to think at all about the principles of representative government. I am a liberal because liberalism seems to mean faith in the people, confidence that they will manage their own affairs far better than those affairs are likely to be managed by others.'

There was spontaneous applause, with voices from the back of the hall calling,

'Hear! Hear!'

Elsie turned to Annie and winked.

'I believe the most effective way forward is by lobbying and talking rationally to MPs we know to be sympathetic to women's suffrage. I also believe that a large part of the present anxiety to improve the education of girls and women is due to the conviction that the political disabilities of women will not be maintained. It is therefore our duty to make women's education a priority in our struggle.'

Millicent Fawcett spoke for a further fifteen minutes to an enrapt audience, until Vesta Tilley appeared on the stage again to announce the interval. Annie smiled at her friends from the munitions factory as she pushed past them to where Vesta Tilley now waited at the side of the stage. Greeting her warmly, Vesta introduced her to Mrs Fawcett, who ushered her to the rear of the stage and offered her a chair.

'Miss Gingell, I remember you well from my last visit to Saffron Walden, and I believe that you have been rather busy since then.'

She paused and brushed a strand of hair from her forehead.

'I understand that apart from your suffrage work, you were employed in a local munitions factory, as well as nursing and ambulance driving both at home and on the front line, not to mention your work with the Actresses' Franchise League, where I believe you were a great favourite with the troops, and of course, your current sterling work with war horses'.

She paused again before continuing:

'I was hoping that you might help me out this evening, as the member who had agreed to speak about her war work has been taken ill.'

Annie felt her face flush under the piercing gaze of the older woman.

'Well ... well, yes. But there are lots of other girls who've done the same. I ... I haven't got anything prepared, and I haven't done any public speaking before, apart from talking to the girls at the factory.'

'I am sure you will find something to talk about, Miss Gingell! We need women like you to talk about the highly skilled and dangerous work they have done. You, and others like you, are our greatest asset in our struggle for the vote.'

She stepped back and, taking Annie's hands in hers, smiled.

'So, you will do it, Miss Gingell?'

Annie's heart pounded against her ribcage as she followed Millicent Fawcett up the steps to the centre of the stage. There was a gasp from Elsie Manning and the girls from Howell's as Annie stood timidly before them.

Mrs Fawcett smiled and, lightly placing her hand on Annie's shoulder, turned to face the silent audience.

'I'd like to introduce you all to Miss Annie Gingell, who has very kindly agreed – at the last minute! – to talk about her recent war service, both at home and at the front.'

Annie froze, her mind a blank. She stared at the back of the hall, trying to think of something to say. Elsie Manning, her old friend from the munitions factory, suddenly stood up and, turning to the audience, stammered:

'St..standing before you is one of the bravest women I know. She saved the lives of a lot of us up at Howell's when we 'ad the explosion, and she made us girls think about how we 'ad the right to be paid the same wage as the men doing the same job as us!'

A number of women began a quiet clap, which grew into a loud symphony of hands. Elsie waited until there was quiet.

'And that's all I know about her war work. She 'asn't talked much about all the other things she's done'.

She turned to Annie and smiled.

'Tell us, Annie!'

Annie took a deep breath and, in a voice that didn't sound like her own, began with an apology.

'I'm afraid I don't have the way with words that Mrs Fawcett has, and all I've done is what lots of other women have done.'

It was nine o'clock before Annie left the stage, to a standing ovation. Mrs Fawcett embraced her warmly and then made her way back onto the stage.

'Well, I think you will agree that Miss Gingell has been an inspiration to us all. We need more women like her to come forward and join us. There are many opportunities. For example, you may like to join the Actresses' Franchise League. If you'd like to be considered for a new entertainment Cecily Hamilton has prepared for our troops, please see Cecily – raise your hand Cecily! – at the back of the room as you leave.'

A murmur of interest spread along several rows.

'Perhaps you might like to help with lobbying Members of Parliament who we know to be sympathetic to our cause. Or if you're returning from France or are working in nursing or a munitions factory, in fact if you're doing any job previously considered impossible for women to undertake, come and talk to other women and men about what you're doing. We need to carry on campaigning peacefully and passively throughout this war, at the same time as making people aware of the heroic war work being carried out by women.'

She looked to the back of the room.

'If you would like to become involved in any way, please see Leena Ashwell, who is also at the back of the room.'

Leena raised her hand as a number of heads turned to acknowledge her.

Mrs Fawcett thanked everyone for coming and then, raising her voice slightly, declared:

'Please remember that we Suffragists should help to work for military victory and not stand idle. It is the time for resolute effort and self-sacrifice on the part of every one of us to help our country. However, we must also remain true to our cause and prove ourselves worthy of citizenship and the vote! Thank you.'

As one, the audience erupted into loud applause. There was a scramble to join the lengthening queue to speak to committee members at the exit. Millicent Fawcett joined Annie as she stood to leave.

'Miss Gingell, that was splendid! I do hope that you will be interested in helping to lobby our parliamentarians. We need women from all backgrounds who are able to influence others.'

'But I haven't got the writing skills that you have Mrs Fawcett, and you said lobbying involved writing to Members of Parliament.'

'Annie, may I call you Annie? We can help you with that. But you have proved yourself more than capable of writing already. The article you wrote for our December issue of '*The Common Cause*' last year was very well received by our readers. As for letter writing, that is only one aspect of lobbying. You have the verbal powers to make people sit up and listen. If we can be seen as thoughtful, intelligent and law-abiding, we will gain the respect of Parliament. Annie you are ideal. Please think about what I've said, and if you are willing to take up your committee work with us again, we can discuss financial remuneration then.'

She pushed a card into Annie's pocket and turned to leave, shaking outstretched hands as she pushed her way through the queues to the exit. As Annie was about to join the factory girls outside, Cecily Hamilton left the group of women surrounding her and grabbed Annie's arm.

'I've signed you up for the troops' new entertainment. Please say you'll do it. We're planning to take it to Walden Place Military Hospital again like last year. The staff said that we were a real tonic for the men, so we've agreed to perform in one of the wards this Easter. Rehearsals start in two weeks, Wednesday evenings at seven o'clock here.'

With that, she pushed a script into Annie's hands and went back to the women gathered around her.

Walking home, Annie thought back to the events of Christmas Eve 1915. It seemed such a long time ago now, but the memory of locking eyes with Arthur moments before he disappeared from the hospital and her desperate efforts to find him up at the 'Big 'Ouse' would live with her forever.

Wiseman's Farm
January 31st

Annie unhitched both horses and, avoiding the newly ploughed furrows, led them across to the stables at the edge of the farmyard. Shutting the smaller horse into his stall, she led the large black into his, then dragged the half-door shut. She lifted one of the stallion's mud-encrusted hooves and began scraping away the cloying Essex clay. She could hear Mr Wiseman in the barn opposite, clearing space for a delivery of seed potatoes. The sudden crack of an air rifle startled the animal. Annie slumped as the horse's hoof shot from her hand as the terrified creature reared up, pinning her against the wall. She raised her free hand in a futile attempt to protect her head from the stallion's flailing front legs as he half-turned, his mouth set in a hideous grin.

'Whoa, whoa, it's alright, it's alright,' she cried softly.

Her voice betrayed her. She knew he could smell fear and was now lost to her, haunted by his own battlefield nightmare. She tried to curl herself into a ball, waiting for the pounding hoof to land. It came. A shocking crack on her ribs and left arm, which she'd now curled around her neck in an effort to protect the back of her head. As she fought to stop herself crying out, she heard Mr Wiseman at the stable door, then his footsteps approaching the stallion's stall. The footsteps halted, then there was another ear-splitting bang and the enormous animal fell to the floor, its left flank partially burying her. Mr Wiseman forced open the stall door, which had jammed against the horse's rump. Raising the gun a second time, he edged over to the panting animal.

'Please, please don't kill him, Mr Wiseman! He's just frightened!'

Ignoring her, he knelt down, pressing the gun into the flesh between the stallion's eyes, and pressed the trigger. With a loud sigh the animal shuddered and lay silent. Mr Wiseman stepped over its warm carcass and, grabbing a muckraking spade, levered the horse's body up enough for Annie to pull her legs free.

'Put your arms over my neck and I'll carry you out.'

Annie's ribs screamed as she took a breath. Her left arm felt like an electric current had ripped through it. She clung to Mr Wiseman, who carried her into the farmhouse and laid her on a sofa. He then disappeared. She could hear his voice in the hallway.

'I need an ambulance. I have a young woman here who has

been trampled on by a horse. Yes, she is conscious, but she's in a lot of pain. Yes, I'll keep her awake and warm. It's Wiseman's Farm, Thaxted Road, Saffron Walden. Quickly please!'

He returned with a blanket and wrapped it around Annie.

'I'll get you a cup of tea.'

Returning with a steaming brew, Mr Wiseman lifted it up to Annie's mouth to help her take a sip.

'It's alright, Mr Wiseman, I can manage with my right arm.'

She tried to swallow but the hot tea spilled down the sides of her mouth, scorching her chin and neck.

'Why did you kill that poor horse, Mr Wiseman?'

He perched on the edge of a shabby leather armchair opposite her, then, with fingers splayed over his knees, leant towards her.

'I had to Annie. Once a horse has reacted like that, you just can't trust it.'

He sighed and stared down at the threadbare piece of carpet placed in front of the armchair to protect the linoleum beneath it.

'I feel that I have to take responsibility for what happened. I shouldn't have shot those rats in the barn. I didn't think, and I should have thought. For that I truly apologise, Annie. Had I thought, I might have realised the noise would startle the horses, even after all these weeks away from the battlefields.'

Annie's hand shook as she tried again to sip the tea.

'Let me help you, Annie, you'll spill it all over you.'

'What a terrible waste of life!' she muttered, as she was carried out to the waiting ambulance. As the driver cranked the engine into life, Mr Wiseman climbed into the back of the vehicle and knelt down next to her.

'Annie, I'll follow the ambulance and then go to your parents' house and let them know what has happened.'

Annie sank back on the stretcher. Tears for the stallion rolled down the sides of her face, wetting Mr Wiseman's blanket, wrapped around her like swaddling.

Saffron Walden Cottage Hospital

She woke hours later to find Pol and Gruff anxiously sitting at her bedside.

'Gruff, look, she's awake!'

Pol's voice echoed in the lofty ward.

'You gave us a fright young lady!'

A tube had been inserted into Annie's right side. Blood trickled into a glass container on the floor beneath the bed. A large splint supported her broken arm, which had been so tightly bound it was difficult to feel her fingers. She tried to lift her head but a sharp pain forced it back on to the pillow. The cloying smell and taste of chloroform lingered in her mouth and nose.

'The doctor said you've got two broken ribs. He said they pierced your right lung and that's what's caused the bleedin'. You could 'ardly breathe when they brought you in, there was so much blood in there!'

Pol jabbed her finger towards Annie's ribcage.

'We've brought you some snowdrops we picked this morning. Now you're awake I'll go and get a nurse to put them in a jug or somethin'.'

As she left the room, Gruff hauled himself out of his chair and leant over his daughter's bed. In the harsh morning light his beard looked like pencil strokes drawn on the side of his face. His anxious hooded eyes, mired in wrinkles, softened as he gently grabbed Annie's free hand. His face was creased with anxiety.

'Now don't you try sittin' up, love, the doctors 'ave said you've got to lie still and rest.'

'I'll be alright, dad, don't you worry, I'll be back on me feet again before you know it!'

Pol appeared with Annie's flowers in a small chipped yellow jug. She placed them next to Annie's bed.

'Now, look at them, they'll cheer you up, love!'

****

Pol came to visit every day and, when word reached Howell's, Elsie arrived with a card from the girls. Putting it on the bedside table, she stepped back to scrutinise the tube leading from Annie into the blood-splattered bottle on the floor next to the bed. She grimaced and focused instead on her friend's bandaged arm.

'What 'ave you been up to now, Annie?'

Without warning, tears streamed down Annie's face, wetting the neck of her nightgown.

'It's my fault, Elsie. That poor horse! I should have been able to calm him down. He trusted me. I should have tried harder!'

'Now Annie, I don't know what you're talkin' about, but I'm sure you're blaming yourself for something you couldn't 'elp.'

'It's one of the war horses I'd been training to plough, up at Wiseman's Farm. He panicked when Mr Wiseman shot some rats. He reared up in 'is stall when I was getting the mud off 'is hoof and I got trapped. I tried to calm him down but he must 'ave thought he was back at the front. I, I couldn't ....'

Her voice trailed off.

'Mr Wiseman shot 'im, and it's all my fault!'

She winced as she wiped fresh tears away with the back of her hand.

'I'll never forgive myself, Elsie.'

'I'm sure Mr Wiseman did what was best, Annie. You could 'ave been trampled to death!'

February 8th

It was Annie's second week in hospital. The tube had been removed from her side and the nurses had allowed her to get up for a short while each day. She was sitting in a bath chair by the window, staring out at the dreary brick houses across the road, which cast long cool shadows on to the street, when there was a sudden commotion at the other end of the ward. Annie turned to find Vesta Tilley and Cecily Hamilton at the door of the ward, discussing whether they'd come to the right room. They scanned the beds looking for Annie and then, spotting her, strode over. In an immaculately clipped voice, rather too loud for the lofty hospital ward, Vesta boomed,

'Oh, you poor girl, whatever happened to you?'

Annie opened her mouth to speak. Instead a chain of coughs and a sharp pain zipped through her chest.

Cecily leaned forward and, in a voice like a stage whisper, asked:

'Are you alright, my dear? Would you like me to get someone?'

'No, no need, I'll be alright in a minute, thank you.'

Vesta scouted round the ward and found a couple of seats,

which she dragged over to Annie's bath chair. She pushed one over to Cecily and the two women sat down and waited for Annie to compose herself. Then, flashing her ambushing smile, Vesta took Annie's hand and gushed:

'There really is no need to explain. Your friend Elsie has already given us the details of your accident. It's so very pleasing to see that you are making good progress.'

The peace of the ward had been shattered by the arrival of the two Suffragists who, when addressing an audience were awe-inspiring, but amongst the sick and distressed patients in the ward, were overwhelming.

'Can I ask you to speak a little quieter please? There are a lot of sick people in 'ere who need calm.'

Vesta's eyes cut briefly to Cecily and then, in a honeyed voice, she answered:

'I am so sorry my dear, forgive me. I sometimes forget when it is appropriate to lower one's voice. It isn't very often that someone pulls me up like that. I admire your ability to talk so frankly, if sometimes rather bluntly!'

She paused and then stared at Annie, shark-eyed.

Annie, we have a proposal. Whilst you are holed up in here, we wondered if you might agree to spend some time writing a few letters, to lobby a number of politicians. It's awfully good to see that you have full use of your right hand. We would of course help in any way we can until you feel confident to work independently.'

Cecily then leaned forward and, lowering her voice, whispered:

'We would of course pay you. We wondered if thirty shillings a week would be sufficient?'

Thirty shillings a week was half as much again as Annie had been earning up at Wiseman's. She swallowed hard before answering.

'I'm not sure how much longer I'm goin' to be in 'ere, and Mr Wiseman will be expecting 'me back at the farm.'

'Most of our committee members work on a part-time basis, lobbying in its various forms two days a week, and then giving talks in the evenings, usually twice or three times a month. This arrangement allows them to continue with their part-time war work, which is of course also very important. The sum we have offered is for part-time work only, Annie.'

'It's a lot to think about. Can I have a few minutes?'

'Of course, my dear.'

Vesta grabbed her bag and then smiled at Annie.

'I don't think you'll need too much coaching. Then, when you're fit enough, you can join us at the local committee rooms. We'll leave you for half an hour or so and then come back.'

With that they stood, scraping their chairs along the wooden floor before marching purposefully out of the ward.

February 9th

The following evening Fred appeared. Removing his cap, he hovered awkwardly in the doorway. Annie's heart smiled as Sister ushered him over to her bed. He now stood taller than Gruff. He winked and went to sit on the side of the bed but quickly stood up again when he saw Sister glaring at him.

'She thinks you'll make the bed dirty, Fred. Go and get a chair from over there. They're for the visitors.'

With shoulders hunched, he returned with a chair and dropped it on the floor next to Annie's bed.

'Shh, Fred, there's sick people in 'ere. They don't want to hear that racket.'

Fred's face flushed as he settled down next to the bed.

'Well, 'ow are you, Annie?'

'A bit sore, so don't make me laugh!'

'When are you comin' 'ome then?'

'I'm hopin' middle of next week if everything's alright. How are you all getting on at 'ome?'

Fred grinned.

'Well, mum's gettin' in a bit of a stew havin' to queue for everythin' – bread, meat, butter, cheese, everything. There was a bit of a to-do up at Salmon's yesterday. Mrs Farnham tried to jump the queue when it looked like the ham was runnin' out. Said her need was greater than mum's. Well, mum wasn't 'avin' any of that. Mr Salmon had to separate them!'

Annie tried not to laugh.

'Well, I wouldn't want to get into a row with mum when she's got the wind up, that's for sure!'

'Me and dad went to the 'orse fair on the Common yesterday. I got Will Osborne to clip Kitty's coat and, seein' as Mr Coe was there, I got 'im to roughen her hooves to stop 'er slippin on the icy roads. It cost a bit, but had to be done. But now I'm earnin' more ....'

Annie raised her eyebrows, realising he was itching to tell her his good news.

'Mr Sillet's given me a proper job! He's teachin me 'ow to make the new bread they're 'avin to sell, and how to make the puffs. I 'ave to get to work early, gettin' the dough ready and greasing up all the tins and then, when it's baked, I 'ave to go and deliver it. I've got one of them bikes with a big basket on the front! I 'ave to take it out to the villages and even the Big 'Ouse. Mind you they don't need so much these days, what with most of the staff doin' war work or fightin'.'

'Well, that's really good news, Fred! I bet mum and dad are pleased! But how are you fitting it in with helping dad with the rounds?'

'He's starting the round later, when I've finished.'

'Well, good for you Fred! It's a lot of work though, what with the allotment as well. How's that going then?'

'The winter turnips are doin' well and should be ready to lift in a few weeks. Dad 'as just put more in. The spring greens, onions and carrots are beginning to push up as well. Mum says the rent's just gone up. It's now 4s 9d a week! So we need all the money we can get from dad's costermongering. Me leavin' school 'as been a bit of a blessin'.

'Well, I've got some good news too. I've got a new job working for the women's group who are fightin' for votes for women and they're goin' to pay me thirty shillings a week for writin' some letters and giving a few talks every month. Then, when I'm properly back on my feet, I can go back to the farm as well.'

Fred suddenly reached into his pocket and brought out a rolled-up poster, which he unfurled and held up so Annie could read it. There was a picture of a woman carrying a bucket, standing next to a calf. She read it out loud:

'For Food Production, Forage and Timber
The help of British women is urgent and indispensable.
Recruits required immediately for the Women's Land Army
ENROL TODAY
Full particulars and application form at nearest Employment Exchange
ASK AT THE POST OFFICE FOR ADDRESS'

‘I never thought you’d want to go back to working with ‘orses after what ‘appened up at Wiseman’s. I’ve ‘eard that they’re paying Land Army girls £1 a week for part-time work, just when they’re needed. I can go to the post office and get a form and find out more if you want.’

Annie reread the poster.

‘Well, you might as well. I’ve got nothing to lose by finding out a bit more. You could ask Mr Wiseman when you’re up there if he’s thinking of taking on any Land Girls. Thanks, Fred!’

Shortly after he left, Annie tried to finish the letter she’d been writing to the Prime Minister. Again, she got no further than the first two lines before screwing up her paper and throwing it on the floor next to her bed. Sister came scurrying over.

‘What on earth is this all about?’

Annie’s face crumpled.

‘It’s no good. I’m not cut out for writin’ clever letters. I just want to write to Arthur! Why hasn’t he answered my last letter?’

‘Is Arthur your young man?’

Annie showed her the string ring on her left hand.

‘He gave me this, and I ‘aven’t seen him since!’

‘Now now, dear, don’t go upsetting yourself. Write to him again and I’ll make sure it gets posted as quickly as possible.’

Annie dried her eyes and turned to a fresh sheet of paper. She didn’t want to alarm Arthur, so pretended she was writing from home.

6 Middle Square
Castle Street,
Saffron Walden
Essex

February 9th, 1917

Darling Arthur,

I hope this letter reaches you, wherever you are. I expect by now your leg has healed and you've been sent back to fight. I wonder if my last letter reached you, as I haven't heard from you since you wrote in December. I tell myself it's because your battalion has been moved from the Somme, as I read that the battle there finished last November.

I've been busy helping mum and dad, and I'm pleased to say dad's back on his feet again and working hard on our allotment. We're growing early turnips and spring vegetables to sell. Fred, my younger brother, is working with dad now, and has also got a job with our baker's and is getting paid regular money. I've been working on a farm, helping to retrain war horses they've brought back from the front to help farmers with their ploughing. There are food shortages and farmers have been told to plough up spare land to grow more wheat and potatoes.

I had a little accident on the farm when one of the horses kicked me, but I'm alright now. I'm going to do another entertainment for the troops at Walden Place this Easter, and I even gave a short talk about my war work a couple of weeks ago to our local branch of the National Union of Women's Suffrage Societies. I was very nervous but I think it went alright.

We won't ever get over losing Stanley but the family are all helping out and I think mum and dad are over the worst. I think of you every day and pray that you will come back safe. Please write and let me know you are still alive.

Your loving Annie

Annie folded the sheet of paper and put it in an envelope, then addressed it to Corporal Arthur Scoggings, c/o The Royal Essex Regiment, France. She knew that if his battalion had been redeployed the Forces Post Service would forward it to him. She placed the envelope on her bedside table for Sister to pick up when she did her evening rounds.

February 11th

Annie took out her writing pad and began listing the points she wanted to make to the Prime Minister. Having done that, she reread the sample letter Vesta had given her the previous day, which showed how to set out a formal letter. She copied the layout and the wording at the head of the sample.

National Union of Women's Suffrage Societies
SAFFRON WALDEN AND DISTRICT FEDERATION
42 King Street
SAFFRON WALDEN
Non-Party and Non-Militant
President: Lady Rochdale

February 11th, 1917

The Right Honourable David Lloyd George

'Right. Now what?' She thought. *'It's all very well writin' that bit, but 'ow do I put what I want to say?'* She decided to go back to her list of points and just write them down as if she were talking to Elsie or someone. Balancing the paper on a book open on her lap, she began:

Sir,

Despite Mr Asquith's declaration of support for our movement, nothing has happened. We hope that you, Sir, as our new Prime Minister, will take notice of the growing support both from the trade unions and a growing number of politicians. I think this is mainly due to the role of women in the war effort. As you know, women are tackling a large range of jobs, from cleaning hides in tanning factories, to packing shells in munitions factories, loading coke in gas works and driving ambulances at the front, as well as nursing and looking after our soldiers. I think you will agree, Sir, that women are proving themselves to be every bit as capable as men in carrying out work which, before the war, no one would believe them able to do.

We are a peaceful, respectable branch of the Suffrage Movement and, unlike our more aggressive sisters (the Suffragettes), Suffragists believe in reasonable discussion. With that in mind, I would like to invite you to a meeting to be held at Newport Village Hall, Newport, Essex, on March 3rd, beginning at 7.00 p.m., when a number of our members will be talking about their war work.

I look forward to hearing from you and remain your loyal servant,

Annie Gingell (Miss)

February 13th

Having hung her saturated coat on a peg outside the ward, Vesta Tilley sat opposite Annie, who'd been wheeled into the bay window next to her bed. Vesta fiddled with strands of sodden hair that clung to her forehead as she reread Annie's letter to Lloyd George. Hailstones bounced off the window as the sky turned gunmetal grey. The dimmed hospital lights did little to lift the cheerless atmosphere that had descended on the ward. Annie studied Vesta's face, trying to read her thoughts. Finally, Vesta passed the letter back to her.

'Well, Annie, I'm very pleased to see that you've used the template I gave you. I have to say that for a first draft your letter is both engaging and heartfelt and, in general you have chosen your words well. We do not wish to appear aggressive, but need to adopt a firm stance too. In that respect, I think you have achieved the correct tone. There are just a few minor changes I'd like to suggest, however.'

Vesta read the letter again, crossing out and replacing a couple of sentences before passing it back to Annie. Then, reaching into her bag, she took out a large manila envelope.

'Annie, I wondered if you might like to join a small group of us on a trip to the Ladies' Gallery at the House of Commons on March 10th? Parliament will be sitting to debate recommendations made at the recent Speaker's Conference concerning votes for women. You'll find a copy of the report in this envelope.'

Waving the damp envelope in the air, she passed it to Annie.

'We're urging all members to write to the Prime Minister to show our support for the recommendations that have been made. Now, can I rely on you to write once you've read the report, Annie?'

'Of course, you can. I'll do it today after I've rewritten my other letter.'

Vesta stood and peered out at the rain cascading off a nearby roof. She then turned to Annie and pointed to the envelope.

'You will also find a petition in there which has been circulating whilst you have been in hospital. It is designed to show the Government that we support the recommendation that changes should be made to current voting regulations to allow women householders over the age of thirty to vote. It is by no means perfect but it's a start, and I'm sure you will want to add your name to it.'

She paused.

'I also need a covering letter to attach to the petition, and I wondered if you might do that?'

'I have only written one letter to the Prime Minister. Isn't there anyone more experienced who should write it?'

'Annie, I have asked you as I know you have the ability to write well. And we need new voices! There's a sample letter in the envelope to help you. Now I'll leave you to it. I'll call back tomorrow to collect both letters and the petition, duly signed. I do hope you'll be well enough to join us for our trip to the Ladies' Gallery in March.'

'*You bet I will be*!' Annie muttered to herself.

That evening, having read the report of the Speaker's Conference, Annie was furious. Its recommendations were so far from being ideal that she found it almost impossible to sign the petition. Finally, however, in a spirit of solidarity she reluctantly scrawled her name beneath Vesta's bold signature. She then rewrote her corrected letter to Lloyd George, taking care that her handwriting was neat and that she hadn't made any spelling mistakes. Finally satisfied, she tucked it into an official envelope ready for Vesta to collect the following morning. She then begrudgingly started to write a second, shorter letter supporting the proposals made by the Speaker's Conference. By now her hand was throbbing and the dim light above her bed cast shadows across the sample letter that Vesta had left to help her. Her eyes ached as she struggled to grasp the meaning of several unfamiliar words and formal phrases used in the sample. After three attempts at drafting a letter of her own to accompany the petition, she sighed and finally took out a sheet of headed notepaper from the envelope and started to write.

The Right Honourable David Lloyd George

February 13th, 1917

Sir,

In view of the recommendations regarding the franchise about to be made by the Conference on Electoral reform, we beg to submit for your consideration the enclosed Memorial, which is in the following terms:

We, the undersigned, urge the necessity of enfranchising women in any proposed electoral reform brought forward during the war, so that they shall take part in the election of the parliament which will deal with the problems of reconstruction after the war.

Signatures have been invited not from the general public, but from well-known and representative people. The signatories number about 4,000 influential persons. Many of these are men and women who before the experience of war conditions were indifferent, even hostile, to the often-expressed demand of women for some share in the political life of the country.

I am, Sir,

Your obedient servant,

Annie Gingell (Miss)

Reading it through, Annie felt as if it had been written by someone else. *Had she relied too heavily on the sample letter?* As she tried to decide if she should change the wording, Sister appeared at the ward door.

'It'll be lights out in five minutes, ladies.'

She folded the letter in two and slipped it into a third envelope before leaving it on the bedside table. She would look at it again in the morning.

February 18th

Gruff tied Kitty and the delivery cart to a pillar outside the entrance to the hospital and then made his way to Annie's ward. He was stopped by Sister, who happened to be coming down the stairs.

'Ah, Mr Gingell, I gather you've come to take your daughter home?'

'Gruff took off his cap and stuffed it in his pocket.

'Yes, Sister, her carriage awaits!'

He pointed to the delivery cart, just as Kitty deposited a warm pile of dung on the paving stones outside the entrance.

Appalled, Sister glared at Gruff.

'Mr Gingell, would you please remove both that horse and its droppings? Whilst you are doing that, I will tell Annie that you are here. Please make sure that she doesn't do anything strenuous for the next fortnight. She needs to rest.'

With that, she disappeared into the ward.

Pol had lit the fire in the front room and put a blanket out on the comfy chair. Annie slowly lowered herself into it and put her feet up on the cane footstool brought down from Fred's room.

'Now you sit there and I'll bring you a nice cup of tea.'

Annie felt quite weak and her ribs ached. She wanted to laugh out loud as she heard Gruff telling Pol about Kitty disgracing herself outside the hospital, but instead settled for a wide grin.

Still smiling, Pol brought Annie's tea and settled herself next to the fire.

'Now, Annie, Sister up at the 'ospital says you've got to rest, so we'll 'ave no talk about you doin' anything for the time being except resting.'

Gruff had put Kitty back in the stable and came into the room carrying a large manila envelope.

'I just saw the postman. This is for you.'

Annie's eyes shot towards the letter, but she knew immediately it was too big to be a soldier's letter.

Gruff placed it on Annie's lap and squeezed her shoulder.

'Don't worry, love, he'll write when he can. Do you want me to 'elp you open it?'

It was a script and list of songs for the soldiers' entertainment to be performed on May 4th. Cecily had underlined the songs she thought Annie could sing, but had also enclosed a note saying she would understand if she only felt up to taking a minor part.

Newport Village Hall
March 3rd

Annie arrived early at Newport Village Hall. Despite it only being 6.30 p.m., a queue was already forming outside the entrance door. She wheeled her bicycle round to the rear of the hall and slotted the front wheel into a rack at the far end of the shed. Checking she had her speech in her shoulder bag, she looked for a side door to the backstage area. She gave three sharp knocks and waited. The door was finally opened by Gertrude Baillie-Weaver, President of the Saffron Walden District Suffrage Society.

'Ah, there you are, Annie. I thought we might quickly run through part of your speech with you on stage, to check the acoustics in the hall.'

Annie's stomach flipped. She ran her hands over the tight bun in the nape of her neck and tucked some damp wisps of hair back into the bone hairgrip Pol had lent her for the evening. The dull ache in her ribcage reminded her that she hadn't fully recovered. Her ribs felt sore and she'd found herself short of breath cycling up the hill to the hall. She mustn't laugh because that really hurt. However, she had spent the past two weeks writing and practising her speech, and nothing was going to stop her now. Taking the two sheets of paper from her bag, she stepped up onto the stage as Mrs Baillie-Weaver walked to the back of the hall.

'Right, Annie, if you'd like to start.'

Annie took a deep breath in but the indrawn air caught in her throat. She coughed, sending a sharp pain through her chest. She swallowed hard and began reading. Her voice felt thin in the lofty hall. It didn't feel like her own voice at all.

'Annie, Annie! Please look up whilst you are reading. You must look at your audience.'

She tried again, pausing several times to look up.

'That is much better, but do try to sweep your eyes around the audience. It makes everyone feel you are talking directly to them.'

She paused and smiled.

'But well done, Annie! No doubt the prospect of addressing an audience with a politician in the front row is daunting, but do remember you are amongst friends.'

She turned to Lena Harris and Mabel Jones, who would shortly be joining Annie on the stage and who'd arrived whilst she'd been practising.

'I am sure that your fellow speakers agree with me when I say that you will be absolutely fine, Annie!'

Lena and Mabel nodded and smiled, and the warmth of their smiles calmed her. She'd taken comfort knowing that Vesta Tilley had cast a critical eye over her speech the previous day and had changed some of the language, but had left it essentially in her own words. Vesta now appeared from behind the stage and briefly went through the running order. Annie was to speak last, after Lena and Mabel. Gertrude then cleared her throat and, checking the clock at the back of the room, turned to the three of them.

'I'm sure you'd all like to know which politician will be joining us tonight. It's the MP George Fotherby, a man known to be sympathetic to our cause. He should be here any moment now with my husband Harold and several other active members of The Men's League for Women's Suffrage. We must thank you, Annie, for Mr Fotherby's attendance this evening. Unfortunately, the Prime Minister was unable to come in person, but he has indicated some support by passing your letter on to Mr Fotherby.'

There was a sudden knocking at the side door. Gertrude rushed to open it and returned with George Fotherby, a tall imposing man, probably in his early thirties, with a fine beard and moustache. He was accompanied by Harold Baillie-Weaver, followed by a small contingent from The Men's League for Women's Suffrage. Annie recognised Mr Fotherby immediately but was shocked to discover that the man she'd seen several times at the farm, talking to Mr Wiseman, was their local MP. Gertrude ushered the men into seats in the front row, before briefly introducing the speakers and indicating that the doors were now to be opened. The hall rapidly filled as women rushed to find seats with a clear view of the stage. The audience fell silent as Mrs Baillie-Weaver took to the stage.

'I'd like to welcome you all to our meeting this evening. I would also like to give special thanks to our local Member of Parliament, Mr George Fotherby, and to the members of the Men's League for Women's Suffrage who have joined us tonight.'

There was a shuffling as women in the audience craned forward, trying to get a view of the special guests at the front. Gertrude then continued:

'I'd now like to introduce our first speaker this evening, Miss Lena Harris.'

Having given a confident talk about the Suffragist movement and how it differed from the better-known Suffragettes, Lena acknowledged the applause before handing the podium over to Mabel Jones. Annie, sitting to the side of the stage, ran her hands over her lap, leaving dark sweat streaks on the pale blue fabric of her skirt. Mabel gave an overview of the activities of the local suffrage group, outlining the need for new members to assist with lobbying, sending letters, and organising petitions and events. She finished by giving details of how to become a member. The audience had been sitting in silence but clapped enthusiastically, nodding to one another as Mabel returned to her seat at the side of the stage.

Gertrude then stood and, still clapping, walked to the podium.

'I'd now like to invite one of our new committee members to talk about her experiences both at home and at the front. She has worked in a local munitions factory, as a VAD nurse at a military hospital, an ambulance driver both at home and in France, as a nurse in a field hospital and latterly has trained ex-war horses to work on the land. Please welcome Miss Annie Gingell.'

There were cheers from the back of the hall. Annie stood,

her heart pounding, her left eye twitching. Trying to hold the two sheets of paper still, she looked out to the audience and focused on the back row, where Elsie Manning and several girls from Howell's factory were sitting, smiling encouragingly at her. She grinned first at them and then, having swept her eyes around the hall, placed the quivering sheets of paper on the podium.

'We have come a long way since 1914, when Elsie Maud Inglis, a qualified surgeon and supporter of women's suffrage, offered her services to the Royal Army Medical Corps and was told to 'Go home and sit still!' Undeterred, however, she went on to set up the Scottish Women's Hospitals to treat troops in both Serbia and Russia.'

She paused and shifted her gaze to the audience.

'I could talk about other inspirational women, but I am here to talk about my own small part in serving our country and, in doing so, hopefully to demonstrate that women are capable of doing jobs that before the war would have been considered unthinkable...' Pausing later, she glanced at the clock at the back of the room, suddenly aware that she'd been speaking for almost twenty minutes. She cast her eyes around the room and to her astonishment realised that the audience were following her every word. Heartened, her voice grew stronger.

'The present time is one of great opportunities and great responsibilities for women. It is also a time to prove ourselves worthy of a vote! I can think of no better way to sum up than to quote Millicent Fawcett, whose wise words inspired me to recognise my own strength, and the strength of many women whose voices have never been heard. I quote:

'I firmly believe that as mothers, women have been given the charge of the home and the care of children. Women are therefore by nature, as well as by training and occupation, more accustomed than men to concentrate their minds on the home and the domestic side of things. But this difference between men and women, instead of being a reason against their disenfranchisement, seems to me to be the strongest possible reason in favour of it. We want to see the home and the domestic side of life count for more in politics and in the administration of public affairs than they do at present. However, a war almost invariably suspends all progress in domestic and social legislation. Two fires cannot burn together.'

Annie paused, glanced up and then back at her paper.

'And so, to conclude (and these are now my words), I believe that feminism isn't about making women stronger. Women are already strong. It's about changing the way we and the world perceive that strength. Thank you.'

Led by George Fotherby, the audience rose to their feet. Finally, as the applause dwindled, Gertrude stood and asked people to be seated. All except George Fotherby sat. He turned to the audience and, in a voice of cut glass, addressed them all.

'I would just like to say a few words before you leave. As you know, the issue of votes for women has been debated by Parliament many times over the past ten years, including the three years that we have been at war. As you know, there has been little obvious progress. However, I feel compelled to inform you that there is growing support for women gaining the vote, mainly due to the political recognition of women's roles in the war effort. These excellent efforts have strengthened the case our last speaker has so eloquently made. Also, the peaceful and respectful way that the Suffragists are carrying out their campaign has gained considerable support from trade union officials and politicians within the Labour movement.'

Again, the audience rose to their feet, clapping warmly.

As Annie went to leave, Elsie and the women from Howell's factory clustered round her.

'Well done, Annie, you 'aven't lost your touch!'

Annie grinned.

'I hope you lot are all joining up.'

'We just 'ave.'

A number of other women broke away from the queue. Having added their names to a growing list of new members, they gathered round her, wanting to show their support. As she chatted to them, Annie noticed two young girls standing shyly listening to the older women. She smiled and approached them.

'It's so nice to have such young people interested in our cause. How old are you girls?'

The two girls blushed and then the older one spoke up.

'I'm fourteen and my sister is twelve.'

'Well, I hope you enjoyed the talks and will come again.'

They grinned at each other and nodded to Annie.

'We live next door, so our mum let us come on our own as it's not far.'

Annie smiled again and replied:

'I'll look forward to seeing you next time then, and perhaps you could bring your mum too.'

It was sometime later that Annie finally managed to get away. Leaving the hall, she shivered, the cold night air striking her hot cheeks like a smack. As she went to the bicycle shed a woman came down the path of the adjoining garden holding a torch. She shone it at Annie, and then leaned over the wall separating her garden from the village hall and exclaimed:

'My little girls were extremely proud that you spoke to them tonight, and they came home quite ardent Suffragists!'

'And very glad I am to hear it! Perhaps *you'd* like to come to our next meeting?'

'I'm not sure my husband would like that. He only let the girls come tonight because he didn't know what the meeting was about.'

'Well, it would be very nice to see you if you can come, Mrs....?'

'Thompson, Gladys Thompson.'

'What are you doing out there in the dark, Gladys?'

'Oh, that's my husband I'd better be getting back indoors.'

With that, she disappeared inside.

Annie dragged her bicycle from the rack and switched on her light, which shone weakly, only just lighting up the ground in front of her. She set off home, the knot in her stomach finally having untied itself. As she turned on to Sparrows Hill a car overtook her and then pulled in. A tall figure emerged from the car. She recognised him immediately. George Fotherby approached her.

'Miss Gingell, I hardly saw you, your light is very weak. Can you even see where the side of the road is?'

'Only just!'

'Well, let's put your bicycle in the back and I'll drop you home.'

'Thank you, but no. I'm almost home now, and you don't want my rusty old bicycle in the back of your clean car.'

'It really is no trouble at all. I'll just open the back windows to make more space for your wheels. I'm sure my car will be able to tolerate your bicycle for a short while. No, I absolutely insist! Now if you get off, I can load it in through the back.'

Annie watched as he lifted her bicycle up and eased it on to what looked like a leather-covered back seat. She was glad the darkness hid the extent of the bright orange rust that coated the frame of her ancient bicycle. Having shut the door and checked the wheels weren't pressing against the car's leather hood, he jumped in and, leaning across, opened the passenger door, patting the seat for her to sit down. It was nothing like the draughty old field ambulances she was used to driving. The interior smelled of polished wood and rich leather. She settled herself into the soft seat and stole a sideways look at the man who was driving her home.

'Right, Miss Gingell, where to?'

'Just carry on this road until we come into Saffron Walden. When we get to the Common go left and straight, then up Museum Street and that will bring you on to Castle Street. You won't want to drive down there mind, so you could just drop me off on Museum Street and I can walk from there.'

They continued in silence for a short while before she felt him glancing across at her.

'Well, Miss Gingell, I did enjoy your talk this evening. We need women like you to address us in the House. Have you thought about sitting in on one of our debates? You can sit in the Ladies' Gallery.'

'Strangely enough I am planning to do just that next week. I think it's the 10th March.'

'Oh yes, the Speaker's Conference Report.'

They had arrived outside the Old Rectory on Museum Street.

'Thank you, Mr Fotherby, I can jump out here.'

He unfolded himself on to the narrow road and pulled the bicycle out, then brushing himself down, pushed it over to where Annie stood on the pavement.

'Here you are.'

'Thank you, but look you're covered in rust!'

Without thinking, Annie started to brush the orange marks off his suit.

'I'm really sorry, Mr Fotherby, your suit is ruined! And after you've been so kind as to give me a lift.'

'Please don't worry, Miss Gingell, it really is nothing. The suit can be cleaned.'

Suddenly aware that her actions might have been a little too familiar, Annie grabbed the bicycle, took hold of the handlebars and began to walk away. As she reached the junction with Castle Street, she turned and found him staring at her. He smiled and waved as she thanked him again and turned down Castle Street.

Houses of Parliament
March 10th

Annie, Vesta and Cecily huddled together, rereading the report of the Speaker's Conference on Electoral Reform. Vesta then stood and turned to the women sitting below them on the staircase leading to the Ladies' Gallery. Waving the document in her left hand, she cleared her throat.

'Ladies, whilst we wait to be admitted I thought it might be appropriate to briefly summarise the report of the Speaker's Conference on Electoral Reform, which I am sure is the reason that most of us are here today. For those of you who have already seen this document, I would ask your forbearance whilst I briefly refer to its contents.'

She paused and pushed her glasses further up the bridge of

her nose.

'During twenty-six sittings the Conference examined the case for giving returning disenfranchised soldiers the vote. As you may know, before the war only 40% of men had the right to vote and, of that 40%, many have now become disenfranchised as they are serving abroad and no longer meet the residency requirement. The cross-party Conference has recommended that this situation be remedied and, in recognition of their service to their country, they all be given the vote.

Both Liberal and Labour politicians argue that this right to vote should be extended to other workers on militarily useful service and, following pressure from women's suffrage campaigners, it has become necessary to consider women too.'

There was a round of applause as Vesta squashed herself back between Annie and Cecily. The stone stairs leading to the Ladies' Gallery had chilled them through. Cecily blew on her hands, her breath condensing in a white cloud. Rubbing her hands together, she smiled at Annie.

'Don't worry about feeling cold now. Once we're allowed into the Gallery, you'll soon warm up. It's horribly hot and stuffy up there. I always come away with a headache.'

'How much longer will it be before we can go in?

'We won't be allowed into the Gallery until the Members are all in the Chamber and the debate has begun. So, it might be a while yet. It's always a good idea to arrive early to be at the head of the queue but, when we do get in, make for the front row, otherwise you won't see a thing.'

Finally, there was the sound of a heavy door opening. As one, the women sitting on the steps below them stood and, brushing down the seats of their overcoats, prepared for the scuffle. Having secured front row seats, Annie was shocked to find an ornate brass grille running the entire length of the Ladies' Gallery, which was set high above the chamber below. They sat with their faces pressed tightly against the brass grille, barely able to see the Members' benches. Behind them, women stood peering over their shoulders trying to get a glimpse of the proceedings. The Gallery itself was tiny, only designed to accommodate twenty women. Vesta leaned over to Annie.

'Now you know why we call this the cage.'

'But why the grille?'

'Apparently it's to stop the men seeing us. In case they are distracted. Rather like being in purdah in the House of Commons!'

Annie wasn't sure what 'purdah' was, but that didn't stop her feeling indignant.

'How dare they treat us like this, packed in here like animals!'

The debate droned on for over an hour, with little hope of the women at the back of the Gallery seeing or hearing anything at all. Annie and her companions were able to catch snippets of some of the speeches but found it almost impossible to follow the proceedings. As she pressed her nose against the grille again, Annie caught sight of rows of men sitting comfortably in seats below, and opposite them.

'Who are all those men in the Gallery opposite?' she hissed.

'That's the Strangers' Gallery. It's open to the public, but not to women it would seem.'

Vesta leaned over to face the women behind and, feigning surprise, announced:

'Ladies, notice that the men in the Strangers' Gallery have an unobstructed view of the Chamber and the Speaker.'

'Where *is* the Speaker?' Annie asked.

'Directly below us. His seat is, of course, on the floor of the Chamber and above him is the Press Gallery'.

'So why are we relegated to this hot, suffocating birdcage up in the gods? Aren't we members of the public as well?'

Annie twisted her neck around the brass post in front of her in a futile attempt to see the Speaker. As she was about to sink back on her seat, George Fotherby rose to his feet to address the Chamber.

She squeezed her face tight up against the grill and cupped her ears to catch his words, which were lost in the melee of shouted comments from both sides of the House.

'I can't hear what he's saying!'

She strained again to catch his words.

'Mr Prime Minister, I beg to move 'That this House records its thanks to Mr Speaker for his services presiding over the Electoral Reform Conference and is of the opinion that legislation should promptly be introduced on the lines of the resolutions reported from the Conference.'

'Hear! Hear!'

A number of MPs from both sides stood to show their support.

The Speaker then replied but his voice failed to carry up to the Ladies' Gallery. His words were completely inaudible. By this time Annie's throat felt like sandpaper and her head thumped. Cecily turned to her and then Vesta.

'I think that is probably the end of the debate and I've had enough for one day. If you don't mind, I think I will make a move.'

Annie hadn't wanted to be the first to give up on the proceedings, so breathed a sigh of relief when Vesta agreed that they'd done their absolute best to hear and see what they'd come for and so there was little point in staying any longer. They made their way down the narrow back stairs to the St Stephen's public exit and had just stepped out into Old Palace Yard when the smiling figure of George Fotherby approached them.

'Ah, ladies, I was hoping to catch you all. I wondered if I might give you a lift back as I'm heading to Saffron Walden myself.'

Annie smiled as he beamed at her and pointed to his car parked opposite them at the back of Westminster Abbey. Thanking him and feeling very relieved not to have the walk back to the Embankment underground station, Vesta, Cecily and Annie followed him over to the sleek Model-T car parked on the other side of the road. Opening the rear door, he invited them to get in.

'Right ladies, jump in!'

Cecily and Vesta slid across the leather upholstered back seat, leaving the front passenger seat for Annie, who sat peering over the dashboard at George Fotherby, as he bent over to engage the starting handle into the engine. On the third turn it spluttered into life and he slipped smoothly into the driver's seat. He released the handbrake and gently revved the engine before gliding out of the parking space into the road. Annie stole a glance at his hands as they curled around the steering wheel. She liked his hands. They were capable hands. They slowly made their way out of the city centre. It had been raining heavily whilst they'd been in the Chamber but the dull grey afternoon did nothing to dampen Annie's spirits as they drove along the rain-puddled Embankment. The gutters flowed with muddy water, which sprayed out on to the pavement as they drove past a group of women pedestrians, splattering them with filthy water. They glared at George Fotherby, who continued his guided tour, pointing out buildings and landmarks to his amused passengers, completely oblivious of the trouble he had caused. Catching the eye of one of the women, Annie mouthed:

'I'm so sorry!'

Annie had only ever read about the iconic buildings that lined the banks of the Thames, which now, seeing them for the first time, overwhelmed her. They were all far grander and more imposing than she had ever imagined. She gazed through the rain-soaked windows at the bustle of the river, drinking in each new slice of London life as they passed. Suddenly, without warning, George Fotherby stopped his running commentary, slowed the car down and briefly turned towards Annie before collapsing into fits of laughter.

'Well done, ladies. I congratulate you on having finally woken up those old dinosaurs in Westminster!'

He turned to Annie and winked.

Annie turned to face Cecily and Vesta before moving back and replying:

'But we haven't woken them up nearly enough yet! The recommendations of the Speaker's Conference doesn't give *me* a vote, or thousands of other women like me who are under 30 years of age, or women who don't own a property, or women who aren't married to a property owner, or women who don't pay more than £5.00 rent a month, or women who haven't got a university degree! Are we to remain disenfranchised?'

There was a stunned silence.

'Also, it's high time something was done to treat the women who choose to visit the House of Commons with a little respect. They shouldn't have to endure being packed like sardines in that stuffy cage up in the gods, behind an enormous grille which prevents them from hearing much, let alone seeing much of what's going on!'

George Fotherby's eyes cut to Annie.

'Well, what a spirited young woman you are, Miss Gingell!'

His eyes briefly rested on her lap and Annie realised that she was fiddling with the string ring on her left hand.

The following day Annie drafted a letter to Sir Alfred Mond, the First Commissioner for Works. After two attempts, her letter still wasn't in the formal style Vesta had shown her. Finally, she took a sheet of headed paper and decided to write exactly what she wanted to say, as she wanted to say it.

Sir Alfred Mond, First Commissioner for Works

March 11th, 1917

Sir,

I spent two hours yesterday in the Ladies' Gallery at the House of Commons, which was a very unpleasant experience. So, I am writing to ask a few questions, which I have listed below.

Why should a woman, when she wants to hear a debate in the House of Commons, be expected to sit in a hot, airless cage just under the ceiling, while the men in the Strangers' Gallery sit in a much bigger, comfortable gallery facing the Speaker and with a clear view of the proceedings?

Why too, should she be hidden away in half-darkness, behind an enormous grille, which makes it almost impossible to see anything unless she is in the front row?

Why is she expected to sit on cold stone steps while waiting for the debate to begin before she is allowed to enter the Ladies' Gallery? I have been told that the men have a waiting room. Why is there not one for women?

Why does the Gallery have no proper ventilation?

The House of Commons is an institution designed by men for men. We have had to fight even to be allowed into one very small part of the building and, even then, we aren't considered to be there. Sir, can I ask you this...if women are expected to obey laws, why should they not have a say in how those laws are made?

I know that I speak for many women when I ask you to remove the grille in the Ladies' Gallery as a matter of urgency.

I look forward to hearing from you and remain your loyal servant,

Annie Gingell (Miss)

Having finished the letter, she made a copy and addressed it to George Fotherby.

Deputation to 10 Downing Street
March 29th

As the early morning mist began to lift over the Thames, Annie and fellow representatives from the National Union of Women's Suffrage Societies joined a growing throng of women on the Embankment. The air buzzed with excitement as groups of war workers from over thirty suffrage societies, unfurled banners and shuffled into a ragged queue, grouping themselves behind their individual banners as they were raised into the drizzle-heavy air.

There was a sudden flurry of movement as the short plump figure of Millicent Fawcett appeared, wearing the red, white and green sash of the NUWSS. She made her way towards the front of the queue and, holding an oversized megaphone, addressed the women:

'Good morning and welcome! It is indeed heart-warming to see so many different suffrage societies represented here this morning, united in our resolve to support the recommendations recently made by the Speaker's Conference regarding the franchise of women. The recommendations made may not be as all-inclusive as we might like, but I think I can say that we would greatly prefer an imperfect scheme that can pass to the most perfect scheme in the world that cannot pass.'

A round of applause was abruptly silenced by the voice of a passing man cutting through the air.

'You are a disgrace! Your men should be keeping you under control!'

Then a woman clutching a button-eyed dog joined him and shouted:

'Get back to your homes!'

'This *is* my home!' Annie screamed.

The woman scowled at Annie and then, raising her hand, hailed a taxi as it sliced past them.

Recognising Annie, Millicent Fawcett gave a wry smile.

'Ah Miss Gingell, perhaps you and Mrs Baillie-Weaver would like to bring your banner and join me at the front of the procession this morning?'

Annie grabbed her banner and, followed by Gertrude, joined Mrs Fawcett, who leaned towards her and whispered, 'Two words to remember this morning, Miss Gingell: strength and dignity.'

Annie hoped that the women standing nearby hadn't heard the reprimand. She busied herself straightening her sash, and then she and Gertrude raised their red, white and green banner into the air.

Mrs Fawcett stood back to read the wording:

NATIONAL UNION OF WOMEN'S SUFFRAGE SOCIETIES
PRESIDENT MILLICENT FAWCETT
LAW-ABIDING SUFFRAGISTS

Nodding her approval, she signalled for other groups to fall into line behind them as the procession steadily started to snake its way along the Embankment towards Parliament Square. The weight of the banner soon made Annie's damaged arm ache. She realised it still hadn't regained its full strength but was determined to keep her banner high in the air for all to see.

By the time they reached Parliament Square a glimmer of winter sun had forced its way through the cloud, briefly casting a pink flush on the face of Big Ben and beneath it the ancient buildings of the Houses of Parliament. Annie's heart felt it would burst as they drew closer to Downing Street, and the unmistakeable figure of Emmeline Pankhurst, resplendent in her sash of green, white and violet, joined them at the head of the procession. Shoulder to shoulder, she and Millicent Fawcett led the deputation into Downing Street.

A podium had been set up in front of the Prime Minister's residence. The women, standing six-deep, fell into a church-like silence. All eyes focused on the burnished black door of Number 10. Four newsreel cameramen had set up, two each side of the door, and were adjusting their tripods ready to film Lloyd George as he stepped out into the street. A slight frost sparkled on the step as the door finally opened. The women surged forward, craning their necks to catch a first glimpse of the Prime Minister's stocky figure as he stepped quickly up to the podium. The unforgiving morning light accentuated the deep lines pleating his face, yet highlighted pale-blue hooded eyes, which smiled warmly as he scanned the sea of banners, flags, rosettes and sashes in front of him. The horn of a passing Thames barge cut through the air as Lloyd George cleared his throat to speak.

'Good morning, ladies. I would first like to welcome you all here this morning.'

He paused as another barge sounded its horn.

'I am delighted to announce that a compromise has been reached by the Coalition Government regarding the issue of the franchise for women. Yesterday the House of Commons voted 385 to 55 that women over the age of thirty who are householders, wives of householders, occupiers of property with an annual rent of £5.00, or graduates of British universities, should have the vote. I have this morning already instructed the Government draftsmen to draw up a bill to introduce early legislation based on these recommendations.'

He paused until the scattered applause died down.

'Every leader of every party in the House of Commons took part in the debate and expressed their support for the enfranchisement of women. The Government whips were not put on, so the outcome was the result of a free vote. This has been a triumph for suffrage!'

Annie's heart pounded as she stepped forward.

'Mr Prime Minister. Sir...can you please tell us why the recommendations go little way to enfranchise women like myself who are under 30 and are not property owners or university graduates. Are we to remain unrepresented?'

Lloyd George ran his hand across the neat white moustache that lathered his upper lip. He lowered his voice and fixed his gaze on Annie before replying:

'I consider that the proposed age bar for women voters is illogical and unjustifiable. However, I do strongly advise you all not to challenge the recommendations made by the

Speaker's Conference. If you push for votes on the same terms as men, there is likely to be strong opposition from anti- suffrage MPs. For the present time, rest assured that the tide has turned!'

Millicent Fawcett shot Annie a warning glance, just as a woman standing behind Annie tapped her on the shoulder.

'These proposals are timid! We shall continue to demand that women be enfranchised on the same terms as men!'

Annie nodded, smiled and turned away as the Prime Minister thanked them all again and disappeared inside.

Millicent Fawcett walked next to Annie as the deputation left, on its way back to the station.

'I thought you might like to know that several anti-suffrage Conference members have resigned and have been replaced (by the Speaker) by pro-Suffragists like the Labour MP George Fotherby, who has been particularly active in pushing through this legislation.'

She paused.

'Miss Gingell, I applaud your hard work and passion for our cause, but unfortunately change is usually rather slow in coming. We have only achieved a partial victory. However, mark my words, we will continue to work tirelessly with strength and dignity, but above all with patience.'

She then turned back to Emmeline Pankhurst, and Annie caught up with Cecily and Vesta, who slipped her arm into Annie's and gave it a squeeze.

'Well, you certainly asked the question that we all wanted to ask, Annie. I hope Mrs Fawcett wasn't too dismissive just now. Sometimes I think she's forgotten what it's like to be young and full of passion for our cause. Don't lose that passion, Annie!'

Cecily grabbed her other arm and, steering the three of

them away from the noisy crocodile of women making their way along the embankment, they stopped to watch a group of coal barges plying their way up the river.

'Annie, we're looking forward to hearing you speak in Dunmow next week. We need your enthusiasm to stir things up a bit there. Mr Fotherby has agreed to join us again and is hoping that you'll attract a younger audience, some of whom may have heard you speak in Newport and may have invited their friends along.'

France
April 2nd

Conscious that he could be robbed of his leave at any moment by a stray shell or an emergency, Arthur swiftly gathered up his things and made his way to the leave train, which would take him to the coast. Once on its way the train trundled along as slowly as a funeral procession. Peering out of the window at fleeting cameos of small farmsteads, animals grazing in fields and farm workers going about their work, Arthur felt dislocated from his surroundings. He was sweating profusely and fidgeted uncontrollably. An older serviceman, probably in his forties, sitting opposite, leaned over and in a matter-of-fact voice said:

'You look as if you've got a touch of leave fever.'

'What do you mean by that?'

'Don't worry, lad, I've had it myself. It will get better. It's not easy going from trench life back into civilian life.'

Arthur leaned back in his seat and smiled weakly at the man.

'So that's what you call it? How long did it last for you?'

'Well, it took a while. I couldn't sleep or stop fidgeting for a few weeks. You got a girl waiting for you?'

‘Yes. But I haven’t seen her since last year, when she was working as a VAD nurse at the military hospital in Etaples. Her brother was killed, so she went back home to help her mum and dad. She doesn’t know I’m coming. I’m hoping to surprise her. ‘

‘Well then, I expect as soon as you see her, things will feel a whole lot better. They did for me! You look all-in, lad. You should try to get some shuteye before we reach the coast.’

Arthur was woken by the grinding of brakes as the train shuddered to a halt. The man opposite stood to take his bag from the overhead luggage rack. He turned to Arthur.

‘Have you got your pass ready, lad?’

Arthur reached into his rucksack and pulled out two sheets of paper, one certifying that he was vermin-free and the other confirming that he was entitled to ten days’ leave. The carriage rapidly emptied as men rushed to join the queue at the dockside, impatient to have their papers checked and to grab a seat on the vast dazzle steamer that waited to take them back to England. Arthur thought back to his first Channel crossing months before, when he’d stood on a deck with scores of eager young men, thirsty for adventure. He wondered how many of them were still alive.

****

As the White Cliffs of Dover came into view, men left their seats to go up on deck to catch a first sight of home. A cheer went up as the boat finally docked and the men scrambled to grab a seat on the leave train waiting for them at Dover dockside station. This train ambled along even more slowly than the French one and the men were growing impatient.

‘Could ‘ave walked faster than this!’

‘My bleedin’ leave will be over before we get to Victoria!’

Arthur grinned and mopped the beads of sweat from his forehead. He closed his eyes and imagined walking up Castle Street, knocking on Annie's front door, and the moment they would throw their arms around each other. His heart leapt remembering the smell of her, the flush of her cheeks and the feel of his arms curled around her waist, her breasts pressed against his chest.

The train finally pulled into Victoria Station. Hordes of men poured out on to the platform and scattered like khaki-coloured ants, back to their own families and loved ones. They were met by crowds of well-wishers giving out packets of cigarettes and bars of chocolate. A buffet with hot drinks had been set up at the end of the platform. Arthur made his way to the Underground and, having bought a ticket, dumped his rucksack on the platform and fixed his gaze on the tunnel from which the train would appear. There was a rumble and clatter as it finally swept into the station and a crush as soldiers jostled with regular commuters to grab a seat. Arthur felt far too edgy to sit down, so chose to stand until the doors opened at Liverpool Street. Having just managed to catch the Saffron Walden train, he sunk back into a seat and, with growing unease, counted the stations to Saffron Walden. Finally, the train began to brake and a man sitting on the opposite side of the carriage picked up his briefcase and stood by the carriage door. As they came to a standstill, he pushed the door open and climbed down on to the platform, followed by Arthur. Several other passengers spilled out before the guard checked the doors, raised his flag and blew his whistle. The train slowly chugged out of the station as Arthur stepped out into Station Street. He looked around him. The row of terraced houses leading up to the station looked exactly as they had the day he'd left for France. Nothing around him had changed, except himself. His mouth felt dry, his hands shook and he struggled to breathe. His heart raced. He stood for a moment, forcing himself to listen to the air travelling down his windpipe into his lungs, hoping to block out the echo of his heart pounding in his ears.

Having finally composed himself, Arthur slowly walked towards the town centre, along streets that were familiar, but unfamiliar. He reached the top of the Common and watched several women taking washing off lines and throwing it into baskets. They chatted and laughed as they picked up their laundry and walked back towards the town, and home.

As he stood watching them there was a sudden movement beyond the rows of washing lines. A sleek Model-T car pulled up by the side of the Common and a tall, striking figure in a smart suit got out. He opened the passenger door for a woman walking along the Ashdon Road. She flashed him a flirtatious smile and slid into the front seat, before the man closed her door and jumped in next to her. The two of them then set off, heading out of town. Arthur hid behind a line of washing and then, peering out from behind a damp army shirt, he realised that the woman was Annie.

Who was this man with the smart car and fancy suit? Why wasn't he out there helping his country like most self-respecting men? She seemed very pleased to see him, he thought. He looked down at his own worn khaki jacket and creased trousers. *How could he compete? What had he expected? Had he really thought she'd be waiting at home in case he turned up at her door?* The battalion's long march to Arras, followed by an intense Lewis gun training course, had given him little time to reply to her last letter. *How could he have not found the time to write? She probably thought he was dead. What a fool he'd been*! He walked to a nearby bench facing away from the lines of washing, threw his rucksack on the ground and slumped on to its splintered seat. Hugging his arms around himself, he doubled over, tears streaming down his face. This was the end of all his dreams

He wasn't sure how long he'd sat there, but the air had become knife-sharp and ugly dark clouds were banking above a tangle of trees lining the Common. The rows of now-empty washing lines were beginning to disappear into the dusk as he wiped tears from his face and picked up his rucksack. He wandered aimlessly towards the town. It had been almost a year and a half since he'd first made his way to Church Street, to Mr and Mrs Luckings's house, looking for a bed. It was nearly dark when he knocked on the door of number 36. The portly figure of Mrs Luckings opened the door and peered through the dark at the wretched soldier standing on her step.

'Well, I'll be dammed. If it isn't young Arthur Scoggings! Come in lad, you look as if you've had a hard time of it.'

Dunmow Community Centre
April 2nd

There had been a good turnout for the meeting and Annie was thrilled to see a queue of young women forming behind a table, where Vesta added their names to a growing list of new NUWSS members. Cecily sat behind another table, writing down the details of a few women interested in joining the Actresses' Franchise League, and a representative of the local Women's Agricultural Committee who'd spoken about the Women's Land Army sat at a third table as a large group of women waited to enlist for farm work.

George Fotherby had rounded off the evening with a positive report from Westminster and now stood beaming at Annie as she finally managed to break away from two women who'd cornered her, wanting to know more about the Suffragist movement, having apparently thought they were coming to listen to a group of Suffragettes. He placed a hand on her shoulder and winked at her.

'Well done! I don't think they'll be in much doubt about the difference between the two groups now!'

'You wouldn't believe the number of women who still see us as a group of terrorists!'

Squeezing her arm, he laughed.

'Well, I think you disabused them of that idea! Now, if you're ready to leave, I've parked outside.'

'I must just say goodbye to Vesta and Cecily. They haven't got far to walk home and said they'd lock up tonight.'

Having agreed to go along the following evening to the first rehearsal of the upcoming soldiers' entertainment, Annie joined George Fotherby, who'd cranked up the car engine and now sat waiting for her outside. Seeing her, he leapt out and round to her door, opening it with a flourish. The two of them then headed off in the direction of Saffron Walden. Annie sat quietly for a while, reflecting on how the meeting had gone. She then turned to him, noticing once again his capable hands on the steering wheel.

'This is very kind of you, Mr Fotherby.'

'It is my pleasure, Miss Gingell. I thought the evening went rather well. You must have been very pleased to see so many younger women present tonight. You certainly are able to attract an audience!'

He paused and appeared to be thinking. She caught him glancing again at the string ring on her left hand, before returning his eyes to the road ahead. She turned away and studied the fields and hedges lining the road as they passed and wondered where Arthur was at this moment, and what he'd think if he could see her now, in the dark, alone in the car of a man she barely knew. George Fotherby suddenly turned to her again.

'I hope you don't mind me asking you, Miss Gingell, but do you have a young man, a soldier perhaps?'

Annie was shocked by the bluntness of his question and hesitated before answering.

'Well, yes, I do. His name is Arthur. But I don't know if he's alive or dead. I haven't heard from him since before Christmas. Every day I come home hoping a letter has arrived. I've written to him but I've heard nothing. I don't even know where he is. Last time he wrote he was recovering in a military hospital near the Somme, but that battle ended last November and I don't know where they sent him after that.'

'Well, no news is generally good news, Miss Gingell.'

Without warning, tears were cascading down Annie's face. She furiously swept them away with the back of her hand, as he pulled off the road, up a narrow farm track, and stopped the car. Reaching into his pocket, he thrust a handkerchief into her hand.

'I am so sorry, Miss Gingell. I didn't mean to upset you.'

Annie blew her nose and through her tears spluttered:

'No, no, it's not your fault. This not knowing is what's so terrible. I'm just tired of pretending everything is alright. I'm trying to be strong but sometimes it just, well, it all gets on top of me. I'll be better in a minute.'

Blowing her nose again, she peered across at him. The light was rapidly fading as he leaned over and wrapped one arm around her shoulders. She couldn't make out the expression in his eyes but sensed his kindness and concern. She felt warm and safe. Instinct told her that he was a man she could trust. She surprised herself, as weeks of pent-up emotion poured out and this man who was almost a complete stranger sat quietly and listened.

'I keep having this dream. There's a procession of pale, thin soldiers, with bandages over their eyes. They're dragging other dead soldiers behind them, around shell holes, through oozing mud. Then I'm standing in a field of headstones watching as a grave swallows Arthur up!'

Another wave of tears engulfed her. He pulled her close and, curling both arms around her, gently rocked her.

'Shh! shh! It'll be alright. I'm sure you'd have heard if something untoward had happened to him. There must be a very good reason for his silence. He'd be a damned fool not to want to return to you, Annie Gingell!'

The smell of his cologne soothed her. The strength of his arms comforted her as a torrent of tears ran down her cheeks. He leant forward and gently took the handkerchief from her and wiped her eyes.

'Now, I'm going to get you home. You'll feel a lot better after a good night's sleep.'

Annie sat back in her seat as he held the steering wheel and put the car into reverse. Without thinking, she stretched out her hand and placed it on top of his.

'Have you got anyone waiting for you when you get home?'

His body tensed and then he slumped back into his seat and thought for a while before answering.

'I did have. I was engaged to be married. She was a VAD nurse like you. She was killed when a shell hit the hospital she was working in.'

'I am so sorry! Mr Fotherby, here you are listening to me feeling sorry for myself, when you must be suffering much more than me. At least I still have some hope, but for you...'

She leant forward and closed her fingers over his.

'Her colleagues told me that she wouldn't have known anything about it. She died instantly, which does give me some comfort.'

In the moonlight Annie could see grief etched across the lines of his face as he stared out at the gathering darkness.

'How long ago?' she asked.

He sighed before answering.

'It was Christmas Eve 1915. A year and a half ago, but it feels like yesterday.'

Looking down at her hand on his, he sat up and turned to her.

'Now we must get back, your family will be wondering where you are.'

As she went to remove her hand from his, he turned his hand over and briefly caught her fingers.

****

Arthur

Wrapped in a cloud of cold air, Arthur stumbled into Mrs Luckings's house, struggling to hold himself together.

'Have you got a room for the night, Mrs Luckings?'

'Of course we have, lad. Put your things down, then come through into the kitchen and I'll make us a nice cup of strong tea. You look as though you could do with one.'

Hearing Arthur's voice, Mr Luckings appeared in the hallway. He took a moment to recognise the distraught man standing in his hallway, mopping his forehead with a hand that shook violently.

'Hello lad, whatever has happened to you? Come and sit down.'

He led the way into the warm kitchen and pulled out a chair.

'Here sit down, lad.'

Arthur sipped the tea, spilling it on his trousers. Taking the cup, Mrs Luckings held it up to his lips as he drank. They sat silently, waiting for Arthur to gather himself together.

'So, what brings you back to Saffron Walden, Arthur?'

Mrs Luckings put the empty cup on the table and shot a glance at her husband as Arthur put his head in his hands and stared blankly at the surface of the scrubbed tabletop. He finally lifted his head and, speaking slowly, forced the words out.

'I've got ten days' leave. I thought I'd surprise Annie – that's my fiancée. I didn't expect to find her with someone else!'

Mr and Mrs Luckings had listened to a few young soldiers spilling their hearts out to them about doomed love affairs, so waited patiently for Arthur to bare his soul.

'What do you mean, lad?'

'I saw her at the Common, getting into a Ford T car, driven by some smart toff in a suit.'

'Well, that doesn't mean anything. He could be her cousin, or a just a friend. You can't just go jumping to conclusions like that, son.'

'It was the way she smiled at him. I could tell what he was thinking.'

'Now lad, you look as if you've had a hard time since we last saw you, and it isn't easy slotting back after what you've seen and had to do. You're probably not thinking straight. You need to find out who he is and where she was going before you think the worst. There's probably a perfectly good explanation.'

Arthur looked at them both and smiled weakly.

'You're right, maybe I'll do just that.'

'Well, I'll show you to your room and when you've tidied yourself up a bit and had a bite to eat you need to go round to her house and see her.'

Arthur washed and shaved, then picked at the sausage roll Mrs Luckings had set out for him in the kitchen, before heading out.

'Good luck son!' Mr Luckings called out from the sitting room.

Arthur decided to walk through the churchyard to Castle Street. The moon cast an eerie glow on the tombstones lining the graveyard in front of St Mary's Church. The clock struck ten as he walked down the narrow alleyway leading from the churchyard into Castle Street. He'd never been to Annie's house before, but knew it was number 6 Middle Square. His legs felt ready to give way and his heart thumped as he stepped down onto the pavement of Castle Street. He stood looking up the road trying to decide which way Middle Square would be when the Ford T appeared, slowly making its way up the street. He darted back into the dark alleyway and peered round the corner of a large Georgian house that faced the road. The car came to a stop a few feet away and the driver got out. He opened the passenger door and Annie stepped out. They stood talking briefly before she stood on tiptoes and hugged him. He returned the hug and, in the moonlight, Arthur was able to see a smile pass between them before she broke away and ran into Middle Square, turning to wave to him as she went. The man got back into the car and drove up the street, passing close to where Arthur hid. As he passed, Arthur was able to see the finely chiselled profile of the man, who he guessed was in his early thirties.

Arthur turned back along the dark alleyway and into the

silent graveyard. The moon hovered above a large yew tree standing to the side of the path leading up to the church door. He sank down on to the cold stone steps of the church, worn down by generations of worshippers, and stared at the ancient tombs in front of him. He envied the peace of their occupants. The church clock chimed eleven as he dragged himself to his feet. The cold night air had chilled him through, and he shivered as he trudged back towards Church Street.

How could he have believed he could step back into the old world? The old world had gone forever, and people had moved on. During his darkest days at the front he'd been sustained by dreams of returning to Annie, and that lost world. *How was he going to survive now*? He reached the Luckings's house and quietly let himself in, creeping up to his room and throwing himself onto the bed, burying his wet face in the pillow.

The following day he caught an early train and headed home to Manchester, where he would spend an agonising few days with his parents before returning to France, robbed of his will to survive. His parents believed their son's low spirits were due to the harsh discipline of army life and the horrors that he'd had to endure and that his depressed state would surely pass.

****

Annie

On her way out the following afternoon Annie waylaid the postman, who was making the second delivery of the day. Once again, she crossed her fingers behind her back and asked if there was anything for her.

'I'm afraid not, Annie. You still waitin' to hear from that young man of yours?'

Uncrossing her fingers and forcing a smile, she replied:

'Yes. I'm still waiting.'

Holding up a letter addressed to Arthur, she waved it in front of him.

'I'm just about to post another letter to him, but I don't know where he is. I just hope the military postal service forwards it to his unit.'

'I'm sure they will, and I'm sure he'll write just as soon as he can. Don't you worry. No news is good news, luv!'

Annie had grown tired of people telling her that no news was good news. It really didn't feel like that to her. She dropped the letter into the box at the end of the road, silently praying that it would reach Arthur, wherever he might be. She then headed towards the United Reformed Church Hall for the first rehearsal of the soldiers' entertainment. She held her copy of the song sheet and ran through the words of *'Going to the Derby,'* the costermonger's song she'd been practising with Gruff, who'd helped her with the costermonger's back slang he used with his friends.

There were several new faces at the rehearsal, women who'd recently joined the Actresses' Franchise League and had been given chorus parts by Cecily. Annie recognised a few of them from the Dunmow meeting and welcomed them with a smile. She then sat back on a pew and watched as Cecily took them through the opening chorus of *'Let the Great Big World Keep Turning'*.

Her thoughts kept returning to the previous evening and to the feel of George Fotherby's arms around her. Despite herself, she felt a fluttering in her stomach. She was certain he'd caught her fingers in his, and that he'd held that smile a little too long as they'd said goodnight.

She suddenly realised that Cecily was calling her on to the stage. Pushing all thoughts of George Fotherby to the back of her mind, she waited for the pianist to play the first bar of *'Going to the Derby'*. As Gruff had suggested, she imagined herself at Saffron Walden market and shouted her costermonger's cry, before launching into a boisterous rendition of the old music hall favourite. Cecily applauded loudly and shrieked:

'You sound just like Marie Lloyd herself!'

The rehearsal over, Annie took the long route home. She needed to sort out the tangle of conflicting emotions coursing through her. *Surely, she was imagining that George Fotherby had any feelings for her. Why would anyone like him be interested in someone like her? Besides, if Arthur was still alive, she was promised to him, and that was that. It was nothing more than vanity, allowing herself to be flattered by the attentions of George Fotherby, a man who himself was grieving for his dead fiancée.*

Arriving home, she wrote another letter to Arthur.

Arras, Northern France
April 15th

The sun was edging its way into the sky, forming silhouettes of the few skeletal trees remaining in no man's land. An eerie silence hung in the cool morning air. Arthur took out his watch.

5.30 a.m. Thirty minutes until zero hour and the start of a forty-eight-hour bombardment. Arthur and his men heaved a hefty Lewis gun into position, forming the rear of a diamond-shaped fighting formation. Arthur guessed that this new strategy had more to do with the huge shortage of manpower as a result of the Somme offensive than it did to clever military planning. He'd qualified as one of the newly trained Lewis gunners and now wore the badge on his arm. He'd selected nine men as assistants to help move the gun forwards at the rear of the creeping diamond formation. Two grenade throwers formed the top of the diamond, a sniper, scout and nine riflemen the left flank, and nine riflemen, a grenade thrower and bomb launcher made up the right. They waited silently for the order, each man lost in his own thoughts. Arthur felt that he was peering over the edge of a precipice. His survival meant nothing to him now. He felt detached and numb.

6.00 a.m. Zero hour. A whistle broke the silence. Defying the gravitational pull of despair, Arthur ordered his men to advance, letting loose an inferno of explosives as they inched forwards. A whine drew close, followed by a vivid flash and the hard metallic crash of an exploding bomb. If Private Brown had cried out, Arthur hadn't heard him. He only felt his body relax and a sigh gurgle into the mud as his face sunk into its depths. The bomb had burst on his side. Arthur called him but there was no answer. He turned him face up. Blood oozed from his neck and head as it fell limply to one side.

'Put your masks on!' Arthur yelled.

There was another blinding explosion, which was to be the last thing Arthur would remember ...

Waking up in a casualty clearing station sometime later, his skin itched unbearably. His eyes had been bandaged and felt sore and swollen. He shivered and realised that he was no longer wearing his uniform. His body felt damp. His hair wet. He couldn't feel his right leg. Seeing him awake, a young nurse came over to check on him. Sensing her beside him, Arthur turned to her. A searing pain shot from his mouth to his cheeks, and then to his eyes. The skin on his face felt stretched and tight, his lips cracked as he struggled to speak.

'Where am I?'

'You're in a degassing unit, Corporal. To decontaminate you we've had to remove your clothes and shower you. I'll get you a fresh uniform when we've finished dressing your wounds.'

'Why have I got bandages over my eyes and face?'

'You were hit by a mustard gas shell. We had to irrigate your eyes. You'll find it difficult and painful to look into the light for a number of weeks to come, and the skin on your face is blistered. Try not to speak. Your skin needs to rest in order to heal.'

'I can't feel my right leg.'

'That's because it's in a splint and the nerve endings have been affected by the gas. You also have a number of burns over your body, which have blistered. We'll be sending you home tomorrow. It usually takes six to eight weeks to recover from mustard gas burns. You're lucky to be alive, Corporal.'

Arthur's thoughts had become tangled in the cobwebs inside his head, and he had no interest in how long it might take his body to recover this time round. He wished he'd been killed.

****

During the sea crossing the rolling motion of the boat comforted him. He shut his eyes and dreamed that Annie was rocking him backwards and forwards in her arms. He was woken up by a sudden loud juddering, as the boat docked and he was carried on to a waiting ambulance train. Knife-sharp bolts of pain shot through his body as the train lumbered along, jostling the racks of wounded men as it went. His back sagged and he couldn't raise his left knee to relieve the constant cramp in his leg, the bunk above him being only a few inches away. After what seemed to be several hours, the train finally rumbled to a halt.

'Where are we?' he called.

A woman with a plummy voice, who must have been standing next to his stretcher, answered:

'We're at Saffron Walden Station, in Essex.'

Arthur froze.

'We're taking you to Walden Place Red Cross Hospital. It's a jolly nice hospital, in beautiful surroundings. I think you'll enjoy your time there.'

As he waited to be lifted out of the train, Arthur prayed that he'd be transferred somewhere else, somewhere unknown, somewhere he could quietly disappear and, if he survived, start again. His stretcher was finally lifted out and into a waiting ambulance, where he lay until the last man was stretchered in, and then the ambulance was cranked into life, sending a bolt of pain through Arthur's wounded leg and blistered body. The plummy-voiced nurse attempted to lower her voice as she talked to the driver.

'Watching them being unloaded is such a sad sight. I can't bear to see them crawling along, bowed and listless. The burns cases are always so dreadful. These men left England fine, alert young soldiers!'

The ambulance took a sharp turn. Several men groaned as it shook and rattled its way up what sounded like a gravel drive before grinding to a halt. The rear doors were opened and Arthur felt his stretcher being lifted out and carried inside, where the plummy-voiced nurse announced,

'All those with crayoned crosses on their foreheads are mustard gas cases.'

Two weeks later – Walden Place
May 4th

The men's iron-framed beds had been moved together to form a line of patients stretching the length of the ward. A stage had been erected in front of a large ornate fireplace at the far end of the room, with a walkway running from it to the door, separating the bedridden from a number of men in bath chairs, who'd been wheeled in. Those able to walk sat in chairs lined up behind them and a few others, preferring to stand, lolled against the back wall next to Matron and the nurses fortunate enough to be on duty. Arthur's eyes and face were still bandaged and sore. His burns itched as the skin beneath the blisters struggled to heal. It was of little interest to him, but he had noticed a slight sensation returning to his wounded leg. He'd said little since arriving and found little to talk about now, as he listened to the babble of excited voices all around him. The sound of brisk footsteps passing the end of his bed and moving towards the stage silenced the men. The footsteps crossed the floorboards of what he thought must be the stage. A man with a cultivated voice addressed the audience.

'Good afternoon, ladies and gentlemen. We are indeed very fortunate to have back with us, by special request, members of the Actresses' Franchise League, with a wonderful new entertainment for you. So, without further ado, I'd like you to welcome the ladies who have worked so hard to bring this show to you today.'

The room filled with loud wolf whistles and cheers as the women made their way past Arthur's bed and up to the stage, singing the opening chorus of *'Let the Great Big World Keep Turning'*. Soldiers to either side of him joined in the singing.

One of them turned to him.

'Come on mate, cheer up, you must know this one. Join in! It'll make you feel better.'

Arthur was grateful to be able to hide behind his bandages. He gave a slight nod and went to turn away.

'There are some real bobby dazzlers up there, mate. Pity you can't see them, eh? You can use your imagination though!'

The soldier turned away again and joined in the lusty applause as the song ended and the women broke into *'There's a Big Lot of Sunshine Coming Soon'*. Arthur's wounds throbbed as he tried to shut out the women's voices and kill a mounting feeling of dread. The show moved on with three other favourite numbers, before the man with the posh voice announced the penultimate song.

'I now have great pleasure in introducing the multitalented Miss Annie Gingell, who is going to sing a very popular song, made famous by none other than Marie Lloyd herself, *'Going to the Derby!'* A huge cheer went up as Annie stepped forward and belted out her costermonger's cry, before launching into song.

'Cor, get an eyeful of 'er!' the man next to Arthur exclaimed.

Those in the audience who were able stood and wolf-whistled whilst others applauded loudly. The piano then sounded the first few notes of *'Goodbyee'* and the ward erupted with the sound of throaty voices singing together.

As the women left the stage they fanned out, chatting to men in beds and others in bath chairs. The soldiers who'd been standing at the back of the room swarmed round them, flirting outrageously as the women slowly made their way to the end of the ward. As Annie neared the exit, she spotted a man almost completely bandaged from head to foot. The soldier in the neighbouring bed called out.

'Ere Miss Gingell, 'ave a word with 'im will you. He could do with cheering up. He hasn't got much to say for himself though.'

Arthur sensed Annie moving towards him. His heart thumped against the wall of his chest. He felt he'd been buried alive. She leaned over and gently held his blistered hand but, hearing him gasp, released it again. As she did, his fingers brushed against a small, string ring on one of her fingers.

The man standing next to her then quietly whispered.

'I think perhaps you should leave him in peace. He's not well.'

'I hope your burns soon heal,' she muttered as she left his bedside and stepped out into the lobby, where she was mobbed by a group of young soldiers eager to catch a closer look at her.

Arthur lay still, replaying the electric moment his finger had brushed against the ring, his ring. *Had he imagined it? Had his burned fingertips fooled him? Was she still wearing it*? He hardly dared to think it possible.

Outside in the lobby Matron Winter was ordering the men back to their wards as the last of the women left. Below his open window, Arthur could hear Annie's laughter floating up into the evening air. It was followed by the grinding of a starting handle and an engine spluttering into life. A car door opened and closed, followed by a second door. A man laughed and said something he couldn't make out. He strained to hear, his brief moment of hope fading with the crunching of tyres on gravel, as the car sped off down the drive and out on to the road.

****

Four weeks later – June 3rd
Walden Place

'Good morning, Corporal Scoggings. I have some good news for you. We will be removing the splint from your leg today. We will also start taking the bandages off your eyes for a few hours each day.'

Matron Winter propped a pair of wooden crutches up by his bedside.

'I've brought up a pair of crutches for you. One of the Red Cross nurses will remove your splint and help you get used to walking with them.'

She turned to go and then, looking back at Arthur, gave a brief smile.

'Oh, and you will be moving to one of the ground floor rooms, with a lovely view over the gardens. Things are looking up, aren't they Corporal Scoggings?'

Are they? He thought. He gave a half-hearted nod and turned away as she moved on to speak to a man at the far end of the ward.

He was woken by the unfamiliar voice of a young Red Cross nurse, who introduced herself as Nurse Atkinson.

'I've come to take your leg out of that awful splint. It will take a while before you'll be able to walk without crutches but it's a start, Corporal Scoggings.'

She paused, waiting for a reaction. When there was none, she smiled and gushed:

'And it means you'll be able to get out into the garden and get some fresh air. That'll cheer you up a bit!'

Will it? he thought.

'Now stop feeling sorry for yourself and try to lie still, so I can cut the bandages binding your leg to the splint.'

Set free, his leg hung limply over the side of the bed as Nurse Atkinson carefully unwound the bandages around his eyes. The sunlight pouring in through the window felt like a flashbulb exploding in his face. Instinctively he turned away from the scorching light and buried his face in his hands.

'You just need to give your eyes a chance to adjust. They'll feel sore for a while yet and you probably won't be able to focus properly.'

Nurse Atkinson bathed his eyes, then rubbed a foul-smelling ointment into his face.

'Can I have a mirror please, nurse?'

She hesitated, and then disappeared, returning with a small tortoiseshell hand mirror. Holding it up to his face, Arthur peered at the red-rimmed lashless eyes that stared back at him, the whites the colour of mustard. He ran his fingers over dried-lentil scabs at the corners of his mouth and the taut eggshell skin stretched over cheekbones that appeared to be popping out of his skull. His fingers snagged on patches of stubble that had sewn themselves into the cracks of his patchwork skin.

'Thank you, nurse', he said, passing the mirror back to her.

'You might not look like an oil painting right now, but you'll catch the eyes of the ladies by the time you leave here, mark my words, Corporal Scoggings! Now, let's get you on your feet and I'll help you down the stairs.'

She picked up the padded wooden crutches from beside his bed and eased them under his armpits. His blurred vision caused him to almost miss a step as they cautiously made their way down the short flight of stairs to a small room on the ground floor. Arthur was given a bed at the far end of the room, next to a tall sash window which looked directly out on to the lawns at the front of the building. He shaded his eyes and stared out of the window. Several beds had been moved out on to the terrace. Men with arms in slings, and others with crutches and missing limbs, milled around the grounds, smoking and relaxing. A few canvas deckchairs had been set out, and a group of soldiers gathered together, enjoying the morning sun. His eyes watered and the bright light hurt his swollen eyes. He shut them, then lay down on the bed, thankful to be alone and to be able to retreat again into the silent, self-absorbed man he had become. He was woken by a beaming Nurse Atkinson leaning over his bed, holding a small pile of letters.

'These are for you, Corporal Scoggings!'

Despite his poor vision, Arthur recognised Annie's bold handwriting. He gasped and stared at the letters, unable to bring himself to open them.

'Would you like me to open them for you?'

He nodded.

'There are three letters here. Would you like me to open the oldest one first?'

He nodded again.

She placed the first letter on his lap and the two others on his knees, then left him alone. Returning an hour later, she found him staring at the unread letters.

'Haven't you read them yet, Corporal Scoggings?'

'I can't, I can't read them.'

'Would you like me to?'

He nodded and fell back on to his pillow, staring up at the ceiling.

Nurse Atkinson quietly read out Annie's letters, glancing across at Arthur, trying to read his expression. The letters hit him like a gunshot. Having read the third one, she put them on his bedside table and turned to him. Tears were flowing down the sides of his disfigured face, soaking his pillow.

'I know the lady who wrote these. Annie Gingell was at school with me. It sounds like she's desperately waiting to hear from you. Why didn't you speak to her when she was here a few weeks ago? Would you like me to tell her you're here?'

'No!' Arthur replied, leaving no space for what she was going to say next.

'But surely you want her to know you are alive. Don't you think she deserves to know?'

'I said no!'

'Well, let me change your dressings, and then I'll leave you alone.'

That night Arthur woke screaming, on the ragged edge of a recurring dream.

The following morning – June 4th

The fresh morning air stung his cheeks. Arthur pulled his service cap down over his eyes and, leaning heavily on his crutches, walked to a wooden bench in the shade of an arching copper beech tree. Propping his crutches up on the edge of the seat, he sat down heavily, stretching his wounded leg out in front of him. The rough woollen hospital uniform irritated the tender new skin covering much of his shin and calf muscles. He took out the last of Annie's letters, written only four weeks before and, screwing up his eyes, forced himself to focus on the quivering page he held in his burned fingers. His head thumped as he tried to understand the conflicting emotions rampaging through him.

Why had she told him about this George Fotherby fellow if she was carrying on with him? Why was she still wearing the ring he'd given her if she was carrying on with him? Maybe Mr and Mrs Luckings were right, he might just be a friend. Would she still love the man he had become? Would he dare to believe her if she told him she still loved him?

With these thoughts in mind, he watched three soldiers throwing stale bread for a mother duck and her seven ducklings, who'd found their way into the grounds from a nearby pond. He found himself smiling. He looked around at a swathe of cream cow parsley, oak and ash trees bursting into leaf, aware of the sound of bees working a bush next to him. A single bee buzzed in circles above his head, flew off and then returned to circle him again. New life was bursting out all around him. He grabbed his crutches and headed back to his room, his heart savage with hope. *He wouldn't let mistrust poison their relationship. He would get better and, when his wounds had healed, he would find Annie. In the meantime he needed to let her know he was still alive.*

6 Middle Square
June 7th

Annie kicked off her muddy boots and stepped out of her overalls. She pushed open the kitchen door to find the room empty. A letter was propped up against a small vase of wild flowers in the centre of the kitchen table. Annie recognised the writing immediately and tore open the envelope, before collapsing into a chair.

Manchester
June 4th, 1917

My darling Annie,

I am writing to say how sorry I am that I haven't written before. The truth is that I have had another setback and am recovering at my parents' house in Manchester.

I never, ever, thought this would happen to me, but I'm sorry to say that I've suffered with my nerves since being hit by a mustard gas shell in May.

Unfortunately, the new respirator gas masks we were given in March didn't prove up to the job, and I've had problems breathing since. My burns are healing now and each day my eyes improve.

I'm telling you this Annie, as I know you would rather hear the truth. Please don't worry about me, and please don't write just yet. I don't think I'm up to hearing from you just now.

I hope you are safe and busy. I think about you all the time, but please wait until I write again before you try to contact me.

Rest assured, beloved, that despite what has been thrown at our love, I believe that it is holding its own and it will endure.

Your loving Arthur

Sobbing, Annie threw the letter down and screamed:

'He's alive! He's alive!'

Then, with tears rampaging down her face, she thumped her hands on the tabletop. What does he mean he isn't up to hearing from me? Why ever not?' What does he mean 'despite what has been thrown at our love'? I haven't thrown anything at it. What am I supposed to think?

Her hand shook as she reread the letter, this time noticing the shaky handwriting.

The swollen kitchen door juddered open as Pol appeared, carrying an armful of turnips from the allotment. Seeing the expression on her daughter's face, she dropped the muddy vegetables in the sink.

'You opened it then?'

Annie thrust the letter in front of Pol.

'Let me just wash me 'ands, luv.'

Pol quickly rinsed her hands at the kitchen sink and then picked up the letter.

'He's still alive, Annie, that's wonderful! You don't look very 'appy about it though.'

'Yes, he's alive and of course I'm really, really, pleased, but why won't he see me? He doesn't even want me to write to him!'

Pol leaned over and encircled Annie in her arms.

'He's trying to protect you, luv. He wants to wait until he's mended before he sees you.'

'But he should want me to help him, to be with him. Surely, he knows me well enough to know that whatever he looks like will make no difference to me. I'll still love him.'

'But he says he's suffering with 'is nerves, Annie. You must have seen enough young soldiers, scarred inside as well as outside, to know how it changes a man.'

'But I could help him.'

'He sounds like a very proud young man. It's probably best to let him get in touch when he's ready, luv.'

Annie folded the letter carefully and put it back in the envelope. Holding back tears, she sighed and turned to look up into Pol's eyes.

'I suppose you're right. But I'm so cross, mum. Do you think I'm being selfish? I'm hurt and I'm angry for me ... but he's the one who's suffering! I'll try to be patient.'

Pol smiled at her daughter.

'You'd better get yourself tidied up. You look like you've just come in off the fields.'

'But I have just come in off the fields, mum!'

Annie slept fitfully that night, haunted by lines of men, eyes bandaged, their skin a bluish-grey, trudging into the hospital at Etaples. She heard the laboured breathing, the efforts to expel the yellowish green frothy fluid that threatened to drown them and through which they inhaled and exhaled air into their lungs with a gurgling noise. She awoke calling Arthur's name, her heart pounding.

June 8th

Annie usually enjoyed the four-mile walk to Wiseman's Farm, but today she mulled over Arthur's letter. The strength of her reaction had both shocked and surprised her. As she walked along, deep in thought, George Fotherby's car pulled up beside her. The early morning sun reflected off his windscreen, blinding her momentarily. He rolled down the window and called out:

'I'm on my way to the farm to check the stock. Mr Wiseman fears we may have an outbreak of ringworm. Jump in and I'll give you a lift!'

Annie slid in beside him. She'd hoped to have more time to think and would rather have walked.

'You didn't hear this from me, Miss Gingell, but I understand that Sir Alfred Mond has taken note of your rather strongly worded complaint and petition concerning the grille in the Ladies' Gallery. He has requested authorisation for a sum of £5.00 to have it removed. Well done you!'

He leaned over and squeezed her arm. But rapidly withdrew it as Annie blurted out:

'Arthur's alive! He's alive!'

Annie looked across at him. *Had he flinched?*

'Well, well, that's wonderful news! Where is he?'

'He's been injured and is recovering from mustard gas poisoning. He's convalescing now at home with his parents, but has trouble with breathing, and his eyesight's been affected. He doesn't want to see me, says he's not ready. My mum says it's because he doesn't want me to see him like that!'

'She's probably right. We men are *so* proud.'

He stopped the car and rolled up his sleeves. The skin on both arms was puckered and tight. He bent over and showed her his right leg, where the skin had been stretched so thinly, she could see his veins.

Annie gasped.

'You were burned too?'

'And that's only the half of it ... but I'm one of the lucky ones, I can cover my scars.'

Annie looked again at his hands, the hands she'd admired and described as 'capable'.

'But your hands are untouched.'

'I was wearing asbestos gloves.'

'So that's why you're not fighting.'

'I was invalided out two years ago. It was when I was recovering that I became interested in politics.'

'And the farm?'

'Well, that's been in my family for years. My father didn't actually farm it. He was more of a gentleman farmer, but I was always much more involved before the war. Now I just oversee things but let Mr Wiseman run the day-to-day.'

'Well, I'm so sorry to hear how much you must have suffered, George.'

She found herself blushing.

'I hope you don't mind me calling you George.'

'I don't mind in the least, Annie. I hope you don't mind me calling you Annie!'

He winked, put the car back in gear and set off towards Wiseman's Farm.

'How do you like being a Land Girl then, Annie?'

'It's hard work but I do enjoy being out in the fresh air, knowing I'm helping with the war effort, and it makes a break from the round of speaking, lobbying and letter writing that I have to do. Mr Wiseman is very flexible and usually only asks me to work three days a week, which allows time for my other work.'

'They pulled into the farmyard and as Annie opened the car door, he turned to her with a wan smile.

'I *am* very pleased for you, Annie!'

There was a lump in her throat as she made her way towards the farm office. *How could he be so pleased for her when his own life was still so full of grief and pain*?

Walden Place
June 17th

Arthur's facial wounds had healed as well as could be expected and the livid scarring had begun to fade. After eight weeks of treatment his eyes were still sore and sensitive to bright light but were now able to focus. He could swallow the daily prescription of charcoal biscuits without gagging and had begun to taste food again. The damage to his leg had left him with a limp and a slightly stooped gait. When tired, he shuffled like a nervous ice skater and suffered spells of uncontrollable shaking, his teeth chattering like a monkey. Some days his hearing loss and the constant humming in his damaged eardrums drove him to distraction, but he had broken out of his silent world.

It was when he was on one of his daily walks around the

hospital grounds that he saw her. He hid behind the trunk of a large oak tree and, with blood pounding painfully against the new skin on his face, he watched as Annie walked past him with another young woman, who so resembled Annie Arthur guessed she must be her younger sister Nora. The two women were dressed smartly and strode purposefully towards the gate leading out into Abbey Lane, in the direction of Audley End House. He leaned against the trunk and waited for the shaking to stop.

'Are you alright, mate?'

'Yes, I'm just getting my breath back, that's all.'

The soldier helped Arthur over to a bench and sat down next to him.

'You looked like you was hiding, the way you jumped behind that tree when you saw them ladies.'

Arthur folded his arms, hoping to stop the shaking.

'She mustn't know I'm here!'

'Who mustn't? Was it one of them ladies?'

'She doesn't know I'm here, and I don't want her to see me until I look a lot better than this!'

He pointed to his damaged face. The soldier leaned back and, squinting against the sun, scrutinised Arthur's scars.

'Come on, mate, there's not a lot wrong with you. If she loves you, she won't even notice your scars.'

'It's not just the scars you can see, it's the ones you can't see I'm worried about. I don't trust myself yet. I don't want to frighten her.'

'Look 'ere, we've all got scars like that, but she'll understand. War changes a man.'

Walden Place
July 1st

Matron Winter appeared in the dining room and made her way over to where Arthur sat alone, finishing breakfast. She pulled up a chair and, pushing a small package into his hands, sat down next to him. Seeing 'Ministry of War' franked across the top right-hand side of the package, Arthur guessed what was inside. His hands shook as he tore back the wrapping paper to reveal a small box containing a silver War Badge, given to all wounded soldiers deemed unfit for further service. There was also an official letter, informing him that he had been honourably discharged from the army. The news both shocked and surprised him, but his overriding feeling was one of relief.

'Well, that's the end of your war, Corporal Scoggings! So now it's time to think about what you're going to do when you leave here.'

Arthur had spent many sleepless nights wondering just that. He'd only ever known life in service before the war but, with the scarring of his face and body, he knew that being a footman was no longer an option. One of the doctors had suggested he should write to Audley End House and enquire if they had any other openings.

'I'm planning to find out if there is anything going at Audley End House. I worked as a footman there before the war.'

'Well good for you, Corporal Scoggings – and good luck!'

She swept out of the room, leaving Arthur to finish his tepid mug of tea.

Audley End House Kitchen Garden
July 5th

Gabriel leaned back on his spade and watched a large

bumblebee working the comfrey bush tucked away in a wild corner of the kitchen garden. Lavender bushes bordering the central pathway, separating the fruit and vegetable gardens, buzzed with several varieties of bees and the espaliered apple trees hugging the garden wall were alive with worker bees filling pollen sacs to take back to the hive. His fascination with bees had never left him and he drew comfort from their busy presence and wisdom. As he stood watching them, there was a rustling behind him. He turned to find a youngish man with a pronounced limp walking towards him.

'Hello, Gabriel.'

Gabriel regarded the man. His voice was familiar and there was something about the slightly lopsided smile that reminded him of someone.

'It's Arthur, Arthur Scoggings, Gabriel. You probably don't recognise me.'

'Of course I recognise you, Arthur!'

He held out his hand and felt the rough scar tissue covering Arthur's fingers, as they shook hands.

'You look as if you've had a hard war, Arthur.'

'Not half as hard as a lot of others, Gabriel. But my war's over and I'm looking for work. I know I'd be no good in the House now but out here I think I could be of some use.'

Gabriel tried hard not to peer at Arthur's scars but couldn't help remembering the handsome man he'd been.

'I'll go and find, Mr Coster. Just you wait 'ere a minute and I'll fetch 'im.'

Arthur sank into a garden bench. His body felt heavy and ached all over after the short walk from Walden Place. He began to feel less confident and wondered if he really was ready for any form of physical labour. But as he listened to the sound of bees and watched several cabbage white butterflies fluttering around a nearby bush, enjoying their short, three-week lives, he felt at peace.

Mr Coster appeared from the vine house at the far end of the garden and walked towards him, removing his muddy gloves. He beamed and slapped Arthur on his back, sending a shooting pain through his neck and into the back of his head.

'It's good to see you, Arthur. How are you, lad?'

'Well as you can see, I'm not quite the man I was, but I survived!'

'Gabriel tells me you're looking for work in the garden.'

'If you'll have me, I'd be happy to learn from you both. I've never been a gardening sort, but if the war has taught me one thing, it's to appreciate the beauty of life. I can now see why you love what you do'.

'Well lad, we are looking for some extra help. It won't pay as much as I expect you're used to, and I'd have to check with Her Ladyship first, but I'm sure she'll be happy to 'ave you back.'

He thought for a moment before asking:

'Where are you living, lad?'

'I'm still at Walden Place, but they'll be discharging me soon.'

'So, you'll be needing somewhere to live then?'

'Well, yes. I wondered if there'd be room in the bothy. I only need a bed and somewhere to put a few clothes.'

'Right you are, lad. I'm sure Gabriel won't mind some company. Now you get off back to the hospital and I'll be in touch just as soon as I've cleared things with Her Ladyship.'

With that, he shook Arthur's hand and returned to the vine

house.

Wiseman's Farm
July 8th

Annie walked into Mr Wiseman's office to find him in conversation with George Fotherby. Seeing her, both men smiled.

'Ah, Annie, I'm getting the charmer in this afternoon and I wondered if you and your girls would like to watch him in action?'

'A charmer? I'm not sure I understand what you mean.'

'We've had several outbreaks of ringworm in the past and have called on the services of Mr McDermott, the charmer. A lot of farmers don't believe me when I tell them that this man simply has to spit on the infected cow, make the sign of the cross on the ground, and off it goes in a flash!'

Annie laughed, believing Mr Wiseman to be joking, but instead George Fotherby spoke up.

'I know it's hard to believe, Annie, but my father used him when he was alive and, despite all my reservations, I've used him and can completely assure you that it works!'

Annie's 'girls' were a gang of four Land Girls whose work Annie supervised. Between them they'd learned how to milk and look after cows and other young livestock, to shoe horses, to follow a horse and plough, to trap moles, and to use various heavy farm implements. Annie had recently learned how to drive the new motor tractor, George Fotherby's pride and joy. He turned to face her and asked,

'I wondered if you'd like to give a demonstration of how to drive the new tractor as one of the attractions at your upcoming show in Bishop's Stortford on August 11th? It would mean driving it there, which might take a while, but it would certainly be a great crowd puller!'

Annie felt a little dubious, but nodded in agreement.

'Miss Talbot, the Director of the Women's Branch of the Board of Agriculture, will be there and I'm sure she would be very interested to see one of the new machines in action.'

George smiled at Annie and walked out into the farmyard to check on the young cattle displaying the telltale rings around their eyes.'

'So, bring your girls along at two o'clock this afternoon, and if it works you could also mention his services!' he called over his shoulder.

Audley End Kitchen Garden
July 10th

Arthur's back ached. Sweat poured down the creases in his patched face as he worked in the heat of the vine house. He'd been given light work since taking up the junior gardener post and was finding the work both satisfying and calming. Today he picked out rogue weeds that had grown up around the base of the ancient vines, whose roots protruded out of the open ground-level windows and into the soil outside. Gabriel appeared at the open door, carrying a trug of early vegetables.

'I wondered if you'd like to take these vegetables up to the 'Ouse, Arthur? You know which door to take them to I expect?'

Arthur straightened up, feeling relieved to have an excuse to have a walk. His leg felt stiff and his hands ached. He smiled and remembered watching Annie taking in the garden produce from the shy young Gabriel. He picked up the trug and made his way out of the garden and up to the service yard, where a young laundry maid was hanging out washing. Hearing him approach, she turned and smiled broadly at him. He stopped in his tracks, his heart leaping. It was Annie's sister, Nora! He returned her smile and then skirted past her and the laundry door, to the scullery. He knocked and waited for the young scullery maid to open the door. She grimaced at seeing his scarred face and then, colouring slightly, smiled and took the trug from him, before quickly shutting the door. He pretended to be checking the game larder in the yard outside the scullery, as he waited for the laundry maid to go inside. He then quickly left the yard and returned to the kitchen garden. Gabriel was checking the beehives and Mr Coster deadheading a bed of early roses as he made his way back to the vinery. The shocked look on the scullery maid's face unsettled him. That evening, as he and Gabriel ate a meal of bread and cheese, Arthur asked:

'Gabriel, do you think I should write and warn Annie about how different I look? The young scullery maid was shocked when she saw me today.'

'No, of course not, Arthur. If she loves you, and I'm sure she does, it will make no difference at all.'

'Is there a laundry maid who looks very much like Annie, Gabriel?'

'Yes, of course – Nora Gingell! She's been 'ere a few weeks now. I don't have much to do with the inside servants, apart from when I 'ave to take the fruit and vegetables down. She seems a lovely lass though.'

'Well, if you do talk to her, please don't tell her who I am, Gabriel. I'm not ready yet.'

'Right you are then. Your secret's safe with me.'

Higham's Farm, Bishop's Stortford
August 11th

Annie climbed down from the tractor and looked for George Fotherby and Mr Wiseman. It had taken well over an hour to drive from Wiseman's and her buttocks ached from sitting astride the large metal seat designed for a male posterior rather than that of a woman of her slight proportions. George Fotherby greeted her with a wide grin.

Annie jumped down and stretched her back.

'I hope you've asked someone else to drive this thing back. My behind is killing me!'

He laughed.

'Don't worry, Annie, I didn't expect you to drive both ways. Mr Wiseman will drive it back. You can come with me. Oh, and by the way, good news! The grille in the Ladies' Gallery was removed yesterday.'

'Hooray!' she exclaimed. 'Now where should I park this monster?'

Mr Wiseman appeared with a plan of the site and a list of which events would be happening where. Hearing Annie's question, he pointed to the far right-hand corner of the field.

'You're over there, so I suggest you head over with the tractor and get parked up. Your demonstration is down for two o'clock, which gives you plenty of time before your talk at the end of the afternoon, around four. As you can see a small stage has been set up. It should be high enough for people to see you. Your gang are here and are setting up in the left-hand corner over there.'

He turned and headed in the direction of the entrance, where a tall slim woman was walking towards them.

'Ah, that must be Elizabeth Talbot.'

George Fotherby shot off and greeted her with a hearty handshake, before bringing her over to Annie.

'Annie, I'd like you to meet Miss Elizabeth Talbot, the Director of the Women's Board of Agriculture.'

'Annie smiled and shook her hand.'

'Miss Gingell is one of our Land Girl gang leaders and has responsibility for four field workers, who will be demonstrating their skills here today. Miss Gingell will be showing the time-saving uses to which our new motor tractor is being put.'

'Good morning, Miss Gingell. I've heard so much about you. I'm looking forward to seeing you putting that wonderful new tractor I see over there through its paces later on.'

Annie smiled.

'Miss Gingell, as you know only too well, women have already proved themselves to be capable of taking on so many roles that were previously carried out only by men. But the many skills on show today will send a further strong message that women are both capable and deserving of the right to vote. Furthermore, it will highlight the nonsense it is to exclude women from jobs because of their sex.'

She then turned to George Fotherby, who was waiting to introduce her to the women setting up their demonstrations in different parts of the site. She looked back towards Annie.

'I shall look forward to your closing address later this afternoon. Good luck, Miss Gingell!'

The event had attracted a number of local farmers, landowners and gardeners, including Gabriel, Mr Coster and Arthur. Arthur had taken to wearing a wide-brimmed hat, which partially covered his face, protecting his eyes and translucent skin from the glare of the summer sun. But perhaps more importantly, it allowed him to deflect the pitying gaze of strangers. He had nervously accepted the offer of a day off and a ticket to the event, knowing that Annie would be speaking. He had made Gabriel and Mr Coster promise not to let her know he was there, so they'd split up at the entrance and arranged to meet up at the end of the show.

Arthur lurked in the shadows as Annie, wearing a wide-brimmed hat, trousers, boots and overalls, drove the gleaming new tractor into the ring. Jumping down from the seat, she smiled warmly at the crowd.

'Good morning, ladies and gentlemen. You see before you the new Model F Fordson tractor, imported recently from America by Mr George Fotherby for use on his farm near Saffron Walden. Farmers are already calling it the Model T of the soil! It is designed to lift the drudgery out of farm work and is capable of harvesting more land in less time, therefore enabling the farmer to increase food production at a time when German submarines continue to threaten our food supply.'

There were nods of approval as the crowd milled around, admiring the tractor's sturdy design. Annie attached a single-furrow plough to the rear of the tractor, before climbing back into the driver's seat and asking the crowd to move back. She drove the engine forward a short distance, demonstrating the speed at which it was able to plough, then replaced the plough with a harrow, and finally with a seed drill.

'As you can see, the tractor is able to do the work of two horses in half the time. It has a small turning circle, so is able to turn sharp corners. It can also be used for towing a haycart, hauling logs, coal, or even bricks.'

She turned off the engine, jumped down and was

immediately surrounded by farmers wanting to get a closer look at the tractor. She was now hidden from Arthur's view, so he moved away into the crowds. He longed to let her know he was there, to speak to her and to hold her again, to claim her as his fiancée. But the pride he felt for her was mingled once again with the lingering doubts that continued to haunt him.

By four o'clock the crowd had gathered around the small stage. A poster had been nailed to a tree to the back of the stage. It depicted a woman walking behind a shire horse guiding a single-furrow plough. Arthur pulled his hat down and read the slogan:

NATIONAL SERVICE WOMEN'S LAND ARMY
GOD SPEED THE PLOUGH AND THE WOMAN WHO DRIVES IT.

He then moved to the back of the crowd as George Fotherby, whom Arthur recognised immediately as the man in the Ford T car, Miss Talbot and Annie climbed up on to the stage. George Fotherby smiled and stepped forward.

'Well, ladies and gentlemen, what a day it's been! Now, I know you haven't come to listen to me, so I'd like to introduce the lady responsible for organising this wonderful event, Miss Elizabeth Talbot, the Director of the Women's Board of Agriculture.'

There was a burst of applause as Miss Talbot stepped to the front of the stage.

'Ladies and gentlemen, what we have seen today has been just a sample of women's skills and achievements. I would venture to say that women have been, and continue to be, the backbone of our society, and in recent years they have turned their hands to jobs previously considered unthinkable for a woman, with both fortitude and grit'.

There was a burst of applause, after which she turned,

smiling, to Annie.

'And now I'd like to introduce a lady who has been a munitions worker, ambulance driver and nurse. She has now turned her energies to the women's suffrage movement and continues her support of the war effort by working as a Land Girl. Please welcome Annie Gingell!'

Annie stepped forward and, directing her gaze to the back of the audience, spotted two familiar faces. She gave Gabriel and Mr Coster a warm smile before speaking.

'I hope you have enjoyed today's demonstrations, showing the type of work the Women's Land Army have tackled in recent months. To name but a few, milking, shepherding, tree felling, thatching, ploughing, animal husbandry and mole trapping. I hope you enjoyed watching the women farriers at work as much as I did, and the wonderful display of farm machinery used by our female workforce.'

There was a movement at the back of the audience. Annie looked up to see a figure in a wide-brimmed hat who'd been standing behind Mr Coster move away and walk towards the exit. There was something familiar about the man's gait that threw her for a moment. She quickly returned to her speech, focusing on the centre of the crowd.

'If there are women in the audience who are interested in joining the Land Army, every village has a registrar who keeps a list of local women farm workers and the skills they have to offer. The WLA have training centres and special short courses at existing agricultural colleges that give an introduction to work on the land. So if you are interested, please pick up a list of registrars from the desk next to the exit as you leave. Finally, please remember that every woman who helps in agriculture during the war is serving her country as well as the man who is fighting in the trenches or at sea!'

When the applause had died down, people began to make their way to the exit. Annie noticed a number of women picking up the list of village registrars.

Arthur waited behind a small outbuilding, where he could watch people leaving. As Gabriel and Mr Coster appeared, he joined them to walk to the station.

'Well, whoever would've thought that the Annie Gingell we knew would be driving tractors and ambulances! It just goes to show what some of these little women are capable of.'

Mr Coster turned to Arthur, who was walking silently behind them.

'What's the matter, son? You should be proud to see your young lady doing so well.'

'I am Mr Coster, I really am. That is if she is still my young lady. Looking at what she's become makes me feel even more inadequate. Look at me, what will she think of the broken wretch I've become? She fell in love with a very different man to the one I am now.'

Gabriel put a hand on his shoulder.

'Now Arthur, you mustn't think like that. You've suffered a great deal for your country and have served it well. That must make you feel you've achieved something very worthwhile.'

'No Gabriel, all it has made me realise is the futility of it all. I saw so many young men die in the most horrible way, all for what? No, my generation has sacrificed its youth for nothing!'

They walked on in silence. As they approached the station a Ford T sailed past.

In the passenger seat sat Annie.

6 Middle Square
Saffron Walden
August 15th

Annie flopped into the chair by the range and tugged off her shoes. Her feet ached. The Underground had been packed and hot. She checked for post. Nothing for her.

Pol passed her a cup of tea and then took out a brown paper bag from the cupboard.

'Salmon's had some slab toffee. Seeing as Nora's coming home for the night I thought we could have a bit of a treat. Go on 'ave a bit, that'll buck you up!'

Annie plunged her hand into the bag and took out a piece of the brittle toffee.

'Did he have to hit it with a hammer? It's all in little sharp pieces!'

'It's the only way to break it up, Annie. I told him our Nora's coming home for the night, so he put a bit extra in.'

She sat back and for a few minutes they silently sucked the sweet, sticky toffee.

'Well, is that doing the trick, luv?'

'I suppose so.'

She swallowed a final piece of toffee and turned to face Pol.

'It was good to sit in the Ladies' Gallery and to be able to see and hear what was going on at last, but everything takes *so* long. Even though Parliament are moving closer to a positive vote, every new bill has to be debated and passed by both Houses, the Commons and the Lords. So many of them are just diehard, anti-Suffragist old men with no intention of changing their ideas. Everything takes so long!'

She paused.

'And still no letter from Arthur. How much longer am I

expected to wait?'

The door was suddenly kicked open and Nora, flushed from her walk, swept in, giving her mum and sister a big hug.

'Well, look at you, all grown up, miss!'

Pol gave her another hug and poured her a cup of tea. Annie smiled at her sister.

'Well, how are you finding it up at the Big 'Ouse then?'

Nora held out her hands. They were red raw.

'Look at my 'ands. I'm up to me elbows in dirty water most of the day, and when I'm not doing that I'm bent over a hot iron. It's 'ard work. But the other laundry maid, Frances, she's nice.'

She took a sip of tea.

I'm up at five o'clock in the morning to check the fire under the copper, and if it's gone out I 'ave to light it again. Then there's all the sorting, soaking and scrubbing. It's never-ending. The family aren't even there at the moment. They're up in London for the season but they send all their dirty washing back on the train for us to do. And we're only getting board wages, but we're still doing the same amount of work!'

Pol rested her arms on her youngest daughter's shoulders and sighed.

'Well, at least you're earning, Nora. What about the other servants, what are they doing if the family aren't there?'

'Some have gone with them. Two of the junior kitchen maids are still cooking for us servants, and the garden staff are all as busy as ever. There's a new man working in the kitchen garden. He must have been badly burned in the war. He brought some vegetables down to the service yard the other day when I was hanging out some sheets. His face gave me such a shock! Emily the scullery maid told me his name is Arthur and that he used to work as a footman at the Big 'Ouse before the war....'

Annie's tea spilled over her lap as she spun round to look at her sister.

'What did you say?'

Startled, Nora glanced across at Annie.

'I, I said there's a new gardener called Arthur who used to work up at the 'Ouse as a footman before the war.'

'No, no, what did you say about his face?'

'I said it's badly burned, that's all.'

She sought out Pol's eyes but they were focused on Annie, whose face had drained of colour.

'Now Annie, that doesn't mean it's the same Arthur, it could be someone else, and just a coincidence.'

Nora put her head in her hands.

'Oh Annie, I'm so sorry, I didn't think, I really didn't.'

Annie put her cup down on the table and went over to the sink, her back stiff with the effort to suppress her tears. Staring out of the window, she fell apart.

'What if it's him, mum? What if that's the reason he doesn't want to see me?'

Pol wrapped her arms around her daughter, trying to find words of comfort.

'I've got to go up there! I've got to find out if it is him.'

'Not tonight you're not. Wait until the morning, Annie. Things will seem much better in the morning.'

August 16th

Annie stole out of the house whilst it was still thick with sleep. She knew that what she was about to do was probably wrong, but knew she was going to do it anyway and she didn't want anyone trying to stop her. She made her way down Castle Street, crossed the High Street and into Freshwell Street, heading towards Audley End House. The early morning sunlight sliced through the line of beech trees at the edge of the estate, dappling the path in front of her. She hitched up her skirts and climbed over a stile and into the orchard behind the kitchen garden. It was still early and rags of mist hung over the ancient fruit trees. She wiped her dew-soaked boots, brushed a layer of newly cut grass from the hem of her sodden skirt and froze as voices drifted over the high brick walls of the kitchen garden. She ran her hands over her hair, pushing a few strands back behind her ears and, with heart pounding, stepped out of the sunshine and into the shade of the garden. A man wearing a wide-brimmed hat and corduroy jacket and trousers leaned over a potting table, picking side shoots off a tray of young tomato plants. He didn't hear the crunch of her feet on the gravel path as she crept closer.

'Arthur?'

He spun round, pulling the brim of his hat down over his face with fingers that trembled like moths' wings.

'How, how did you find me, Annie?'

Unflinching, Annie stared at the scarred face of the man she loved.

'Well, Arthur Scoggings, I've got a bone to pick with you! How long have you been here without letting me know?'

'I didn't think you'd want to see me looking the way I do now, Annie.'

'Come here, you silly man!'

She threw herself into his arms, knocking his hat to the ground. She ran her fingers over his damaged face, tracing the lines of rough skin that formed the joins in his face. Her fingers hovered over the taut skin stretched over his lips before she gently kissed him. Neither of them spoke as they clung silently together.

'I don't want your pity, Annie,' he whispered into her ear.

'What are you talking about, Arthur? I don't care what you look like. I love you for who you are.'

'But you could have anyone you want, Annie – you're so beautiful!'

'But I don't want *anyone*. I chose you a long time ago!'

She kissed him more urgently this time, and he responded, running his hand down her back and over her buttocks, pulling her closer to him.

'I'm frightened to love you too much, Annie', he whispered. 'If you were to change your mind, I don't think I could bear to live.'

'Arthur, how can you even think that?'

He picked up her left hand and swivelled the rough string ring around her finger.

'I only took it off when I really had to Arthur.'

He pulled back from her.

'Look at me, Annie. I mean *really* look at me. Could you bear to wake up every morning and look at my face, feel my rough hands on your body, without feeling revulsion and pity?'

Annie stared at him, the way a lens concentrates light.

'Arthur when I stare at you like I am now, what I see is the man I have loved since I first set eyes on you. When I look into your eyes the light in them hasn't changed, and why should I feel revulsion for a man whose face bears witness to the horrors that have afflicted our generation. I don't pity you, Arthur, I'm in awe of you! You're alive when I thought you were dead, and you've come back to me.'

'Marry me, Annie!'

'Yes, yes. Of course I'll marry you!'

Annie bent over and picked up his hat. Pushing it firmly down over his shock of wavy brown hair, she ducked under its brim and tenderly kissed him again and again. Hearing footsteps approaching the entrance to the garden, she pulled away from him and grinned.

'I like you in that hat. It suits you!'

He laughed, and the crease lines in his face lifted for the first time in months.

'I've got to go now, Arthur. I'm already very late and Mr Wiseman will be wondering what has happened to me. But I'll be finished and back home by six o'clock.'

'Meet me by the Lion Gate at seven then!'

Arthur drew her to him again. They clung fiercely to each other until she pulled away. Letting him go, she laughed, pecked him on the cheek and bounced out of the garden. He watched her go with eyes that rimmed with tears but a heart that sang.

The Lion Gate
Audley End Estate

Arthur waited. She was late. He took out his pocket watch: a quarter past seven. He began to feel less sure of himself. *Had she thought about things and changed her mind*? He lifted his face up to the old Lion, standing astride the gate. The evening sun, which he couldn't quite feel on his face, lit up the ancient creature's dense mane, and a swarm of bees clustered around its proud head. A single bee detached itself from the swarm and hovered above him as he turned to look up the road. His heart lurched as Annie came running towards him, holding on to her hat, her overalls open and flapping behind her. She jumped into his open arms, almost toppling him over.

'I'm so sorry, I couldn't get away....'

'Don't worry, my love. You're here now. I thought we could walk up through the village to St Mark's.'

They sat leaning against the vast trunk of an ancient oak tree growing amongst the ruins of St Mark's chapel. He slipped his arm around her as they sat, watching the sun slowly disappear behind the roof of a nearby barn. He touched her chin and gently turned her face towards him. Her gaze rested on his eyes, which asked, *'Are you sure? Can you really love me as you used to?'* She could feel his fear.

'Arthur, you've got to believe me when I tell you that I love you as much, if not more than when you marched out of the Town Square all that time ago.'

'But Annie, I'm just a junior gardener. I've got nothing to offer you, except my love.'

'Well, that's more than enough for anybody!'

'I've seen what you've become. You've grown, whereas my life has shrunk. I've become a recluse. When I look at you, I see you making a success of everything you do, and I don't want to hold you back.'

'Hold me back! How could you ever hold me back, Arthur Scoggings?'

'No, I mean it. You have to continue living your life, Annie. It's the only way.'

'I will Arthur, but with you!'

Arthur leaned forward and kissed her, first tenderly, then with a fierce passion. Annie felt his burning desire insistent and present, and returned his kiss. At the sound of voices, Arthur broke away and leaned back against the tree. Annie turned to him to find tears rolling down the joins in his face.

'Arthur, what's the matter? Tell me!'

'Annie, these are happy tears!' he spluttered.

As they walked arm-in-arm back along the narrow street of quaint estate workers' cottages, Arthur suddenly spun her round to face him and then, grabbing her hand, led her to a small cottage at the end of a terrace of houses, opposite the tiny village school. Taking a key from his pocket, he thrust it into the door's dull brass keyhole, turning it twice before pushing the door open into a small sitting room with a red brick fireplace. The fireplace felt too big for the room and was inset with a large blackened cooking range. A narrow staircase led upstairs to a single bedroom with a tiny window, looking out on to the school and cottages opposite.

'Do you like it, Annie?'

'Well, yes, it's lovely, but why have you brought me here?'

'Because it's ours if we want it, just as soon as we're married!'

'What?'

'After you left the kitchen garden this morning, I had a word with Mr Coster. I told him you'd agreed to marry me and, before I knew what he was doing, he'd had a word with Mr Yorke, the estate steward, who agreed to let us have this empty cottage as long as I continue to work on the estate!'

Annie's skin was a rash of goose pimples.

'Well, Mr Scoggings, we'd better get married quickly before he changes his mind. It's lovely, Arthur!'

She wrapped her arms around him.

'I thought you said you had nothing to offer me. Well, this is hardly nothing, Arthur!'

'Come and look out the back. There's a privy and a nice little garden!'

They climbed back downstairs and out into a tiny garden, with hollyhocks and lupins tumbling over a cobbled path leading to a small privy.

'It's perfect, Arthur!'

6 Middle Square
September 28th

The wedding had been arranged for December 20th at Littlebury Church. Pol busied herself in the kitchen. She'd pulled her hair into a chignon at the nape of her neck and had changed into a fresh blouse and skirt. Gruff had brushed his mop of white hair and had put on a fresh shirt, and Fred was at the sink, washing the smell of vegetables from his hands. The kitchen door opened with less of a judder than usual, as Gruff had finally oiled the hinges. Annie appeared in the doorway, beaming, and pulling Arthur in behind her.

'Mum and dad, this is Arthur.'

Pol and Gruff smiled nervously as Arthur held out a claw-like hand. Pol stepped forward and shook the hand gently.

'We're so pleased to meet you at last, Arthur.'

Gruff got up from his chair and, grabbing Arthur's hand, pumped it up and down.

'It's good to meet you, son.'

Hearing voices, Fred appeared, drying his hands on a towel.

'Good to meet you, Arthur!'

'Well, come in, come in and sit down the pair of you.'

Pol led the way into the small front room, where she'd lit a fire.

'The evenings are closing in and the temperature soon drops once the sun's gone down, so I thought I'd light a fire. Would you like some tea? And I've made a cake.'

'That would be lovely, Mrs Gingell.'

Arthur perched uncomfortably on the edge of the best chair, facing the fire. Fred pulled up a stool and sat next to him.

'So, you've asked our Annie to marry you then. Have you any idea what you're letting yourself in for?'

Gruff laughed.

'Don't worry lad, she's not that bad!'

Pol brought in a tray laid with the best cups and saucers. Smiling, she cut Arthur a large piece of seed cake.

'Ere we are luv, I hope it's alright. I 'ad to change some of the ingredients. It's getting so 'ard to get stuff, what with the new shortages. They say there'll be compulsory rationing by January of next year.'

Annie passed round the cups of tea, whilst Pol cut more slices of cake.

Arthur sipped his tea, bit into the cake and stared into the fire.

'It's a lovely cake, Mrs Gingell.'

They sat for a moment, savouring the cake and enjoying the warmth of the fire. Arthur then put down his tea and, reaching into his pocket, brought out a small box and gave it to Annie.

'I wanted to give you this while your family are here. It belonged to my grandmother, and mother wanted you to have it, Annie. I hope it's not too big.'

Annie's eyes sparkled as he slid the string ring from her finger and pushed the simple diamond ring on in its place.

'Arthur, it's beautiful!'

Fighting back tears, Pol turned to Gruff.

'Gruff go and get the Christmas sherry out. And get the good glasses from the back of the cupboard, this calls for a toast!'

Gruff disappeared into the kitchen and came back with five small glasses of sherry.

'To Annie and Arthur. We 'ope you'll be very happy!'

'Annie and Arthur!'

Gruff stood and gave Annie one of his bear hugs and then slapped Arthur on the shoulder, making him flinch.

'We'll look forward to welcoming you into our family! And I 'ope she'll listen to you more than she does to 'er old dad!'

October 9th

Annie threw down her pen and, stretching both arms in front of her, rushed downstairs when she heard Arthur's voice in the kitchen. Arthur was still in his corduroy work clothes and clasped his straw hat behind his back. He winked and gave her one of his delicious lopsided grins, which she had come to love.

'It's a lovely evening, Annie, I thought we could have a walk into Audley End village and have a look at the house.'

Pol glanced across at Annie.

'Don't forget you've got that article to finish for tomorrow.'

'Don't worry mum, we won't be long!'

They swept out of the kitchen and into the yard. As they walked down Castle Street the Ford T pulled in next to them, and out jumped George Fotherby. Smiling broadly, he held out his hand to Arthur.

'You must be Arthur Scoggings, the lucky man to have won the heart of our lovely Annie Gingell. How very good it is to meet you!'

'And you must be George Fotherby. I've heard a lot about you.'

The two men shook hands. Then, turning to Annie, George smiled.

'Annie, I know you're writing an article for *'The Common Cause'* and wondered if you could use it as the basis for a talk to the Newport branch of the NUWSS on Friday evening? I could drive you there and back.'

Annie returned his smile and turned to Arthur.

'Perhaps you'd like to come too Arthur?'

She felt him hesitate.

'No, no Annie, I'm afraid I'll be busy up at the garden on Friday evening. Perhaps next time.'

George Fotherby leaned over and shook his hand again.

'Such a shame, Mr Scoggings. But we'll look forward to you joining our next meeting.'

He jumped back into the car and, as it moved off, shouted over his shoulder:

'I'll pick you up at 6.30 on Friday!'

As the car sped off up the road Annie reached for Arthur's hand. She felt him recoil.

'Arthur? What's the matter?'

'Have you any idea how that makes me feel? Seeing you so chummy with a man like him. He was flirting with you, Annie!'

'Don't be ridiculous, Arthur, he was just being friendly!'

They walked on in silence until they reached Walden Place, where a number of wounded soldiers were milling around the grounds. A man who'd shared a room with Arthur shouted over to them.

'Well, looks like you're on the mend, old chap!'

Arthur smiled and waved.

'*If only he knew*', he muttered under his breath.

October 13th

Annie waited on the pavement outside Middle Square. The Ford T turned into Castle Street and pulled up next to her. Grinning, George Fotherby leaped out and opened the passenger door for Annie.

'Your carriage awaits, madam!'

He winked at Mrs Sillet's grandchildren, who stood on the opposite side of the road, watching as they sped off.

'The neighbours 'ave started talking, George. I think it's best you don't pick me up here in future.'

'Your wish is my command, Annie. It was good to meet Arthur the other evening. How is he dealing with his facial disfigurement?'

'I think he's worried that I'll find it hard to love him now. He's trying not to compare himself now with his old self.'

'I can see he must have been a good-looking man.'

'Yes, he was. But to me he's still the same man and always will be.'

'Give him time, Annie. The wounds he's suffering aren't just skin-deep.'

'I know, George. I just hope that when we're married his invisible wounds will start to heal.'

The village hall was already almost full to capacity as they drew up. Annie left George to park the car and made her way into the hall. Mrs Baillie-Weaver breathed a sigh of relief as Annie appeared, and walked over to the side of the stage.

'Oh, thank goodness you're here. I thought you might have forgotten. Are you ready? You're the only speaker this evening, so if we get started on time, we might get away at a reasonably early time.'

She then walked up to the podium, raised her hands for silence and, smiling at Annie, introduced the topic for the evening.

'Tonight I'd like to welcome back Annie Gingell. A woman whose fierce integrity and tireless work has encouraged hundreds of women up and down the country to join together, to promote the absolute necessity of female enfranchisement. She has kindly agreed to talk this evening about her fourteen reasons for supporting women's suffrage.'

There was loud applause as Annie stepped up on to the stage and looked to the back of the hall. George had just slipped in and sat next to Harold Baillie-Weaver. He smiled warmly at her as she placed her notes on the podium and swept the room with her beaming gaze, letting it rest on George Fotherby. Returning his smile, she directed her words towards him.

'I'd like to begin with two thoughts. First, no self-respecting woman should wish, or work for, the success of a party that ignores her. And second, to ask for freedom for women is not a crime.

However, as Mrs Baillie-Weaver has just said, I'm going to talk to you this evening about why I support women's suffrage. Having thought very carefully about this, I eventually came up with fourteen reasons, which formed the basis of an article published this week in the WUSS journal '*The Common Cause*', copies of which are on sale at the back of the room.'

A number of women turned to the back of the hall and then to each other, nodding.

'I thought it best that I just read my list of reasons and then, if you have questions, we can open the evening up for discussion.'

There were nods of approval as the audience focused on the strikingly confident young woman standing in front of them. Annie cleared her throat and began to read:

'The Fourteen Reasons for Supporting Women's Suffrage:

1. Because it is the foundation of all political liberty that those who obey the law should have a voice in choosing those who make the law.
2. Because Parliament should be the reflection of the wishes of the people.
3. Because Parliament cannot fully reflect the wishes of the people when the wishes of women are without any direct representation.
4. Because most laws affect women as much as men, and some laws affect women especially.
5. Because the laws which affect women especially are now passed without consulting those persons whom they are intended to benefit.
6. Because laws affecting children should be regarded from the woman's point of view as well as the man's.

7. Because at every session, questions affecting the home come up for consideration in Parliament.
8. Because women have experience which should be helpfully brought to bear on domestic legislation.
9. Because to deprive women of the vote is to lower their position in common estimation.
10. Because the possession of the vote would increase the sense of responsibility amongst women towards questions of public importance.
11. Because public-spirited mothers make public-spirited sons and daughters.
12. Because large numbers of hard-working, intelligent, thoughtful women desire the franchise.
13. Because the objections raised against them having the franchise are based on sentiment not on reason.
14. Because, to sum all reasons up in one, it is for the common good of all.'

There was rapturous applause as Annie replaced her notes on the podium and warmly acknowledged the listeners as, one by one, they stood, clapping loudly. Finally, she held her hands up and indicated that people should be seated. There was a brief shuffling and sharing of hushed comments as the audience settled back into their seats.

The question-and-answer session finally over, Annie left the stage buoyed up by the success of the evening and excited to see so many of the audience queuing for a copy of '*The Common Cause*'. George waited in the car and whisked her away as the women began to filter out of the hall in chattering groups.

'Well done, Annie! Another resounding success.'

As they reached the Common, George pulled up by the kerb for Annie to get out. Winking, he turned to her.

'Would you like to get out here, Miss Gingell? We can't have the neighbours talking now, can we?'

'No, we can't!' she retorted. She turned to him and found his pale-blue eyes gazing at her. He crossed his arms and leaned back in his seat, still staring at her.

'I'm trying to decide, is it because of, or in spite of, you being the defiant, rebellious, spirited young woman that you are, you manage to captivate and win over any audience, no matter what their background. It's a gift, Annie, it truly is.'

'Well, thank you for the lift, George.'

Closing the car door behind her, she made her way down Museum Street and back home.

7 Audley End Road
November 15th

Fred and Gruff pulled up next to number 7 Audley End Road.

'Whoa there, Kitty! Woah!'

The horse came to a standstill as they jumped down from the delivery cart. Annie came to the front door and stared wide-eyed at the large jumble of furniture piled up in the back of the cart.

'I 'ope it's all going to fit in!'

'You're alright, luv, we'll do our best to get it all in, and if it don't all fit, Mr Reed said we could take some of it back and he'd refund our money. Now you two, give us an 'and with this bedframe, will you?'

An hour later, as they dragged the final piece of furniture, a tea chest full of kitchen pots and pans, through the narrow front door, Arthur appeared in his gardening clothes, his shirt sleeves rolled up, revealing the damaged skin of his forearms.

'Looks like I've missed all the excitement then!'

'Well, we thought we'd save you the bother, Arthur.'

Arthur glanced around the tiny room now, full of dark oak furniture. Annie beamed at him.

'Well, what do you think, Arthur?'

'I think it will be grand,' he smiled.

Having finally managed to move a chest of drawers up the narrow staircase, the four of them perched on packing boxes and shared two bottles of beer and a stack of cheese sandwiches Pol had packed up in a basket. Looking around the room, Annie frowned at the yellowing walls and dingy red lino.

'We'll need to give the walls a lick of distemper and take up this lino before we put everything in its proper place. That should brighten things up a bit.'

'We've got plenty of distemper in the garden storeroom. I'll ask Mr Coster if we can use some of that, and then we can have a go at the weekend.'

Arthur squeezed her arm and eased himself up into standing. Gruff and Fred picked up the basket and, looking round the room, nodded before heading to the door.

'Well, Annie, we need to make a move. Your mum will be wondering what's happened to us.'

Arthur shook them both by the hand and gave Annie a hug before locking the door behind them. Having helped Annie into the cart, he set off back to the bothy. The clip-clop of

Kitty's hooves echoed along the narrow street as Gruff turned the cart round and headed back to Middle Square

December 20th
Littlebury Parish Church

The December rain screamed against the church windows. Inside, candles lining the aisle flickered, casting quivering shadows on the small congregation, who craned their heads to see Annie and Arthur, now man and wife, slowly make their way out of the church. Gruff, uncomfortable in his scratchy woollen suit and starched white collar, stood awkwardly to lead both families outside for photographs. Tears ran down the folds of fat in his face. Pol, wearing her best green velvet suit and matching hat, grinned, rolled her eyes and offered him her handkerchief. Mr Scoggings stood and turned to his wife, a plump woman with cheeks the colour of a rash and, helping her to stand up, smiled broadly, his currant-like eyes disappearing into his face. Fred, wearing a borrowed suit from Mr Sillet, with trousers a little too short, and Nora, in one of Annie's old linen frocks, followed behind. The remainder of the congregation then fell in line at the rear.

The photographer fussed around, placing guests to either side of Arthur and Annie, who giggled as the raw afternoon wind lifted her skirts, revealing her underskirt. Behind them the church reached up as if trying to grab the dark clouds hunched above its tower. Having taken photographs of both families and the few friends, who now stood shivering, eager to move on to the pub, the photographer called Annie and Arthur over for a final picture of everyone. Arthur, placed in the centre of the group, fiddled with his newly grown moustache and turned to Gabriel, standing behind him, who pointed up at a single bee circling above Annie and Arthur's heads.

'I told 'em you was to be married today.'

Arthur grinned and turned back to Annie, who had slipped her hand in his. Their eyes met and something passed between them.

'Ladies and gentlemen, this will be the last photograph, I assure you! Now please look this way, at the camera.'

Fred had agreed to take the bride and groom from the pub to their new house. He'd placed a garland of ivy around the old horse's neck and had polished her hooves until they shone. Pol had tied red, white and blue bunting around the edge of the delivery cart, and Gruff had covered the old wooden seat with a straw cushion, wrapped in a brightly checked tablecloth.

'Mr and Mrs Scoggings, your carriage awaits outside', Gruff announced, before walking unsteadily to the pub door and throwing it open.

'Oh, look at Kitty all dressed up to the nines, and the cart looks lovely!'

Annie laughed and grabbed Arthur's hand, dragging him outside. Holding her hand, he stepped back and helped his wife into the cart before climbing in and kissing her warmly on the lips. The bar had emptied and the guests had spilled out on to the pavement, cheering and waving as Kitty slowly moved off down Castle Street, with Annie and Arthur waving to neighbours who'd come out to see them off. Mr Salmon was waiting outside his shop and pushed a large brown bag into Annie's hands.

'That should see you alright for a few days!' he shouted up to them.

Inside were a selection of sweets, a Madeira cake and a bottle of white wine.

As they turned into the High Street Annie shouted:

'Thank you, Mr Salmon, all my favourites!'

Then, turning to Arthur:

'I hope you're going to carry me over the threshold when we get home!'

As they pulled up outside number 7, Arthur jumped down and opened the door.

'Right Mrs Scoggings, come here!'

As Arthur lifted a giggling Annie over the threshold of their new home, Fred urged kitty on, leaving Arthur to shut the door.

1918

January 11th, 1918

Arthur whistled as he waited for the kettle to boil. Upstairs, Annie lay half awake. She smiled and turned over, listening to the street waking up. A letter dropped onto the mat by the front door. She heard Arthur pick it up before bringing two cups of tea up to the bedroom.

'Good morning, madam!'

Leaning over the bed, he put one cup down on the stool on her side and then put the second on his, before climbing back into bed and warming his feet on her.

'You're freezing!'

'Well you'd better warm me up then!'

They'd slept naked. She shivered as his cold hands cupped her breasts. She pulled him close and kissed his face, running her hands over his cold body. He moaned:

'That is so nice. I love you, Annie Scoggings.'

When he rolled off her, she lay with her face on his chest, listening to his ragged breath and racing heart. He lay there for a few minutes, then sat up and looked deep into her eyes.

'Promise me that you'll never leave me, Annie. I couldn't bear it!'

'Why would I want to leave you, Arthur?'

'You might find someone else, without a damaged smile and wrecked body.'

She kissed him tenderly and peered into the blue depth of his eyes.

'But I love your crooked smile, and your patched body! Now are we going to have that tea before it's completely cold? And can I see that letter?'

'Oh yes, I almost forgot.'

Passing it to her, he lay back against the headboard and watched as she balanced the tea on her knee and ripped open the envelope.

'It's from the Committee. The enfranchisement Bill has passed through the Lords, by 136 votes to 71! There's nothing to stop the final act going through now.'

'That's wonderful, Annie. Well done!'

Clinking their cups together, they gave a toast to women and drank the lukewarm tea as the enormity of her news sunk in.

February 6th

George Fotherby pulled up outside number 7 Audley Road. Annie opened the door and beamed at him. Standing behind her, Arthur dressed in his work corduroys, eyed up George's smartly cut suit, greeted him with a mumbled 'Good morning', then, kissing Annie, set off down the road towards the estate.

'I'll see you later!' he called.

'I hope I'm not too early, Annie. It's a big day today, and I didn't want us to be late.'

'I'm all ready, George.'

Jumping in beside him, she leaned over and squeezed his arm.

'I could hardly sleep last night. This is such a momentous day. I hardly dare believe it's true!'

'Well, Annie, the *Representation of the People Act* will become law today and I for one don't want to miss any of it.'

'Me neither!'

The Ladies' Gallery was packed to capacity by the time the

Speaker rose to his feet. To a hushed house he announced:

'As from today, the *Representation of the People Act* becomes law, enfranchising all women over the age of thirty with the minimum property qualification, and all men over the age of twenty-one. In total 8.4 million women have gained the vote!'

A loud cheer went up from the Ladies' Gallery. Vesta gathered up her skirt and climbed onto her seat. Beaming, she shouted:

'Ladies, today you have witnessed history in the making. You will be able to say to your grandchildren, "I was there"!'

Cecily, Gertrude and Annie joined the other women hugging each other, delighting in the moment. Annie looked down and caught the eye of George Fotherby, who was smiling up at her.

Later that day

George dropped Annie off at the top of the road. As she was about to step out of the car, he leaned over and grabbed both her hands.

'Well done!'

He paused.

'This is, of course, only the first step. As you know, the *Qualification of Women Act* is to be debated shortly and, when the time comes, which it surely will, I hope you will consider standing for election. We need spirited women like you in Parliament.'

Annie laughed under his scrutiny and released her hands from his.

'I'll think about it. Thank you for the lift, George.'

Arthur was sitting staring into a blazing fire, his face ruddy in the firelight, as she bounced through the front door, intoxicated by the events of the day. His gaze shifted to her, his eyes dead. He patted the seat next to him, wanting her to sit down. Instead, she gently placed her hands on each side of his face and tilted his head up towards her. She kissed his warm forehead, his eyes, his cheeks and mouth, before holding his head close to her stomach. He broke away from her embrace and stared up at her.

'I suppose I should say congratulations. Congratulations for becoming the strong woman that you are, congratulations for having achieved your goal, congratulations for having won the heart of a handsome young MP, who runs you around in his smart car!'

'Stop, Arthur! Just stop it!'

She sunk into the chair beside him and held both his hands in hers.

'Arthur, what do I have to do or say, to make you believe that it's you I love. You're my husband!'

'And what sort of husband am I?'

'You're *my* husband. Now I'm going to put the kettle on, and you can tell me about your day.'

Wiseman's Farm
July 17th

Annie jumped down from the tractor and, pushing her hair back off her forehead, grabbed a shovel from the pigsties. She drove the ten Gloucester Old Spots out into the field, where they dug their snouts into the muddy wallow, their curly tails quivering with delight. She shovelled the foul-smelling muck into her wheelbarrow and wheeled it over to the midden at the far end of the yard. As she returned to the sty, George Fotherby turned in through the five-bar gate and pulled up next to her.

'Good morning, Annie, you look like you've got a lovely job there!'

'I know. I don't think I'll ever get used to the smell of pigs!'

'I'm glad I caught you, Annie. I was wondering if you were thinking of coming to listen to the debate tomorrow?'

'You mean the *Qualification of Women Bill*?'

'Yes. I did rather hope you'd be coming. I can give you a lift.'

'Thank you, George, but I won't be coming tomorrow. We have our first lot of prisoners of war arriving to help out on the farm, and I promised Mr Wiseman that I'd help out here.'

'Oh yes, of course, he did mention it. That's a pity, but I'm sure there'll be another opportunity before the Bill goes to the Lords. You know how slowly things move.'

Annie had jumped at a chance to help Mr Wiseman show the POWs the ropes and was secretly pleased to have an excuse to avoid George Fotherby. When she arrived home that evening a pair of rabbits hung from an old hook in the garden wall. Arthur was unloading a small barrowful of vegetables he'd wheeled over from the estate kitchen garden. He looked up at her and flashed his crooked smile.

'Give those rabbits a few days to ripen a bit and they'll make a good stew.'

Annie eyed the eggs, fresh spinach, onions and carrots he'd laid out on the table and returned his smile.

'That's wonderful, Arthur!'

'So, I am useful for something then?'

'Did I ever say you weren't useful, Arthur Scoggings? But I do feel guilty, having all this good food, when rationing is hitting everyone so hard.'

'Just enjoy it, woman!'

The following morning a letter addressed to Arthur dropped on the mat. He checked the postmark. It had come from

Manchester but he didn't recognise the writing. Sitting down at the table, he placed his half-drunk cup of tea on the tabletop before tearing open the envelope. Upstairs, Annie heard a loud wail and hurried down in her dressing gown. Arthur was sitting with his hands covering his face, his body racked by loud sobs.

'Arthur, whatever is the matter?'

He pushed the letter towards her. She picked it up and read:

12 Walmer Terrace
Salford
Manchester
July 15th, 1918

Dear Mr Scoggings,

It is with great regret that it falls on me (your parents' neighbour from Walmer Terrace) to inform you of the sudden death of your parents, within two days of each other, from what is now being called the Spanish Flu.

The only word of comfort I can offer you is that their suffering was short and, as far as I understand it, they didn't know of each other's death.

I send you my sincere condolences and trust that you will make the necessary funeral arrangements. I will, of course, help in any way I can, but am myself now living in isolation. I fear there will be many more cases, so beg you to act speedily before funeral parlours are overwhelmed.

Yours sincerely,

Frank Smith

Annie gathered Arthur into her arms and held him until his sobs subsided.

July 23rd

There were only a handful of people at the funeral. Three of Arthur's brothers, a spinster aunt, a distant cousin and neighbours from either side of the small terraced house, where, forty years before, Arthur's father had carried his mother over the threshold. At the graveside they threw earth on the two coffins, lying side by side, before making their way to the *Fox and Hounds* public house for sandwiches and tea. Conversation sagged. Arthur, self-absorbed, lost in remembering and mourning the past, hunched over his cup, avoiding the pitiful glances of the small group of people gathered together to share memories of his parents' lives.

****

Back at home in Audley End village, Arthur sat terse and brooding. His face turned away from Annie as he struggled to deal with a flood of emotions. She leaned in towards him and, taking his face in her hands, peered into his eyes.

'You're wearing your 'don't talk to me eyes', Arthur.'

While he gazed at her, the tears rimming his dull eyes overflowed as he buried his head in his hands.

July 28th

An invitation had been dropped through the door of number 6 Middle Square. Pol sat at the kitchen table, holding the buff-coloured card in her hand, scarcely able to read through blinding tears. She heard Gruff's heavy tread on the stairs and wiped the tears away with the back of her hand. Silently, she held the invite out to him as he appeared in the kitchen doorway. Alarmed, Gruff grabbed the card and read the invitation that had come from the Lord Mayor.

It was to a gathering in the Town Square, followed by a service in the parish church on 4th August, to mark the fourth anniversary of the start of the war.

He threw it down on the table.

'But the bloody war isn't over yet. Are we supposed to be celebrating the last four years?'

'No, of course not Gruff, look at it again. It's to mark the occasion as a Day of Remembrance, and it says it's a tribute to the 'Sons of the Empire' who have fallen in the war. That's our Stanley, Gruff.'

Their eyes cut to the framed photograph sitting on the dresser. Stanley, in his oversized field hat, stared proudly out into the kitchen. Swallowing back tears, Gruff patted Pol on the arm.

'Alright luv, we'll go, of course we'll go.'

Saffron Walden Town Square
August 4th

Families of the bereaved stood stiffly in their Sunday best, waiting for the Mayor, resplendent in red robes and his gold chain of office, to begin. Finally, he paused for a moment, studying the silent mourners, before clearing his throat.

'We are gathered here today to remember the many brave young men who have proudly marched out of this Square during the past four years. We meet here today, as a community united in both grief and immense pride, to remember the sons who did not return.'

There was a ripple of movement as parents bowed heads, joined hands or wiped eyes. The mayor paused until the raw emotion stirred up by his words subsided, before continuing:

'I'd now like you all to stand, as I read out the names of the fallen. This will be followed by two minutes silence to remember each one of them. We will then move up to the church for a special service of remembrance.'

There was the sound of muffled sobbing as, one by one, the names were read out. Pol grabbed Gruff's arm, digging her fingers into his flesh, as Stanley's name resounded around the Square. Finally, the last name was read out and the sound of a bugle playing the *Last Post* filled the morning air, marking the beginning of the two-minute silence. With heads bowed, bereft parents silently pictured their beloved children. The silence was suddenly broken by the screams of a woman in the front row.

'I can't bear it! It's too much to bear! No parent should have to mourn the death of a child!'

A number of people sitting nearby gathered around the distraught woman, who fell senseless to the ground.

SPANISH FLU

October 20th, 1918
Saffron Walden

Pol's face had drained of colour. She slammed the newspaper down on the kitchen table. The headlines, in bold capitals, announced the first cases of Spanish Flu in the town. Gruff appeared at the kitchen door and, seeing the stricken look on Pol's face, picked up the paper and sank into his chair, his heart pounding.

Pol stared at him as he tried to digest the news.

'Gruff, they've started spraying the pavements and buses with disinfectant. Castle Street School, the Boys' British School, South Road Girls' School have all closed. If you feel ill you've got to isolate yourself. What are we goin' to do, Gruff, if we get ill and can't work? Or worse still, supposing it gets us like it did Arthur's parents, what will 'appen to our Nora and Fred?'

'Come on, luv, we're made of tough stuff, it'll take more than some flu bug to kill us off!'

'It says there probably won't be enough coffins or gravediggers, Gruff! 'Aven't we all suffered enough? What have we done to deserve this?'

'You're talking like we're all doomed. Come on, luv, we'll fight this thing, just like we have this bloody war!'

'But what about, Arthur? He's not a strong man, how would our Annie cope if anything was to 'appen to 'im?'

October 31st

Pol moved into the small sitting room, where she'd made up the fire. The rich smell of pheasant stew, made from the carcass of a young pheasant the gamekeeper had given Arthur, filled the house. Fred and Gruff would be home soon so, leaving the stew to simmer on the range, she picked up the local paper.

SPANISH FLU
RADWINTER FARMER DIES WITHIN 24 HOURS OF DOCTOR BEING CALLED

Gripping the edges of the newspaper, Pol studied the smiling face of a youngish man dressed in running clothes. The short article beneath the photograph filled her with terror. She'd thought the endless reports of war dead had numbed her, but her hands shook as she digested the horror or what was now threatening to overwhelm their lives. She leaned forward and poked the fire, muttering to herself.

'Everything is vanishing, everything.'

She turned as the kitchen door juddered open. Fred and Gruff appeared, ruddy-faced, wrapped in a cloud of cold air, which settled round her feet.

'Well, that's a welcome smell, Pol....and you've lit the fire!'

Gruff hurried over to the fire and warmed his hands. Fred lifted the lid of the stew pot, took a spoon from the drawer and dipped it into the rich gravy, swallowing a large mouthful before kicking his boots off and warming his feet by the range.

'Listen to this!'

Pol's voice quavered as she read:

'Radwinter farmer Laurie Drysdale, aged 38, a most healthy and robust man, who had been an Essex county cross-country champion, died of the flu within just twenty-four hours of the doctor being called. Three of his five children are also thought to be ill with the flu. The day after his death

on Wednesday, the Drysdale's fifteen-year-old servant, Lily Palmer, complained of a cold. Again, the doctor was called but Lily died on Friday, just one day after the doctor's visit. They will both be buried at Radwinter Road Cemetery on Saturday at 2 p.m., following a short church service at 1.00 p.m. Due to the highly contagious nature of this disease it is urged that only close family members attend the service.'

'And listen to this:'

'Saffron Walden is getting considerably more than its share of the flu. The outbreak is, in fact, becoming serious.'

Fred had come through and was now sitting on a small stool next to the fire. He made balloons of his cheeks, held his breath and then exhaled slowly.

'Mum, 'aven't you 'eard what's 'appened to the Duberrys at number 26? They lost four people this week!'

'Not Frank?'

'Yes. And Alice, Emma and Sarah.'

Pol hugged herself and rocked in her chair, peering at the smoke from the fire, which swirled like a dark whisper up into the chimney.'

'Tell me, what has this generation done to deserve this?'

ARMISTICE

Audley End House
1 p.m. November 11th

Loud cheering drifted over the kitchen garden walls, as the sharp peal of bells from St Mary's cut through the murky November afternoon. The cheering swelled as the two laundry maids, their hands wet with suds, abandoned their sinks. The dairymaid left her butter half-churned and Mrs Warwick, the cook, took the turbot steamer off the hot plate and called to the kitchen maids, who, wiping their floury hands on their aprons, followed her out on to the front lawn to join the house staff, who were chanting, cheering and slapping each other on the back.

'It's over! The war is over! Peace at last!'

Arthur threw down his spade as Gabriel and Mr Coster came running from the orchard. The bells of St Mary's had now been joined by those of St Mark's, creating a cacophony of joyous sound.

'It's over! The war is over!'

The three gardeners ran to join the house staff, who had formed a ragged circle. Arthur and Gabriel squeezed in between Nora and Isla, the scullery maid. Nora turned and hugged Arthur, as they joined hands and sang *'Auld Lang Syne'* at the tops of their voices. Arthur's hat was suddenly pushed over his eyes and he spun round to find Annie beaming at him.

'What news!' she shouted.

She slipped her hand in his and joined the circle, as it broke into *'Pack Up Your Troubles.'* Annie looked at Arthur and felt her eyes rim with tears. She leaned over, squeezed his hand and planted a kiss on his cheek.

'I am so proud of you, Arthur!'

Gabriel suddenly broke away from the circle, pulling Isla and the others behind him, leading them to the far end of the estate and the gate leading into Abbey Lane. The sound of bells grew louder as they neared the town and joined an impromptu procession parading through to the Market Square. People burst out of houses waving flags, blowing whistles and cheering as they joined the snaking line of jubilant revellers. As they turned into the High Street, clerks left their stools and hurried to join the procession, shop assistants came scurrying pell-mell to join the throng. A great flood of joy and enthusiasm passed like electricity from person to person. They moved along King Street and into the Market Square, where the Mayor stood on a makeshift platform, smiling from ear to ear, as more and more people poured down side streets to join the crowd. Looking around, Annie spotted Gruff, Pol, and Fred standing at the opposite side of the Square, next to a group of men on crutches. One by one they were lifted up above the crowd, supported by their fellow soldiers from Walden Place hospital. The crowd clapped wildly, cheering, as the men acknowledged them with modest waves. Annie raised both hands in the air, hoping to attract her parents' attention, but they were helping to steady one of the young soldiers as he was lifted back down into the crowd. Pol passed the man's crutches back to him and, taking a handkerchief from her overall pocket, wiped her eyes. Shouting above the cacophony of bells, sirens and whistles, the Lord Mayor bawled:

'For so many of you, the weeks, months, years of hourly fear, hoping for the best, but always half-expecting the worst, has finally come to an end. After fifty-one months of fighting, today we have cast off the shackles of war! Today will be a celebration of life. A celebration of the lives of the one hundred and fifty-nine sons of Saffron Walden who laid down their lives so bravely that we might live in peace and freedom!'

There was a roar from the crowd as people waved flags, hugged each other and cheered. He held up his hands for quiet before continuing:

'There will be a Service of Thanksgiving at three o'clock in the church this afternoon and a Service of Remembrance tomorrow evening at six. And now I will leave it to your consciences as to how you behave today!'

There was another roar as the crowd burst into the National Anthem. Standing behind Annie and Arthur, two young lads shouted to each other above the noise.

'The war has ended too soon! I was supposed to go to the front next week, now I've got *no* chance to fight. Bloody armistice!'

Arthur spun round, glaring at them.

'So, you wanted to fight, did you? Wanted to be a hero, did you?'

He felt their revulsion as they stared at his disfigured face. Pointing to his scars, he hissed:

'Well, this is what war does to you. You want to look like this, eh? Believe me, there is nothing glorious about war. Just you remember that!'

The two young men hung their heads and sloped off through the crowd. Arthur stared at his hands. They shook uncontrollably. Annie held them tightly in hers, and gently guided him over towards Gruff and Pol. Seeing them, Gruff called out.

'Come 'ere and give us a hug!'

Picking Annie up, he spun her round, nearly knocking the man next to him off his crutches.

'Who'd 'ave thought it, this bloody war is over. Peace at last!'

Pol grabbed Arthur and hugged him so tightly he could barely breathe. Tears had lodged in the lines beneath her eyes.

'It must be a proud day for you, Arthur!'

Fred patted him on the shoulder and Gruff grabbed his hand, wildly pumping it up and down.

'We're very proud of you, lad!'

Arthur smiled wearily but didn't reply.

****

Outside the church, groups of townspeople who weren't regular churchgoers, feeling it was just the right place to be, clamoured to squeeze into the aisles, sides and rear of the ancient building. People gathered around the open door, trying to catch a glimpse of the altar and to add their voices to the throng as the refrain of '*Land of Hope and Glory*' rose into the air, drowning the stirring melody of the organ.

On Castle Street Gruff and Fred helped to hang brightly coloured bunting along the houses. Every family had dragged chairs and tables into the street to form a single long bench running from *Salmon's Stores* up to the *Five Bells*, which had already opened its doors. An assortment of mismatched tablecloths, laid with a random selection of plates, mugs, cups and glasses, waited for neighbours and their families to change into their Sunday best clothes to mark the occasion. Gradually groups of residents spilled out of the church and joined those already seated, as Pol, Nora and Mrs Bolton from number 32 carried out large platters of ham sandwiches and pots of tea. Reggie Salmon filled a bag with enough tuffins for each child in the street, then hauled four crates of beer and one of sherry out of the shop and on to the pavement, before sticking a large notice up on the door.

'PEACE! – NOTHING ELSE MATTERS – OPEN ON WEDNESDAY.'

'Perfectly put Reggie, I couldn't 'ave said it better meself!'

Examining the crates of alcohol, Gruff winked at Reggie.

'I 'ope that isn't the watered-down stuff they've been trying to get us to drink!'

'Don't you worry, Gruff, today calls for the real stuff! Pass it round, will you? And get Fred to give out the tuffins to the kids.'

By eight o'clock tables had been dragged up onto the pavement. Outside the *Five Bells*, Alf Turner, Ernie Bolton, Gruff and Fred heaved the pub piano out on to the road. Ernie rolled up his shirtsleeves and, with fingers working the keyboard, belted out the *'Tiger Rag.'* Borrowed light, streaming out from blackout free windows, and candles in jars, arranged haphazardly on tables along the pavement, cast long shadows, as young and old neighbours pushed back chairs and jigged to the rhythm of the music. Annie tried to find Arthur, wanting to drag him up to dance. She scanned the groups of friends and checked the pub and the kitchen of number six. There was no sign of him anywhere. She found Nora dancing with Albert Sillet. Pulling her to one side, she shouted above the noise:

'Have you seen Arthur?'

'I think I saw him going up the alleyway into the churchyard a while ago, but I haven't seen him since.'

Annie darted off up the alleyway and into the graveyard. There was no sign of him there, so pushing open the huge oak door to the church, she crept in and spotted Arthur sitting on a pew staring at the altar. The vast stained-glass windows of the nave glowed in the candlelight, casting flickering shadows over the choir stalls. She slid in next to him but he continued to stare ahead, transfixed by some inner force.

'Look at me, Arthur!' she whispered.

Slowly he turned towards her. She couldn't read the expression in his eyes. They were talking to her, but she couldn't read what they were saying.

'Arthur, come back from wherever you are. Talk to me.'

He shook his head.

'What do you want me to say? That I'm enjoying the party? That today's a wonderful celebration of the futility of war? I can't, Annie, I just can't! Are we supposed to celebrate the slaughter, the loss of all those young lives? For what? Are all those people out there dancing and singing worth the sacrifice, the sacrifice our generation has made? Do they deserve it?'

He turned to her, his eyes blazing.

'There are parents out there who lost their sons. They're dancing and singing! Your parents, your brother and sister are out there laughing. It disgusts me! Have they forgotten Stanley so soon?'

'Of course they haven't, Arthur. Nor has anyone forgotten those they've lost. But life has to go on. Stanley wouldn't want us to spend the rest of our lives mourning him. He'd want us to live! We must make him proud of the people we will become, can't you see that?'

Arthur's face crumpled as she held him to her, his body shaken by each wave of grief as it washed over him. They sat locked in each other's arms until his body calmed. The ragtime piano and laughter echoed through the silent church, as a deadly invisible enemy continued to spread its evil fingers over those celebrating victory, like the savage last breath of a storm.

November 15th

The King's Telegram had been delivered to the Bolton family at number 32 Castle Street. Ernie Bolton had just finished breakfast when he spotted the young telegram boy leaning his bicycle up against the house. With his face draining of colour and heart thumping against his ribcage, he rushed to open the door and grabbed the buff-coloured telegram silently pushed into his quaking hands by a lad who couldn't meet his eyes.

'We regret to inform you of the death of Private Charles Bolton at 10.55 a.m. November 11th 1918 at Etaples Military Hospital. Cause of death: Influenza.'

Ernie sank onto the floor, propping himself up against the door. Mrs Bolton appeared from the kitchen, and seeing her husband slumped over, clutching the telegram, she fell to her knees.

'No, no, it's not true! Tell me it's not true!'

Mrs Bolton's screams could be heard up and down Castle Street. Mrs Sillet had seen the telegram boy's bicycle outside the Bolton's house. A chill had passed through her as she imagined the scene inside her neighbour's house. By midday word had spread.

'He was only nineteen! Dying of this Spanish Flu, five minutes before the Armistice! Those poor souls. And they was 'avin such a good time the other night. Who'd 'ave thought the hand of fate could be so cruel?'

Pol sighed and, looking round the table at the stricken faces of her two youngest children, gathered them to her and silently prayed.

November 16th

Advice posters issued by the Board of Health appeared in shop windows and on public noticeboards around Saffron Walden. On the morning of November 16th Pol joined several Castle Street residents clustered around the new poster in Reggie Salmon's shop window. She read with mounting alarm the stark advice it gave:

EPIDEMIC

SPANISH INFLUENZA

THIS DISEASE IS HIGHLY COMMUNICABLE

IT MAY DEVELOP INTO SEVERE PNEUMONIA

- *THERE IS NO MEDICINE WHICH WILL PREVENT IT*
- *KEEP AWAY FROM PUBLIC MEETINGS, THEATRES AND OTHER PLACES WHERE CROWDS ARE ASSEMBLED*
- *KEEP THE MOUTH AND NOSE COVERED WHILST COUGHING OR SNEEZING*
- *WHEN A MEMBER OF THE HOUSEHOLD BECOMES ILL, PLACE HIM IN A ROOM BY HIMSELF. THE ROOM SHOULD BE WARM BUT WELL VENTILATED*
- *THE ATTENDANT SHOULD PUT ON A MASK BEFORE ENTERING THE ROOM OF THOSE ILL OF THE DISEASE.*

George Pledger broke the silence.

'Well, looks like I'll have to shut up shop. Frank Duberry was in the pub the night before he died of it.'

Albert Sillet glanced nervously around at his neighbours.

'And we were all out in the street celebrating only a couple of nights ago. God knows how many of us have got it and don't know it yet!'

Pol stared up at the two men.

'You're right, Albert. I was walking past the *Five Bells* just now and Mrs Turner's been taken ill this morning with the chills and a headache. Mr Turner is out there now putting straw down on the street to deaden the noise of the horses' hooves.'

The bell above the shop door jangled as Reggie Salmon appeared with the morning papers. He stacked them up on a rack outside the shop, then turned to George Pledger, who was anxiously scanning the headlines of every paper.

'I've just been reading the papers, George. All of them are saying the same thing: that there were lots of cases of Spanish Flu during the summer but it was hushed up as they didn't want to it to affect morale. Apparently, it was over here, and in France, Germany and Spain, in June. They say there were 100,000 cases in six weeks up North. Then it seemed to go away, and they hoped it had burned itself out. But by September, with all the transport ships bringing back our troops and nurses from the front, they reckon they brought it back with them. Probably a lot of them caught it on the ships.'

Pol picked up a paper.

'Put it on the tab will you, Reggie.'

She glanced at the front page and sighed.

'This is just piling more tragedy on top of the tragedy we're already suffering! When will it all end, Reggie?'

November 23rd

A week later Arthur's throat was raw. To the touch his forehead burned and his cheeks had taken on the colour of a deep red rash. Despite an extra thick blanket Annie had draped over him, he shivered, unable to get warm. Annie recognised the symptoms. She'd nursed soldiers at Etaples before there was any talk of Spanish Flu. She'd been laid low herself for a week with flu-like symptoms, which she hoped had given her some immunity. She propped Arthur's head up on his pillow and gave him two aspirin, prescribed by Lord Braybrooke's personal doctor, who'd been called to examine him.

'As you know, Mrs Scoggings, there's nothing I can give him, apart from aspirin, which will help alleviate the symptoms. I'm sure you're aware that it may develop into severe pneumonia. Keep his room warm but well ventilated, give him plenty to drink and wear a mask to cover your nose and mouth when you're with him. Do not visit your family or go out unless you absolutely have to. This disease is highly infectious.'

Arthur slept fitfully, waking on and off, feeling that he was drowning in his own bodily fluids. He called out to Annie, who bathed his face with cold flannels and held his hand.

'I feel like I'm being crushed to death, Annie.'

'Shh, Arthur, shh! Try to sleep.'

'No, Annie. How can I sleep when I'm so angry and bitter? My youth has been taken from me. My life taken from me, and for what? I'd hoped we'd have children, watch them grow up and then grow old together. Why is it that men have to spoil what is lovely in the world?'

'Not everything, Arthur. We still have each other.'

The grief she was already feeling made her heavy with tiredness. She leaned over and kissed his forehead, tightening her grip on his hand, hoping to forestall the inevitability of what was to come.

By the following morning Arthur's skin had begun to take on a bluish hue as he struggled to breathe. He reached out and took Annie's hand in his. It felt clammy and cold, like snakeskin.

'So, this is the end of all our dreams, Annie.'

'No, Arthur. You mustn't think like that.'

She leaned over him, cradling his head in her arms.

'You know as well as I do, that it's ...'

His voice trailed off as a chain of coughs shook his body. She wiped the blood splatters off his mouth and stroked his ravaged face as he struggled to speak.

'Be happy, Annie, live your life to the full, you've still got so much more life to live. Make me proud of the woman that you'll become.'

Annie's hand clung to Arthur's as she felt him letting go.

'No Arthur, no, not yet!'

His body heaved as a final gurgling breath marked the end of his life. Annie slowly lifted his head back on to the pillow and gently pulled his half-open lids over his eyes. She sat, holding his hand, until it grew cold. Outside, the voices of young children playing drifted through the tiny bedroom window. And for one moment she thought she heard the click of the door latch downstairs and Arthur's footsteps on the tiled floor, leaving.

Littlebury Church
November 29th

The sun was fingering the skyline as Arthur's coffin was carried through the silent graveyard into the church. There were only a handful of mourners. The fear of catching the flu had spread, making all but those closest to the deceased reluctant to leave the safety of their houses.

Sitting in the front pew, flanked by Pol and Nora, who'd

each grasped one of her hands, Annie turned to watch as the coffin, supported by Gruff, Fred and Albert Sillet on one side, and Gabriel, Mr Coster and Reggie Salmon on the other, made its unsteady way down the aisle to the altar. She was surprised to see Vesta, Cecily and Gertrude Baillie-Weaver sitting together at the back of the small church. She caught Vesta's eye and smiled wanly before turning to watch the coffin being placed on a pedestal directly in front of her. As Reggie Salmon walked past to his seat he leaned over Nora, and squeezed Annie's shoulder. She looked up and met his eyes. His sympathy warmed her.

Standing beside the newly dug plot, Annie sank into Gruff's arms as the grave swallowed her dead husband. They each threw a handful of earth on to the coffin, hitting it with a dull thud. As the last spadeful of earth was tamped down over the coffin and the wooden cross hammered into the earth, Annie placed a single bouquet of white lilies on the grave, whilst a final prayer marked the end of the simple service. There was to be no wake. Annie, wiping her face with a borrowed handkerchief, halted the tracks of her tears as she thanked those remaining, and spotted George Fotherby at the far side of the graveyard. Bowing his head, he walked towards her.

'I wondered if I could offer you and your family a lift back to Middle Square?'

It had begun to rain and heavy grey clouds were banking over the graveyard.

'That's very kind of you, George.'

December 3rd

Annie turned down the offer of remaining in the house at number seven Audley End Road. In the days after the funeral, she moved frantically about its tiny rooms, as if movement could stop the truth from settling. She opened the tiny wardrobe they'd shared and took out Arthur's orphaned clothes, holding them to her nose and breathing in the smell of him, before carefully folding and placing them into the wooden trunk they'd kept at the foot of their bed. She'd agreed to return the keys to the estate office after clearing the house of the few pieces of furniture they'd so recently bought from Reed's. She waited for their van to arrive. As she stood at the back door, she heard the sound of a car pull up outside. The front door opened and the figure of George Fotherby filled the room.

'I wondered if I might help move a few of your belongings back to Middle Square.'

'That's very kind of you, George, but I can't let you take the risk of catching the flu. Reed's have very kindly agreed to take back the furniture we bought from them but they'll be spraying it all before they take it away.'

'I'll be alright, Annie! I'm pretty resilient, and if I'm prepared to take the risk, then there isn't a problem, is there? Now, what needs to go to Castle Street?'

'Not much actually. We've got no room at home to store anything, so the only thing is the trunk over there.'

He grabbed the metal handle and dragged it to the door. Annie helped him lift it over the threshold and between them they managed to force it into the back of the car.

'I hope your leather seat won't get scratched by this old thing.'

'Don't worry, nothing a bit of polish won't fix.'

As he slammed the car door shut, Reed's van appeared and parked behind him.

'I'll be back to pick you up when I've dropped this off.'

'Thank you, George, but I think I'd like to walk if you don't mind.'

'Oh yes, of course. I expect you'd like some time on your own.'

He moved off up the road and drove off with the trunk perched on the back seat.

An hour later, Annie took a look around the tiny cottage and locked the front door for the last time.

Middle Square
December 5th

It was strange to be back home in Nora's tiny room, under the rafters. Annie was grateful for the quiet space it gave her to grieve. She'd kept the string ring Arthur had made for her and now wore it on her ring finger, together with her engagement and wedding rings. She lay on her tiny bed and fiddled with the string ring. Arthur's words kept filling her head.

'Be happy Annie! Live your life to the full. Make me proud of the woman you will become!'

How could she ever be happy again?

1919

July 29th, 1919

Spanish Flu, having infected most people who hadn't already been affected, had begun to burn itself out, mutating to almost like normal flu. People had finally begun to go about their lives without looking over their shoulders. But another crisis was looming ....

Wounded soldiers in their hundreds were returning to a country wrecked by war. Little thought had been given to the needs of these vulnerable men, many of whom were now ill-equipped to return to their former jobs. No provision had been made to retrain or rehabilitate these ex-servicemen.

Infuriated by this, Annie joined the Labour Party and became a prospective Labour MP, to campaign on behalf of wounded soldiers.

October 9th

George Fotherby sounded the horn of his car as he waited for Annie. She finally appeared and slipped into the passenger seat. He leaned over and squeezed her hand before putting the car into gear and setting off.

'I'm not sure I'm ready for this, George.'

He smiled and winked at her.

'You'll be fine, Annie. You're passionate about your cause, and that's when you're at your best.'

They parked in front of the new YMCA building in the centre of Cambridge and were met by Vesta, who rushed out to meet them. Hugging Annie, she showed them into a large hall, which was only half full.

'There may not be many here, Annie, but those who are, are pretty fired up! Now you'd better go backstage and be ready to start in five minutes. I'll introduce you.'

Annie felt her knees buckling, but was encouraged by George's warm smile as she stepped up to the podium.

'Men are beginning to cluster on benches outside in the street. They're bored and apathetic. They fear unemployment, destitution but, most of all, the shame of being unable to provide for their families! Is this the way to treat our returning heroes?'

Pleased to see some of Annie's spirit returning, George smiled to himself, as the audience, many of whom were wounded ex-servicemen, warmed to the young woman addressing them.

'We have to rely on voluntary organisations such as the YMCA to offer retraining and the hope of finding employment for our returning wounded soldiers. How can that possibly be right?'

'Hear! Hear!' shouted a man on crutches, who had propped himself up at the back of the room. 'I've been reduced to selling matches to try and keep the wolf from the door. What are our Government doing to help us?'

'Nothing!' another amputee sitting in the front row shouted. 'They were only too happy to send us off to war. No expense spared then, but now they don't know what to do with us. This is how they repay us!'

Annie paused, waiting for silence, then held up a poster, but noticing several blind men in the audience, read it aloud:

'DON'T PITY A DISABLED MAN
FIND HIM A JOB!

Phone Red Triangle Employment Bureau – or your local employment office.'

A blind man in the front row shouted:

'There are no jobs for the likes of us!'

'We're on the scrap heap now!'

Annie smiled.

'Well, that's where you're wrong. We in the Labour Party are lobbying for a number of rehabilitation centres to be set up where amputees can learn new skills. For example, electrical engineering, carpentry and motor mechanics, which will equip them to return to civilian life. We are in the process of setting up a home for those men blinded by mustard gas, where they can learn Braille, which will enable them to train for active employment. Our slogan is *'Hope welcomes all who enter here'* and will be displayed at all the retraining centres currently being set up. I urge you all to pick up one of the leaflets by the door as you leave. Thank you for listening.'

Several of the men stood to applaud, soon followed by a number of others. As she joined George and was about to leave the hall, a man came slowly towards her, leaning heavily on a crutch.

'Bless you, Annie Scoggings!'

His left arm had been amputated from the elbow, but he held out his right hand.

'Private Jones. I served with your husband in France. I knew it had to be you giving the talk tonight. He talked about you so much. We were friends despite him being my superior. I just wanted to let you know what a brave man he was and how his men loved and respected him. He would be very proud to know what you are doing to help us all.'

Annie's eyes filled with tears as she thanked him, before allowing George to lead her out and into the car.

1922

Three years later
November 11th, 1922
St Mary's Church, Saffron Walden
Remembrance Day

As the church clock struck eleven the town fell silent for two minutes, before the names of every man inscribed on the War Memorial at the top of the town were read out.

The Mayor, followed by local MP George Fotherby, laid wreaths, before the crowd silently made its way down the High Street to the church. The families of the one hundred and fifty-nine local men killed during the four years of war filed silently into its cavernous interior. Pews rapidly filled with neighbours and friends, wearing black armbands. Grief etched as clearly on their faces as it had been three years before, and now gathered together to remember their dead on this first Poppy Day. Annie, Fred and Nora sat next to Pol and Gruff, towards the back of the church. The congregation waited silently, some craning their necks to get a better view of Reverend Johnson as he finally climbed up into the pulpit. At the same moment the side door of the church creaked open as George Fotherby, looking flustered, crept in and squeezed in next to Annie. She shuffled up to make space for him. He patted her hand and spread his long legs out into the aisle.

'Sorry!' he whispered.

Reverend Johnson cleared his throat and swept the congregation with smiling eyes, directing his gaze at many individuals who had not only lost loved ones during the war, but also to the Spanish Flu. He tried to include everyone.

'We are gathered here today to remember the brave young men of Saffron Walden who fought so valiantly on our behalf, for our futures. We must not allow the slow, grinding pulse of grief, to overwhelm us. We must not let the optimism in the British way of life disappear forever. Instead, we must live in hope for the future and live our lives to the full, to honour those who gave up so much for us ....'

There was the sound of muffled sobbing as they opened their hymn books for the final hymn, '*The Lord is My Shepherd*', then, as the congregation sat with heads bowed, a lone bugler performed the '*Last Post*', which had been played at the end of the killing. One hundred and fifty-nine poppies were then released from a balcony high up in the roof. Annie gripped George's hand as the last poppy drifted down and came to rest on the floor, like the last soldier falling into the mud of the trenches. Above their heads a single bee flew in circles over them. The church grew quiet and, after a minute or two of silence, a baby began to cry.

EPILOGUE

Disabled

He sat in a wheeled chair, waiting for dark,
And shivered in his ghastly suit of grey,
Legless, sewn short at elbow. Through the park
Voices of boys rang saddening like a hymn,
Voices of play and pleasure after day,
Till gathering sleep had mothered them from him.

****

About this time Town used to swing so gay
When glow-lamps budded in the light-blue trees,
And girls glanced lovelier as the air grew dim,—
In the old times, before he threw away his knees.
Now he will never feel again how slim
Girls' waists are, or how warm their subtle hands,
All of them touch him like some queer disease.

****

There was an artist silly for his face,
For it was younger than his youth, last year.
Now, he is old; his back will never brace;
He's lost his colour very far from here,
Poured it down shell-holes till the veins ran dry,
And half his lifetime lapsed in the hot race
And leap of purple spurted from his thigh.

****

One time he liked a blood-smear down his leg,
After the matches carried shoulder-high.
It was after football, when he'd drunk a peg,

He thought he'd better join. He wonders why.
Someone had said he'd look a god in kilts.
That's why; and maybe, too, to please his Meg,
Aye, that was it, to please the giddy jilts,
He asked to join. He didn't have to beg;
Smiling they wrote his lie: aged nineteen years.
Germans he scarcely thought of, all their guilt,
And Austria's, did not move him. And no fears
Of Fear came yet. He thought of jewelled hilts
For daggers in plaid socks; of smart salutes;
And care of arms; and leave; and pay arrears;
Esprit de corps; and hints for young recruits.
And soon, he was drafted out with drums and cheers.

****

Some cheered him home, but not as crowds cheer Goal.
Only a solemn man who brought him fruits
Thanked him; and then inquired about his soul.

****

Now, he will spend a few sick years in institutes,
And do what things the rules consider wise,
And take whatever pity they may dole.
Tonight he noticed how the women's eyes
Passed from him to the strong men that were whole.
How cold and late it is! Why don't they come
And put him into bed? Why don't they come?

WILFRED OWEN

ABOUT THE AUTHOR

Christa Skinner lives in Saffron Walden. After teaching for many years at international schools in Brussels and Basel, as well as state schools in the UK, she worked for several years at Audley End House and the Imperial War Museum, Duxford. She is married with two children.

Printed in Great Britain
by Amazon